Barvick Falls

Rob McInroy

With best wishes

Rob McInroy

Barvick Falls © 2025. All rights reserved. The right of Rob McInroy to be identified as the author of the Work has been asserted in accordance with the Copyright, Designs & Patents Act 1988.

This first edition published and copyright 2025
by Tippermuir Books Ltd, Perth, Scotland.
mail@tippermuirbooks.co.uk – www.tippermuirbooks.co.uk.

No part of this publication may be reproduced or used in any form or by any means without written permission from the Publisher except for review purposes. All rights whatsoever in this book are reserved.

ISBN 978-1-913836-54-2 (paperback).

A CIP catalogue record for this book is available from the British Library.

Project coordination and editorial by Paul S Philippou.

Cover design by Rob McInroy.

Co-founders and publishers of Tippermuir Books: Rob Hands, Matthew Mackie and Paul S Philippou.

Text design, layout, and artwork
by Palimpsest Book Production Limited, Falkirk, Stirlingshire

Text set in Times.

Printed and bound by CPI Antony Rowe.

This book has been printed in the UK to reduce transportation miles and their impact on the environment. It has been printed to comply with the Forest Stewardship Council (FSC) Chain of Custody requirements and paper sourcing from responsibly managed sources.

'Better to remain silent and be thought a fool than to speak and to remove all doubt.'
Attributed to Abraham Lincoln

or

'I like better for one to say some foolish thing upon important matters than to be silent. That becomes the subject of discussion and dispute, and the truth is discovered.'
Denis Diderot

Reader, you decide.

Praise for Rob McInroy

Burials and Other Stories
'A dark and very well-crafted mini thriller.'
Rachel Seiffert, author of Booker Prize shortlisted novel The Dark Room

Moot
'Trust me when I say read this book.'
Jim C Mackintosh, poet and 'Scots Writer o the Year' 2024

'As evocative as it is thrilling.'
Nick Quantrill, author of the Joe Geraghty novels

Barossa Street
'A powerful and resonant novel that explores the prejudices and injustices of the time and their impact on policing. Dark, thrilling and sinister, it will keep you guessing until you reach the last page.'
C L Taylor, Sunday Times bestselling author of The Accident and The Lie

'Part murder mystery, part gritty crime, part immersive historical fiction – 100% excellent.'
Dan Malakin, author of The Wreckage of Us and The Box

Cuddies Strip
'Very much a contemporary novel. It deals with misogyny, it

deals with institutional corruption, it deals with the problem of policing. I highly recommend it.'
Val McDermid, bestselling Scottish crime writer

'I read this wonderful novel with a tear in my eye. I could hardly bear to read the ending but it was beautiful.'
Cathi Unsworth, author of That Old Black Magic and Weirdo

Also by Rob McInroy

Fiction
Cuddies Strip (2020)
Barossa Street (2022)
Moot (2024)
Burials and Other Stories (2024)

Non-Fiction
'Cormac McCarthy and the Cities of God,
Man and the Plain' (unpublished PhD thesis,
University of Hull, 2013)
*One Final Hurdle: A Fans' History of
St Johnstone FC* (2014)
*An Odious Campaign: The Ross and Cromarty
By-Election of 1936* (2025)

About the Author

Rob McInroy is primarily a novelist. He was born in Crieff, Perthshire, and his fiction is mostly set in his home county, particularly Crieff, the Knock Hill and the River Earn. He is the author of the acclaimed Bob and Annie Kelty series of historical crime fiction which follows the central characters from the 1930s to the 2010s.

In 2018, he was a winner of the Bradford Literature Festival Northern Noir Crime Novel competition with an early draft of *Cuddies Strip* and this first novel was subsequently longlisted for the Crime Writers' Association John Creasey First Blood Dagger Award.

He has an MA in Creative Writing and a PhD in American Literature, both from the University of Hull. He currently lives in Yorkshire.

Acknowledgements

I would like to thank my editor Andrew Mackenzie and his editorial team, Amisha Deb and Kirsty Laverac, for their careful and detailed assistance in the editorial process. I've been fortunate to have Andrew oversee three of my books, and he is a delight to work with.

My thanks to Strathearn Arts, the Crieff and Strathearn Museum, and Innerpeffray Library for their continued support.

My thanks to Paul S Philippou and Tippermuir Books for taking on Bob and Annie Kelty and ensuring their story can continue.

For my Auntie, Greta Fyfe

Saturday, 2 September 1939

A Day of Waiting

Immersed in sleep, dreaming uneasily of war, Bob Kelty assimilated the sound of banging into a dream of raised hands surrendering to a waving pistol. He woke with a start. There was a sharp rapping noise whose source he could not identify. He sat up.

'What time is it?'

He focused for a few seconds on the luminous hands of the alarm clock by the bedside until they began to glow. Eight o'clock.

'Damn,' he shouted, leaping from the bed. 'We've slept in.' He pulled on his tweed dressing gown and slid his feet into grey slippers. Annie shifted in the bed.

'What you sayin?'

'Those damned blackoot curtains.' He ran downstairs and pulled back the curtain covering the front door of the Cloudland Café. Leslie Comer, headscarf covering her hair, waited, frowning.

'Did I disturb your rumpy-pumpy?'

'Certainly no.'

She laughed. 'Dinnae sound so scandalised. You're allowed, you ken. You *are* merried.'

'No on a Seturday mornin.'

'Ach, you young anes.' She stepped past and hung her coat on the coat stand and placed her headscarf over it.

'It's thae blackoot curtains,' Bob said. 'The room was pitch black. We didnae wake up.'

'Well, get oot my road and let me get thae scones made. Awa and mak yoursel decent, man.'

Bob quickly checked but his dressing gown was in place, modesty maintained. Leslie had a habit of teasing Bob and Annie, recognising in them an innocence she, thirty years older, found old-fashioned. By the time he retreated upstairs, Annie was in her dressing gown, stirring porridge.

'You micht hae wakened me,' she said.

'I would, if I'd been awake mysel.'

'Thae blackoot curtains.'

The previous night had seen the first compulsory blackout, following the German invasion of Poland that morning. Bob had spent an hour taping strips of *The Strathearn Herald* around the edges of the windows of their flat and running downstairs to check for light escaping onto James Square, returning and repairing, then checking again. They had spent the rest of the evening in claustrophobic silence, staring at the sullen blackout curtains. Somehow, the curtains seemed to drain light from the room so that, although there was the same illumination as usual from their standard lamp and the coal fire, they seemed to be peering at one another through caliginous gloom.

Bob filled the kettle and set it on the range. He tried to act as though nothing was different, as though the sun was shining on an ordinary day, but the near certainty of war was impossible to ignore. Indeed, he couldn't understand why the declaration hadn't already been made. The Anglo-Polish agreement was explicit: in the event of military action against Poland, Britain would intervene. The invasion had come at 4:45 the previous morning and this delay was inexplicable. The uncertainty added to his concern. For the past four or five years, European tensions had been building and, since the Munich conference the previous year, there had seemed an inevitability about war but, now it was almost on them, the idea seemed too massive, too irremediable to be possible. Only twenty-one years after the last slaughter, barely a generation, and they were about to do it again? Bob knew he would have to concentrate on deflecting the darkness that would seek to infest his mind once more. There was something seductive, insidious, about the way his despondency could grow until it was almost a physical presence within him. He had laboured against it for years, since the death of his father, and he knew that, however happy he felt on the surface, he was never far from a descent, as he termed his moments of despair.

'We'll be fine,' Annie said, gripping his hand, conscious as always of her husband's shift in mood.

From below, there was a rapping on the front door of Cloudland once more. 'Leslie's there,' Bob said. 'She'll get rid of them. Probably Pat the postie.'

'We're no up that late.'

'True.'

'Mr Kelty, Mrs Kelty.'

They both looked up in surprise. Standing in the kitchen doorway was Mrs McNeill from the Women's Voluntary Service. She noted their dressing gowns with ill-disguised disapproval.

'We slept in,' Bob explained. 'The blackoot curtains. Made aathin dark.'

'That's the intention.'

'What can we do for you?'

Mrs McNeill was a small, terrier-like woman with sharp features and piercing blue eyes. She wore a checked suit and a knitted turban hat and had the air of someone used to being in control. Such was the confidence that came with being a doctor's wife, Bob supposed. She sat at the kitchen table and indicated to Bob and Annie to do likewise.

'You're no doubt aware,' she said briskly, 'that the evacuation of children from our main cities began yesterday?'

'Aye,' said Annie, 'There's some here already. Puir mites.'

'More will arrive today and tomorrow. Crieff burgh and its landward areas have been detailed to take three thousand children from Glasgow.' She looked around the kitchen and stood and walked into the hallway. 'May I?' she said and without waiting for permission she looked into each room in turn. 'Just the two bedrooms,' she said.

'Aye,' said Bob. 'There's only me and Annie for now.'

'I'll have to put you down for just one child. That bedroom is very poky.'

'Eh?'

'From Glasgow. You'll have to take one. Go to the Public School tomorrow at four. Mrs Liversedge will allocate your child.'

'Do we hae to?' said Annie.

'You do, yes.'

'As you say, it's gey poky.'

'It's your civic duty, Mrs Kelty.'

Annie bristled and looked to Bob. "Civic duty" was one of those phrases people of a certain class used when speaking to people of Bob and Annie's class as a way of making them conform. She resisted the urge to make a tart rejoinder. She had submitted an application to join the WVS a week before, after concluding it was time she played a greater part in the town's daily life, and dealing with the likes of Mrs McNeill was one of the vexations she would have to endure if her membership was approved.

'Aye,' she said. 'Fower o'clock.'

'I'll see myself out.'

Bob turned to Annie as Mrs McNeill clattered down the stairs.

'That's twa bairns you'll hae to look after, noo,' he said.

Annie laughed. 'Awa and tidy up your toys.'

*

Mid-morning, and Cloudland was quiet, as though Crieffites were waiting for news, lives interrupted. Bob spread *The Courier* on the table by the window and read of the German invasion of Poland. Danzig had been attacked and, near the border, the town of Weiluń had been badly bombed in probably the first action of the war. Buildings had been destroyed, including a hospital. Bob remembered Weiluń from his friend Jozef Kawala at the International Rover Scout Moot in Monzie a few weeks before. Jozef was an excitable young man from Danzig, and his parents lived in Weiluń. He had been certain the Germans would attack there and Bob had tried to reassure him the town was so small there was no reason they should. What did Bob know?

'My first husband fought in the last war.' Leslie Comer lit a Woodbine and sat beside Bob. 'Palestine. It ruined him, made him the bastard he was. You cannae kill people and then juist switch aff and go back to normal when it's aa ower. It affects you.'

'Must do.'

'If aa you young men, you juist turned roond to the auld men and telt them, "no, we winnae fight your stupit war for you", the world would be a better place.'

'That winnae happen.'

'How no? Mak it happen. Somebody has to mak a stand.'

*

'You're new?'

Mary Kemp turned apprehensively to the source of the enquiry, an elegant young woman seated at a dressing table beside a window in the Barvick Falls lodging house, overlooking the Comrie road and MacRosty Park.

'Beg your pardon, miss, I didnae ken there was onyone in.'

'Even hard-working schoolteachers are allowed some leisure at the weekend.'

'Of course. I didnae mean. . .'

'What's your name?'

'Mary Kemp.'

'And when did you start here, Mary Kemp?'

'Juist this week. I used to work. . .'

'Welcome. My name is Miss Carrington. I think we'll get along just swimmingly. All I ask is that you keep out of my room. . .'

'Mrs Mitchell, Miss, she asked me to clean aa the rooms. . .'

'I'm sure she did. She's such a darling. The thing is, I'm very partial to my privacy. Most particular, in fact.'

'I wouldnae want to get in trouble. . .'

'And you shan't. If you're asked, you can say my room has been cleaned to within an inch of its life. Look around.' She gestured to the spacious, well-furnished bedroom, high-ceilinged in typical Victorian fashion. A gramophone player stood against a side wall next to a hand basin, a mahogany wardrobe and matching sideboard on the opposite wall. Trinkets covered the sideboard. They looked expensive. Facing the window was a narrow bed with a pink bedspread.

'As you can see, there's nothing to clean.' Lorna Carrington tapped ash from her Players' cigarette into a round, glass ashtray. 'Shut the door on the way out, there's a sweetie.'

*

Sandy Disdain pushed a wooden wheelbarrow up the High Street, bending low to give himself propulsion. The wheelbarrow was laden with flowers and vegetables – potatoes and onions carefully wrapped in old newspaper, bunches of dahlias and roses, verbena and gaudy chrysanthemums lightly tied with string. He seemed barely out of breath. Bob, rushing to catch him as he crossed the road at the Pretoria Bar, wheezed heavily.

'You've a fair lick on there, man,' he said.

Sandy turned and nodded and carried on walking down Church Street.

'What's aa this in aid of?'

'Flower show.'

'I thocht it was cancelled. The war.'

'Better bloody no be. I've carted these things aa the way fae the Laggan.'

'I'll buy any ingins you've got.'

'Efter. Come by the hall at six and you can hae whatever you want. Save me cartin them hame again. Some roses for the wife an aa.'

'Good idea. We're haein to tak an evacuee the morn. She's frettin.'

'An evacuee? The war's no even started yet.'

'No, but they started shiftin bairns fae Glesga yesterday.'

'How?'

'They reckon the first thing the Germans'll do is bomb the big cities. Glesga'll be important acos of the shipbuilding.'

'It'll be months afore there's ony bombin.'

'That's no what they're sayin.'

Predictions were gloomy. Based on the bombing campaigns in Spain, notably in Barcelona, Guernica and Madrid, it was feared that an aerial attack on the British mainland could begin within days of the outbreak of war and lead to tens – maybe hundreds – of thousands of casualties. Hospitals were already being emptied of non-urgent cases in readiness.

'They'll say onythin to frighten us,' said Sandy. 'Keep us under control.'

'Aye, you could be richt.' They stopped outside the church hall. 'I dinnae suppose you hae any transport, do you?'

'If I had transport, d'you think I'd be usin a wheelbarra?'

'Aye, good point. Pity. I've to pick the bairn up fae the school the morn. It'll hae a case of claes and such. It's a sair fecht fae the school aa the wey up to James Square.'

'What time?'

'Fower o'clock.'

'Leave it wi me.' With that, Sandy picked up his wheelbarrow once more and steered it through the doorway into the church hall.

'Grand,' said Bob. He retraced his steps uphill to the High Street and sauntered back to James Square. On impulse, instead of returning to Cloudland, he turned right and entered the Burgh Surveyor's office in a neat, sandstone building next to the bank. Two rooms on the ground floor, overlooking the square, had been given over to the Crieff ARP Wardens for their headquarters. Gordon Eadie, Head Warden, and Ian MacNaughton, lead Warden for bombing and fire precautions, were studying a large Ordnance Survey map of West Perthshire taped to the rear wall. Archie Watters and Eddie McAndrew were playing rummy at a small table in the middle of the room. Bob went to the makeshift kitchen next door where Ronnie Francis was standing over a large kettle that was about to boil.

'You makin a brew? Bob asked.

'They said you were a bit of a detective.'

'Has there been ony announcement yet?'

'No last I heard. Twa o'clock news. Nothin.'

'Dinnae ken what's keepin them.'

'I wouldnae be in too much of a rush for war to start.' Ronnie was forty, saw nine months of action on the Western Front in 1917 and 1918, had spent the next twenty-one years trying to forget it.

Bob gestured next door. 'I see the high-heid-yins are studying the terrain. They expectin the Nazi invasion fae Monzie?'

'Tap o Turleum. Five hundred parachutists.'

'How would they get across the Earn?'

'Rubber dinghies.'

'They've got it aa planned.'

'Unless they come on a Wednesday.'

'Wednesday?'

'Women's Voluntary Service meetin in the Institute, ten o'clock sharp. Pity the man wha interferes wi that.'

'Aye, richt enough. Annie's lookin at joinin.'

'Turned into a bossy besom?'

'She ay was.' He paused. 'She needs to be. I need tellin.'

'Well, in that case get the tea made.' He draped the dish cloth he was holding over Bob's arm and went next door. Bob filled the teapot and placed six cups and saucers on a tray and carried it through. Eadie and MacNaughton had joined the others seated around a circular table. Ronnie moved aside to allow Bob to place the tray on the table. No one else moved or acknowledged him. He pulled up a chair and sat behind Ronnie.

'I don't like it,' said MacNaughton. 'We should have declared war by now. Chamberlain's been chickening out for two years. Now he's at it again. Makes us look like cowards.'

'Talkin of cowards,' said Archie Watters, 'war hasnae even been declared yet and the first conchie's crawled out of the woodwork.'

Robert Bain, a farm worker from Wick, had become the first person to be placed on Scotland's conscientious objectors' register. Would you interfere with a man who tried to kill your father, he was asked. No, he replied. If attacked yourself, would you turn the other cheek? Yes, he replied, although he disliked the religious connotations of the question. Bob had followed the case with interest, thought Robert Bain a perceptive and temperate young man. The ARPs discussed conchies for some time, agreeing they were cowards, every one. Bob remained quiet.

'We need to step up patrols,' said Eadie. 'We had nowhere near enough men out last night. Good God, the town was lit up like Blackpool illuminations. People have no idea how to erect blackout curtains. If the Jerries had come over last night there'd be nothing left of the town.'

'We're not at war yet,' said MacNaughton.

'And you think that would stop Herr Hitler? There's a man who won't play fair. I want twice the number of patrols tonight.

Kelty, ring round and get half a dozen more volunteers. The Fifth zone was especially bad last night. Get extra men in there.'

The Fifth zone was Bob's. He tried – unsuccessfully – not to take it as a personal affront.

*

As dusk fell, Lorna Carrington descended from the train and walked up the main road to the Lochearnhead Hotel. A few evacuees, all boys, newly arrived that day from Springbank in Glasgow, were running rampant by the lochside. All was dark, the bright lights usually adorning the front of the hotel eclipsed for the blackout. Lorna walked round the building towards the rear. Smells of cooking emanated from the kitchens – fish on the menu tonight, probably cod like she'd had last week on her evening out with a special gentleman. *That evening.*

Memories assailed her. Memories she would fight away. *Registration. Mr and Mrs Jones. Concierge grinning at them, unbelieving. Dinner. Retiring upstairs. Doing That. It. The beast with two backs.*

She shuddered. *And next morning, concierge, smug again. 'Back home to your wife now, sir?' he'd asked, looking at Lorna. Looking through Lorna. The men laughing. Him looking at his property.*

Bastards. Bastards. Somebody would have to pay.

The back of the building, with a line of trees and the rising bank of the hill, was darker still than the front. Fifty feet away, on its own, was a wooden outbuilding, a two-storey barn with enormous wooden doors, into the right hand of which was cut a smaller door for easier ingress. She tried the handle. It was open. She went inside and switched on a small pocket torch. In front of her rose dozens of bales of hay, neatly piled one on the other, ready to sustain the hotel's animals through the winter.

Or not.

I am come to send fire on the Earth.

She pulled a rag stopper from a milk bottle filled with paraffin and poured its contents over the nearest bale. Then she took a copy of the *Glasgow Evening Times* she had salvaged from a litter bin in Barvick Falls that morning, property of Miss Glass, a Glaswegian who, although she had resided in Barvick Falls for thirty years, still insisted on keeping up with news from the dear green place. Lorna ripped a few strips from the topmost pages and took out a box of matches. *Newspapers. What were they for, anyway? They didn't tell the truth. Only news. Two different things.*

For we can do nothing against the truth, but for the truth.

She lit the newspaper fragments and, stepping back, dropped them on the paraffin-soaked bale. A sheet of flame whooshed into being and the bale started to crackle as fire spread through the dry straw, shooting up its hollowed insides. With a leap, the flames travelled onto a second bale and engulfed that, too. Smoke billowed around her. She stood and admired her handiwork, then reflected that she needed to get away before her clothing was tainted with the smell of smoke. *The pressure. The promise.*

But I have a baptism to be baptised with; and how am I straitened till it be accomplished!

She pulled her blue shawl around her. Reluctantly, she turned and walked back towards the still-dark hotel, dropping the newspaper outside.

I had the knowledge. I have the knowledge. I will spread the knowledge.

*

Bob studied the sombre outline of the terrace block in Milnab Street. A waning gibbous moon gave sufficient light for him to walk without difficulty. He imagined things might be trickier in a few weeks, with a new moon and the start of winter weather. His evening had been easier than the previous night, only three lights visible through blackout curtains and the occupants all apologetic when he knocked on their doors to advise them. A quick walk the length of Milnab Street as far as the mill and he'd be finished for the night.

He detoured behind the end of the squat terrace to check the rears of the properties. The building nearest him blocked the moon and he stumbled over some loose stones on the rough path. Above him, he saw a light in the roof of the nearest house. He went back to the street and his heart sank when he realised whose house it was.

Isa Lawson.

He knocked on her door and waited. The door opened.

'What?'

Isa Lawson was in her seventies, a cantankerous shrew of a woman perennially in a black shawl. She had harried her husband, Fred, into an early grave years before and to this day berated him to anyone who would listen for abandoning her.

'You've a light on, roond the back.'

'What's it to you?'

He pointed to the armband over his jacket. 'ARP,' he said. 'You need to put a blackoot curtain ower the windae.'

'And how the hell am I supposed to do that? It's a skylight.'

'You'll hae to tape it to the wall.'

'And ruin my guid paintwork? It's no as if I've a man to fix it, is it?'

'Well, if you cannae cover it, you'll juist hae to no use the light.'

'It's the lavvy. How am I supposed to wipe my arse in the pitch dark?'

'I'm sure you can find it.'

'Dinnae cheek me, you wee bastard.'

'I'll speak to Jack McOmish the morn. He'll come and fix you up in no time.'

'And you'll pey for it an aa?'

'Five minute job. It'll cost you nae mair than sixpence.'

'Sixpence might no be much to you, laddie, but I'm a widow-woman. I havenae got onyone bringin in a wage. You young anes dinnae gie a fig for us auld folk. I tell you this, I'm gled I'm on the wey oot.'

'Just let Jack in the morn. He'll sort you.'

'Awa and stick your bollocks in a mangle.' She slammed the door in his face and Bob reflected the conversation had gone about as well as he could have hoped.

*

Sergeant Braggan was already in a bad mood when the woman entered Lochearnhead police station. Not local, a young woman in a blue shawl and grey coat, standing in the doorway and barking across the room at him as though she were addressing a lackey, something about the Lochearnhead Hotel.

'Come in and let me take down the details.'

'There are no details to take down. Just a bunch of those Glasgow hooligans making mischief behind the hotel.'

'And you are?'

But when he looked up she was gone.

*

The sound of pipe music drifted down King Street as Bob made his way home. He continued to James Square in search of the source and found Sandy Disdain and Pipey Oldham by the Murray Fountain. Seated beside them were Mary Kemp and Leslie Comer.

'Evenin all,' Bob said.

Sandy offered Bob a hip flask. Bob sipped from it. Whisky, neat.

'That clears your sinuses,' he said.

'You didnae collect your ingins.'

'No, I didnae hae time. I was workin at the ARP. Did you win?'

'Won wi the dahlies and the Pentland Firths. Second or third for aathin else. Your ingins are there if you want them.' He gestured to a parcel at the foot of the fountain wrapped in an old *Perthshire Advertiser*.

'Grand. What aboot the roses?'

'Nah.' He looked momentarily coy, an incongruous sight for this usually featureless man, and then glanced towards Mary Kemp who, Bob noticed, was clutching four cut roses. Bob smiled.

'Hello Mary,' he said. 'I didnae see you there.'

'Aye, that happens.' She became aware of the roses in her hand, of Bob looking at them, of how he might interpret that, and she laid them on the bench beside her and looked away.

'I didnae mean to gie her them,' Sandy whispered to Bob. 'She got the wrang end of the stick. Didnae hae the heart to tak them aff her.'

Bob reflected that such a demonstration of diplomacy was rare for Sandy Disdain. He patted his shoulder and leaned round him. 'How's Doctor McNeill's?' he said to Mary.

'I dinnae work there ony mair.' She looked suddenly panicked. 'I didnae get the sack...'

'I never supposed you would. So whaur are you noo?'

'Barvick Falls.'

'That's ane of the hooses on my ARP route. And Mrs Mitchell's ane of my regulars in Cloudland. She's got three or fower folk bidin wi her, has she no? You'll be gey busy.'

'Four. Aye.'

Silence filled the space where Mary would have been expected to continue the conversation. Bob, no great conversationalist himself, looked to Pipey Oldham.

'Awa and get your pipes,' said Pipey. 'Jine the party.'

'What's it in aid of?'

'Last night of freedom. They'll declare war the morn. And aa this...' He gestured around him, at the Murray Fountain, the High Street, King Street straight and steep, and beyond it, hidden by darkness, Turleum and the Ochils. 'It'll be years afore we're back to ordinar. If we ever are.'

'Five minutes,' said Bob, and he rushed downhill to Cloudland and gathered Annie and his pipes. By the time they returned, half a dozen locals had joined Sandy and Pipey, a couple with tenor drums and one with a fiddle, and the ragtag band struck up *The Braes of Ochtertyre*. Bob played a favourite tune, *Struan Robertson's Salute*, a lament as old as the Battle of Bannockburn. Annie sang *O Rowan Tree*. After considerable encouragement, Mary Kemp sang *The Old Rugged Cross* and Annie cried at the frailty of her voice. Sandy had everyone laughing with *The Haggis o Dunbar* and Fordie Williamson, a traveller stopping in Crieff for the tattie-howking, sang *MacCrimmon's Lament*. The ensemble breezed into *Miss Murray* and *Glenturret Glen*. After an hour, they stopped for cigarettes and pipes and reflection.

'Will it really be war?' asked Mary.

'Aye,' said Bob. 'I'm afraid so.'

'I'm scared.'

'Me an aa. It's hellish. You juist want it to stop. Want Hitler to see sense. See what he's doin. Goin to do.'

'My brither's seventeen. Dick. A year younger than me.'

'He'll no be called up.'

'No yet. But in a year's time? You think the war'll last that long?'

Bob was certain it would but, even in the darkness, Mary's eyes and tight mouth betrayed her fear better than any words. 'When Hitler sees we're no goin to back doon, he'll most likely stop,' he said. 'That's what cowards do.'

'I doot it,' said Sandy. 'He's been plannin this for years. Aathin up to noo – Austria, Sudetenland, Czechoslovakia – was juist buildin up to this.'

'Will he bomb here?' said Mary.

'Aye, maybe.'

'Oh my, how will I get my mither's shoppin?'

'We'll be grand,' said Bob. He picked up his pipes and played *Cock of the North* and then *Bonnie Dundee*. What would war be like? When would there be peace? He played on, emptied his mind of fear, filled it instead with love and companionship. And when, just after midnight, a thunderstorm brought a premature end to their entertainment, Bob and the forty or so souls communing in complete darkness had managed, for a short while anyway, to shake free the dread that had hung over them all day. That dread would return, redoubled, in the hours that followed but, for now, exulting in the rain falling from a mild autumn sky, they felt happy. The world turned. Tomorrow was another day.

Sunday, 3 September

A Day of Declaration

At first light, Sergeant Braggan studied the charred wreckage of the Lochearnhead Hotel's barn. 'What a bloody mess,' he said to Harry Rodgers, the hotel manager. Looking up at the scant remains of the roof, he pushed aside the charred door and entered. 'Paraffin,' he said. 'Smell it?'

'Bastards,' said Harry.

'It wasn't you, was it? Insurance job?'

'It's no insured. It's juist a barn.'

'That's rough.' They went back outside and Braggan bent and picked up a newspaper. '*Glasgow Evening Times*,' he said. 'There's bits been ripped off it. This is what they started the fire with. Probably dipped it in the paraffin and lit it.' He looked back at the lochside, the group of children playing beside it. 'The woman last night said there were Glasgow boys messing about. Bloody keelies. Here five minutes and they've started their nonsense. I knew this would happen.' He marched off, furious that his quiet life was going to be interrupted for the duration by a bunch of feral children.

*

'Well done, Kelty.' Gordon Eadie marched into ARP headquarters where Bob was checking the timetables posted on the wall. 'I walked Zone 5 last night. Only one light, in Milnab Street.'

'Isa Lawson. I'm callin Jack McOmish this mornin. Sendin him roond to fix it.'

'Capital.'

Ronnie Francis strode into the office, removing his bunnet and unbuttoning his coat. He sighed theatrically. 'You've got your wey, then,' he said to Bob. 'Prime Minister's broadcastin at eleven. You ken what that means.'

Bob checked the clock on the rear wall. Ten to eleven. In a moment of absolute clarity, he knew he didn't want to be here, among relative strangers, when he heard the most important announcement of his life. He picked up his bunnet and strode out of the ARP office and crossed the bottom of James Square to Cloudland. He sprinted upstairs and switched on the wireless in the living room.

'What is it?' said Annie, pinnie wrapped around her waist, her hands white with flour.

Bob sat and gestured to Annie to join him. He held her hand, oblivious of the flour. After an introduction from a BBC presenter, Neville Chamberlain's plummy voice filled the room.

'I am speaking to you from the cabinet room at 10 Downing Street. This morning the British ambassador in Berlin handed the German government a final note stating that unless we heard from them by eleven o'clock that they were prepared at once to withdraw their troops from Poland, a state of war would exist between us. I have to tell you now that no such undertaking has been received, and that consequently this country is at war with Germany.'

That was it. No preamble, just the bald truth – "this country is at war with Germany". Chamberlain carried on talking but Bob had stopped listening. The announcement ended and *God Save the King* played. Bob switched off the wireless. Out on the Square, three headscarfed women walked past, deep in conversation. They hadn't heard yet, didn't know the calamity that had befallen them, the years of war and strife to which they had been committed in the name of – what?

'That's that, then,' said Annie.

'Aye.'

He held his breath and closed his eyes. War. The very word frightened him. Not the physical danger, although that was terrifying indeed. What truly frightened him was what war would mean for humanity, for Jock Tamson's bairns, for love and beauty and truth. Those fragile gems would stand no chance in the charnel house the world was about to become. An age of innocence was over and Bob knew, one way or the other, his life would never be the same again.

*

In the entrance hall of Crieff Public School, an elegant staircase split in two halfway up and turned through ninety degrees to form separate entrances to the upper floor, at either end of a long corridor.

'Michty,' said Annie, 'this is grander than Hillyland School.'

'You here for a bairn?' said a young woman with spectacles in horn-rimmed frames that looked old-fashioned on her young face. 'Upstairs on the right. Miss Carrington's classroom.'

They ascended the stairs and turned right turn and stood before Miss Carrington's room. Bob exhaled heavily.

'Ready?' Annie asked.

'No really.'

He knocked on the door and entered. Annie followed. A roomful of children stared at them from six neat rows of desks. The room smelled of stale sweat. A woman sat at the teacher's desk, a younger woman standing behind her, clutching a clipboard.

'Mrs Liversedge?' said Bob. 'Mrs McNeill sent us.'

'And you are?'

'Mr and Mrs Kelty.'

The younger woman checked her clipboard. 'Two children,' she said. Annie and Bob exchanged glances and Bob shook his head.

'The Jardine twins,' said Mrs Liversedge. 'I'll be glad to see them out of the way.' She clapped her hands. 'You boys,' she shouted, gesturing to a pair of lads, identical, about nine years old with skinheads and furious expressions. They were filthy.

'I'm no goin wi him,' said one.

'Baldy cunt,' said the other.

Bob turned to Mrs Liversedge. 'There's been a mistake. We only have room for one bairn.'

'We'll be the judge of that.'

'You were. Mrs McNeill yesterday. She visited and said we only had space for one bairn.'

'It says two here,' said the younger woman, gesturing to her clipboard.

'Well, it's wrang. Oor hoose was "poky", she said. One bairn.'

'Oh, for goodness sake,' said Mrs Liversedge. 'Vera, go down to the secretary's office and telephone Mrs McNeill. She'll be at the Scout hut. Find out what's what. We haven't time for this palaver.' She glowered at Bob and Annie as though this were somehow their fault. Blushing, Vera rushed from the room and Bob turned to the children.

'Hello aabody,' he said. No one replied. Rows of sullen faces stared at him. Each child was wearing an overcoat and most wore hats of some description. They had cases or bags or parcels wrapped in paper, either on the floor beside them or rested on the desk in front of them. Most, but not all, had a gas mask.

'Are you all fae Glesga?' Bob continued. Again, there was silence. Finally a brown-haired girl spoke.

'Finnieston,' she said.

'Finnieston aye? Is that in Glesga?'

'Course it is.' She rolled her eyes at her neighbour, a pretty girl with jet black hair. The black-haired girl stared at Bob but her expression remained hostile.

'Most of the children come from shipbuilding families,' said Mrs Liversedge. 'Very deprived. The lads you're taking, their father died in an accident at the shipyard. They're a bit wild. You'll need a firm hand.'

Bob looked at the Jardine twins. They glowered back at him and Bob knew he was in no way capable of managing them. He felt for Annie's hand and gripped it. War had been declared and now he was being called on to act as a parent when he still felt much like a child himself. The classroom door opened and Vera returned, out of breath. She stood in front of Mrs Liversedge like a naughty schoolchild about to explain herself.

'Mrs McNeill confirms – just one child.'

Mrs Liversedge took the news as if it were a personal affront. 'This is too much,' she said. 'Looking after three thousand children is difficult enough without this incompetence.' She peered at the children in front of her.

'You,' she said, pointing to the black-haired girl. 'What's your name?'

'Ellen.'

'Ellen what?'

'Ellen Laing.'

'Ellen Laing what?'

The girl looked mystified. She shrugged.

'"Ellen Laing, miss",' said Mrs Liversedge. 'Surely you call your teachers "sir" or "miss"?' Ellen shrugged again. 'Very well, Ellen Laing. This is Mr and Mrs Kelty. You'll be staying with them from now on. Say hello.'

Ellen said nothing.

'Come along, child,' Mrs Liversedge said, an irritated edge to her voice. 'We haven't all day. Chop-chop.'

Ellen rose hesitantly, clutching a gas mask to her stomach.

21

On the desk was a bundle that appeared to be wrapped in old wallpaper and tied with string. She stepped forward and stood beside Bob and Annie, not looking up at them.

'Hello Ellen,' Bob said. He stretched out his hand. 'Nice to meet you.'

She didn't take his hand. She was grubby, dirt beneath her fingernails and a tide mark around her neck. Bob took her bundle of clothing. It was surprisingly light.

'Let's go,' he said. 'I'll warn you noo, Crieff's built on a hill so aaplace you want to go you hae to climb to get there. You're alright the day, though. I've arranged a lift hame. Special treat. D'you fancy a wee hurl in a car?'

He opened the classroom door and ushered Ellen and Annie out and followed them down the stairway. A young woman emerged from the headmaster's office, her hair neatly permed. She was wearing a crisp green tunic and looked most elegant. Bob smiled and Lorna Carrington returned his smile before glancing at Annie and staring for some moments at Ellen.

'Good luck,' she said and sashayed up the stairs.

They exited into the playground and Bob looked for Sandy Disdain. He was leaning against the Commissioner Street wall, smoking a Capstan.

'Sandy,' he said. 'Thanks for helpin.'

Sandy indicated behind him. 'Your carriage awaits.' Waiting at the kerb was an open wooden cart hitched to a morose-looking horse with blinkers.

'What the hell's that?' said Bob.

'Your transport.'

'It's a horse and cairt.'

'I ken.'

'I thocht it was a car.'

'I never said it was a car.'

Ellen backed away, horrified. 'Huv I come to the olden days?' she said.

Bob laughed. 'You might think that, hen,' he admitted. 'We're probably no as fancy as your Glesga weys.'

'I'm no goin on that hing. It's mawkit.'

Bob looked at her frowning face. 'It'll be fine,' he said. 'We'll be hame in five minutes. It's juist up the hill.'

Annie inspected the cart. It was indeed filthy, grass and weeds strewn over it, and clods of earth, a worm wriggling through one of them. She had worn her good swagger coat and best frock to make an impression on their evacuee and there was no way she was getting onto that cart.

'I'll awa to Campbell's and see if they've ony pies left,' she said. 'The lassie's probably famished.'

'Can I come wi ye?' said Ellen.

Annie hesitated and said no. 'Stay with your Uncle Bob,' she said.

'He's no my uncle.'

'Aye well, we'll work out what you can call us. On you go.' She gave a wave and hurried along Commissioner Street. Bob tossed the bundle of clothing onto the cart and grabbed Ellen and lifted her aboard. He handed her the gas mask and she sat near the front, clutching her bundle once more. She didn't speak. Bob and Sandy clambered onto the front of the cart and Sandy took the reins and flicked them over the horse's flank. It raised its head and began to move and they progressed along Commissioner Street, overtaking Annie just before the King Street junction. She waved but Ellen sat staring backwards, impassive. Sandy manoeuvred onto King Street and they began their ascent.

'It's no quite what I expected but thanks onywey,' said Bob.

'What are you goin to do wi her?'

'Nae idea. I dinnae ken much aboot bairns. Even when I was one I never played with the other bairns. I suppose we'll see what interests she has. Maybe you could tak her oot wi you some time.'

'What, rabbitin?'

'Aye.'

'A lassie?'

'How no?'

Thingwie Johnstone, leaning against a lamp post outside the police station to catch his breath, hailed them with a wave. 'Hoi,' he shouted, pointing behind them. 'You've lost somethin.'

They both turned and looked behind them. Sprawled on the dirt road, staring back at them furiously, bundle by her side, was Ellen. Her clothes, already grubby, were now filthy. She wiped hair from her face. Sandy pulled up and Bob jumped out to retrieve her.

'People are lookin at me,' she seethed. 'Make them stoap.' She glowered at Bob, her expression a combination of rage and embarrassment. Her hands were fisted so tight her knuckles were white. Bob pulled her to her feet and deposited her, once more, on the cart.

'Sit further back,' he said. 'I did think you were a bit close to the edge.'

'It's a pity ye didnae think to mention it.'

'Aye, richt enough. You'll find I'm no the most practical man.'

'Just fuckin get me oot of here.' She stared at the dusty road, ignoring the crowd gathered around her.

Sandy set off once more and they arrived a minute or so later at Cloudland, where he declined the offer of a cup of tea. 'Need to get this thing back afore Tam Jarvis notices it's missin.' He flicked the reins and the horse began to trot uphill to the High Street. Bob opened the door of Cloudland and led Ellen upstairs to the flat.

'This is your room,' he said, showing her into the spare room. 'Got the bed specially this morning fae Neil's showroom. We havenae ony blankets for a single bed yet so we've just used doubles for noo. That's why they're hingin aa the wey to the floor.'

She didn't reply, only stood and stared at him. She seemed petrified. 'You've a wee set of drawers here. Let's put your stuff away.' He untied the wallpaper-covered bundle. It was virtually empty, a pair of pants, a pair of socks, a vest and a pinafore that was surely too small.

'Is this aa you've got?' he said. Again, she didn't reply. He put what there was in the top drawer. Everything was old and soiled, threadbare to the point of uselessness. He studied the girl, her dirty clothing, scuffed shoes, socks with no elastic, a frock with at least two holes in it. She would need everything new. With relief, he heard Annie returning from Campbell's and they went to the kitchen to greet her.

'Last pie in the shop,' she said, sliding it onto a plate. 'Here you go, lassie, you'll never hae tasted onythin like this afore, I promise.' She cut the pie in two, revealing a dense layer of minced lamb and semi-congealed fat, held together by a pastry cup. Ellen looked dubious but she took a small mouthful and chewed meditatively. Then she took a fuller mouthful and chomped on it greedily and with another two bites the pie was gone.

'Good?' said Annie.

'Mingin,' said Ellen.

'I'd like to see how fast you can eat somethin you like,' said Bob.

Ellen licked her fingers and looked around the kitchen as though in search of more food. 'I prefer a piece,' she said.

'I'll mind that,' said Annie. 'Jam? Or cheese?'

'Lard.'

'I'm sure we could rustle that up,' said Bob. 'Have you mony of your pals wi you? Fae school?'

'Wan of them was killed on the wey here. Fell aff the train.'

Bob and Annie exchanged glances. 'Is that right?' said Bob.

'Willie Wood. Lives the same close as me.'

'Did they no stop the train?'

25

'Aye. But he was deid already. They stuck him in the guard room.' She spoke matter-of-factly, scratching her arm and shoulder.

Annie shook her head at Bob. This was clearly not true, but she didn't think there would be any benefit in pursuing the point. 'Any other pals?' she said brightly.

'I dinnae hae pals.'

'How no?'

'Naebody likes me.'

'I'm sure that's no true.'

'An how would you know?'

'I never had pals at school either,' said Bob.

'Why doesn't that surprise me?'

'You'll mak new friends here.'

'Wi teuchters? That'll be fuckin right.'

'We're no awfae keen on swearin in the hoose.'

'Can I do it in the cludgy then?'

'The toilet's in the hoose.'

She looked at him, scandalised. 'That's mingin. Who wants the smell of keech in the hoose?'

Annie gave a strained smile. 'At least we hae it to oorsels, dinnae need to share. And it doesnae smell bad. . .'

'I suppose your keech smells of perfume?'

Annie sighed. 'I'm beginnin to see why you dinnae hae ony friends.'

'I didnae ask to come here. I dinnae want to be here.'

Bob picked up his pipe. 'Aye, it's gey strange for us aa. But we'll get used to each other. . .'

'Get to fuck.' Ellen jumped to her feet and ran for the door, slamming it behind her. Moments later, her bedroom door slammed, too.

'I'm thinkin we micht hae been better wi thae twins,' said Bob.

*

Mary had worked a twelve-hour shift at Barvick Falls because Bessie, the other maid, was unwell. Although Mary had only been working there for a week, she was already beginning to suspect that Bessie's illnesses might not be rarities. Mrs Mitchell didn't seem to care as long as the work was done and that left Mary to pick up the strain. She crossed the landing to the bedroom she shared with Bessie but before she could reach it the door to Miss Carrington's room opened.

'Thought I heard you stalking about,' Lorna said. 'You're no ballet dancer.' She held a cigarette in her right hand in the fashion of Hollywood starlets and blew smoke across the landing. 'What time do you finish?'

'I've just finished, miss,' Mary replied wearily.

'Come and share a sherry with me.' She turned and re-entered her room without waiting for a reply, leaving Mary to view her retreating back helplessly. All Mary wanted to do was get to her room and steep her feet in a pail of hot water. Sherry? She'd never drunk sherry in her life. She followed Lorna with all the foreboding of a convict entering the condemned cell.

'I hope you didn't think me rude yesterday.' Lorna poured two small schooners of sherry and handed one to Mary. 'I'd like for us to be friends. Most of the people here are ancient. Miss Glass is virtually senile. Mr Henderson is a vile old man and that nurse of his – well I wouldn't want her nursing me, that's all I can say. And the other maid, Bessie, she's frightfully common, don't you think?' She sat on the pink bedspread and gestured to the seat by the window. 'Not our class of girl, am I right?'

Mary sipped her sherry. It wasn't what she expected. She'd taken a mouthful of her father's *Lamb's Navy Rum* the previous Hogmanay and thought that was how all alcohol tasted. The sherry was so sweet she feared it might glue her mouth shut. She stared at the glass, pondering how she would ever be able to drink it all. Lorna saw her.

'Lovely, isn't it? *Sandeman's*, frightfully expensive but an admirer buys it for me.'

Mary wondered what kind of admirer would purchase alcohol for an unmarried woman. That seemed – she wasn't sure of the word – decadent? She felt out of her depth. She needed to escape.

'Yesterday,' Lorna said. 'You know I was here all day, don't you? If anyone asks.'

Mary knew no such thing. How could she? She twisted her sherry glass in her hand. 'Aye,' she said. 'I think so, aye.'

'Good girl. All day and all evening. Remember. We're going to be such friends.' Lorna flashed a smile that disappeared almost immediately. 'Have you ever thought of going into teaching?' she said. 'It's a good career for a woman. Especially if she doesn't intend to get married.' She stared at Mary. 'And you don't look the marrying sort.'

'I was never awfae good at the school.'

'You don't have to be. That's the joy of it. The little brats, they don't know anything. You only have to keep one stage ahead of them. It isn't hard.'

'I dinnae think I could keep them under control.'

'Oh, that's the easy bit.' She reached into a satchel beside her bed and pulled out a leather tawse, a good foot and a half in length, with three thick tines at one end. 'This is your best friend.' She laughed and strapped her left hand lightly with it. 'Don't suppose you ever got the strap?'

'Certainly no.'

She laughed again and handed the tawse to Mary. Mary was astonished by its weight and the stiffness of the leather. She had seen boys strapped often, six times on each hand, and now she felt the tawse she couldn't conceive how painful that must have been.

'Well,' said Lorna, winking at her, 'be a good girl and I shan't have to use it on you.'

*

'Ellen.' Annie knocked on the bedroom door. 'I've filled you a bath, ben the kitchen.'

'I'm no needin a bath.'

'It's Sunday nicht.'

'So?'

'Sunday's bath nicht.'

The door swung open and Ellen stood framed in the doorway. Her expression was fierce but her eyes were rimmed red and Annie could tell she had been crying. She reached her hand out.

'Come on,' she said and led her into the kitchen. On the floor, beside the table, a tin bath was half-filled with water, steam rising from it.

'I'm no gettin in there.'

'You hae to, hen. We're takin you to Perth the morn to buy you some new claes, but you'll need a wash first.'

'I'm no getting in there!' She yanked her hand free of Annie's and sped back to her room. Bob, hearing the commotion, emerged from the living room. Annie shook her head.

'I dinnae ken what to do.'

'She'll settle. Juist gie her some time.'

'She needs a bath. She's clarty.'

'I ken, but no the nicht. She's up to high doh with the worry.'

Annie looked at the closed bedroom door. 'I suppose,' she said. 'I'll juist get her ready for bed, then.' She hesitated at the door, deciding what to say to the girl. 'There's fresh watter in the bath if you want,' she said to Bob.

'I'm no gettin in there!'

'Bob Kelty!' Their laughter broke the tension. Annie entered Ellen's room. 'You've had a long day, hen, what say we get you ready for bed?'

'I'm no needin my bed.'

'You dinnae need to put the light off yet, we'll just get you tucked up nice and cozy. Let me tak your frock off.'

'Get to fuck. Nobody's goin to tak ma frock and pinch it while I'm dossin.'

'Naebody's goin to pinch. . .'

Ellen leaped across the bed and ducked low and slipped past Annie. Before Annie could move she bolted out of the front door and clattered down the stairs. 'Witch!' she shouted. By the time Bob and Annie could follow, the front door was open and Ellen had disappeared.

'Damn,' said Bob. 'You bide here in case she comes back. I'll look for her.' The square was bathed in evening sunshine, the air still warm. Bob tried to think where Ellen would go. Down King Street, probably, back the way they had come that afternoon. She would choose somewhere familiar. He marched downhill as far as Commissioner Street and stopped. A signpost directed the way to the railway station. Perhaps she'd gone there, intent on finding a train back to Glasgow. He trotted downhill and at the station he checked the Up and Down platforms but there was no sign of her. Sighing, he made his way uphill again and walked towards the school. The gates were locked and the building lay in darkness. The ghosts of poachie beds, squares numbered one to ten, were marked on the playground in chalk, remnants of the school year past, faded now and awaiting a new cohort to take on the mantle.

He climbed Duchlage Road and checked at the bus station but, apart from a drunk Hallie Newton awaiting the Muthill bus, it was deserted. He passed the church hall, scene of Sandy Disdain's flower show triumphs the previous day, and at the High Street he turned left into the town centre. The place was quiet. He headed back towards Cloudland, pondering what to do next, and saw Ellen sitting on the stone steps at the Murray Fountain, knees drawn up, cradled by her arms, her chin nestling against them. He sat down beside her.

'See that,' he said, pointing to a hill far in the distance. 'That's Turleum. We're surrounded by hills here. Everywhere you look. I'll tak you up the Knock and show you.'

'Whit's the Knock?'

This was the first time she'd responded without hostility. 'The whole of Crieff's built on a hill called the Knock. Aa the wey up there. . .' He turned and pointed behind them. 'That's the tap of the Knock. We'll soon hae you fit, livin here.'

'I dinnae want to live here.'

'I ken. But the high-heid-yins, they're worried Glesga'll get bombed. They're juist lookin oot for you.'

'I can look after mysel.'

'I dinnae doot it.' He took out his pipe and filled the bowl and tamped it. He lit it and smoke curled into the air around them.

'Seez a shot of your pipe?'

'I dinnae think so.'

'My faither lets me smoke his fags.'

'How auld are you?'

'Near twelve.'

'Far too young. I didnae start till I was fourteen.' He handed her the pipe. 'Dinnae inhale. Just tak it into your mooth and let it roll aroond, then blaw it oot.'

Ellen studied the bowl of the pipe, making herself cross-eyed in the process. She gripped it with both hands as she took in a draw of the smoke. She held it in her mouth, then let it out in a rush.

'Aye?'

'Aye.'

'Dinnae tell Annie I let you do that.'

'She's a witch.'

'She isnae. Really. She's the kindest person I've ever kent. You'll see.'

Ellen inhaled again, this time drawing the smoke into her lungs. She choked and coughed and Bob took the pipe from her and patted her back gently.

'How long ye gonnae keep me here?'

'It's no us that's keepin you, hen. But I'd say until aathin's safe again.'

'And when will that be?'

Bob stared all the way down King Street. He looked up at Turleum, turning indistinct as darkness began to settle on the strath. *When everything was safe again.* He wasn't sure anything had ever been safe. Not really. The sign above Cloudland stood out in the square, its bright red cursive script modern in comparison to everything else around. Cloudland. Home. A place of safety. Refuge. Love. A sanctuary from the hustle of life, the decisions, the relentless drive of time, those interactions with people, every one a strain, a drain on his mental resources. And those were the good days. Now, the country was at war. The world would follow. This would be a war not fought on battlegrounds, in trenches, army against army. This war would be fought in the streets, the homes, the hearts of ordinary people, people like Annie, like little Ellen, frightened and angry and lonely, lashing out, unable to distinguish between kindness and indifference. *When everything was safe again. When everything. . .*Without knowing why, he started to cry, tears of helplessness in a world not tuned to his wavelength, tears of despair and tears of hope, tears for better days and worse, for now and beyond. Tears for the war. Tears for the child. For himself and Annie. For Turleum and the Ochils and Strathearn, for Crieff, quiet wee toon, suddenly, irrevocably, a warzone. He wiped his eyes and looked at Ellen.

'Fuckin weirdie,' she said.

*

Lorna Carrington threw down the newspaper, angered by a report on the conscientious objector, Robert Bain, in which his stance was supported by a Minister of the Church of Scotland. The second death awaited the coward Bain and his ilk, the *lake which burneth with fire and brimstone*. Lorna hated cowardice, and she also hated the Church and its mealy-mouthed morality. *Turn the other cheek. Love thy neighbour.* She hated the hypocrisy of a religion that encouraged dictatorship in the home and democracy at large. She hated her father, the Reverend David Carrington, Wee Free Minister, home dictator and bully, misogynist and misandrist, a man for whom charity was a word on the page to be lied about until the last trump sounded and all but he were condemned to the eternal fires.

Lorna stared out of her window at the darkness enveloping the town. She replayed the fire in Lochearnhead. Those sounds, so sharp, so violent, so vital. The smell. Smell of destruction. Division. And such sights. Flames destroying everything in their path.

Fire was a beautiful thing. *For our God is a consuming fire.*

Lorna Carrington was going to build some fires.

Monday, 4 September

A Day of Meetings

'How did you sleep?' Bob laid down his *Courier* and smiled as Ellen sat at the kitchen table.

'Terrible,' she said.

'How?'

'Too quiet.'

'You should've said. I'd hae got my bagpipes oot.'

'You play the bagpipes?'

'I'll show you later.'

'Please don't. Ma faither was right. This really is teuchter country.'

'You've maybe no seen the best of us yet. Noo then, porridge for breakfast.' Her eyes widened. 'Is that teuchter as well?' She nodded.

Annie placed three bowls of porridge on the table, all different sizes.

'Look,' said Bob. 'Goldilocks and the three bears.'

'Who?' said Ellen.

'You've never heard of Goldilocks?'

'Nut.'

'She must be a teuchter thing an aa.'

'Don't make a fool of me.'

'Sorry, I didnae mean to. Eat up. We're takin you shoppin.'

They were only supposed to provide food and incidentals for

Ellen, for which they would receive 10/6 a week, to be collected from the Strathearn Institute each Saturday but, the night before, as they studied the contents of her wallpaper package and the condition of her frock they knew remedial action was necessary.

'It's a Crieff holiday the day,' Bob said, 'so we hae to go to Perth.'

'What's a Crieff holiday?'

'Aa the shops are shut.'

'What for?'

'A holiday.'

Ellen looked at him in bemusement. 'How can a town go on holiday?'

*

The Ministry of Agriculture was encouraging farmers to plough ten percent more of their land to help with the war effort. That was bad news for hunters like Sandy Disdain, meaning there would be fewer fallow fields for snaring rabbits. Sandy adjusted his gamebag on his shoulder and leaned into the shallow slope of a field bordering the Horseshoe Drive. This was too near town, too near civilisation, but he would soon have no option but to snare such areas. He stopped by a tumbledown drystane dyke and surveyed the field opposite, run to grass for the season. He studied the pattern of rabbit runs, heading northwest across the field towards another wall at the far corner, then he climbed the dyke and jumped into the field.

He stopped at the first rabbit run and gauged where to set his snare. Into the dry ground he heeled a wooden peg, attached to which with rope was a looped coil of finely spun copper wire. He set the snare so that the loop was about six inches in diameter, then fixed a hazel tealer into the ground, aslant, and settled the snare into a V-shaped notch in the top. He positioned the snare and sat back. He readjusted it and then, satisfied, pulled the next snare from his gamebag and moved on.

'You there.'

Lorna Carrington, on her daily walk, stood on the Horseshoe Drive behind the wall Sandy had just climbed. She wore a blue shawl over her hair and a red, wide-lapelled princess coat.

'Come here,' she said.

'I've juist been there. Noo I'm goin ower yonder.' He pointed over his shoulder.

'What are you doing?'

'Mindin my ain business. I recommend it.'

'Are you setting snares?'

Sandy looked at the snare at his feet, and then at the one in his hand, and then at the forty or so in his gamebag. 'What gies you that idea?'

'It's deplorable. Killing animals is criminal.'

'Aye well, there's a war on. We'll be needin every bit of food we can get afore lang. You micht change your tune when you're sittin at the table wi nothin on your plate.'

'You're a barbarian.'

'I shoot them an aa, if that's any better.' He took out a Capstan and lit it. Although he was enjoying the argument, he knew there was no point prolonging it. He turned and headed for the next rabbit run.

'Don't walk away from me!'

'I've work to do.'

'I'll report you. To. . . To the farmer.'

'I am the fairmer.'

*

Bob recognised an old friend and colleague, Jimmy Wright, driving the Perth bus when they arrived at the station, and shook his hand as they stepped on board.

'I guess you'll be cuttin your timetable?' Bob said. 'Wi the war?'

'Nae doot. I'm no carin. I'll be retirin soon.' He gestured to the bus waiting at the next aisle. 'That's the day's mystery tour. Probably the last ane of them until this is aa ower.'

'Whaur's it goin?'

'Glesga.'

'Thank God we didnae book that. The lassie's juist come fae there, haven't you Ellen?'

'I want to go back.'

Jimmy studied Ellen as though she were some exotic creature. 'I hear there was ane of them killed on the train here. Fell aff afore Falkirk.' Annie and Bob looked at one another, then at Ellen. She gave them an insolent smirk.

They sat on the back seat and Ellen watched startle-eyed as town gave way to country, to field after field, the farmers with their threshers, bringing in the harvest. The heatwave they had enjoyed for the past few weeks showed no sign of abating and there was a haze in the air, the sky a cloudless expanse of blue. Clydesdales, muscular and imposing, dragged the threshing machines and Bob felt a pang of loss. In a different world it would have been him tending those heavy horses, inheriting the job from his faither, making his living from the land. In that world, of course, he would never have met Annie, and that wouldn't do, not at all but, watching the horses now, he couldn't deny the feeling that his life was somehow diminished.

On the descent into Perth, Ellen seemed to relax, as though the sight of buildings and streets was returning her to normality. The area around Tulloch had changed since Bob had lived in Perth, new streets rising from what had once been farmland. Bob pointed out Muirton Park, home of St Johnstone football club but Ellen showed no interest. They disembarked outside the Sandeman Public Library.

'I used to work there,' Bob said. 'For aboot five minutes until I got the sack.'

'Whit d'you get the sack fur?'

Bob considered. 'Tryin to do the right thing,' he said finally. 'That's ay gettin me into bother, one wey or the other.'

They went to Davidson's on George Street, where Annie had had her clothes bought for her when she was a bairn. She smiled at the assistant, an elderly woman she was sure she recognised from years before, but the smile wasn't reciprocated. The assistant glared at Ellen as they studied the frocks on display.

'Could we try this on?' Annie said, holding up a green dress.

'No her, you cannae,' the assistant said, staring at Ellen. 'She's filthy.'

'She's no filthy.'

'She's no tryin on any clothes in here. Is she ane of those Glesga keelies? Lord knows what diseases she's got.'

'Fuck off, you old hag,' said Ellen. She ran from the shop and Bob remembered her response the day before when she fell from the cart on King Street. "People are lookin at me. Make them stoap." It was an anger born of embarrassment, he knew. He rushed after her.

'Some folk are juist stuck up,' he said. 'We dinnae need to bother wi them.'

'Auld cunt,' said Ellen. Annie glowered at her as she exited the shop and she looked back to see whether the shop assistant had heard. The woman was staring at them frostily.

As they retreated up George Street, Annie's mind whirred. She bent down to Ellen. 'Listen, hen, we really need to buy you some new claes. You'd like that, would you no? But these shop assistants, they're awfae pan-loafy. Can I tak you to the public baths and just tidy you up a wee bit? No a bath nor nothin, juist a quick dicht.' She stroked Ellen's cheek. 'We'll only be five minutes, and then you'll be allowed to try on the nice frocks. Aye?'

With relief, she realised Ellen didn't resist as she started walking again and in a couple of minutes they arrived at the public baths and wash-house in Mill Street.

'I'll wait for you here,' Bob said and Annie and Ellen entered the baths. Annie had never set foot in the place before and wasn't sure what to do.

'You alright, hen?' A young woman, younger even than Annie, sat in a booth near the entrance. She had the most startling pale blue eyes. 'Quick wash is it?'

'Aye,' said Annie.

'A penny. Through there.'

She paid the penny and stepped through an arched doorway marked "Ladies" into a large, insufferably hot room, separated into small booths, cordoned off by half-walls rising about five feet in the air. In each booth was a wide, rectangular sink with a single copper tap. Annie put the plug in the sink and ran the water. It was scaldingly hot and she shoogled the water with her hand as though this might somehow cool it. There was a small pile of cloths, clean but old and yellowing with age, and she took the top one and floated it in the water. She squeezed off the excess and wiped it across Ellen's neck. 'Alright?' she said. Ellen said nothing. Annie recharged the cloth and scrubbed the grime from her neck, then gingerly wiped it across Ellen's face. Ellen backed away but didn't resist, and Annie wiped her face clean and stepped back.

'There,' she said, 'what a bonny lassie.' For an instant, she detected a glimmer of pleasure on Ellen's face before it was overtaken by her customary scowl. Only an instant, but long enough. Annie smiled and bent down. 'Hands noo,' she said, and she wiped her hands and then her knees and legs as far as the socks which dangled around her ankles. She stood up.

'Pretty as a picter.'

Back outside, Bob was puffing on his pipe as he watched the arrivals and departures at the Sandeman Library. Although Ellen looked much cleaner, he chose not to remark. They went to Christeen Reid's on South Methven Street and bought three pairs of socks and three pairs of pants. Ellen stroked them over and over until the assistant had to take them from her to wrap them. She tried on three tweed frocks and hated them all. 'They're jaggy,' she said.

'Nice and warm for the winter,' said Annie.

Ellen picked up a frock on the next rail. 'This,' she said. It was red with small white spots and larger, golden circles. The waist and squared neck were patterned with half a dozen narrow bands of red and yellow bounded by wider bands of deep purple. She tried it on and the effect was bright and chic, counterpointing the darkness of her hair.

'Juist the dab,' said Bob.

'Can I keep it on?'

'Aye, I dinnae see why no.'

In Carmichael's, Ellen tried on several pairs of shoes before returning to the ones she had tried first, reddish-brown patent leather with dainty buckles at the side. They matched the frock perfectly. Annie looked at the price.

'Seven and nine,' she said. 'That's awfae dear.'

'I've some money put by for a new fiddle bow,' Bob said. 'We can use that.'

After buying new toothbrushes for everyone in Blair's, they pondered what to do next and agreed that they should visit Bella Conoboy. The Conoboys were old acquaintances of Bob and Annie and had looked out for Bob when he first arrived in Perth as a laddie following the death of his father. Victor Conoboy had died a few weeks earlier and they hadn't seen Bella since the funeral. Although Bella wrote every week, Annie was concerned how she would be bearing up on her own.

Dozens of soldiers were digging trenches on the North Inch, opposite the Conoboys' residence on Rose Terrace. Mina, the maid, opened the door and escorted them inside. Bella was in her accustomed seat by the fire, bookcases behind her, her current book, *Goodbye to Berlin*, on the round table beside her. Bob could barely bring himself to look at Victor's empty chair. Bella rose and embraced Bob and Annie and turned to Ellen.

'And who is this charming young lady in the beautiful frock?' she said.

'This is Ellen Laing,' Bob said. 'She's staying with us.'

'An evacuee?'

'From Glasgow.'

'Finnieston,' said Ellen.

Bella bent and shook Ellen's hand. 'Lovely to meet you, Ellen. I'm Bella, so our names are quite similar. That means we're going to get on splendidly. You're from Finnieston? Does that mean your daddy works in the shipbuilding?' Ellen nodded. 'That's a very important job, isn't it? I expect you're missing your family. Do you have brothers and sisters?'

'Naw.'

'Everything must seem very strange. Here all on your own. Would you like some lemonade?' Ellen nodded. 'Perhaps you can go with Mina and help her with the drinks?' Mina stood at the door and waited until Ellen joined her and the two left the room.

'She's frightened,' said Bella.

'Yes,' said Bob. 'And it's makin her aggressive and difficult.'

'It isn't her fault.'

'I know.'

'We're no awfae good at this parentin lark,' said Annie. We couldnae even get her to tak a bath last night.' She explained about Ellen's temper tantrum, her refusal to get in the bath, running away, and the difficulty they'd encountered in Davidson's as a result.

'Leave that to me,' said Bella.

Bella had lost weight. Some of the lustre had gone from her eyes. She seemed slower. 'How are you keeping?' Annie asked.

'I miss him terribly, if that's what you mean. But I get by. Mornings are so quiet. Breakfast. No one to discuss the news with. And, heavens, what news there is, what tragic, tragic news. And the evenings are long. No one to help with the crossword. But right now the only thing I can think about is this wretched war. All those young men. . .' She turned to Bob.

'You must look after yourself,' she said. 'No cause is worth the loss of your life. Do you hear?'

'Yes.'

'But do you hear? Do you know what I'm saying?'

'I do.'

Mina and Ellen arrived with the drinks and they sat quietly, drinking, thinking, remembering. The pulse of history was in the room, young Tom Conoboy lost to war before he was even a man, Victor Conoboy, dead a matter of weeks after a lifetime of public service, Bella Conoboy, the most decent, honourable woman Bob had ever known, wounded by existence, refusing to submit, locked in a lifetime of grief and despair.

'Tell me, Ellen,' said Bella, 'do you read?'

'Nut.'

'What a shame. Let's see what we can do about that.' She approached her bookcases and studied them for some moments before extracting a slim volume. She handed it to Ellen.

'This was a favourite of my son's when he'd have been about your age.'

Ellen took the book wide-eyed and held it as though trying not to exert any pressure on it or leave any marks. As she had done with her pants and socks in the shop earlier, she stroked it meditatively.

'*The Secret Garden*,' Bella said. 'I think you'll like it. I expect everything's very odd to you at the moment. You might understand how the little girl in the book feels.'

Ellen opened it. Inside was an inscription, "To Tom, love Mummy and Daddy, Christmas 1911."

'Tom, is that yer son?'

'Yes.'

'Won't he mind?'

'I'm sure he'd have been delighted to see it being enjoyed again.'

Ellen looked as if she was about to speak again, but instead she walked across to Victor's chair and sat down. Bob looked in alarm at Bella to see if this was permitted but Bella wore an amiable smile.

'Now,' she said. 'This is a very big house and there's lots to see. Come with me.' She reached out her hand and Ellen looked at her quizzically before jumping off the chair. Placing her book carefully on the arm, she followed Bella into the hallway.

Bella gave Ellen a tour of the house from top to bottom. They looked across Rose Terrace at the soldiers digging on the Inch.

'Why are they doin that?' Ellen asked.

'Foolishness, my dear. Foolishness.' She led her to the bathroom. 'This,' she said, pointing to an enamel bath that took up an entire wall, 'is my pride and joy. We had it installed a couple of years ago. Running hot water. As much as you need.'

Ellen looked at it in astonishment. 'Ye could swim in there.'

'You probably could. What do you think? Would you like to try it out?'

'What, huv a bath in that?'

'Yes.'

'I've never hud a bath. No a real one.'

'One that you could lie down in?'

'Naw.'

'You can in there. Put your head underwater. Pretend the world isn't there. All you can hear are your own thoughts.' Ellen continued to look in wonderment. 'Would you like to?' Without waiting for an answer she turned the taps. Above them, the pipes rattled and a moment later water began to gush into the bath, at first, vaguely brown-coloured but quickly clearing. Ellen could smell the heat, almost metallic. She dipped her hand in the rapidly-filling bath and pulled it away with a grimace. Bella smiled.

'Let's cool it down a touch,' she said, turning the cold tap up and the hot tap down. It took five minutes before the bath was filled and Bella turned to Ellen. 'Now then,' she said. She unbuttoned the new frock and lifted it over her head. Beneath, Ellen still wore the grimy vest she had arrived in. Bella removed that too and stifled a gasp when she saw the state of the girl's skin. There were patches of eczema on her back and arms and there was a red circle on her underarm which Bella thought was ringworm. The girl was desperately thin, her shoulder blades jutting out as though trying to escape. Bella stroked a patch of eczema.

'That must be terribly sore,' she said. 'Poor love. We'll need to see what we can do about that.' She peeled off Ellen's pants and socks and took her hand. 'In you go,' she said. Holding on to Bella, Ellen stepped into the bath.

'If you need more water, or if it gets cold, just shout for Mina.' Ellen sat stock-still in the bath, her knees drawn up, as Bella closed the door and retreated downstairs.

'Where is she?' Annie asked.

'Having a bath.'

'How did you get her to do that?'

'Turn something into a playground and a child will play with it.'

'I hope she doesnae make too much mess.'

'I hope she does.'

The adults continued to talk as the afternoon progressed, their conversation punctuated by girlish screams and yelps and the sound of splashing water. Annie apologised but Bella waved her away.

'The house hasn't been this alive in twenty years and more,' she said, sitting contentedly in her chair. 'Children, you see, they can resolve any worries, if you let them.'

*

'So much disruption for these poor children.'

'What?' Lorna turned on the stair. That old buffoon Mr

Henderson was approaching, followed by his wretched nurse. They rented all three rooms on the second floor of Barvick Falls and Lorna was certain the man was lecherous because of the way he constantly tried to engage her in meaningless conversation.

'These poor evacuees,' Mr Henderson continued. 'Uprooted from their homes, brought a hundred miles away, made to live with people they don't know. What a thing to do.'

'Would you rather they were blown to smithereens in bombing raids?'

'I'd rather there were no bombing raids.'

'Well, it's too late for that.'

'It's never too late for common sense to prevail.'

'You'll be wanting us to negotiate with Hitler, I take it?'

'Would that be so wrong?'

'Where has it got us so far?'

'Perhaps we haven't negotiated properly.'

Lorna shifted her satchel to her other hand. 'You don't negotiate. You fight. You don't ask. You take. That's the way of the world.'

'What a world.'

'What a world indeed. A beautiful one.'

And the violent take it by force.

*

Bob rapped gently on Ellen's door. 'Can I come in?' he said.

Ellen was in bed, wearing her new pyjamas, her frock folded on the dressing table chair. Her vest was on the floor. Bob picked it up.

'I think we need to throw this awa,' he said. 'By the look of it, it's aulder than I am.'

'Nothin's that auld.'

'Cheeky madam.' He gestured to the book. 'Are you enjoyin it?'

'It's too hard.'

'I'll maybe help you wi it. Read it wi you.' She didn't agree, but she didn't say no either.

'Why do you speak posh to her?' Ellen said.

'Who?'

'That woman.'

'Mrs Conoboy? I dinnae.'

'Aye, you do. You even said I came from "Glasgow".' She repeated it for effect, trying to sound refined. 'Gleeesgoooow.'

'I dinnae,' he repeated but he knew she was right. He always had. And he didn't know why.

'Why does she no leave the hoose?'

He looked at her in surprise. 'How did you ken that?'

'She kept sayin "so and so came roond" or "thingummy does that for me". That made me think she didnae go oot. So I asked her if she enjoyed doin the gairden and she said naw, she didnae spend much time oot there. But all the time she was speakin she was lookin at it, like she wanted to be oot there. And her seat's placed so she can see straight oot.'

'You're a wee detective,' said Bob. He had been surprised when Ellen had asked that question. It was probably the first time she'd spoken unbidden since she'd arrived and it seemed a most unusual thing for a child to ask. 'Mrs Conoboy has something called agoraphobia,' he explained. 'It means she's scared to go ootside.'

'Why?'

'It's just something she's had for years.'

'Since Tom died?'

'How on earth d'you ken that?'

She gestured to her book, the inscription inside. 'When I asked if he'd mind, you and yer missus looked a bit funny, like ye was needin a jobbie. And then Mrs Conoboy said, "he would huv been pleased". Makes it sound like he's deid, no?'

'He was killed in the war.'

'Are you gonnae fight in the war?'

'I dinnae ken.'

'My faither winnae huv to fight because he works on the docks. That's a reversed occupation.'

'Reserved occupation.'

'That's whit I said.'

'So it was.'

He left her a few minutes later, studying her book, and went back to Annie in the living room, still thinking about fighting and reserved occupations. The government had produced a list of occupations where, even if a man was of an age to be called up, he could remain in his current employment. It included obvious professions like farm workers, poultrymen, fishermen or ambulance drivers, but more unusual ones too, like accountants, bookstall attendants or French polishers. And, of course, men like Ellen's faither who would build the ships that would wage the war.

Following government advice, Bob had stuck brown paper around the central lampshade on their standard lamp, reducing further the light it emitted, leaving the room mired in gloom. The blackout curtains hung heavy and intrusive. There was a weight to this way of living, a density that was, even this early, exhausting. He opened up *The Courier* and peered at it in the half-light. On the inside back page was news that football was now at a standstill, the season stopped "in the meantime". Bob's beloved St Johnstone had won 3-0 against Aberdeen on Saturday. Who could tell when their next match might be? In the Stop Press, there was an announcement stamped onto the paper in red ink:

S.S. ATHENIA WITH 1400 PASSENGERS ON BOARD, HAS BEEN TORPEDOED 200 MILES WEST OF HEBRIDES, AND HAS SUNK.

He handed the paper to Annie and she read it. 'What does that mean?' she asked.

'It means the Germans have sunk a civilian ship.'

On the hour, they switched on the wireless and an announcer intoned in a sombre voice to which they were already becoming accustomed.

'. . .loss of the ship *Athenia*. The passenger liner was steaming away from England towards Canada when it was struck twice off the coast of Ireland. Ships in the vicinity have sailed to the scene and are reported to have picked up survivors but it is feared there will be many civilian deaths.'

Bob felt like he had been hit with a hammer. Yesterday, the war had felt distant, remote, more hypothetical than real. He felt insulated from it. Now, he realised that was a foolish notion. This was a disaster. No, it was much, much worse than that. The *Athenia* was sailing towards Canada, and therefore away from any European war zone. What's more, she had set sail before war was even declared. The majority of her passengers were women and children, most of them foreigners returning to North America. Germany had begun by bombing towns and villages in Poland and now, with the war barely two hours old, here was an act of international piracy.

'This is the way it'll be,' he said. 'We're in the grip of primitive law and there's nae escape. I ken that. We'll get mair brutal. Mair terrible. Baith sides. What the Germans are doin noo – the *Athenia*, Weiluń – we'll end up doin an aa. By war's end we'll be bombin German cities, killin German bairns. In the name of humanity. We'll convince oorsels that oor cause is just and that the end justifies the means. And maybe it does. Maybe Hitler's too big a monster to be left undestroyed. But there are bairns and women in Germany the day – right this minute – livin blameless lives who will be killed by us. In oor name. Children no even born yet. Born only to die because humanity has lost its humanity.'

'It'll no come to that.'

'We live less than an hoor fae Glencoe. You ken what happened there. To Scots. . . By Scots. . . Humans are capable of onythin.'

Bob thought back to a few weeks before, in the aftermath of the affair at the Scout Moot when he'd been interrogated by some mysterious government individuals, all of them consumed by self-righteous certainty over the rectitude of their position. "By Christmas, it's likely the country will be at war," he'd been told, "and as soon as that happens we will have total power." *Total power.* The state. Already the Emergency Powers Act had given government carte blanche to act "in the national interest", with *Habeas Corpus* suspended and parliamentary elections cancelled. The National Registration Act would compel everyone to offer identification on request and provide the authorities with information on their current employment. All theatres, cinemas, football grounds and places of entertainment had been closed down. Dissent was not allowed. There was no other way to describe this – overnight, Britain had become a dictatorship.

'You'll get called up,' Annie said at last.

'Aye.'

'And then what?'

Bob had thought about little else all evening. Under the terms of the Conditions of Service Act, the Territorial Army, the new Militia and the regular army had been merged into a single force. All army reserves and volunteer reserves had been called up. There was to be immediate legislation to conscript all fit men between eighteen and forty-one, assimilating them one year at a time. Bob reckoned, aged twenty-five, he would be called up in about March. Would he fight, or would he make a stand, be a conscientious objector?

A conscientious objector or, depending on your viewpoint, a coward.

*

Lorna followed Sandy Disdain from a distance, irritated by the swagger in his walk. She watched him cross a recently harvested field, hayricks punctuating the expanse, the ground hard and powdery after so many dry days. He approached a small cottage perched on the hillside and entered without knocking. Lorna nodded with satisfaction and walked downhill until she reached the farmhouse. She stood beneath a horse chestnut tree. The villain had told her he was the farmer. That was obviously a lie, since he didn't live in the farmhouse, but the cottage was on the farmer's land so he was no doubt an employee. In Lochearnhead, when an employee had dared show her disrespect the hotel had to pay the reckoning. Here, the same must apply. Responsibility rested with the farmer, for hiring an animal murderer.

He would have to pay the price.

Tuesday, 5 September

A Day of Flames

'Take off your frock.'

'Nut.'

The nurse, an untidy woman in her forties with a hair lip, remained impassive. 'That wasn't a request. Do as I say.'

Ellen fixed Annie with a look of pure hostility, as if to suggest this was her doing. To an extent, it was, Annie supposed. She was *in loco parentis*, after all, even if the idea of being a parent was baffling to her.

'Is this necessary?' she asked.

'We've been seeing all sorts of infestations. Impetigo, tubercular sores, even VD.'

'A bairn in Crieff has VD?'

'Well, that wasn't in Crieff, no. . .'

'Ellen hasnae anythin like that.'

'Then there won't be any problem with her taking her frock off.'

St Fillan's Hall on Ford Road was long and narrow and afforded no privacy. Half-a-dozen children, including two boys, were in various stages of undress and undergoing examination. Annie undid the buttons on Ellen's frock and gestured for her to stand, sliding the frock down as she did.

'I hate you,' Ellen said quietly.

The nurse studied Ellen's back and upper arms and looked triumphantly at Annie. 'Eczema,' she said.

'Aye, a wee bit of a rash. Have you onythin to treat it?'

'Just make sure she doesn't scratch it. Mittens in bed, if necessary. Keep her out of draughts. And direct sunlight. No shellfish or oily fish.' She looked at Ellen. 'Are you constipated?'

'Eh?'

'Your bowel movements?'

'Eh?'

'How often do you go to the toilet?'

'When I need a keech.'

'Every day?'

'I dunno.'

The nurse looked over her head at Annie. 'Give her California syrup of figs. You can get it in Harley & Watts.' She continued the examination, pulling at Ellen, lifting each arm in turn and causing her to squeal.

'There,' she said, pointing to the circular lesion on the inside of Ellen's upper arm. 'That's ringworm.'

'I havenae got worms,' said Ellen.

'No. Ringworm isn't caused by worms. We used to think it was, hence the name, but it's a fungal infection.'

'Is it sair?' Annie asked.

'Itchy,' said Ellen.

'What can we do for it?'

The nurse turned Ellen around. 'Garlic. Mashed up in a tablespoon of olive oil and a tablespoon of honey. Twice a day. And wash. Body and clothes.' She made this sound like a rebuke and Annie bristled.

'We bath twice a week, thank you very much. And a clothes wash every Friday.'

'Good for you.' She finished her examination by checking Ellen's tongue, then her feet and hands, and measuring her height and weight. This information was noted in a large ledger and Annie couldn't conceive what possible use it might have. All she could reflect was that, yet again, after Ellen had begun to mellow through the morning, following an argument about porridge at breakfast, something had happened to sour her temper. Parenthood, she was discovering, meant constantly managing mood swings and conflicting emotions. She helped Ellen back into her frock and took her hand as they exited onto Ford Road.

The Misses Seaton, Beaton and Miller, dressed for midwinter in this hottest of Indian summers, were perched outside, studying the arrivals and departures with obvious disapproval. They afforded Ellen a look of sheer disdain.

'Have you ladies nowhere better to go on a fine day like this?' Annie said. She knew it was a mistake, knew that everyone in Crieff cautioned against taking on the dreaded spinsters, but their casual disapprobation incensed her.

'Did you hear how she spoke to us?' said Miss Miller.

'Disgraceful,' said Miss Seaton.

'Disgustin,' said Miss Beaton.

'She's fae Perth, mind,' said Miss Miller. 'Common as muck, and wi that feckless husband of hers. Him that plays the bagpipes like he's torturin them.'

'I pity the Glesga urchin that has to stay wi them,' said Miss Seaton.

'Oot of the fryin pan into the fire.'

'Leave her alane, ye auld witches,' shouted Ellen, standing in front of them and glowering.

'Did you hear thon?' said Miss Seaton.

'Such muck, comin oot the mooth of a pretty wee thing an aa,' said Miss Miller. 'Contrary wee madam.' The spinsters swooned and Annie, part horrified, part delighted by Ellen's behaviour, tugged at her and dragged her onto Burrell Street and then King Street.

'And if you think you're puttin mittens on me,' said Ellen, 'you can fuckin think again.'

*

Sandy Disdain threw his deerstalker onto a table by the window of Cloudland and rested a gamebag bulging with rabbits on the floor. Blood seeped from one corner onto the floorboards.

'Could you no hae taken them to Low's afore you came in here?' said Bob.

'It'll wash aff.'

Bob placed a mug of extra strong tea on the table and sat beside him.

'Did you hear about Gertie and Fordie Williamson?' Sandy said.

'What?'

'Deid. Run ower last night, ootside the Golf Course. Pushin their cairt up to Callum's Hill in the blackoot. Lorry fae Perth didnae see them, ran them ower.'

'Damn me. We only saw Fordie on Seturday.'

'Aye, and he sang *MacCrimmon's Lament*. . .'

'He did. "Nae mair forever". Prophetic or what?'

'I tell you, this stupit blackoot's goin to kill mair people than the bloody Germans ever will. There was a wifie killed in Perth on Monday. Someone in Glesga an aa. And Embra. But it's juist us ordinary folks that's coppin it so that doesnae matter.'

'Aye, the government says jump and we hae to jump. It's no wey to live.' Bob picked up his mug and carried it to the kitchen at the rear of Cloudland. 'D'you want somethin to eat? I've fish pie that didnae sell the day. We're haein that. There's plenty, if you want your tea.'

Sandy looked at the clock on the wall. Four-thirty. His mither was at the market and she'd told him to get the tatties on by five.

Fish pie, though, he hadn't had fish pie in months. 'How no?' he said.

*

Late afternoon, Lorna watched the cottage on the Laggan Hill for an hour until she was satisfied there was nobody inside. She approached the front door silently and, holding the letterbox open, dropped a note inside. She eased the letterbox shut again and stepped back and returned the way she had come. This was the risky part of the operation. This was where everything could unravel. It wasn't strictly necessary, but Lorna was aroused by the additional drama.

Be strong and of a good courage.

*

'It's aa I've heard aa day,' said Bob that evening after. Ellen had gone to bed. 'Aabody who's come into Cloudland – "Keelies this, Keelies that". They're getting the blame for aathin. Jinky Ford's chickens had their necks wrung last nicht. Wha d'you think got the blame?'

'There was a spate of that last year, was there no?' said Annie. 'Harry Roy's. Erchie Jackson.'

'Exactly. But no, it was the Glesga bairns did it. Gie it a few days and it'll be them started the war. He folded *The Courier* over his lap. 'I'm sure they're no aa angels and they're no the cleanest people I've ever seen. . .'

'It's juist the same when the tinkers come for the tattie-howkin.'

'Aye. Ootsiders. . .'

'"Cannae trust them". Betty Copeland was sayin a group of Glesga laddies were blamed for startin a fire at the Lochearnhead Hotel the other nicht. Some woman reported them. Said she saw somethin fishy at the back of the hotel. When the polis got there, the byre was on fire. Arson. Could smell the paraffin fae the road. . .'

'That'll be Sergeant Braggan. Good to hear he's got some real polis work to do for a change.' Sergeant Braggan was an old adversary of Bob's, someone who sorely tested his resolve to think only the best of everyone. Bob studied the newspaper headlines. Countries around the world were aligning themselves in the war. Romania, Spain, Norway and Sweden had declared neutrality. Yugoslavia was mobilising its army. Rhodesia's Territorial force and reserves had also been mobilised. Egypt and Iraq had severed relations with Germany. Bob sighed. With the world in such turmoil, the last thing he wanted was uproar in Crieff, too, but the forced integration of three thousand Glaswegians in their community had pretty much dictated that would be the case.

The door opened and Ellen's face peered in at them. 'What does "contrary" mean?' she asked.

'Contrary?' said Bob. 'Opposite.'

'That doesnae make sense.'

'How?'

'It's in ma book. The lassie in it is called contrary. One of thae witches the day called me that.' She wore a fierce expression, jaws clamped shut and eyes unblinking. She was fated to be forever thought angry, Bob realised, when in truth she was frightened and lonely.

'Come on, then,' he said. 'Let's get you back into bed and I'll hae a look at it.'

When she had settled in bed, Bob sat beside her and picked up the book and started to read what Basil said to Mary:

"Mistress Mary, quite contrary,
How does your garden grow?
With silver bells, and cockle shells,
And marigolds all in a row."

'See? What does that mean?'

'He's teasin her. Sayin she's difficult.'

'They called me that the day. I'm no difficult.'

Well you're no exactly easy, Bob thought.

'Why are people horrible?' Ellen asked.

'It's the war. And all of a sudden there's three thoosand folk billeted in the toon. That's almost as mony as live here onywey. So people are gettin used to it. . .'

'It's no oor fault we're here. They dinnae need to be so nasty.'

Bob turned back to the story. 'They're bein nasty to Mary in the book an aa,' he said. 'But maybe, once they get to ken her better, folks'll like her mair. Shall we read on?'

'Aye.'

'D'you want to read or shall I?'

'You. But show me wi yer finger what ye're readin.'

*

On her journey through the parks, Lorna saw nobody and considered this a good omen. The day had been fine, Indian summer continuing and the sky all but cloudless, but the moon was waning and its illumination of blackout Crieff was growing dimmer by the day. Her battered, grey coat contained three milk bottles, each filled with paraffin and stoppered with cloth remnants. In the inside pocket was Saturday's *Glasgow Evening Times*, carefully removed earlier from Miss Glass's bin. As she turned onto the Laggan road, a fragment of cloud briefly slid across the moon, throwing the area into complete darkness. Lorna listened to a silence that was dense and almost mystical. Across it came a rustle of branches. Creak. The trace of something travelling through the undergrowth, invisible and untouchable. She felt a momentary doubt about how she might get into and out of the fields but doubt gave way to determination, as it always did. Lorna Carrington was not a woman to be stopped by mere practicalities.

'Push,' she said into the darkness. It was an explanation and an instruction, perhaps even an imprecation.

She had identified her targets the previous night, watching from beneath the sweet chestnut tree. She stood under that same tree now and waited, checking whether anyone had been alerted to her plans. There was noise from the farm behind her but that seemed only the sounds of daily living.

'Go.'

She clambered over a stone dyke and crossed a field, the rough ground bristling and cracking with the detritus of the wheat hairst. Hayricks loomed in the darkness like voids in space. She walked to the top of the slope and selected a rick and pulled a bottle from her coat. She poured paraffin over the rick and lit a strip from the newspaper, letting it catch before dropping it onto the rick. After a moment, there was a visual and aural whoosh and flames took hold, blue and purple, deepening to red in the paraffin-soaked epicentre and fading to yellows and greens as the flames spread outwards and upwards.

She stepped downhill a hundred yards or so and selected another rick. In the distance, she fancied she could see the outline of the farmhouse but this could have been her imagination. Wishful thinking, hoping the inhabitants were having a grand view of the destruction of their property. She doused the rick in paraffin and lit it and watched with satisfaction as she lit a newspaper scrap and dropped it and the rick became submerged in flame. Behind her, the first rick was well ablaze, flames leaping feet into the air as if in a rabid dance.

She felt an intense excitement and a delicious ache in her thighs. Two fires lit the blackout sky, twin beacons in an expanse of darkness. She crossed into the field nearest the farmhouse and arrived at another hayrick and emptied the third bottle of paraffin over it. Again, she lit a newspaper scrap and settled it on the paraffin-soaked hay and thrilled at the sound of ignition.

Burning up the chaff with unquenchable fire.

Above her, voices rang out, two or three, all male. She dropped the newspaper and hurried to the foot of the field and climbed onto the Laggan road. The voices were more agitated now, barking orders. Three fires raged on the hill as Lorna strode calmly through the blackness towards town.

*

Flames roared fifteen feet into the black sky from the tightly bound hayrick. Searing heat repelled men carrying buckets, frantic figures framed by the fire's light, chiaroscuro in gold. The crackling as each sheaf in turn succumbed to fire seemed to coalesce to make the strangest whirring noise. It sounded mechanical. Deafening.

'You're wastin your time,' shouted Sandy Disdain. Malky Bennett threw his water over the rick. The flames sizzled and, for an instant, twisted and turned blue, but then they licked higher and higher yet.

A hundred yards uphill, the first hayrick was now reduced to molten heat, pulsing against the darkness of the night. To their west, in the low field nearest the farmhouse, the third rick was still ablaze. In the east, two miles distant, Crieff lay in darkness.

Malky Bennett threw his bucket to the ground.

'At least the Jerries didnae choose the nicht to bomb us,' said Sandy.

He and Malky watched for an hour while the fires burned themselves out. They smoked pensively, each wondering why someone would have done this, and whether they would return to do more damage another night.

'It'll be thae bloody Glesga bairns,' said Malky. 'This kind of thing didnae happen afore they got here.'

Sandy could think of at least three instances of farm arson over the past couple of years but chose not to argue. He watched Malky stride back to the farm and turned for home himself. A rustling sound alerted him to a newspaper lying close to the smouldering hayrick. He picked it up and tucked it into his back pocket and headed uphill, whistling The Black Bear. His mother was standing at the kitchen table as he entered the house, holding a piece of paper.

'It's a pity you were late hame,' she said. 'Or you micht hae seen this.' She pointed through the window at the smouldering hayrick. 'Your man who did this, he sent us a warning first.' She handed Sandy the paper and he read it:

I will gain my vengeance on you. Tonight I will burn down your hayricks and you will see I am serious. By the end of the week, I will have burned down your Dairy, whether you have a police cordon around it or not, as my highly complicated and scientific method of fire-raising cannot fail.

Sandy pulled the newspaper from his pocket. The *Glasgow Evening Times*. He looked again at the letter. 'Heidcase,' he said.

Wednesday, 6 September

A Day of Waiting

Sandy and Malky Bennett surveyed the burnt-out debris at first light. Smoke still coiled from the remains, heat rising into the chill of the morning. Sandy showed Malky the anonymous letter. 'Heidcase,' he said, repeating his observation from the previous night.

'A heidcase who set fire to three ricks. How do I ken he winnae do what he says and go for the dairy?'

'A hayrick's ae thing. Mischief. But settin fire to a buildin, that's somethin else. . .'

'I cannae tak the chance.'

Sandy suspected the culprits weren't Glasgow evacuees but he showed Malky the *Glasgow Evening Times*, hoping that might make him rest easier. A group of children was less frightening than an anonymous adult, surely? Easier to manage.

'It's juist bairns,' he said. 'Muckin aboot.'

'I dinnae ken,' said Malky. 'It probably is. But I cannae tak the chance.'

'No,' said Sandy. 'Leave it wi me. I'll speak to some folk, see if we can get a guard set up overnicht. First few nichts onywey. If we hae people watchin the dairy naebody'll get in.'

'Aye. And you need to go and tell the polis an aa.'

'Sergeant Rudd? That'll put the fear of God into the arsonist, richt enough.'

'Aye well,' said Malky, 'he's the best we've got.'

*

'Why are the lambs cross?' Ellen was studying the front page of *The Strathearn Herald*. The paper dwarfed her tiny frame.

'What lambs?' said Bob.

She pointed to an advert for the Crieff Livestock Mart for three thousand cross lambs from well-known hirsels in the neighbouring area.

'Whit are they cross fur?'

'Well, they're goin to be killed and eaten so they're probably a bit in the huff, but that's no what it means. Cross lambs are cross breeds. A mix of different types.'

'Ye get different types of lambs?'

'Aye. Blackface, Hielan, Cheviot. Lots of them.'

'Whit do they look like?'

'Lambs?'

'Aye.'

'You dinnae ken what a lamb looks like?'

'We don't get many sheep in Finnieston, but.'

'I suppose no.'

'Bob,' said Annie, 'how d'you no tak Ellen to jine the library? She's fair enjoyed *The Secret Gerden*. Maybe she'd like another book.'

Bob and Ellen had taken to turns to read *The Secret Garden* aloud and it had been a great success. Bob discovered he had a facility for accents although, in truth, he had no idea how a Yorkshire accent was meant to sound. When Ellen read, her delivery was slower and Bob could tell it took a great deal of concentration for her to get through the words. Once he had explained a word to her, though, she retained it. And throughout she asked thoughtful questions. What was wrong with Colin? Could Dickon really speak to the birds? When they were reading, Ellen was a different person, inquisitive, friendly, calm.

'That's no a bad idea,' he said.

'And maybe you'll find a book wi picters of animals in it.'

'What's a library?' said Ellen.

'A place where you can borrow books.' Ellen looked blank and Annie explained. 'You borrow a book and tak it hame to read, and when you're finished it you tak it back and get another ane.'

'Is that real?'

'Aye.'

'Whit's the catch?'

'Nae catch.'

'Come oan, then.' She leaped up and thrust her feet into her shoes. 'Come oan,' she repeated, more firmly. Bob laughed at her excitement.

'Don't laugh at me,' she shouted.

*

Sergeant Rudd handed the letter back to Sandy. 'It's thae Gleswegians,' he said.

'Thon's no a bairn's writin,' Sandy replied.

'There's plenty mithers here wi them. Causin havoc.'

'How would a mither torch a hayrick?'

'How would onybody?'

'I'm thinkin we need to keep a watch on Malky's dairy. For a few nichts onywey.'

'You do, aye.'

'We do,' Sandy said slowly.

'You're no expectin any help fae me, are you?'

'What, the polis? Preventin crime?'

'Can you imagine what that would do to my overtime budget? Aa nicht for what, three or fower nichts? I cannae do it, man. I could maybe lend you PC McAnuff, but to be honest you'd be better on your lain.'

Sandy snatched up the letter and stood. 'Helpful as ever,' he said.

Sergeant Rudd smiled. 'A wee birdie was tellin me you were seen wi your shotgun up the Hosh the other day.'

'No me,' said Sandy, too quickly.

'Thocht so. Keep your neb clean, son.'

*

The Taylor Trust Library on East High Street was a cramped and dark building whose low ceilings created a sense of claustrophobia. Working behind the counter was Eliza Burrell, daughter of Elsie, a regular in Cloudland. Bob handed over fourpence for a year's subscription for him and Ellen.

'You can take two books at a time,' Eliza explained. 'You can choose now while I write out your cards.'

Ellen stared at the rows of books, still baffled by the process. 'How do they know we'll bring em back and no just sell em?' she said.

'Wheesht,' said Bob, 'You'll get us barred. They juist trust us.'

'It's like magic.'

'It is, aye. Dinnae ken why I didnae join afore.'

'Ye've me to thank fur that, then.'

'Thank you very much, miss.' He bowed elaborately, like a French aristocrat of old. A couple of borrowers, old women in hats and wearing the permanent expressions of disapproval that were almost a uniform for people of that generation, tutted loudly.

'Now who's gonnae get us barred?' said Ellen.

She selected *The Incredible Adventures of Professor Branestawm* and *The Family From One End Street* and Bob chose *The Case for Federal Union* and *The Children's Book of Farm Animals*. Eliza stamped them with the due date and put the book cards inside their readers' tickets and filed them in a large wooden tray that dominated the front desk.

'Due back in two weeks,' she said.

Bob looked at Ellen, virtually overcome with excitement. 'We'll be back lang afore then, Liza,' he predicted.

*

Bob sat in the kitchen of the Laggan cottage and read the letter twice. 'Wha sent it?' he said.

'Nae idea,' said Sandy.

'What did he do it for?'

'Nae idea.'

'How did he put the note through your door, no fairmer Bennett's?'

'Nae idea.'

Bob gestured to the much-torn *Glasgow Evening Times*. 'Whaur would he get a Glesga paper fae?'

'Nae idea.'

'You're no bein much help.'

'You're supposed to be the brains.'

'God help us if that's true.'

They walked to the wheatfield, Sandy lighting a Capstan from the butt of the previous one. A reek of burning filled the air. The charred remains of the hayrick still smouldered, soil beneath blackened and charred. Sandy pointed out the second and third burnt hayricks.

'You can smell paraffin,' he said.

'Aye.'

As they crossed the field to the second rick, Bob spotted something glinting among the wheat debris. He picked up a milk bottle labelled in red *McLaren's Dairy, Duchlage, Crieff*. He sniffed it.

'Paraffin.'

By the edge of the field, near the second fire, they found another bottle, also from McLaren's but of an older vintage, with a wider, squatter shape and the logo faded after many hundreds of washes.

'I guess it doesnae tell us onythin we didnae already ken,'

Sandy said. 'Three fires wouldnae spontaneously combust so there must hae been somethin caused it. At least noo we ken what.'

'And that maks it less likely it was Glesga bairns did it,' Bob replied.

'How?'

'Whaur would they come by twa McLaren's milk bottles?'

'Aye.'

They crossed into the low field where the remains of the third rick stood, less charred than the others, evidence of partial success by the Bennetts and Sandy in dousing it. Nearby, they found a third bottle. Bob picked it up with a handkerchief and put it in his inside pocket. He scratched his head.

'"My highly complicated and scientific method", your letter called it. Doesnae seem that scientific to me. Bottle of paraffin and a match.'

'Well, scientific or no, it worked.'

'So now we hae to worry aboot the dairy bein next. How's Malky takin it?'

'He's petrified. He only built that dairy last year. A hunnert pound it cost him. He's still peyin it aff.'

'I expect he's worried aboot his faimly an aa.'

Sandy reflected for a moment. 'Maybe. I hadnae thocht of that.'

*

Lorna switched off the gramophone player and returned the gramophone to its paper sleeve. She owed two months' hire purchase on the player and she thought she might pay some of it off soon. Show willing. She sat down at the window but stood up almost immediately, unable to relax, unable to concentrate. She checked the time. Near enough.

It shall come to pass and I will do it.

She picked up her coat.

*

At two in the morning, Sandy, Bob and Malky Bennett stood around a brazier in the yard outside Malky's dairy, warming their hands on a fire that was slowly dying. Behind them, on the Laggan road, laughter and loud conversation thrummed among forty or fifty locals who had been waiting since nightfall for the arsonist's arrival. Bob peered at them through the gloom.

'This is a waste of time,' he said. 'Naebody in their richt mind would try and burn doon your dairy wi half of Crieff camped ootside.'

'If it was your café he'd threatened, would you be so damned sure?' replied Malky.

'Aye, I ken. But he's no goin to show.'

'He's right,' said Sandy. 'I dinnae suppose the heidcase reckoned on this much interest. The danger time'll be the weekend, when aabody's got scunnered and gone awa. That's when we need to keep guard. The noo,' he gestured towards the road, 'that lot are doin the job for us.'

'Richt enough,' said Malky. 'You boys awa hame and get some rest. I'll juist bide here a whiley longer.'

*

Among the watchers on the Laggan, mostly men with bottles of beer and hipflasks to help while away the hours until the arsonist's arrival, was Lorna Carrington. The collar of her overcoat was pulled up, Mr Henderson's homburg, which she'd taken from the coat rack at Barvick Falls, pressed on her head. She cursed these imbeciles and their incessant chatter and pointless speculation. *Go home, go home*, she implored them, but she realised there was no possibility of that happening just yet. She hadn't anticipated how much tumult the fires would cause and she calculated now that it might take three or four days before the excitement died down.

By Saturday, she thought. *Saturday. Command fire to come down from Heaven.*

Come what may

Thursday, 7 September

A Day of Provocation

'Miss Carrington?'

Lorna walked on as though she hadn't heard. In her experience, people who accosted her in the street seldom had honourable intentions. She felt a tug on her elbow and turned round with exasperation. Facing her, wheezing slightly, was Mr Salmond from Salmond's Emporium on King Street.

'Your gramophone player,' he said. 'You're two months behind on your hire purchase payments.'

'Oh, Mr Salmond, I'm so embarrassed. I can only apologise. What a terrible position to put you in. It's all my fault, of course. My schoolteacher's salary. . .'

'Aye, I'm sure it's no easy for ony of us the noo, the wey the world is. . .'

'You are sweet to be so understanding. But I promise, I will pay my dues as soon as I possibly can.'

'That would be grand, miss, thank you.'

'I'll be in the shop tomorrow, without fail. Good day, Mr Salmond.'

She bowed her head and walked on. She looked around to see if anyone had witnessed the scene. The gormless maid from Barvick Falls, Mary, was on the other side of the street, watching. Anger rose in Lorna. A few weeks' overdue payments on a wretched gramophone player. In the middle of a war. With an arsonist on the rampage. Had the old buffoon nothing better to occupy himself with? As it happened, she had been intending to make a payment today, but he could whistle for it now.

*

'Now then, young man,' Mrs McLaren greeted Bob from behind the counter of McLaren's Dairy on Comrie Street, opposite the war memorial, neat in her starched white overall. 'What d'you think of this?' She gestured to a lozenge-shaped contraption to the right of the counter. 'Brand new. Our patent ice cream maker. Top quality. D'you want some?'

'No the noo, but I've a fancy the faimly would love some. I'll bring them by.'

'Faimly?'

'Evacuee. Wee lassie called Ellen.'

'Oh, puir man. I hear they're awfae people.'

'So folk keep sayin, but Ellen's a wee smasher.' *When you get used to her.* He settled a string bag on the counter and pulled out two of the three milk bottles he and Sandy had retrieved. He left the third in the bag.

'These are yours,' he said, settling them with the logo facing Mrs McLaren.

'They are. Jings, whaur did you dig this auld thing up?' She picked up the bottle that was shorter and squatter. 'We stopped makin this design lang syne. Back in the twenties. Havenae seen ane of these in years.'

'So you wouldnae still be usin this?'

'No, if that came back we'd tak it oot of circulation. It looks auld and tattered. You can hardly read oor name. And it's a different shape fae oor usual bottles. Wouldnae fit in oor modern trays.'

'So how would someone come by this?'

She held the bottle up to the light and shook her head. 'I can only think it's been lyin aboot in somebody's hoose.'

'Could you tell whaur?'

'Nae idea. We just fill the bottles and put them on the milk floats and send them oot on the rounds. Could be onywhere in Crieff. Or Gilmerton, Madderty, Muthill. How did you come by them, onywey?'

'You've heard aboot Malky Bennett's hayricks?'

'It's aa folk were talkin aboot yesterday.'

'Well, these were used by the arsonist to set the ricks on fire. Filled wi paraffin.'

A look of consternation crossed Mrs McLaren's face. She sniffed the bottle and nodded. 'I hope you dinnae think we had onythin to do wi it?'

'If you did, you'd be the maist glaikit criminals in history. Wi your name plastered aa ower the only bits of evidence?'

She smiled mischievously. 'Aye, but could that no be a double bluff? Throw you aff the scent?'

'Dinnae go sayin that to Sergeant Rudd. Even as a joke. He'd probably believe you.'

'I was at the school wi Danny Rudd. Nice laddie, but no awfae bright. How he made it to sergeant I've nae idea. Could I keep these bottles? Especially this ane?'

'You can hae these twa.' He picked up the string bag containing the third. 'I'll hing on to this, if you dinnae mind. I'll gie you it back in a whiley.'

*

'I saw you in the street at lunchtime, miss.' Mary curtsied as Lorna passed her on the stairs of Barvick Falls. 'King Street. I waved but you didnae see me.'

'Of course I saw you. But I was hardly going to acknowledge you in the street, was I?'

'Of course not, miss. Sorry.'

Lorna walked on but turned back and stood on the same step as Mary. 'If you're to be my friend you have to learn to be a bit more cultured. You can't really believe I'd be seen in public with you, the way you look? Your hair, girl. When did you last have it permed?'

'In the summer.'

'Have it done. Immediately. Understand?'

'Yes, miss.'

*

'School starts on Monday,' Annie said to Bob. 'Twa shifts, mornin and efternoon. Ellen's efternoon.'

'We'll hae to get her a uniform.'

'We cannae afford it.'

'We can get a scarf at least. And a pullover. She'll need somethin warm. Thon frock's nice but it's no awfae practical.'

'I'll go to Palmer Valentine's the morn.'

'I dinnae want to go to school,' said Ellen.

'I dinnae blame you,' said Bob. 'I hated it an aa.'

'Bob,' reproached Annie. 'That doesnae help. Did you no like the school in Glesga?'

'Nut. Whit's the point? Who cares?'

'Was there ony lessons you liked?'

'Nut.'

'What aboot English?' said Bob. 'You're doin grand wi your readin.'

'That's just to gie me somethin to do. Pass the time.'

Bob was convinced there was more to Ellen's reading than passing the time. After two days, she'd already returned *Professor Branestawm* and *One End Street* and was now devouring *Little House on the Prairie*. Bob had watched her as she read, the book spread across her thighs, finger tracing the words as she silently mouthed them. Her concentration was so fierce she didn't even notice Bob watching her. At all other times, her levels of self-consciousness were such that she was aware of everything around her, anticipating the next indignity. Reading took her out of herself.

'D'you ever write your ain stories?' he asked.

She sneered. 'Don't talk saft.'

'I used to write stories when I was your age.'

'I bet they were shite.'

'They certainly were. But I was ay the hero in them. Beatin all the folks I didnae like in real life.'

'I could write aboot you two, then.'

'We're no that bad, are we?'

'This toon's a hellhole.'

'You'll be grand when you get to the school and mak new pals.'

'I'll never make pals.'

Bob thought back to his own childhood, moving to Perth at the same age Ellen was now, similarly confused, afraid, alone. He'd thought the same thing and, in truth, he never did make many friends. But he met Annie and that was enough.

'You only need ae friend,' he said. 'As long as it's the richt ane. You'll see.'

'Ellen,' said Annie, looking flustered, 'can you go doon to Cloudland and ask Mrs Comer if she can start half an hoor early the morn's morn?'

When Ellen had gone downstairs on her mission, Annie turned to Bob. 'She's never goin to mak friends if she's rude all the time. "I could write aboot you two." How rude was that?'

'She didnae mean it.'

'Stickin up for her winnae help. I ken what you're doin. You see yoursel in her. But if you'd behaved like that your gran would hae skelped your bahookie. The Conoboys wouldnae hae stood for it, either. It winnae help her, lettin her get awa wi bein rude aa the time.'

'I ken. Things'll be better when she's at the school. We're aa she's seen so far. It must be borin for the sowel. There's no much for her to do.'

'How d'you no tak her on your ARP roond wi you?'

'I'm no supposed to. In case onythin happens.'

'The Germans arenae goin to bomb the nicht. And it'll be good for her to see the layoot of the toon, even if it is dark.'

'I'll ask her, see what she says.'

Bob was dubious that Ellen would consider two hours of walking the streets of Crieff to be an attractive offer but, to his surprise, she expressed enthusiasm. Half an hour later, wearing one of Annie's cardigans beneath her coat for warmth, she joined him as they left Cloudland.

The moon was still just under half full and there was no cloud. The night was warm. As they passed the small cottage next to McLaren's Dairy, Bob spotted a light from an upstairs window. 'That's Mrs Kiddie,' he said. 'Lovely woman, but awfae forgetful. Heaven knows how often I've had to return her gloves or scarf when she's left them in Cloudland.' He positioned himself outside her living room window and began to sing:

As I passed by your window
In the dark of the night,
It surprised me to notice
A streak of bright light;
Now I really must warn you
It's my duty, you know
That unless you're more careful
You'll spoil the whole show.

'Did you make that up?' said Ellen.

'Aye.'

'Just as well ye've a café to fall back on.'

'What did I tell you aboot bein rude?'

'That's no rude. That's the truth.'

'Sometimes they can be the same thing.'

The living room window opened, flooding the street with light, and Mrs Kiddie's head appeared. 'What nonsense is this?' she shouted.

'ARP Warden, Mrs Kiddie. Just advisin you there's some licht showin at the tap of your windae. You'll need to put some mair newspaper ower it or get a thicker blackoot curtain.'

'Have you seen the price of thae curtains? Daylight robbery.'

'It is, aye. But *The Herald's* only sixpence. That'll dae the job juist as weel. I'll call by the morn and see you've done it.'

'Awa wi you!'

'See you the morn.'

'Why do we huv a blackoot?' Ellen asked as they walked downhill past the war memorial.

'So's the Germans cannae see whaur oor toons are and drap bombs on them.'

'Why wid they drop bombs here?'

'That I dinnae ken.' In the distance, on Milnab Street, he saw another upstairs light and this time it was evident no attempt had been made to block it out beyond the normal, thin curtain.

'That's Thingwie Johnstone,' he said, resignation in his voice. 'Gaupit auld scunner. Come on.'

'Ye're no goin to sing to him an aa?'

'Horses for courses, hen. I dinnae think Thingwie would appreciate my singin.'

'I'm no sure that wifie did, either. Why's he called Thingwie?'

'Because he's got a hellish memory.' He knocked on Thingwie's door and waited. It took some time before a short, distracted-looking man appeared. He was completely bald and he wore a string vest over trousers hanging low from a pair of ill-fitting braces.

'What?' he said.

'You've a light showin. Up there.'

'And?'

'You need to put it oot. Put up a blackoot curtain. Like you were telt.'

'I never go in that room.'

'You must be in it, the light's on.'

'I was lookin for somethin.'

'So you hae to put up a blackoot curtain.'

'What would I do that for, if I never go in it?'

'But you have been in it.'

'Only this aince.'

'And wha's to say you willnae need somethin else oot of there anither time?'

'And wha's to say I will?'

'Look, I'm no arguin. . .'

'You bloody are, you wee upstart. Right this noo. You're standin on my doorstep and arguin the toss like some jumped up wee Sergeant-Major.'

Ellen, growing bored with the contretemps, joined in. 'You're no exactly a giant, yoursel,' she said.

'Cheeky wee besom. Are you the lassie fell aff the cairt? I'll skelp your backside if you gie me any mair of your impudence.'

'Gaupit auld scunner.'

'What did you call me?'

'It wasnae me said that. It was him.' She pointed at Bob. 'Comin doon the road.'

Thingwie rounded on Bob. 'Did you?' Standing on his doorstep gave him an unaccustomed height advantage and he used it to good effect, lamping Bob with a thunderous haymaker punch which knocked his head sideways. Bob collapsed to the ground like a tree stricken by a storm and lay motionless. Thingwie cursed and held his right fist in his left hand, shaking it furiously.

'Look what you've done to my knuckle, heid-the-baw.'

Ellen looked at Bob's prone body, then at Thingwie. She kicked his ankle and he howled in pain. She kicked his other ankle and then the first one again, as Bob started to come round on the pavement, groaning and holding his head.

'What's goin on here?'

The three protagonists turned to see PC McAnuff marching warily towards them, truncheon out, moonlight showing fear on his features.

'This horrible mannie beat up my uncle,' Ellen said. Bob staggered to his feet, clutching the wall for support.

'It's fine,' he said.

'No, it isnae,' said Ellen. She kicked Thingwie once more and he raised his hand to her but saw PC McAnuff brandish his truncheon and stopped.

'No, it isnae,' agreed PC McAnuff. 'We cannae hae people goin aboot duffin up ARP Wardens. You'll hae to come wi me, Thingwie.'

'You're never arrestin me for that?'

'I am.'

'I play thingwie wi your faither every Seturday.'

'The bools, I ken. But maybe no this weekend. I reckon you'll get seven days for this.'

Thingwie glowered at Bob. 'This is your fault.'

*

Lorna felt desperation as she marched along the Laggan road to the Bennett farm. The shouts and bursts of laughter suggested the crowd of observers was no smaller than the previous night. She pulled her shawl over her hair and sidled to the back of the congregation. Beer and whisky were being consumed with relish and the group was growing raucous. Malky Bennett strode out of his yard towards them, gesturing.

'Naethin's goin to happen,' he said. 'Can you no aa go hame? I've bairns tryin to sleep in there. We've to be up at fower for the milkin.'

'And miss the excitement?' someone yelled from the group. Lorna bit her lip, her mood growing ever darker.

'Save me from these cretins,' she said. She turned and marched back towards town.

Friday, 8 September

A Day of Conviction

'Tell me again, what did he hit you for?' Annie stood at the kitchen table, hand on her hip, staring first at Bob and then at Ellen. Bob had already explained twice about Thingwie Johnstone's haymaker punch but Annie was convinced there must be more to the story. Thingwie was well-known to be bad-tempered but Annie had never heard of him being aggressive. Not even in drink.

'I called him a gaupit auld scunner.'

'How?'

'Because he is.'

'Maybe so, but how did you feel the need to tell him?'

'Ach, it juist slipped oot.'

Annie turned to Ellen. 'Did you hae ony part in this?'

'No, she didnae,' said Bob.

'I asked her.'

'He called him a gaupit auld scunner,' said Ellen, aware that Bob appeared to be trying to minimise her role in the proceedings and happy to play along.

'What for?'

Ellen shrugged. 'It's just him bein him. He does stupit things.'

Annie took a breath to argue but Bob nodded. 'I do. Weel-kent for it.' He raised an eyebrow at Ellen. Ellen's face remained impassive.

Not for the last time, Annie wondered whether parenting responsibilities were being evenly distributed in this household.

*

'This is awfae good of you, Audrey.'

Mary Kemp sat in the Disdain family kitchen, a tablecloth draped over her shoulders. On the kitchen table was a bowl of water and beside it a pile of pins. Sandy's younger sister, Audrey, stood behind Mary.

'I've only ever done this on mysel, mind.'

'Well, your hair's that bonny, it'll be grand.'

Audrey wet the brush and pulled loose a strand of hair from Mary's hairline. She held the strand upright and ran her brush through it to dampen it, then started to curl the hair round her fingers until she reached the scalp. She used a pin to hold it in place and then affixed a kirby grip for extra security. She repeated the exercise over and over until, half an hour later, the whole of Mary's head was covered with tightly curled and fixed rings of hair.

'Goodness,' said Mary, 'that was a trauchle.'

'We hae to let it dry noo,' said Audrey. She wrapped a scarf round Mary's head and knotted it in place above her forehead.

'How long do we keep them in?'

'Long as you can. D'you hae to be onywhere?'

'No really. It's my day aff.'

'So wha's the lucky lad, then?'

'What lucky lad?'

Audrey laughed. 'You must be doin this for a laddie. Is it oor Sandy?'

Sandy was in the kitchen garden, digging over the plot in which his mother had grown this year's carrots. Mary watched him, his biceps firm in the sunshine. She felt herself blush.

Audrey followed her gaze and laughed. 'Enough said.'

Enough said. Was it, though? Mary continued to watch

Sandy, confident, energetic. Handsome, aye, definitely handsome. A fine catch, especially for someone like Mary. *Someone as plain as me.*

But was she looking for a catch? Or was she just trying to escape? Escape her family? Escape her faither?

*

'Next case.'

Thingwie Johnstone was brought to the bench in front of Justice of the Peace Kenton by PC McAnuff and stood to attention, unable to hide the outrage he still felt at the turn of events.

'What is the charge?'

'William Johnstone, of Milnab Street, Crieff, on the evening of the seventh of September, assaulted an ARP Warden, Mr Robert Kelty, by striking him on the head and knocking him to the ground.'

Mr Kenton shook his head. 'This is a most deplorable occurrence. The country is newly at war and our ARP Wardens – volunteers, mark you – are playing a vital role in ensuring safety on the Home Front. It is quite disgraceful that our brave wardens should be abused in such a manner.'

'He asked for it. . .'

'Silence! I would advise you, Mr Johnstone, not to compound your criminal activity by speaking out in my court in this uncouth manner. Do you admit the charge?'

'Aye, but. . .'

'You admit your guilt? Very well, an example must be made in order to protect our Wardens. I sentence you to ten days' confinement in Perth Prison.'

'Ten days?' He turned to PC McAnuff. 'You said a week, you wee nyaff.' PC McAnuff smiled weakly. Thingwie turned to Justice Kenton. 'Can I thingwie against it?'

'I beg your pardon?'

'Can I mak a thingwie?' He looked at PC McAnuff.

'Appeal?' said McAnuff.

'Aye. Can I appeal?'

'No, you cannot,' said Mr Kenton.

'Your Honour?'

Mr Kenton looked up sharply. Apart from the usher, PC McAnuff and Thingwie, there were only five people in the courtroom, David Phillips from *The Strathearn Herald*, the Misses Seaton, Beaton and Miller and, looking distinctly uncomfortable, Bob Kelty. Bob raised his hand and stood. His eye sported an impressive keeker.

'And you are?' said Mr Kenton.

'Bob Kelty.'

'The ARP Warden?'

'Aye.'

'Come to see justice dispensed. Capital.'

'No, Your Honour. I'd like to speak, if I may. . .On Thingwie's behalf.'

'You wish to speak for the accused?'

'Aye.'

'He assaulted you. Knocked you to the ground.'

Bob took a breath. It was one thing to downplay Ellen's role to Annie, for the sake of domestic harmony, but to do so in court would disadvantage Thingwie. 'He was provoked,' he said. 'Earlier, I'd been speakin to Ellen, the wee Glasgow girl stayin wi us, and I used a rude term to describe Mr Johnstone. Ellen repeated that to him.'

'And what was this rude term?'

'Gaupit auld scunner.'

Mr Kenton reflected for a moment. He turned to Thingwie. 'Is that true?'

'Aye. And the lassie kicked me on the shins an aa.'

'Was that before or after you assaulted Mr Kelty?'

'Efter.'

'Then it is not germane. I can see being called a "gaupit auld scunner" – whatever that means – may have offended you, but it does not in any way excuse your intolerable behaviour.'

'But. . .'

'Another word and I'll increase your sentence to fourteen days.'

'But. . .' said Bob.

'And another word from you and you'll be joining him.'

*

At five o'clock, Audrey unwrapped the scarf from Mary's head. 'Ready?' she said. Mary nodded. Audrey pulled out three of the pins from the top of her head and brushed the hair out, using her fingers to create extra bounce. She worked through them all and stood back to admire her work. Mary's hair, usually long and lank, bounced around her shoulders.

'My,' Audrey said. 'Wha's this beautiful woman sittin in my kitchen? Awa through to my bedroom and hae a look in the mirror.'

Mary, feeling breathless with anticipation, stood slowly, trying not to move her head too much for fear of messing her hair. She went through to the bedroom and sat before the dressing table. She stared at herself in silence, at the transformation Audrey had wrought.

'What d'you think?' said Audrey.

'It's too good for me.'

Audrey rapped on the window and when Sandy, cutting bean and pea plants back to the ground, looked up she gestured to him to come inside. Sandy knocked his boots against the door frame to remove sods of earth clinging to the soles.

'What?' he said.

Audrey gestured to Mary. 'Mary,' she said.

'Aye, I ken.' He looked at Mary. 'You could do wi a haircut. Is it no gettin a bit lang?'

*

After tea, Lorna turned back at Eppie Callum's tree, furious. She had felt sure that the watchers would have lost interest by now but their number had actually increased. There were still dozens of people and a party was in full swing. Lorna was concerned that her plan to attack tomorrow evening might be in jeopardy. She started to walk back to town.

'Did you see the ricks?' A youngish woman, labouring uphill with a baby in a Sovereign pram, smiled too cheerily as she addressed Lorna. Lorna bristled.

'Certainly not. I have no interest in such nonsense.' She swept past.

'Snotty cow.'

Just wait a few years until that brat in the pram is in my classroom, Lorna thought. Then we'll see who's a cow. A young couple approached, hand-in-hand, talking animatedly, and Lorna braced herself for another confrontation. She hurried across the bridge over the Barvick Burn, Doctor McNeill's house beneath her on the right.

'Did you. . .'

'No. . .'

There were perhaps seven or eight groups of people at various points between her and Milnab Mill, seven or eight more opportunities for witless conversation. She detoured down the rough path to Dr McNeill's house and followed the line of the Barvick as it flowed its final few yards before it merged with the River Earn. She walked beneath a fine stone viaduct that towered high over her as the railway line straddled the Barvick. The air was damp and stale. Her footsteps echoed.

A hundred yards or so further on the Barvick reached the end of its journey. It seemed odd to Lorna that the confluence of these two water sources should be so shallow, but you could easily cross the Earn at this point, the river bed clearly visible, stony and ice-cold.

In the distance was the Dallerie Laundry, on the site of the old mill, stone-built, enormous, ugly, running the length of an entire street. She peeled away from the river in the direction of the laundry, crossing two fields. Dusk was settling and as she walked through the old mill site a bat flew past, then another, and another, speeding through the evening in search of sustenance. She passed the laundry and walked up a rough track alongside the old millowner's house.

'This is private land.'

Lorna looked around to find the source of the call. In the middle of the millowner's house, on a landing between the ground floor and first floor, was a large window, and an old man was hanging from it.

'This is private land,' he repeated.

'As long as I am not lodging or camping, there is no offence of trespass in Scottish law.'

'This is private land.'

'Are you simple?'

'This is private land.'

Lorna shook her head with frustration. There was a rage boiling inside her, a lust for revenge against a world that was moronic and dull. She strode up Dallerie Brae to Sauchie, breathing heavily, muttering under her breath.

She was determined, now, that come what may tomorrow would be the day. It had to be.

Because it will surely come, it will not tarry.

Saturday, 9 September

A Night of Reckoning

Lorna, hair wrapped in a tightly bound scarf, made her way in moonlit gloom to the Laggan. Near midnight, the air was bitingly cold. Her fingers ached but she couldn't put them in her pockets because of the bottles of paraffin they contained, one in each pocket to stop them clinking. She walked with her arms folded, fingers sheltered by her coat sleeves. Finally, after four days, it seemed the excitement aroused by the arson attack had dissipated and she encountered no one on her passage down the Laggan. Nor could she hear the raucous sounds of nights previous. A hundred yards from the farm she climbed over a drystane dyke and jumped into the ploughed field beyond. Crouching, she progressed towards the house. Sudden activity in the tree canopy made her start. An owl flew along the tree line and disappeared. There was a strong smell of honeysuckle, sweet and fragrant. Ahead of her, the Laggan farm lay in darkness. The dairy, she knew from previous reconnaissance, was to the rear of the farm buildings, adjoining the main yard. She stole further forwards until she reached the end of the field. Another dyke ran uphill to the foot of the Laggan Hill. Behind the dyke was a rough path and, on the opposite side, down a single-track lane, was a side entrance to the farm. She clambered onto the dyke and jumped over the ditch onto the path. Voices and laughter drifted towards her from the house, presumably the guards that Malky Bennett had mustered to protect his dairy. Idiots. Drawing attention to themselves, helping Lorna to navigate the site and plot her passage to the dairy unobserved and untroubled.

She struck uphill for a hundred yards or so until she reached the foot of the tree line on the Laggan Hill. Following the line, she skirted the edge of the farm and approached from the north. The guards, Lorna felt sure, would not expect this and would be focused on the front of the farm, by the roadside. She stopped and listened for five minutes. There was rustling in the trees behind her, a soughing wind. The same low voices of the guards could still be heard from the far side of the farm. On this side there was silence. Blackness. Chill. She felt the bottles in her pockets. Something close to elation was coursing through her, euphoria, an almost delirious delight in her undertaking.

The soul of the diligent shall be made fat.

A sudden commotion to her right broke the spell and almost caused her to scream. An instant panic rose in her throat, the urge for flight descending on her until she understood the noise had come from an Ayrshire cow penned in the byre to the rear of the yard. She waited until her heart rate lowered to something like normal and crept forwards once more, keeping to the shadows until she reached the edge of the building. She stroked the stone wall reflexively. The dairy was round the corner and she would have to cross the yard to reach it. This was a moment of danger. Keeping close to the walls, she edged into the yard and set off. Moonlight glinted off the otherwise blackened windows of the dairy. There was no noise but Lorna could feel and hear the pulse in her chest. Her hands tingled. She wiped them on her coat. Forwards. Forwards. Thirty feet, twenty feet, ten. Almost there.

Too late she realised the noiseless yard was not a good thing. Too late she realised the previously chatty guards were now silent, and that suggested they were listening. Aware. She looked behind her and saw a shape approaching through the darkness, and another alongside.

She ran.

'Stop!'

She ran on. She pulled a bottle from her pocket and dropped it on the stone surface of the farmyard. It shattered. She dropped the second bottle and it, too shattered. Curses from behind her suggested the broken shards had impeded her pursuers. She could see, through the darkness, the outline of a five-bar gate at the entrance to the farm. Her pursuers were still behind her, close enough for her to hear their panting breaths. There was no way she could stop to climb the gate without them catching her. With no notion of how she could have learned the technique, she ran for the gate and jumped and reached for the top rail and used it to lever herself upwards. She imagined she would in this way be able to vault over it but her technique did not reach that level of proficiency and she found herself straddled on the top of the fence. The collision winded her and pain shot through her knee but she used her momentum to roll over and down the other side and she limped towards the main road. The rattling of the fence behind her told her that her pursuers had not been as adept at clearing the gate and were lumbering over it. She took advantage of her preciously won seconds to race onto the Laggan road. On the right, she knew, was a narrow pathway which led to Lady Mary's Walk and the river. Judging her pursuers would not expect her to know this, or to use the pathway, she pushed into it and started to run blindly into the darkness.

The only way she could tell where she was going was the denser blackness on either side of her where the hedges lined the path. As long as she stayed between these she was secure, or so she thought until she tripped on an exposed stone and fell headlong to the ground, grazing her palms and her right cheek. She lay still for a moment, listening. Please let there be no sound, she thought, but there was, probably a hundred yards behind at most. They were following.

She scrambled to her feet and ran on. The path began to rise and she climbed uphill, her calves and thighs straining with effort. After half a mile or so she arrived at a small cottage, completely isolated in the woods. In the blackout, it was difficult to tell whether or not houses were occupied but Lorna had a strong sense this house was empty. The curtains in the front room were open and the house seemed possessed by a negative energy. Now motionless, she could hear the sound of her pursuers once more and she ran round the back of the house. She tried the kitchen door. It was open. She stepped inside and navigated through darkness into the living room and watched the clearing where she had just been standing. Within moments, her pursuers arrived and stopped. There were two of them, both men. Malky Bennett, smaller and stouter, bent and rested his hands on his knees, wheezing. Sandy Disdain, taller, rangy, stood and looked around. After forty seconds or so, Bob Kelty arrived, much out of breath, and fell to his knees.

'You sure he came this way?' said Malky.

'Aye,' said Sandy, still peering as though he could somehow see through the darkness. Bob, now on all fours, was incapable of speech.

'Well, if he did,' said Malky, 'the only way oot of here is Lady Mary's Walk. And Alec and Vinnie are sat at the bridge at the other end so, when he comes oot, they'll spot him. Let's get back to the fairm. The polis'll be there by noo.'

'We ought to carry on,' said Sandy. 'Stay ahint him.'

'There's nae point. He's no goin onywhere.'

Lorna watched as the three men turned and climbed the path back to the farm. The tall one lit a cigarette. The unfit one lit a pipe. Lorna waited until their glows had disappeared and then she looked around. The house was clearly uninhabited, layers of dust on the furniture, the air stale and dank.

She was relieved to let herself out the back door and return to the clearing. Downhill, a tunnel threaded beneath the railway line and, beyond that, following the line of the river Earn, was Lady Mary's Walk. The sound of the river flowing to her right soothed her agitation and she walked briskly, pondering what the two men had said. The tall one, she was sure, was the one with the snares, the one who had started all this. Hatred of him burned inside her. There were people at the far end of Lady Mary's Walk, the other one had said. That would be at the entrance opposite Mungall Park. How was she to escape, if the only exit was being watched? She came to a small beach by the riverside. An enormous stone sat in the middle of the clearing and Lorna stood beside it to watch the quick-flowing water. The opposite bank was some thirty feet away.

Then the idea came to her.

There was no way she could cross the river here. But downstream, near the entrance to Lady Mary's Walk, where the Earn was met by the Barvick Burn, the speed of the river slowed and the depth fell to no more than a foot. She had seen it yesterday and wondered at it.

'Yes!' she shouted and set off again, taking care because she knew this section of path was riddled with exposed tree roots. Even so, she fell and almost slid into the river, grabbing at a woody root to stop herself. She picked herself up and dusted down her coat. It was filthy. In the distance, a railway viaduct loomed - the one she had walked beneath yesterday and she knew she was almost at the spot. The air grew damper and there was a strong smell of aniseed. The river, previously wide and proud, narrowed as it took a sharp right to meet the Barvick Burn.

Lorna took off her shoes and socks and waded into the water. There was a circular area ahead, not quite an island, but only lightly covered by water. She reached it and looked around. To her left, the path continued for another couple of hundred yards and came out at the park. Alec and Vinnie were waiting there. Lorna waded off the high land into the river and pushed towards the opposite bank. The water reached no higher than her knees and she walked through it with ease. Grabbing a willow tree, she pulled herself onto the far bank and scrambled on her hands and knees until she regained her balance. She stood and looked back the way she had come, over the river. Shivering, she pulled on her clothing again and began to retrace her steps of the day before, following the river along the opposite bank to the one she had just taken, back the way she had come until she reached Dallerie.

As the tension of the chase diminished, in its place a crushing anger overwhelmed her. She had failed. She had not achieved her mission. There was no way she could go back there now, no way she could fulfil her promise. But she had to.

When all this comes true – and it surely will – then they will know that a prophet has been among them.

But the prophet would need a new target for the prophesy to be fulfilled.

And, as she walked past the Dallerie laundry buildings, without consciously thinking about it she knew they must be that target. She whistled *Little Brown Jug* as she approached the old millowner's house and the rise towards Dallerie Brae and the road to town. She didn't spot the watcher in the millowner's house. Even if she had, she wouldn't have been concerned. She had already moved on.

For the LORD God of recompenses shall surely requite.

Sunday, 10 September

A Day of Discovery

'We damn near had him,' said Bob.

'Must hae been a Powderhall sprinter to get awa fae you, Sandy,' said Annie. She and Ellen listened intently as Sandy and Bob relayed the events of the previous evening. In the yard, Malky Bennett was sweeping up the broken glass from Lorna's bottles. Beside him was a small girl, about Ellen's age, with an explosion of brown hair. She waved at Ellen but Ellen ignored her.

'How did he get awa?' Annie asked.

'We lost him. He went doon there. . .' Sandy pointed to the track off the Laggan road.

'That taks you to Lady Mary's.'

'We Aye. And there's only ae wey oot of there.'

'At the park.'

'Whaur Alec and Vinnie were stationed.'

'And they didnae see him?'

'Not a soul passed through there last nicht. Alec swears to it.'

They walked down the track, all the while proposing ways the arsonist could have escaped. Perhaps he hadn't gone down this path at all? Went up the Laggan Hill instead? No, said Sandy, he definitely came this way. They arrived at Norrie Smith's house, the scene of a tragic occurrence a few weeks previously which was wrapped up in the Moot camp adventure in which Bob and Sandy had become embroiled.

'I was that oot of breath last night,' said Bob, 'I didnae even realise this was whaur we ended up.'

'Aye, you did seem awfae interested in that grund,' said Sandy.

'Wonder if the polis have locked up yet?' Bob walked round the rear of the house and tried the back door. It opened. He rolled his eyes at Sandy. 'Just as well Norrie didnae hae onythin worth stealin.' He was about to close the door when he noticed a mark on the flag floor of the kitchen. He went inside and bent to inspect it.

'Sandy,' he called. 'Footprint.'

Sandy inspected the mark, little more than a smudge on the floor, but almost certainly caused by a foot, one that had trodden in mud on the rough paths outside. They went into the living room and looked out of the window. Annie and Ellen were on the path and Ellen waved. Bob waved back. He studied the floor. There were marks by the window.

'Damn me,' said Bob. 'I think oor man was watchin us the hale time.'

'Laughin, no doot.'

'Probably stayed here aa nicht. Scarpered at first licht, when naebody was lookin.'

'No chance. Malky's aside himsel wi worry. He was watchin the tap of this path aa nicht.'

They looked at one another. 'You think he's still here?' Bob said, his voice low and slow. Without replying Sandy went into the hallway and looked up the narrow staircase. He began to climb. His knees creaked on every step. Bob followed, a pulse beating in his ears. At the top of the stairs Sandy paused. There were two doors, to the left and the right. Both were closed. He opened the left-hand door and strode in. Bob took the right-hand door and peered in from the hallway. The room was dirty and cluttered. And empty.

'Nothin,' he said.

'Nothin here either,' said Sandy. They turned and descended the stairs once more.

'He was definitely here, though,' said Bob.

They rejoined Annie and Ellen outside and walked downhill, through the railway tunnel to the beginning of Lady Mary's Walk and strolled in bright sunshine, the river to their right, retaining wall of the railway on their left. They reached a wide pathway, lined either side by beech trees. The ground was thick with fallen leaves, generation upon generation, slowly turning to powder. Ellen kicked it, scattering leaves all around, and dragged her foot through it, creating a mound of leaves two feet high. Her eyes were wide and she wore an expansive grin.

'Smell that?' said Sandy. 'Like aniseed? That's sweet cicely.' He crouched close to the water and trailed his fingers through a green plant, leaves like miniature ferns. He rubbed the leaves and pressed his fingers to his nose, and then to Ellen's. 'Smell?' he said.

'Smells nice. Can you eat it?'

'Aye. My mither puts it in soup.'

'And rhubarb crumble,' said Annie.

'Feech,' said Sandy.

They walked on and emerged at a small beach by the water's edge, a giant stone, blackened by fire, at its centre. Ellen ran to the stone and climbed on top.

There was a steep banking to their right, covered in scrub and broom and ferns, and Ellen scrambled up it. She hung against a tree and looked westward. The river pulsed steadily, faster in some places, breaking in white waves around stray stones, dense and dark elsewhere. Ellen fell silent. The autumn sun was low in the sky, bright. Its reflections shaded the water gold and black and silver. There were birds singing and Ellen wanted to know what birds they were. She could hear at least three different types, maybe four. There had been overnight rain and smells were rising from the ground, earthy and strong, smells of the soil and leaf litter and bacteria, filling Ellen's senses. She rested her cheek against the bark of the beech tree to which she was clinging. It was cold, but somehow comforting. There was rustling in the canopy above her, leaves in the wind, birds resting. A pigeon cooed. Bob and Annie retreated into shade and Sandy lit a cigarette. Ellen watched them as though they were strangers, as though they were outside her existence. She felt a burst of elation, an overwhelming sense of excitement, almost an enchantment. She had never known anything like this. There was a connection, an affiliation, association. The world had only ever comprised Ellen and her family and the streets and buildings she occupied. An immediate existence, depthless, lonesome. One day merged into another, no change, no opportunity. Here, here she felt something deeper, elemental. Complete. Ellen was appalled to feel tears running down her cheek. She wiped them with her sleeve and blinked, looked away from Bob and Annie in case they saw.

'Look,' said Sandy, pointing across the river. 'A heron.'

Ellen studied the bird. It was impassive, immobile. 'Has it only got wan leg?' she said.

'It's got twa, but it stands on one.'

'Why?'

'The watter's cold. The bird loses heat standin in it, so if it juist uses the one leg, that reduces how much heat it loses.'

'How does it know to do that?'

'Knowledge passed down through hundreds of generations.'

'I thought birds were stupit.'

'They dinnae go to the school. They dinnae work. Dinnae pay tax. Dinnae go to war. How stupit is that?'

'I suppose it wouldnae be a bad life,' said Ellen, climbing down from the tree. 'I wouldnae stand in a river, but.'

'You would if your tea was in it.'

'Whit?'

'They're waiting for a fish or a puddock to come by.'
'To eat it?'
'Aye.'
'I'd like to see that.'
'Come here often enough, you probably will.'

Ellen looked at Bob. 'Am I allowed to come here?'

'Aye, ony time you like.'

'Just dinnae fall in the water,' said Annie. 'No like some I could mention.'

Ellen looked at Bob and raised an eyebrow. 'You?'

Bob grinned. 'A few years ago, aye. But it was grand – I didnae let the picnic get wet.'

'Juist himsel,' said Annie, laughing. 'Drookit, heid to toe.'

'It was a hot day. I needed coolin doon. If we walk on, I'll show you whaur it happened.'

The Earn beside them was wide and calm, flowing gently eastwards. Their path narrowed and was littered with exposed tree roots, making their passage awkward. When they passed the scene of Bob's accident, he inadvertently came within a whisker of repeating the act, securing himself against a tree trunk at the last moment.

'There's that smell again,' said Ellen, running ahead and scouring the bank for its source, pointing proudly to a clump of sweet cicely.

'Very good,' said Sandy.

In the distance they could see the railway viaduct. Ellen stopped and stared at the water. She turned to Sandy. 'Ye said naebody could get oot of here except goin up to the end of the path.'

'Aye.'

She pointed at the water, pooling at the point where the Barvick met the Earn, the waters shallow and clear. 'Ye could get across there easy,' she said.

Sandy studied the pool and looked ahead. The entrance to Lady Mary's Walk was out of sight. 'She's richt,' he said.

'Would you be able to get oot of the watter on the other side?' said Bob.

'Nae bother,' said Ellen. She slipped off her shoes and socks and before Bob or Annie could intervene she was stepping into the water.

'It's freezin,' she said. She paddled through the almost still pool and into the gentle flow of the river as it turned through ninety degrees. She reached the edge and scrambled up the banking and turned back triumphantly.

'Telt you,' she said. 'Piece of piss.'

'Ellen, stop that swearin,' Annie shouted back.

Ellen dried her feet with her hands and slipped her socks and shoes back on. 'Come oan,' she said. 'Your turn.'

'I'm no goin in there,' said Annie, shivering.

'Go up into the field,' Sandy shouted to Ellen, gesturing behind her. 'Cross to the other side, whaur the lade is. There's a gate by the road. We'll meet you there in five minutes.'

They ambled uphill to the start of the walk, where Alec and Vinnie had been watching. 'I think the bairn's richt,' said Sandy. 'That's how he got awa.'

'Definitely a local, then,' said Annie. 'You'd hae to ken the water's shallow there. I've been doon here dozens of times and I've never noticed that.'

'What chance Sergeant Rudd'll accept it's no Glesga bairns noo?'

'Nane at all,' said Sandy.

*

'Can I go back doon the river the morra?'

'You've got the school the morn,' said Annie.

'I dinnae huv to be there till wan o'clock. Can I go in the mornin?'

'You'll get yoursel clarty.'

'I winnae. I promise.'

'You liked it doon there, didn't you?' said Bob.

Ellen thought it was the most magical place in the world. She had experienced something she'd never known before, a kind of transcendence, an awareness that there was more than just the moment. Life happened there. Ellen realised she had never experienced life, not until now.

Today had changed everything.

'It was alright,' she said.

Monday, 11 September

A Day of Beginnings

Lorna studied her face in the dressing table mirror. The graze on her right cheek where she had fallen in her escape from the dairy was unmissable. The grazes on her palms she could conceal but she needed to deal with her face. She applied foundation, then used a puff to dab on complexion powder. She studied the effect. The powder had been applied so thickly she looked artificial, like a doll that had been water damaged. She wiped it off with her brush. Natural looked much better. She would simply have to talk her way out of it. She rose from her chair, feeling stiffness in her legs and back. She wanted to rest, to sleep, to spend the day luxuriating in bed, dreaming about fire and planning her next escapade.

What she really did not want was to have to teach two classes of twelve-year-old schoolchildren.

'Little bastards.'

She put on her coat and hat and took her satchel. The first day of a new academic year was torture, overexcitable and untrained children assuming they were there for their own benefits rather than their teachers. It took weeks to make them malleable. She stopped on the landing as Mary walked past carrying an armful of fresh bed linen.

'Good God, what have you done?' she said. She sighed in exasperation and opened the door to her room. 'Get in,' she said and held the door open. Mary crept past and stood in the middle of the room, head bowed.

'Take that cap off.'

'I'd rather not, miss. It took me ages to get it on.'

'Take it off!'

Mary pulled at her maid's cap and her hair cascaded down to her shoulders. Lorna appraised her, frowning, and Mary felt as though she were naked.

'What on earth is that?'

'Pin curls.'

'And who did it?'

'A friend. Well, a friend of a friend.'

'Not a hairdresser?'

'No, she works in the mill.'

'I specifically instructed you to get a perm. And you've come back with this monstrosity.'

'I'm sorry. . .'

'Have you no sense? Have you no sensibility? I don't suppose you even know the difference between the two words. Can you not see this abomination makes you look like a trollop?'

Mary felt her eyes tearing up. She gripped her cap tightly and stared at the floor, unable to speak or move.

'I told you to get a perm. I didn't expect to have to tell you again but clearly you're not capable of following a simple instruction.' She grabbed a handful of Mary's hair and tugged it hard, causing Mary to buckle at the knees. 'So I shall tell you again. And this time I want all that ridiculous length cut off. You're not a child any longer, even if you behave like one.' She yanked her hair again. Mary yelped in pain.

'Now,' she continued, 'I have some undergarments that need washed and dried so that I can wear them tomorrow.'

'Yes, miss. The washroom will be free now.'

'Excellent. There they are.' Lorna pointed to a pile of dirty laundry on the floor by the dressing table. 'You can take them and do them now.'

'I have my own duties to attend to, miss,' Mary said. 'I have to empty the grates and light the fires, and I've a lot of cleaning to get through. . .'

'Then the sooner you stop jabbering and get my laundry done, the sooner you'll get back to your duties. We'll make this a regular Monday morning task. Leave.'

Mary gathered up the laundry and rushed from the room before she was overtaken by tears. She closed the door and, sobbing, crossed the landing to the stairs. Mr Henderson, descending from his quarters, watched her go. He stared at the closed door to Lorna's room and shook his head.

*

'It was a madman,' said Marnie Bennett, her shock of brown hair waving as she spoke. 'Saturday night, tried to burn doon oor dairy, like he said he would. My faither chased him awa.'

The hayrick fires on the Bennett farm and the attempted arson attack on the dairy were the only topics of conversation among the Crieff children in Miss Carrington's classroom. Nothing as exciting as this had happened in Crieff in their lifetimes.

'There's been a guard on oor fairmhoose night and day,' Marnie continued.' We've even had the ARP helpin.'

'No, you havenae,' said Georgie Murray.

'We have so. My uncle Pally's a Warden. He sorted it.'

The Glasgow children sat at the back of the classroom, ignoring the teuchters in front.

'Whit you wearin that fur?' Alison McGillivray rubbed the sleeve of Ellen's grey school pullover as though it were something noxious.

'They made me.'

'Ye'll no get me in wan of them.' Alison was a year older than Ellen and normally in a different class but they seemed to have been lumped together in the new, makeshift timetable, along with the Jardine twins and three other boys and three girls from Finnieston, plus a group of eight from Springbank School. 'You look like a fuckin teuchter,' she went on.

'Teuchter, teuchter, teuchter,' the Jardine twins chanted in unison, and the other Glasgow children joined in, crowding round Ellen and pointing their fingers in her face. Ellen felt her cheeks start to burn.

'Silence!'

Lorna Carrington strode into the classroom, lean and angular, her movements jerky and erratic, like a poorly controlled marionette. She dropped her satchel and leather tawse onto her desk with a thwack.

'I'll overlook this racket just this once as high jinks on the first day of a new year but never, ever, will I tolerate anything like this again.' She marched down the central aisle of the classroom to the Glasgow contingent and stared at them malevolently.

'You.' She pointed to Alison McGillivray. 'Swap places with George Murray on the front row, by the window.'

'I dinnae. . .'

'Don't dare speak back to me! Move!' Alison shifted from her seat as slowly as she calculated she would get away with and took the seat vacated by George. He ignored her. Lorna turned to Maggie MacMaster.

'You, swap with Rhona Walker, over by the door.' She glowered at Ellen. 'You, with the insolent scowl, down the front, next to my desk. You look like trouble.'

Ellen picked up her things and sat next to the girl with wild hair. The Jardine twins were separated and Lorna carried on rearranging the room until no Glaswegian children remained together. By the time she had finished the room was brimming with hostility.

'This is my second class of the day,' said Lorna, 'and I

will be teaching double shifts from now until Christmas, at the earliest. Do not expect me to be tolerant, or kind, or considerate. You will do what I say, when I say. Is that clear?'

'Yes, Miss Carrington,' intoned the Crieff children. The Glasgow children remained silent. Lorna picked up her tawse and smacked it against her open palm.

'When I ask a question, you will answer. Every one of you. Do you understand?'

'Yes, Miss Carrington.'

Ellen seethed with the injustice of being picked on when she had done nothing wrong. She chewed the inside of her lip and stared at the map of the world on the wall behind Miss Carrington's desk, lost herself in it, imagined herself somewhere else, anywhere, any place in the world far away from this horrible town. She became aware that the Crieff girl seated next to her in the double desk was staring at her. She turned and gave her a baleful glare.

'I'm Marnie,' the girl whispered. 'I saw you yesterday, at the fairm.'

'Silence, child.' Lorna glared at Marnie and then at Ellen. You will notice,' she continued, 'that my face is somewhat grazed. Let that be a warning to you all never to run outdoors. You child, are you paying attention?'

Ellen realised the teacher was speaking to her. She looked up at her, into her eyes, and she saw an emptiness in them that made her shiver.

'Yes, miss.'

*

'I shouldnae say it, but thank heavens she's awa to the school.' Annie sank onto a chair in Cloudland and wrapped her hands around a mug of tea Leslie Comer had brewed for her.

'There speaks the mither of every bairn on the first day of school efter the summer holidays,' said Leslie, laughing. She lit a Woodbine and sat down. There were only two customers in Cloudland, Betty Copland and Elma Mackintosh, each of them nodding their agreement with Leslie's prognosis.

'I'm absolutely worn oot. Thon's been the longest week of my life.'

'Is your lassie alright?' asked Betty Copland. 'Some of thae Glesga keelies have been terrors.'

'Aye, she's grand. I'm just no used to bairns.'

'Ina Harrison was tellin me, her next door neighbour – her whose husband ran awa wi a lassie fae the shows last Games day – she's got three Glesga laddies, and only the one pair of shin atween them. Filthy an aa. Like they've never seen a bucket of water, let alone use ane.'

'And rude,' Aggie chipped in. 'Glenys Maxtone's got a couple of wee anes, and their mither's wi them an aa. Giein Glenys nothin but cheek. Winnae lift a finger to help. "You're bein paid to look efter us," she keeps tellin her.'

'I wouldnae stand for that,' said Betty.

'The hale thing's been a shambles,' said Leslie. 'You hae to feel sorry for them. Some of them dinnae even understand what they're here for. Naebody explained it to them. . .'

'You cannae explain onythin to people like thon. . .'

'Common.'

'Dirty.'

'My Ellen's no in the least bit dirty,' said Annie, tiring of the women's vituperation. This had been the tenor of discussion in town for the past week, accusations and insults being hurled at the Glaswegians, marking them out as all the same. 'Onywey,' she said, changing the subject to something else she was certain would incur their wrath and drag them from further discourse on the Glaswegians, 'did you hear thon government mannie on the wireless this mornin, saying there was nae shortage of food and nae need to stockpile. . .'

'Arschole,' said Leslie. 'If there's a sure wey to mak folk start stockpilin, it's to tell them there's nae need.'

'Exactly. And if there really are nae shortages, what are they makin ration cards for?'

'They're no bringin in rationin, are they?' said Betty.

'They are. It was in *The Courier*.'

'Oh my, I mind rationin the last time. Hellish.'

'It's this National Register,' Annie explained. The deadline for registering under the National Registration Act was little more than two weeks way. 'They're goin to use that to mak oor ID cards. And then they're usin it to mak ration cards an aa.'

Betty shook her head. 'Start diggin up your gairdens.'

*

'Because you're only at school half a day you're going to have to do a lot more homework to keep up.' Lorna leaned back against her desk and enjoyed the looks of consternation on the faces of Primary Six. She sensed already this was not going to be a good class. She preferred children with intelligence and creativity and this bunch looked devoid of spark. Lorna Carrington's philosophy of pedagogy was to ignore the ninety-five per cent who typified the vacuity of humanity and concentrate on drawing out the talents of the remainder. Looking around the room, she saw little to encourage her. The small one with the dark hair, though – Black Alice, Lorna had already nicknamed her because she looked like the Tenniel drawings of *Alice in Wonderland* but for the cascade of hair being black rather than blond – she seemed intensely internal and Lorna knew well that this often suggested some hidden facet which was worth uncovering. The child had spent most of the afternoon studying the map of the world on the wall with a level of concentration that Lorna found irritating and impressive in equal measure. She threw a stick of chalk at her, hitting her on the chest and marking her new pullover.

'Black Alice,' she said. 'What did I just say?'

'We've to write two pages fur homework on workin for a

livin,' replied Ellen, 'somethin we know aboot or want to do when we grow up.'

Word perfect. Lorna couldn't interpret the girl's expression. It wasn't insolence, or arrogance. Nor fear. Nor self-assurance. Something, though, there was something about her.

'What is it on the map of the world that has you so interested?' she asked.

'I was lookin at the right-hand side of America and the left-hand side of Africa and thinkin how well they join up, like they used to be part of the same place.'

Lorna silenced the sniggers and snorts from the Glaswegian children. 'And did you uncover this revelation by yourself or did someone suggest it to you?'

'I just thought of it the noo.'

'You thought of it now.'

'That's what I said.'

'For cheeking me, Black Alice, you will do double homework. Four pages instead of two.'

And that way we'll see, Lorna thought, what is going on in that irritating little head.

*

During playtime and after school on the first day a strict demarcation was established, the Crieff girls and boys on one side of their respective playgrounds and the Glasgow children on the other. Each group regarded the other with hostility. The Crieff girls played poachie, the boys dodgeball. The Glaswegians talked among themselves. Ellen, not friends with any of her Glaswegian classmates, stood alone. She watched the little girl who had introduced herself as Marnie. She was a slight girl with hair so wild it looked as though it had been detonated. She too stood on the periphery of her peers and the two girls caught each other's attention across the divide of the playground. They each turned away.

At going home time Ellen kicked a stone along the pavement

in Commissioner Street, thinking about the day and her new teacher. Miss Carrington seemed to have taken against her and she had no idea why. All she knew was that she had been given double homework for no reason.

'Hello.'

Marnie bounded up behind her, struggling to contain her satchel on her shoulder. One of the buttons on her pinafore had come loose and the front bib was hanging down, revealing a grimy shirt, clearly not new and, this early in the school year, obviously a hand-me-down.

'I'm sorry you got extra homework,' she said.

'I dunno what fur.'

'We have to speak proper in class. "Now" not "noo".'

'Why?'

'"Noo" is slang.'

'No, it isnae. That's just the word fur it.'

'No in class.'

'I hate this place.'

'So do I.'

'But you come fae here.'

'So?'

At Kemp's the butcher's, Ellen looked up King Street. 'I'm goin this way,' she said.

'I can go that wey, too.'

'You live on that farm. It's no up this way.'

'I can still go that wey, though.'

Before she could reply, Ellen felt a sharp blow to the back of her head. She winced and raised her hand as Alison McGillivray sped past.

'Ellen is a teuchter, Ellen is a teuchter.'

Maggie MacMaster came from behind and she, too, slapped Ellen over the head. 'Speak to the teuchters again and ye'll no be allowed to speak to us no more,' she said. She gripped Ellen's jaw and pushed her face towards her. 'Got it, teuchter?' She grabbed her gas mask and pushed her away and she and

Alison ran laughing up King Street. At Bryce's shoe shop Maggie threw the gas mask onto the road.

'Maybe I'd better go this wey after aa,' said Marnie, pointing across Commissioner Street.

'Aye,' said Ellen.

*

Lorna rarely sat in the communal rooms of Barvick Falls but her first day of the new school year had been dispiriting and she thought adult company might improve her mood. The evening concert with the BBC Orchestra was playing on the wireless in the front lounge and the inconsequence of the music was making her reassess her decision. So too was Miss Glass, the old fool grinning like a loon as she conducted the orchestra with her fingers. Lorna was on the verge of leaving when she heard the tip-tap of Mr Henderson's walking stick on the parquet flooring of the hallway. She willed the lounge door to remain shut but it opened and Mr Henderson limped in, followed by his abominable nurse, Miss Salter. This was the first time Lorna had been in the same room as the woman and she eyed her disdainfully.

'Splendid evening,' said Mr Henderson.

'It was,' replied Lorna. She stared out of the window at the sloped garden.

'How is your father?' said Miss Salter.

Lorna turned in amazement. Miss Salter smiled. 'I used to live in St Andrews,' she said. 'I was in your father's congregation. Free Church.'

Shock coursed through Lorna's body. 'You're mistaking me for someone else,' she said coldly. 'I have never been to St Andrews. I come from Mintlaw. My father is not a minister.'

'But he is. I remember you as a child. You and your younger brother. You knew your own mind even then. I remember one time. . .'

Without a word, Lorna rose from her seat, gathered her

cigarettes and lighter and walked out of the room. She returned to her bedroom and threw herself on the bed.

How dare the past intrude on her present?

*

'How was your first day of school?' Bob asked. Ellen was sitting by the fire with a new school jotter open on her knees, staring at a blank page as though in search of inspiration.

'Okay.'

'What's your teacher like?'

She's a complete and utter witch, thought Ellen. *She's out to get me.*

'Fine,' she said.

Friday, 15 September

A Day of Sore Heads

The east-facing wall of the classroom was dominated by three large windows which the ARP had instructed be permanently blacked out. Sheets of opaque blackout paper had been taped together and sealed around the window frames and the effect was a permanent half-light that hung over the classroom. Ellen was engrossed in the map of world nations on the wall when the sound of thirty wooden chairs scraping against the varnished floorboards alerted her to the arrival of Miss Carrington and she, too, stood to attention.

'Good morning, Miss Carrington,' the children chanted.
'Sit.'

As usual, Lorna made a show of placing her tawse on her desk. She had used it only once so far, on one of the Jardine twins, and she had decided that today she should use it again. End the first week with a show of force. Concentrate their minds over the weekend. She marched up and down the rows of desks, handing back the children's marked compositions, a comment accompanying each one. 'Edward Soutar, see me afterwards.'

Ellen felt her palms prickle as she waited for her jotter to be returned. It had been hard, stretching her composition over four pages, especially since she had chosen to write in smaller handwriting than usual to avoid being accused of trying to shirk her punishment, but she was pleased with the result. She was honest about her family's lack of money, the struggle by Thursday and Friday to make ends meet, but she was careful not to overplay their poverty. Her dad was in work and they managed and there were plenty of other families whose fathers were out of work. Ellen didn't want anybody's pity.

Lorna continued the return of the homework. The last jotter she handed out was Ellen's. She threw it onto her desk. The previous evening, she had left marking Ellen's homework until last, hoping it would reveal the hidden depths she imagined Black Alice might possess, but she had been greatly frustrated. The essay was well enough written, with beautifully neat handwriting and perfect spelling and grammar throughout, but there was no spark. Mostly, this was the result of the subject matter.

'Honestly,' she said, 'did you imagine anyone would be interested in the home life of Glasgow Keelies? Shipyards? Manual work? I mean, riveting is hardly riveting, is it? You're living in Crieff, now. Do this again for Monday, but write about more acceptable subject matter for a small, rural town.'

Ellen opened her jotter and stared at the mark in disbelief.

'One for good spelling and one for neat handwriting,' Lorna said. 'Two out of ten. Lowest mark in the class. And we know what that means.' She went to a cupboard at the back of the room and took from it a conical hat, completely white but for a large "D" emblazoned on the front and back. She handed it to Ellen.

'The dunce of the class wears the dunce's cap,' she said. 'Put it on, Black Alice.'

*

The three-legged device looked like an instrument of torture, a black painted column rising three feet in the air, topped by a hoop from which hung thirty or so lengths of rubber, each holding a Bakelite clamp.

'You sure you want all this length off?' Jeanie Armour said, looking at Mary in the mirror. 'It's awfae bonny.'

Mary, unable to take her gaze from the Eugene permanent wave machine, nodded mutely. She didn't want to lose her length, not at all, but Lorna Carrington was not someone to be argued with. She was in a situation from which there felt no escape. She closed her eyes as Jeannie started cutting. It felt like the end of her childhood.

*

Mr Henderson and Miss Salter changed buses at Perth and boarded an Eastern Bluebird to St Andrews. Mr Henderson sucked on a Pan Drop and studied the shifting autumnal tapestry through the window, trees turning bronze and gold and yellow and brown, the fields lying fallow after harvesting, in recovery, the soil dry and powdery. All week he had been greatly troubled by the scene with Miss Carrington on Monday. Miss Salter remained adamant she knew her from St Andrews and furnished him with enough examples of Miss Carrington's antics as a child for him to be assured she was correct. Certainly, she didn't come from Mintlaw, not with that accent. The suddenness and ferocity of her response convinced him there was something seriously amiss. During the war, leading large groups of recalcitrant men, he had seen enough prevarication and bluster to know when a story was being concealed. He was certain they needed to investigate Miss Carrington further.

At the bus station in St Andrews they alighted and walked slowly, Mr Henderson resting increasingly heavily on his stick as they progressed down Westburn Lane to the Free Church. A ladder was laid against a single storey extension to the right of the church and a young man was perched on the upper rungs, reaching high above him. The man spotted Mr Henderson and Miss Salter and descended.

'I won't shake your hand,' he said, waving a filthy hand

in front of him. 'Gutters.' He pointed to a giant beech tree behind them. 'Have to clean them out every week, this time of year.'

Mr Henderson noted with surprise the man wore a dog collar. 'Are you the minister?' he asked.

'Reverend Foster,' the man replied. 'Locum.'

'Where is Reverend Carrington?'

'Not well, I'm afraid. He's been off work for some time now. Do you know him?'

'Miss Salter was formerly a parishioner here.'

'Twenty years ago,' said Miss Salter.

Reverend Foster nodded his head. 'Time hasn't been kind to Reverend Carrington,' he said. 'I'm afraid he's not at all well. Cancer. Lungs. Unlikely he'll be back.'

Mr Henderson rested against his stick. 'And the family?' he said.

'Mrs Carrington is a wonderful woman. So brave. An inspiration. I see her every Wednesday for tea and scones. I believe she provides me greater succour than I do her.'

'And the children?'

'Scott. He still lives in town. Works in the bank. A very fine young man.'

'And Lorna?'

Reverend Foster's expression clouded. He looked up at the guttering, and then at the beech tree. 'Lorna left home some years ago, I understand.'

'To be a teacher?'

'I don't know the ins and outs of it. I wasn't here then.'

'Did something happen?'

Reverend Foster's discomfort was evident. 'I don't know. Honestly. She went away. Up north somewhere. Mintlaw? Is that a place?'

'Was there a scandal?'

'It was felt best she moved away.'

'But you don't know why?'

'There was something about a child. A daft laddie. Something happened to him.'

'What?'

'Honestly, I don't know.'

Mr Henderson was quite certain the minister did know, but he was equally certain the man would never reveal what. He tapped his stick on the ground.

'Is Mrs Carrington in?' he asked.

'I'm afraid not.'

Mr Henderson noticed the hesitancy with which the minister spoke. A lie by someone unused to lying. 'I would rather like to speak with her,' he pressed. 'Miss Salter would like to pay her respects.'

'I can pass on your regards,' Reverend Foster said.

'You're sure she's not at home?' Mr Henderson looked up at the house as though expecting to see her through the window. The house was in darkness.

'She's visiting. Down south.'

Too vague to be true, Mr Henderson knew. He also knew he would not get past Mrs Carrington's sentinel.

'Good day to you, Reverend,' he said and walked off. Miss Salter followed.

*

'Miss, Miss, Alison McGillivray's got lice.' Georgie Murray sat with his arm raised straight above him. Those around him backed away from Alison, their chairs scraping on the floor. Lorna threw her chalk on her table and strode towards Alison and peered at her mousy, shoulder-length hair. A louse leaped from her head onto her desk and, through luck rather than judgement, Lorna managed to slap her hand over it. She turned to Maggie McMaster.

'Go to the janitor's office and ask Mr Smith for a metal bucket. Now!'

Maggie scuttled out of the room and Lorna strode to the

front. She addressed the class with a voice cold and slow. 'I will not allow you Glasgow children to import your filthy habits to this clean-living town. You are found wanting in virtually every regard. Some of you are little better than vermin, and now you bring lice into my classroom!' Her voice rose to a roar. 'Disgusting creatures!' They sat in silent terror as they waited for Maggie's return, while Lorna rifled through the cupboards beneath her desk. She emerged with three McLaren's Dairy milk bottles full of a clear, blueish liquid.

'There's only one cure for lice nits,' she said. 'Paraffin.'

'Fuck off,' said Alison McGillivray.

'It'll be the strap for that, when we're done making you fit for civilised company.' Maggie returned with Mr Smith, who deposited a bucket on the floor by the door. He waited, not sure what was happening.

'That will be all, thank you, Mr Smith,' Lorna said. Mr Smith looked at the bottles on her desk, and at the bucket and seemed to make some sort of connection, but he turned and left without a word. 'You, get over here,' Lorna shouted, pointing at Alison. Alison stood up but remained rooted by her desk. Lorna grabbed her shoulder and pulled her towards the bucket and forced her to kneel beside it, pushing her head inside. Alison's screams reverberated against the metal and echoed around the room as Laura poured the first bottle of paraffin over her head and started to rub the scalp vigorously. She poured the second bottle over as well, and then the third, scrubbing at the scalp all the while and running her fingers through the girl's hair. Floating in paraffin in the bottom of the bucket were a dozen lice eggs.

'Look at that,' Laura shouted, forcing Alison's head close to the level of the paraffin. 'Dirty living causes that. How dare you come here and infest my classroom!' She scooped paraffin over Alison's scalp again and again for five minutes, rubbing it in with her fingernails, scratching the skin, then she sat back on her heels, panting. 'Get up,' she said. 'Go to the toilet and wash your hair out in cold water.' Alison ran from the room, sobbing.

Lorna looked around the classroom, gratified to see horror and alarm on the faces of the children. This would teach them all a lesson. She turned to Black Alice and saw – fury rose in her once more – was that contempt? Or disgust?

'You!" she shouted. She jumped to her feet and crossed to Ellen's desk. 'Did I see a louse flying from your hair just then?'

'No, miss!'

'I did.' She turned to the children surrounding Ellen. 'You saw it, didn't you?' The children either sat mutely or nodded in terrified agreement. Marnie Bennett shook her head.

'I havenae got lice,' said Ellen. She rose from her chair and backed away.

'Come here, wretched child.' Lorna pulled the dunce's cap from Ellen's head and dragged her to the bucket and forced her head inside. Ellen could see the eggs floating in the liquid. She screamed as Lorna thrust handfuls of paraffin over her hair, her fingers digging into her scalp and grazing the skin. The fumes from the paraffin were overwhelming and, although she kept he mouth firmly shut, some of the liquid slid up her nose, causing her to gag and retch. All the while, she screamed inside her head that she hadn't had lice, but she probably would now that her hair was being doused in the liquid used to clean Alison's scalp. She felt as though her head was on fire, from the heat of the paraffin and the raking of Lorna's fingers across her scalp. She began to cry, finally unable to summon the strength to resist. She had no idea how long the ordeal lasted – it felt like hours – and finally she reached a point where she stopped struggling and leant passively into the bucket.

As soon as she did, Lorna stopped.

'Back to your seat, Black Alice, and don't speak for the rest of the day.'

*

Mary felt as though her scalp was burning. First, Jeannie had applied some hideous-smelling chemicals to her newly-shortened hair which started to burn immediately, and then she had threaded strands of hair through Bakelite clamps until her entire scalp was gripped and raised high in the air. She looked as though she was being electrocuted. Then Jeannie started heating the rods and Mary could smell burning and then she felt burning, and she knew she was trapped in this machine, unable to move, and panic started to overwhelm her. She started to cry.

'You're no the first to find the machine difficult,' said Jeannie, stroking her shoulder. 'The things we do to mak oorsels bonny, eh? I hope your lad appreciates it.'

Mary thought about Sandy. She'd be pleased if he even noticed. Of far greater importance, though, was Lorna Carrington's reaction.

*

Ellen's first thought when school finished was to go to Lady Mary's Walk but as she passed Milnab Mill she changed her mind: that was her special place and she didn't want it tainted by the furious thoughts whirling through her brain at that moment. Instead, she carried on to Mungall Park and sat by the curling pond and pulled at blades of grass. Her initial anger had subsided but in its place was a burning resentment. Resentment towards Miss Carrington, towards Crieff, towards anyone who thrust her into the spotlight. She wanted to go through life unobserved, at ease. That wasn't much to ask, to be left alone. Was it?

It was nine o'clock before, cold and hungry, she felt able to return to Cloudland and face the overweening solicitousness of Bob and Annie.

'Whaur hae you been?' Annie screeched. 'I've been worried seeck.'

'Who cares?'

'I care. Whaur were you?'

'Doon the park.'

Annie closed her eyes. 'You're allowed to go aboot, but you hae to tell us. You cannae juist wander aff like that.' Ellen was biting her cheek, staring out of the window. 'Are you okay?' Annie said. She sniffed the air. 'What hae you been doin? You reek of paraffin.'

Ellen knew she couldn't talk about what happened. The shame of it, the humiliation, in front of everyone in class. She would never mention it. She turned and went to her room and closed the door. Almost immediately, it opened and Annie positioned herself to prevent another breakout.

'Explain!'

Just go away. Leave me alane.

'It was some of the Glesga bairns,' she said finally. Anything to make Annie go away and leave her be. 'They were just playin. A bit of fun.'

'Coverin you in paraffin? What fun is that?'

'Just my hair.'

'Juist your hair? That's alright then.' Annie's voice was loud and shrill and she was clearly upset. Somehow, this made the situation worse for Ellen and, without knowing why, she started to cry. Her habitual anger had dissipated and in its place was the melancholy of a child out of place and out of time. Annie sat beside her on the bed and cradled her to her chest. She took her into the kitchen and washed her hair in the tub on the kitchen floor, gently soaping it and squeezing a sponge over it again and again until all trace of the paraffin had been removed. Gradually, she could feel the tension lift from Ellen's body and the child nestled against her. Annie kissed her cheek and held her close and she felt Ellen's small hand gripping her shoulder and in that moment she felt a sense of responsibility greater than anything she had ever known. They remained like that, fused together, for a full minute. Annie patted her hair dry, studying its texture, thinking some of the shine and gloss had been stripped from it. The child was deeply upset, she could tell, and the more she thought about that, the more enraged Annie became.

Saturday, 17 September

A Day of Change

The tree had come down in the big storm of 1923 and was gradually disintegrating, now grass- and moss-covered, slowly breaking down into humus. This skeleton of giant roots, eight feet high, had over the course of a generation become a favourite play area for Crieff's children. Some thirty people were gathered around it now, all clutching scissors or shears or other cutting implements. Harry McKenzie, eighty-three and half-blind, brandished a scythe that hadn't seen a whetstone since Victoria was on the throne. Between him and the others a sensible distance was being kept.

'Today, we are collecting sphagnum moss.' Mrs McNeill's clipped tones rang through the Monzie Estate from her position next to the fallen oak. 'We prefer red moss, and please cut it close to the area of moss itself, avoiding too much woody material. Please do not lose any moisture. Members of the WVS will come round and gather your harvest in these sacks.' She held aloft a hessian potato sack with *Wm Haggart* stamped on it.

'Whit do they want it fur?' Ellen asked.

'They use it for dressin wounds,' Annie replied. 'It absorbs liquid well or somethin.'

'They're gonnae pit weeds in a bandage?'

'Moss is not a weed,' said Mrs McNeill. 'Weeds are

unwanted and valueless plants that multiply in areas where they shouldn't. Mosses are a very ancient and important group of plants.' She frowned at Ellen, who she considered a sullen-faced child with a common Glasgow accent. A call had gone out to WVS groups throughout the country to gather sphagnum moss for the war effort and Mrs McNeill was determined that Crieff, with its profusion of mosses in the nearby countryside, should gather more than anywhere else. Even so, some volunteers were less desirable than others.

'Some of our ladies have provided sandwiches and hot drinks, and lemonade for the children,' she continued. 'We will work until twelve and then have luncheon.'

'That's awfae good of them,' said Annie.

'Big deal,' said Ellen. 'I'd sooner be paid two bob than get a manky sangwich. This is ma labour. I've a right to expect a fair day's pay for a fair day's work.'

'John MacLean's alive and well,' said Bob.

'Who?'

'A great man. Fae Glesga.'

'Are you makin a fool of me again?'

'Honestly, no.' He bent over a clump of moss. 'It's only a few weeks ago I was chasin a murderer through here in the pitch dark.'

'Aye, so ye were.'

'He was,' confirmed Annie. 'Got himsel clouted ower the heid and knocked unconscious.'

Ellen looked him up and down. 'Ye're no much of a fechter, are ye?'

'Seriously hen, if you ever need onyone to fight your corner, choose Annie.'

'I can fight my ain battles.'

'I ken that fine.'

They started to gather the moss. Ellen squeezed some tightly, squealing with surprise and delight at how much water was discharged. It trickled down her arm and she rubbed it into her skin. The moss was surprisingly soft, not at all what she expected when she first saw it, and the water it held was cold and almost velvety to the touch. She rubbed some more onto her bare arms, pressing the moss itself against her skin where the eczema was bad. It felt lovely.

Apart from her, there were only four children present, one of whom was Marnie Bennett. Seeing Marnie immediately reminded Ellen of school and, inevitably, of Friday's experience with the paraffin. It was a memory she didn't want to revisit.

'Dinnae mention Friday,' she instructed Marnie.

'I wasnae goin to,' Marnie replied. 'Miss Carrington's a witch.' She clipped desultorily with her scissors. 'This is borin. At least when you're pickin blaeberries you can eat some. . . And mak warpaint wi them.'

'Warpaint?'

She patted her hand over her mouth and ululated like Indians in the cowboy films. Ellen, who had never seen a cowboy film, was mystified. She hacked at the moss as though it had offended her.

'Your dairy no been burnt doon yet?' she said.

'No yet. I think they scared him aff last week. I juist wish it would aa go awa. I havenae been able to sleep for watchin oot for him.' Ellen thought Marnie did, indeed, look tired. Even her usually wild hair seemed subdued.

'I'm sure it'll by alright,' she said.

After half an hour, two ladies from the WVS came round to gather their efforts, the younger one, in a cream headscarf, lugging a half-full sack behind her and grimacing as though she were dragging an anchor.

'Good show,' the older woman said as she piled the girls' gathered moss inside.

'Good show,' mimicked Ellen when the women had moved out of earshot.

'You Glesga folk are awfae rude,' said Marnie.

'Everybody's rude to us.'

'Cos you're rude to us.'

'Cos you're rude to us.'

'You started it.'

'No we didnae. We just got landed here. I never asked to come to this shitehole.'

'It must be better than whaur you come fae. Slums and that.'

'Who sez I live in a slum?'

'Well. . .' Marnie wasn't entirely sure what a slum was, but she had heard her parents talking about it. 'You live in these big tenement thingwies, aye?'

'Whit's wrong wi that?'

'It's no as nice as here.'

'I havenae seen hellish much nice here.' Ellen thought about Lady Mary's Walk and the river Earn, but that was a secret pleasure, not to be shared with anyone.

'You can run aboot.'

'I can run aboot at hame.'

'Aye, but only in the streets. Here. . .' Marnie gestured at the moor surrounding them. 'There's a loch,' she said.

'Where?'

'Just ower there. There's curlin stanes an aathin.'

'What's curlin stanes?'

Marnie's mother had her back to them. So did Bob and Annie. With a grin, Marnie threw down her scissors and started to run. 'Come on,' she said, and bounded over the moss, her feet squelching in damp spots and sinking into the peat. Ellen looked at Bob and Annie and threw down her scissors and followed. She let out an involuntary yell of excitement.

Annie turned. 'Whaur's she aff to?' she said.

Bob smiled. 'Aff for a play, by the look of it. She's maybe found hersel a wee pal at last.'

*

Three soldiers, volunteers earlier in the year for the 6/7th Black Watch Territorials – now subsumed into the main army and awaiting posting – strolled down the High Street, greeting friends and accepting messages of good luck from strangers. The sight of soldiers in uniform would become commonplace in the months ahead but for now it was faintly exotic. A group of children, making their way home from Sunday school, saluted elaborately and the soldiers reciprocated.

'On whose authority are you licenced to kill other human beings?' Mr Henderson stood in front of Bain's Toy Shop, leaning on his stick, and addressed the soldiers. They didn't reply and he repeated his challenge. His eyes were watery and his voice was thin, but he addressed them defiantly.

'The government's,' said one of the soldiers, a ruddy-faced, happy-looking lad of twenty or so.

'And who grants them authority?'

'The people,' the soldier replied. 'We voted for them.'

'Ah, so we have granted ourselves the authority to kill other human beings. Through the aegis of our government. What do you imagine our Lord thinks of that?'

'Our Lord gave us free will.'

'And if we exercise our free will in such an egregious manner, how do you think He will respond?'

'I dinnae ken what egregious means so I couldnae say.'

'Egregious,' came another voice, a woman's, and the group turned to see Lorna Carrington sneering at Mr Henderson, 'egregious is one of those words that people like to use when they want to inhabit the moral high ground. Leftists and socialists, pacifists and the pious. All four of those descriptions could be attached to Mr Henderson here, my good men, so pay no heed to his wittering.'

'It is those with least to lose who are generally the most certain,' said Mr Henderson.

'I could say the same of you, old man.'

'Indeed, my remaining time on this earth will not be long.

But neither my views nor my actions will result in the deaths of innocent human beings.'

'You think not? You think if we turn the other cheek, the Nazis will stop what they're doing, won't invade anywhere else, won't bomb anyone, won't kill innocent people? You think that if we behave nicely they will, too? You think that? Then you are a bigger fool than I had supposed.'

'Warmongers cannot be conquered by war, Miss Carrington. Only peace can quench their evil desires. If we respond to Herr Hitler by mimicking his methods and waging war, that only serves to feed his arrogance, persuade him his ways must be correct.'

'And while we wait for him to see sense and renounce violence, what happens to all the people who disagree with him? Who aren't like him?'

'Non-violence does not mean doing nothing. It means overcoming evil with good. Justice and goodness and truth will prevail.'

'Mr Henderson, you are a foolish old man, living in the past. These brave lads here, they are the future of this country. You should be proud of them.'

'I will not take pride in the acts of a murderer.'

'Then you should rot in hell for the coward you are.'

Mr Henderson studied her expression but Miss Carrington remained an enigma. 'I went to St Andrews on Friday,' he said. Her expression didn't change. 'I went to the Free Church.' The silence grew uncomfortable. 'There was a locum in place. Did you know that?'

'Why would I?'

'Because your father is unwell. Seriously so. Have you been to visit him recently?'

'My family come from Mintlaw.'

'Why do you not speak the Doric?'

'Because I was taught to speak the King's English. Honestly, I haven't. . .'

'What about your mother?'

'What about my mother?'

'We didn't have the opportunity to speak with her, unfortunately. I would have liked to ask her about you. . .'

'My mother is in Mintlaw. . .' *My mother is in hell, in living hell, a special compartment for the weak and the cowardly, for the craven and feeble, for those who will not open their eyes or their mouths, nor judge righteously, nor defend the rights of the poor and needy.*

'And about the dead boy.'

'Get out of my sight.'

Mr Henderson stood his ground, resting on his stick. 'There is a story to be told about you, isn't there?' he said at length. 'What have you done?'

The interfering bonehead showed no indication of leaving and Lorna, although she considered it a sign of weakness, felt compelled to make the first move. She swept past him without a word and marched in the direction of the Drummond Arms, drowning out the sound of his voice as he continued to harangue her with the insistence of her own thoughts. This was outrageous, unconscionable. This was harassment. The simpleton boy's death was years ago. Trivial. A misfortune. Not something to cast against her years later.

For I will be merciful. Their sins and their iniquities will I remember no more.

*

There was a locked storeroom by the edge of Loch More and a jetty extending into the water. The surface lay still and dense, almost black, glinting silver in the sunlight. By the edge of the loch the girls found three curling stones, beautifully polished and shaped marble topped with a hooked metal handle.

'What d'ye do wi them?' Ellen asked.

'Curlin. It's a bit like marbles, but on the watter.'

'Do they no sink?'

'When the watter's iced over.'

'Ye can stand on the water?'

'In winter, aye. They mark oot a curling rink, and the stanes nearest the jack win. It gets gey rauch sometimes. You can knock the other player's stanes oot the way. My faither's good at it.'

They sat by the water's edge, Ellen stroking her arm slowly and gently with a piece of moss. When she did, her skin didn't itch like normal.

'Can ye swim in it?' she asked.

'Aye. Cauld, though.'

'I'm goin in.'

'It's ower cauld.'

'Ach, away.' She stood up and stretched behind to unbutton her frock and stepped out of it. She pulled off her shoes and socks and scampered to the water's edge. Marnie stood and, shyly, peeled off her own frock and followed suit.

'Ready?' said Ellen. She grabbed Marnie's hand and they both stepped into the water, shrieking as the coldness hit their skin.

'Go right in,' said Marnie. 'And sit doon. It's easier.' She pushed forward three or four paces until the water was up to her thighs then crouched until she was submerged to her neck. She let out a yell. Ellen laughed and hesitated for a moment, but then copied Marnie's movements. The coldness of the water was overwhelming. Initially, she thought it was painful and she was on the verge of screaming, but quickly her body grew accustomed and the cold started to feel, at first, natural and then oddly pleasurable. She pushed forward and glided into the loch and floated for a moment. She had no idea how to swim and she bobbed along, always ensuring she could touch the bottom of the loch. She could feel it dropping away as the loch grew deeper and she remained close to the edge.

'Put your arms oot like this,' Marnie said, demonstrating a breast stroke, and let yourself go. You winnae sink.'

'I will.'

'Dinnae fight it. Juist float. Then move your legs. Like a puddock. That maks you go forward.' She began to swim towards Ellen, showing her the technique, and Ellen tried to copy. At first she sank but she persevered and after a couple of minutes she was gliding across the water alongside Marnie. For quarter of an hour they felt no cold, but then it started to seep into them, first their feet, then arms and legs, then torsos, and they dragged themselves out of the water, shivering and laughing, and lay on the grass in the still bright sunshine.

'What's that?' said Marnie, pointing to Ellen's back. Ellen turned round quickly to conceal it.

'It's just a rash. Etzemer or somethin.'

'Is it sair?'

'Nah. Itchy mostly. Actually, it's much better the day.'

When they calculated it must be lunch time, they returned to the moss-gatherers, giggling and laughing. Bob watched them approach.

'What you been up to?' he said.

'Swimmin,' Ellen replied.

'In Loch More?' he said, incredulity registering in his voice. 'In September? Was it no cauld?'

'Fuckin freezin.'

'Ellen!'

'Freezin.' She reached up and grabbed Bob's bunnet and ran off as he protested. She bent and cut a swathe of moss and piled it into the bunnet.

'What's that for?' said Marnie.

'Later.'

*

As they walked home from Monzie, across the Knock to Ferntower and the top of Crieff, they bumped into Sandy and

Mary, out on their first public walk together and both highly self-conscious. Sensing this, Bob started telling them of their day's moss-picking.

'Of course, this ane was no use,' he said jocularly, jerking his head towards Ellen. 'Too busy swimmin in the loch.'

'Swimmin was it?' said Sandy, and Ellen was sure there was an element of approval in his tone. 'Must hae been gey cauld.'

'Ellen,' warned Annie.

'Jolly cold,' said Ellen in her poshest accent. Sandy picked up on the undercurrent between Annie and Ellen, parent and child. Instinctively, he took the side of the child.

'Jolly enough to freeze your tits aff, I'd hae thocht.'

'Sandy!' said Annie.

Sandy continued without comment. 'The weather's changin,' he said. 'It's dens you should be buildin, noo. So you can shelter when you're oot.'

'How d'you dae that?' said Ellen.

'Find yoursel a good tree that's got a straight branch stickin oot, aboot your height. Then gather aa the fallen branches you can find. Start wi the big anes. Prop them against the tree branch till you mak a circle aroond it. Then start fillin the shape in wi the smaller branches. Weave them in and oot to gie it strength. Then cover it wi leaves and naebody will even ken it's there. You can hide fae aabody in there.'

Ellen looked at Bob and Annie and decided she liked the sound of that. She studied Sandy, his huge, scowling face, his distant expression. He was engaged in the conversation but he still seemed remote somehow, as though he weren't fully there.

'What is it ye dae?' she asked him.

Sandy took out a Capstan but replied before lighting. 'I'm a gamekeeper, I suppose. For the Hydro Estate.' Sandy wasn't officially a gamekeeper but the Hydro tolerated him hunting on their land because it saved them the expense of employing a real gamekeeper. Officially, the family worked on the Laggan farm but Sandy wasn't a man to be pinned down by details like work.

'Can I write aboot ye?'

'Eh?'

'For school. I hae to write aboot someone who works, what they dae, that kind of thing. I wrote aboot my faither, on the shipyards in Glesga, but the teacher wants me to write aboot you teuchters. . .'

'I dinnae suppose she said it exactly like that,' said Bob.

'Can you no write aboot your Uncle Bob?' Sandy asked.

'It needs to be somethin interestin.'

Sandy's usually impassive features almost betrayed a smile. 'Aye, I see your problem.'

'Thanks,' said Bob.

'Well,' Sandy continued, 'here's a deal: if he maks me and Mary a cuppie tea and a scone, I'll tell you aa aboot the gamekeepin.'

'Deal,' said Ellen.

'Do I no get a say in this?' said Bob.

'And whit wid yer answer be?' Ellen stared at him. The intensity of her gaze was almost a match for Sandy's. She was the most curious mixture, Bob thought, a lassie who hated having attention drawn to her, but someone possessed of a ferocious self-determination.

'I feel like I'm bein ganged up on,' he said

'Ye are,' said Ellen, smiling at Sandy. 'So whit's yer answer.'

Bob started to walk towards town. 'Tea and a scone,' he said.

*

At bedtime, Ellen gripped *Little House on the Prairie* tightly as she reflected on the day. Today had been great fun. That day, down the Earn, had been a moment of wonder, a moment for herself, but today had been – enjoyable. She couldn't remember when she'd felt so free and happy. Even those dark thoughts of Miss Carrington had been dispelled. There was nothing to worry about. Nothing to do. Enjoyment was all that mattered. The stuff Sandy Disdain told her about hunting was more interesting than anything she'd ever heard. And Marnie had been nice. She only realised how much she had missed speaking to someone her own age when she was with Marnie at the loch. Bob and Annie weren't the same, the way they constantly fussed over her or tried to teach her things, worrying about her. There was a knock on the door and Ellen sighed. Annie peered round the door and entered, carrying a glass of water which she placed on the bedside table.

'Have you finished your hamework?'

She sat on the edge of Ellen's bed and picked up her jotter. Four pages of beautifully neat writing told the story of Sandy Disdain's work as a gamekeeper, keeping control of the rabbits, preventing them from becoming a menace to farmers. He talked of shooting, snaring, long-netting, ferreting.

'No matter how many you kill,' he'd told her, 'the numbers keep goin up. They're a bloody menace.' That had formed the conclusion to Ellen's essay, in time of war it being more important than ever that farmers should produce as much food as possible. Gamekeeping was an essential job.

'I'd like to be a gamekeeper,' Ellen said. 'Then I could be on my own all day. Live in a den. Hunt and shoot, like Sandy.'

'You seemed to tak to him.'

'I was just askin him questions.'

'No half. He was sayin when he went oot, he's had easier interrogations aff the polis.'

'I want this essay to be good.'

'I'm sure it will be.' She took hold of Ellen's wrist. 'My,' she said, 'your arm looks much better the nicht. Must be all that fresh air.' She gently stroked her fingers across the patch of eczema on Ellen's upper arm.

'It's the moss,' Ellen replied. 'It's lovely.'

'Is that why you brought some hame wi you? Bob was wonderin when he'd get his bunnet back.'

'It stops me itchin.'

'Here, let me put some on your back.' Ellen lay on her bed and rested her head on her folded arms as Annie lifted her pyjama top and gently grazed the moss across her back.

'Nice?' Annie asked.

But already Ellen was asleep.

Monday, 18 September, 1 am

An Hour of Destruction

Lorna lay on her pink bedspread, eyes shut, hands fisted, muscles tensed. She was exhausted but she couldn't dispose her mind. These intrusions into her private domain were an abomination. The nurse, evil personified, the decrepit Henderson, presuming – presuming! – to defile her splendid isolation. The ghosts of memory made flesh – Norman Banks, leering child, peering, intruding. *Flee from me. You shall not devour me.* Above them all her father. Man of God? Man of Good? Man of much admiration. *And no marvel; for Satan himself is transformed into an angel of light.* Mother, mother of mine. *Can a woman forget her sucking child?*

She can, she could, she did, she would.

The rage was in Lorna, a rage provoked, a rage undimmed after five hours of reflection. But she would not be afraid. The right hand of her own righteousness would uphold her. *He hath sent me to bind up the brokenhearted.* All the lost, all the hurt, all the shunned, the shunted, those who live in the margins, who die in the footnotes, whose voices are silent, whose screams are unheard, rejoice for unto you is come this day a saviour.

In the world ye shall have tribulation: but be of good cheer; I have overcome the world.

By midnight, Lorna knew there was no alternative. The ghosts had to be assuaged. So too the pain. The anger.

Fire. Fire. Hallowed fire.

A harvest moon in an almost cloudless sky lent a milk-silver sheen to the vista before her. She waited at the top of Dallerie Brae to get her bearings. The laundry loomed far below, a deathly darkness against the sallow moonlight. The millowner's house and a couple of workers' cottages lined the road leading to the laundry. All else was field, bounded by the Earn to the south and the railway embankment to the west. On the east was the cemetery. She walked down the brae, her footsteps echoing so loudly she fancied they might wake the cemetery dead. Lights were on in the millowner's house, a wide central window revealing a high and turning staircase leading to a grand central landing. The cottages were in blackout darkness. So, too, was the laundry.

The front elevation comprised a single, double-height hall, relic of the former mill, but in the rear Laura had identified some smaller rooms, probably originally for grain storage, in which dirty laundry was waiting to be cleaned. Laura stopped to listen but heard nothing except the sound of the Earn pulsing in the near distance.

She turned her back on the window of the furthest away room and pressed her elbow against the glass. She pulled away and immediately thrust her elbow back against the window. Pain shot up her arm but the glass remained intact. She tried again and failed again. Holding her aching arm, she checked the rear of building and found, in a lean-to against the gable end, a neatly stacked pile of cut logs. She selected the largest, a foot-and-a-half in length. She returned to the window and smashed the log into it with all her strength. The sound of shattered glass exploded into the night, momentarily terrifying her. She composed herself and fumbled in her pocket for the milk bottle she'd taken from the shed at Barvick Falls and filled with paraffin. Reaching through the broken pane, she poured the paraffin into the room. She lit long strips from the *Glasgow Evening Times* and dropped them onto the paraffin-soaked storage room. At first, she thought the fire hadn't taken but then flames began to flicker in the darkness and she watched them following the trail of paraffin and settling at the base of a pile of laundry. After a few seconds, the fire took hold.

'Hoi!'

The shout came from behind her, in the direction of the main laundry and the workers' cottages. 'What are you doin?' He was on her before she could react and she felt his hand rasp across her cheek. Stung, she flailed into the darkness and caught his jaw. He staggered back and Lorna ran, heading for the back of the row, past the lean-to and into the darkness of the fields beyond. She cursed the moonlight and cheered as a cloud floated across the moon, plunging them into darkness. Blindly, she ran across flat fields, straining to hear the sounds of any pursuit. She stumbled and fell as she encountered an unexpected rise in the ground, some small banking, and she paused for a moment, listening. She thought she could hear rustling behind her. She pulled herself upright and pressed on and found herself stepping into nothing and falling forwards.

She found herself on her hands and knees in five inches of ice-cold water and tried to understand what had happened: the lade that served the old mill – she'd landed in the lade. Although the water was freezing, she forced herself to stay still. She could hear heavy breathing as her pursuer approached and she ducked her head below the bank of the lade. Blood was trickling down her cheek where her assailant had scratched her but, as long as she stayed where she was, she was out of sight and safe. She waited, growing ever colder.

'Anything, Gibby?' came a voice from the direction of the laundry.

'Nothin,' replied Lorna's pursuer. 'He's scarpered.'

'I've called the fire brigade.'

'Have you no get the fire oot?'
'Oot? It's damn near oot of control.'

*

Three hours later, Lorna lay in bed looking out of the window at the sky, wishing it were black, unspectacular. The evening had been a disaster. When she set the fire, saw it take, watched it spread, that was like a knife opening up her flesh and releasing the loathing inside her, countervailing the alienation. She felt immense. She felt whole. But all that relief expired in an instant while she was forced to crouch like a cowering animal in the middle of the lade, soaked, humiliated. A failure.

'I am not a failure.'

And let us not be weary in well doing: for in due season we shall reap, if we faint not.

In due season.

Next time.

Monday, 18 September

A Day of Confrontations

Mary stared at herself in the mirror. Even after three days she couldn't accustom herself to the new perm.

'Wha are you?' she said. She was almost physically afraid of meeting Lorna again and having to withstand whatever reaction the perm would arouse. What if she didn't like it? Again? There was nothing else to cut. Nowhere else to hide.

The servants' bell rang on the landing and she looked out of the top glass pane of her bedroom door to see whose it was, praying it wouldn't be Lorna. It was. She wiped her hands across her face and steeled herself, then put on her apron and went to Lorna's door and knocked.

'Enter.'

'Good morning, miss.'

Lorna was seated at her dressing table, looking out of the window at the garden, cigarette in her hand, elbow rested on the table.

'I have some more washing that needs doing. Urgently.'

'I'm no sure I'll hae time, miss.'

'It's over there. It's rather damp and muddy.'

Mary bent over the pile of clothes, trousers, undergarments, shirt, and sweater. She picked them up. They were sodden.

'Whatever happened?'

'That's none of your concern. Just take them away and see

to them.' Lorna still hadn't turned round and was staring distractedly out of the window.

'I. . .I had my hair permed, miss, as you instructed.'

Lorna turned round. She had a scratch on her cheek and she looked tired. She appraised Mary, focusing on her new perm. 'Tallulah Bankhead,' she said. 'Too fancy for you.'

She inhaled her cigarette and blew smoke from the side of her mouth. 'Have my clothes ready by the time I get home.'

*

Sergeant Rudd and PC McAnuff walked through the firedamaged rear of the laundry. The fire had spread from the small room where it had started into the main hall and had destroyed perhaps a dozen bundles of dirty laundry. There would be a few hotels in Strathearn short of bed linen in the coming days.

'Fuckin Glesga bairns,' said Gibby Owen.

'You think it was them?' said Rudd.

'Aye. Look, I found this ootside the windae.' He handed Rudd a torn copy of the *Glasgow Evening Times*. 'And I nearly caught the little bastard. Fetched him a slap on the puss.'

'Would it leave a mark?'

'Dinnae ken. Too dark. We chased him but he got awa.'

'Aye well,' said Rudd. 'We'll find him.'

PC McAnuff shuddered. He knew what that meant: his next instruction would be to speak to the Glasgow families. And that would be a job from hell and no mistake.

*

The soothing sphagnum moss had allowed Ellen to sleep uninterrupted through the night and she was in a cheerful mood when she entered the classroom at one o'clock. She smiled at Marnie as she settled her satchel and gas mask on her desk and eased into her chair.

'Watch oot, it's Scabby Back,' shouted Georgie Murray.

Ellen turned sharply, and Marnie stared at her in horror.
'Did you say anythin?' Ellen hissed.

'No, I promise.'

'Another filthy Glesga mink bringin their diseases to Crieff,' Georgie said. In unison, the Jardine twins raced across the room to confront him.

'Whit did you call us?' one of the twins said.

'Ellen,' said Georgie, ignoring them, 'how did you get on wi your underwater curlin?'

Ellen looked at Marnie with fury and slapped her arm. 'Why?' she said. 'Why wid ye dae that?'

Before Marnie could explain, the contretemps was ended by the arrival of Miss Carrington, throwing open the door and striding into the classroom. Even by her standards, she appeared cross.

'Sit!' she commanded. She slapped her tawse onto the desk and looked round at the commotion, the Jardines bent over Georgie's desk, Ellen glowering at Marnie. 'You boys, return to your seats this instant. This isn't a zoo where you can wander around as you choose. Marnie Bennett, collect everyone's homework jotters and place them on my desk. Black Alice, simmer down. If you get any more angry you'll explode.'

Lorna faced the class. 'You may notice,' she said, pointing to her cheek, 'that I have managed to scratch myself yet again. I expect most of you will be out in the coming days picking fruit and berries, so let my experience point out to you the dangers of getting too close to bramble briars. An inch higher and it could have taken my eye.'

Too bad, thought Ellen. She reproached herself immediately, but in her heart she knew that her initial response was the truest.

Lorna picked up her chalk and turned to the blackboard and began to write:

'Pale Ebenezer thought it wrong to fight,
But Roaring Bill (who killed him) thought it right.'

She turned to the class. 'The words of Hillaire Belloc,' she said. 'So which are you? Are you a Pale Ebenezer, convinced of the purity of your argument, right up to the moment you die for it, or are you a Roaring Bill, pragmatic to the end and winning?' Nobody answered. 'Well? That was not a rhetorical question. I want an answer from every one of you.'

One by one the children raised their hands and each one said 'Roaring Bill.' Only Marnie and Ellen remained. Marnie raised her hand. 'Roaring Bill,' she whispered.

Lorna walked to Ellen's desk and stood in front of her. 'Black Alice?' she said.

Ellen's skin was itching worse than it had for two weeks. She still felt a flush of anger on her cheeks and chest. Yet again, the whole class was staring at her. She was a Roaring Bill, she knew she was.

'Pale Ebenezer,' she said.

Lorna put her hand on her hip and chewed her lip. She shook her head. 'How disappointing you are, child.'

*

Annie watched through the glass window in the door as the children lined up at the front of the classroom and began to sing:

'At the end of the day we stand and pray
Thank you Lord for our work and play.
We try to be good, for we know that we should,
That's our prayer at the end of the day.'

Lorna swung open the classroom door and the children filed past Annie two-by-two, holding hands. Ellen looked startled when she saw Annie, then worried, and finally angry.

'Don't!' she seethed as she passed into the corridor.

Lorna was closing her leather satchel when Annie entered and she looked up sharply. 'Can I help you?'

'I'm Mrs Kelty. I'm here about Ellen.'

Lorna had anticipated the child might tell her guardians what had happened. No matter. She was within her rights. Lice were a menace. 'An intriguing child,' she said. 'I believe she has an excellent brain, but she hasn't yet managed to make the most of it.'

'She needs encouragement.'

'As do all of them. I am very keen to work with my pupils and help them to improve. It's a wonderful privilege being a teacher, seeing these young minds forming, anticipating the adults they will grow into. I couldn't have chosen a happier vocation.'

'Did you know some of the Glesga bairns washed Ellen's heid in paraffin?'

Lorna didn't need to simulate surprise. This wasn't what she anticipated. *Well done, Black Alice*, she thought. *You kept your mouth shut. Good girl.*

'No, I'm shocked. Appalled.' She inclined her head and tutted loudly. She picked up a pile of jotters. 'But I'm not wholly surprised, I'm sorry to say. These Glasgow children, they are almost wholly lacking in standards or basic civility.'

'And what are you goin to do about it?'

'Did she tell you who did it?'

'No, she winnae say.'

'Oh dear, how dreadful.' She glanced her hand across Ellen's shoulder solicitously. 'But I'm not sure exactly what I can do. They're virtually feral, but they have a sort of lowbrow code. I imagine Ellen broke that code in some way and she was punished for it.'

'And you think that's okay?'

'Certainly not. And I'll keep a close eye on Ellen in the next few days, make sure she's safe. But, if I don't know who did it, I'm honestly not sure what I can do.'

Annie scowled in exasperation. 'Ask them wha did it?'

Lorna gave a diffident smile which immediately rankled

Annie. 'First thing tomorrow, I'll raise it with them. But I don't hold out much hope for any admission of guilt.'

They faced up to one another. Annie was perturbed. Everything the schoolteacher had said seemed reasonable. She sounded concerned.

And yet.

Annie had previously thought the woman willowy and elegant. She hadn't noticed how hard-featured and severe she looked, stern even. Cold. There was a disconnect between her words and the way she delivered them, a lack of emotion, empathy. Annie would have hated having her for a teacher.

'Miss Carrington.' Annie's heart was hammering in her chest. 'It's your job to mak sure my lassie is managin at the school.'

'*Your* lassie?'

'Aye. As long as she's bidin wi me, she's my lassie. And naebody's goin to touch her. I'll come and sort it oot mysel if I need to.'

The slight smile re-emerged. 'Ellen is extremely fortunate to have you, Mrs Kelty. If anyone can help her recover from this dreadful experience, I'm sure it's you.'

Lorna exhaled slowly. *Such melodrama*, she thought. *Such little people.*

*

'You don't know me. I'd like to speak to the minister.'

Mr Henderson had had to wait three days for Barvick Falls to be unoccupied to allow him to conduct a telephone conversation in confidence. Even though he was sure the house was empty but for the maids, he spoke quietly.

'Speaking. Reverend Duncan.'

'My name is Harold Henderson. My nurse, Miss Salter, used to be a parishioner in the Free Church in St Andrews. Reverend Carrington.'

'I have heard of Reverend Carrington. A good man.'

'Indeed. And an inspiring preacher. It was related to Reverend Carrington that I wished to speak to you. Or rather his daughter. Lorna Carrington.'

The ensuing pause was long enough to confirm to Mr Henderson that he had found the right place. 'I understand she relocated to Mintlaw some time ago. Naturally, I felt sure she'd be in contact with the church so I thought I would contact you.'

'And why is that?'

'I'm trying to understand something of Lorna's background. And I know that she previously lived in Mintlaw.'

'Lorna did move here about three years ago. She stayed about a year.'

Reverend Duncan's tone was clipped and precise, the voice of somebody taking care to say only what was necessary. Mr Henderson recognised it from the tribunals he had conducted during the Great War, soldiers too frightened to think clearly, saying nothing for fear of uttering a single, incriminating remark. If only those young men had known that their interrogator was as frightened as them, and equally fervent that they should not implicate themselves. Lieutenant-Colonel Harold Henderson prided himself on having never passed a death sentence as convenor of a courts martial.

'I understand,' he continued, 'that when Lorna left St Andrews this was under something of a cloud.'

'I wouldn't know.'

'I'd have thought, when they arranged new accommodation for her in Mintlaw, as a courtesy they would give some detail of what had occurred to necessitate the arrangement.'

'Or perhaps, as a courtesy to Miss Carrington, they decided she could leave whatever emotional baggage she had behind. Start afresh.'

'Well, I'm not sure that is entirely in line with Free Church doctrine, but I can see that might be thought a charitable approach.'

'Mr Henderson, what is it you want?'

'I am concerned about the health of Lorna Carrington. There is something afflicting her today which I think may have roots in her past. I'm seeking to discover what that might be, in order to perhaps offer assistance to her now.'

'And what is this affliction she is suffering?'

'It may be something and nothing.'

'You have just – very politely – chided me for being unforthcoming. And in the next breath you do the same thing.'

'Miss Carrington seems peculiarly determined to remove any connection between herself and her past. To the extent of denying she is Reverend Carrington's daughter or that she once lived in St Andrews.'

'You're sure you have the right person?'

'Quite sure.'

There was a long pause once more and Mr Henderson could picture Reverend Duncan, standing in his hallway, wrestling with his conscience.

'Miss Carrington left Mintlaw of her own volition. But let us say that many locals weren't unhappy about her decision. There was an occurrence in the lodgings where she resided.'

'What happened?'

'I do not feel at liberty to say. The authorities concluded it was a complete accident. . .But there were some who sought to cast doubt on Miss Carrington's version of events.'

'In what way?'

'She denied being in the house at the time of the incident. . .'

'And what was this incident?'

A longer pause ensued. 'There was a tragic occurrence. A young woman died.'

'How?'

'A house fire. As I say, the official view was that it was an accident. . .'

'But?'

'Although Miss Carrington said she wasn't present at the

time of the accident, two people, separately, suggested she was.'

'And did the police investigate?'

'The two people were maids. Known to be hostile to Miss Carrington. Their testimony wasn't considered credible.'

'And what do you think?'

The longest pause of all was broken by Reverend Duncan's soft tones. 'I think that charity dictates I believe Miss Carrington's statement.' There was a heavy sigh. 'All the same, take care Mr Henderson.'

*

After tea, when he relayed the details of his conversation to Miss Salter, she could not contain her concern.

'Surely she's dangerous?'

'Who can say? We don't know what actually happened in Mintlaw. . .'

'Or St Andrews.'

'Indeed.'

'But something did. In both places. That can't be coincidence.'

'No.'

'Should we go to the police?'

'And say what? All we know for certain is that she is lying about who she is. I dare say that's a lot more common than we realise. Plenty of people have skeletons in their closets.'

'She's a cold fish.'

'Indeed she is. But, again, that isn't a crime. Nonetheless, we must keep an eye on her.'

*

In the moments after dusk, leaning against the wooden slats of the shelter shed, Lorna slid her knickers back on. She was breathing heavily.

'Hurry,' she said.

These outdoor trysts were intensely charged for Lorna. The potential jeopardy of being caught *in flagrante* in MacRosty Park was as exciting as anything she had ever known. Twice in recent weeks, dog walkers had passed while she and PC McAnuff pressed themselves against the back wall, not breathing. Once, a labrador had sniffed in the shed and detected them but was pulled away by its owner before it could expose them. She liked that PC McAnuff, twenty and gauche, was terrible at sex but tried so hard, puppyishly doing everything she instructed. Their encounters created an erotic charge she knew could never be recaptured in the bourgeois safety of a bed.

'Tie my shoelaces,' she said, planting her left foot in front of her to allow him to kneel and re-tie the laces of her work brogues. 'Here,' she said, handing him a letter. 'Post this for me.'

He took it and studied the address. 'Dallerie Laundry? What are you sending a letter to them for?'

'It's for the school.'

'Don't they use the Strathearn Laundry?'

'Just checking whether they might do it more cheaply. Saving tax payers' money.' She patted his cheek. 'Off you trot. We'll try again next week, lover boy. You'll get the hang of it one of these days.'

Wednesday, 20 September

A Day of the Harvest Moon

Ellen and Marnie had maintained a frosty silence since Monday. Ellen felt herself tense the moment she entered the classroom and saw Marnie seated at her desk. She assumed the sternest expression she could muster and slid into the adjoining seat, pulling open the lid of her desk and stowing her gas mask inside. She took her fountain pen from her pencil case and rested it on the groove at the top of her desk next to the inkwell.

'Please, I need to talk to you,' said Marnie. Ellen looked away. 'It's no what you think.'

'Alright Scabby Back?' said Eddie Soutar as he pushed past Marnie and Ellen's desks. Without thinking, Ellen jumped up and punched him and Eddie staggered back, caught unawares. He rubbed his jaw and stared at Ellen in amazement.

'Juist as well you're only a lassie or I'd thump you,' he said.

'She's no a lassie,' said Georgie Murray. 'She's a Glesga mink. Lice in her hair, scabs on her back. Scabby Ellen, Scabby Ellen, Scabby Ellen.'

The room fell silent as Ellen strode towards Georgie's desk, clenching and unclenching her fists. She had no idea what she was going to do. At times like this, she felt as though she were outside her own body, not in control of her actions. This was no ordinary anger she felt but outrage at being made the centre of attention.

'Black Alice, sit down.' Lorna marched into the room and made her usual show of dropping her satchel and tawse on the desk. 'Whatever shenanigans you have in mind, save them for the playground. It may be the start of the school day for you, but I've had a full and active morning and I've given the strap three times already. I am not prepared to tolerate any misbehaviour this afternoon.'

Ellen returned to her seat and glowered at Marnie, more annoyed with her now than ever. Marnie rested her head on her crossed arms on the desk, facing away from Ellen.

Lorna opened her satchel and pulled out the class's homework jotters. 'With all this talk of war, children, you must never lose sight of the fact that war is something man declares against himself. It is a noble undertaking to kill a man for moral reasons. *Be not afraid. Let not your hearts faint, fear not and do not tremble.*'

She started to hand out the homework, providing succinct summaries of each as she progressed down the lines. 'Edward Soutar, see me afterwards. I gave you fair warning last week. This time it's the strap.' As before, Ellen's homework was the last to be returned and Ellen waited nervously.

Lorna threw the jotter on her desk. 'Disgraceful. Not an appropriate subject. I have just talked about killing. Killing people in war is justifiable. Honourable, even. Killing animals is not. Killing animals is criminal. Plain and simple. I was going to give you one out of ten for spelling and handwriting, but I took that into account for your last dismal effort, so even that isn't warranted.'

Ellen opened her jotter. Nothing out of ten. She flushed with embarrassment and shut the jotter and stared at her desk, at the carving of "AJ" near the inkwell, decades old, probably cut out by someone who was a pensioner now, dead even. She willed herself into a different space.

'You will do this again,' said Lorna. 'And this time it had better be flawless.'

'Miss,' said Georgie Murray, his hand raised. 'Alison McGillivray's got lice again.'

Ellen screamed. She jumped to her feet and Lorna grabbed for her shoulder but she ducked and pushed past her and fled for the door.

'Come back this instant!'

But Ellen had already made her escape. She ran down the stairs and through the front door into the girls' playground.

*

Eric Haig, from Halley's Taxis, deposited Mr Henderson's wireless on the desk at the rear of Salmond's Emporium. 'I'll wait for you in the taxi,' he said to Mr Henderson.

Mr Henderson thanked him and greeted Mr Salmond. 'Bally wireless,' he said, 'stopped working.'

Mr Salmond turned it around and inspected it. He unscrewed the back and peered inside. 'Straightforward two-valve,' he said.

Mr Henderson, to whom this meant nothing, nodded. 'Can you repair it?'

'Saturday. You're at Barvick Falls, aren't you? I'll have the lad bring it round, save you comin back.'

'That would be most kind.'

'You must know Miss Carrington? She lives in Barvick Falls, too.'

'A schoolteacher, yes.' *And deuced odd, too.*

'Aye, that's the surpsising thing. Owes me three months' HP on her gramophone player. You wouldnae expect that fae a schoolteacher.'

Mr Henderson reckoned that was the least of Miss Carrington's peculiarities. 'I'm sure there's an explanation,' he said.

'She promised me she'd be in yesterday. To my face. And

then didnae turn up. I dinnae want to, but if she doesnae pey somethin soon I'll hae to repossess it.'

Mr Henderson fancied Miss Carrington wouldn't give up her possessions without a struggle. *Bring help when you try.*

*

Ellen could hear Mr Smith's tuneless whistle up in the infants' playground. Cautiously, she swung open the door of his hut at the back of the playground and confirmed it was empty. The hut smelled of oil and rust, and a wooden workbench was cluttered with metal implements Ellen could not identify. She hunted among this chaos until she found a pair of scissors. They were huge, like they were made for a giant, and she tried to grip them with her right hand. They were so big she had to use both hands to open and close them. An empty bucket sat in the far corner and she set it in the middle of the floor and bent over it. She started to hack at her hair with the scissors, half cutting, half chopping, until enormous tufts gave way and fell into the bucket. She worked for ten minutes, her fingers aching and a blister forming on the inside of her thumb. When she was done, her long hair had been reduced to a ragged short back and sides.

'Try washin ma hair in paraffin now, ye bitch.'

*

Although the new Cooperative store on the top of King Street was only about thirty yards from Cloudland, Bob had yet to visit. Cloudland was quiet mid-afternoon and he left Leslie in charge and sauntered round the corner. The advert in *The Strathearn Herald* promised a "special show of autumn goods" and Bob was in need of a new pair of boots so he thought he'd give them a try before going to Bryce's as usual. The doorbell jangled as he entered and the people inside, three assistants and three shoppers, turned to appraise the new arrival.

Among them was Thingwie Johnstone. Bob didn't have time to make a diplomatic exist before Thingwie spotted him, and he gave him a weak smile.

'You're oot, then.'

'Served my time.'

'I'm sorry. I didnae mean that to happen.'

'Water under the bridge.'

'You mean that?'

'If you were on fire I wouldnae waste my piss on you, but I'm no one to bear a grudge.'

'Well, that's big of you.'

'"Big of me" is it, aye? Is that you makin fun of me acos of my size?'

'No. Honestly. No.'

'Baldy fuckin nyaff.'

'Excuse me, sir,' said Mr Denham, the shop manager, buttoned into an over-tight brown overall. 'We'll have none of that sort of language. There are ladies present.'

Thingwie looked around and snorted. 'The only wumman I see in here is Mavis Muirhead.' He pointed to a middle-aged woman in a black coat and blue hat. 'And she's no lady, I'll tell you that for nothin. I mind when she was Mavis Willis, or Mavis Willing as we called her, acos she ay was.'

There was a collective intake of breath in the shop. Mavis Muirhead stepped forward and slapped Thingwie on the cheek, the retort echoing around the shop. 'You always were a little maggot, William Johnstone.'

'Best handjob in toon. Weel kent for it.'

'Willie,' said Bob, resting his hand lightly on the man's shoulder. Thingwie turned, enraged, and with a haymaker the equal of the one a fortnight before, sent Bob sprawling the length of the Cooperative floor.

*

The door standing ajar alerted Mr Smith that someone had been in his shed. He peered inside to check if anyone was still there. His bucket was not in its proper position and he bent over to inspect it. Long clumps of black hair lay in the bottom. His secateurs lay on the workbench. He reached into the bucket. Human hair, no question, and very black. The little Glasgow girl had the blackest hair Mr Smith had ever seen. And she'd had it washed in paraffin by Miss Carrington, a fact confirmed by three of her classmates. Now black hair had been hacked off and dumped in his bucket. Mr Smith lit a Kensitas Club and sat on his stool.

*

Lorna stood before DO MacLean's desk. 'Ellen Laing, headmaster,' she said. 'One of the Glasgow children. A bit of a trial, to be honest. Intelligent, but highly strung.'

'And she just made off?' said Mr MacLean.

'She did.'

'What provoked this?'

'One of the pupils informed me that one of the Glasgow girls had lice in her hair. . .'

'But not Ellen Laing?'

'No.'

'So why did Ellen run away?'

'I really couldn't say.'

Miss Carrington was in her second year at Crieff Public School and Mr MacLean was still not sure what to make of her. Her classes performed well in tests and took a full part in sporting and music activities, something he believed should play a pivotal role in the school curriculum, but there seemed to be little affection for her among her pupils and, as a cohort, they were withdrawn and distant. He had observed her classes on a number of occasions and couldn't fault her teaching, but there was a wintriness to her demeanour. He looked at his pocket watch.

'I will speak with her tomorrow,' he said.

'Very good, headmaster.'

Lorna excused herself and walked into the playground. It was empty, nine or ten poachie beds chalked onto the ground, stones waiting to be used again next morning. She stared at the sky, a solid grey, low and dismal. The headmaster would speak to Black Alice tomorrow. She would tell him about the paraffin. Mr MacLean would support Lorna, obviously, but there would be damage done. Lorna had said she didn't know why Ellen ran away. The headmaster would uncover this lie.

She felt a tightness in her chest that was too, too familiar, drawing her back to her childhood, to St Andrews, the crises, her father, the uncaring beast of a man, a man who never recovered from his disappointment that the Great War was not the War of Armageddon he had prophesied and who took out his frustrations on his family. Life, he said, was nothing but eschatology, waiting for the end times. *Daily living? What of it? Make mistakes? Suffer the consequences. Presume to ask for help? The Lord is all the help you need. Start again? Do you imagine God does not see all? You're suffering? Be afflicted that you might learn His Statutes. Glory in tribulations. Believe with all thine heart.*

Lorna believed and she didn't believe. Her rational mind told her one thing, her inherited Calvinism foretold another.

It is done.

*

By four o'clock, Bob's right eye had almost closed up. The bruise on his left eye from Thingwie's previous assault had only just healed and here he was with a new keeker forming. He looked up as the door of Cloudland opened and Ellen slunk in.

'What happened to you?' they said in unison.

Bob rushed and grabbed her and sat her down at a table

by the window. 'Wha did that to you?' he said, running his fingers through her shorn hair.

'I did it mysel.'

'How?'

'The lassies in my class were gonnae wash my hair in paraffin again.'

'So you cut it aff?'

'In the janny's hut.'

'You dinnae do things by half, do you?'

'Huv ye ever hud yer heid washed in paraffin?'

'No.'

'There ye go, then. Ye're talkin oot yer arse.'

Bob thought it best to ignore the swearing on this occasion. 'What did your teacher say?'

'She didnae see it. I bunked aff.'

'Aa efternoon?'

'Aye.'

'Whaur did you go?'

'That park up the top of toon.'

'Lauder Park? The Taylor Institution folk will hae seen you. Lucky they didnae set the polis on you.'

'They did.'

'Eh?'

'I ran away.'

'You ran awa fae the polis?'

'I wasnae goin back to school to get my heid washed in paraffin, was I?'

Bob sat down heavily, wondering what new revelation might next unfold. 'Well, we'll wait to see wha comes for you first, the heidie or the polis.'

'I'm no carin.' The shortness of her hair made her customary angry expression seem even angrier. She looked ready to erupt. Bob had learned that in such moments Ellen was best left alone. He picked up his pipe and lit it.

'Whit happened to you, then?' Ellen asked.

'Thingwie Johnstone.'

'Again?'

'Aye.'

'Ye need to stick up fur yersel.'

'I ken.'

'At least it wasnae ma fault this time.'

'It wasnae your fault last time.'

Ellen fell quiet. She looked out at James Square, sandbagged and quiet in late afternoon sunshine. She liked to put on a tough façade but Bob could tell she was upset.

'I'll write you a note to tak to your teacher the morn.'

'Sayin whit?'

'Sayin she has to mak sure your pals dinnae pick on you.'

'Or whit, you'll come and sort them oot?'

'Well.' He gestured at his swollen eye. 'I do look like a fechter at the moment.'

'Aye. A shite one.' She turned and faced him. 'Ye think I'll be in trouble?'

'Trouble? You dinnae ken the meanin of the word. Wait till Annie sees what you've done to your hair.'

*

Sandy Disdain sat in splendid isolation on the top of the Knock as evening fell. In fields all around he could see or hear activity, farmers taking advantage of the harvest moon which, for several days in a row, had risen just as the sun was setting, affording continuous light to allow them to maintain their operations. Old Sol began to sink beneath the western horizon, the sky orange and burning, with Ben Vorlich, Ben More and Ben Ledi standing in bold relief, the shape of the world revealed in the day's passing. Sandy, an autodidact who would never reveal to anyone the extent of his self-taught learning, stared into this proud prospect and quoted Sir Walter Scott:

> The western waves of ebbing day
> Rolled o'er the glen, their levelled way;
> Each purple peak, each flinty spire,
> Was bathed in floods of living fire.

Gradually, the sounds of the farmers began to diminish and finally dissolve into the darkness that fell on Strathearn and Sandy Disdain was left alone with his thoughts, his hopes. He had no dreams – the life of such a concrete man could not be measured by abstractions – but he held to the hope that such nights, such moments, such tranquility and peace, might never recede.

*

Once Annie had got over the initial shock and tidied up Ellen's hair with scissors she had to acknowledge it looked quite fetching, in a boyish kind of way. All the same, she had no intention of telling Ellen this, or of letting her off with her actions.

'No allowed oot efter school for a fortnicht,' she said, 'And you'll be up at six every morn to help Leslie mak the scones.'

'I dunno how to make scones.'

'You'll learn soon enough.'

They were seated by the window in Cloudland, finishing off the remains of the rabbit casserole Bob had made that morning. His stews usually sold out, but not the rabbit. Folks were choosy about their meat these days, but give it a few months, Bob reckoned, and they'd be grateful for meat of any sort. Whatever the government said about there being no imminent food rationing, the news of blockades on the Atlantic merchant shipping suggested otherwise. There was a knock on the door and Annie answered it while Bob shovelled the last of the rabbit into his mouth. PC McAnuff stood stiffly at the entrance, as unsure of himself as ever.

'Which of my twa reprobates is it you're efter?' Annie said.

'Mr Kelty.'

'What can I do for you, Willy?' Bob said when it was obvious PC McAnuff wasn't going to divulge his reasons for joining them without being granted permission.

'You had another to-do wi Thingwie?'

'His fist seems awfae partial to my face.'

'He's up in court the morn.'

'Ach no, it was juist a wee bit bother.'

'You'll hae to come. The Justice of the Peace wants to speak to you.'

'How?'

'He wants to ken if you provoked him.'

'Mr Denham can tell him that.'

'Nae doot, but the JP's asked for you personally.'

'Will ye go to jail?' asked Ellen.

'What, for somebody punchin me?'

'Nothin would surprise me aboot this toon.'

'D'you want a bite to eat, Willy?' Annie said. She gestured to the kitchen. 'We've plenty. It'll only go to waste.'

PC McAnuff shook his head but looked at the plates in front of Bob, Annie and Ellen. 'Actually, if it's nae bother? It's been a lang day.'

'Sit yoursel doon.'

'Have you made any progress wi Fairmer Bennett's arsonist?' Bob asked while Annie spooned the rabbit casserole onto a plate.

PC McAnuff sat back and shook his head. 'It's no an arsonist. It's juist thae bloody Glesga bairns.' He remembered Ellen's presence and blushed. 'Nae offence. But ever since they came here there's been trouble galore. Fires. Lochearnhead Hotel. Malky's ricks. Dallerie Laundry. . .'

'Dallerie Laundry?' said Bob. 'What happened at the laundry?'

'Sunday nicht. Glesga bairns set fire to it. Caused a fair bit of damage afore the fire brigade got it under control. Gibby

Owen almost caught ane of them in the act, pouring paraffin through the windae and settin fire to it. He managed to skelp him across the cheek. "A young laddie's face", he telt me. Nae roughness to it.'

Ellen played with her fork as PC McAnuff shovelled the casserole into his mouth as though he hadn't eaten in days. 'Sunday?' she asked nonchalantly. 'Did he actually see it was a laddie?'

'No as such, no. It was dark.'

'And if he caught the laddie in the face, wid he huv left a mark? A scratch or summhin?'

'I couldnae say. Gibby couldnae see. Man, this stew's braw.'

'Rabbit,' said Bob.

PC McAnuff put down his fork. 'Rabbit?' he repeated.

'Freshly snared by Sandy Disdain.'

'I dinnae like rabbit.'

'I dinnae suppose the rabbit's that keen on you.'

Annie watched Ellen, the way she was staring at Willy McAnuff, the sly smile that had started playing around her mouth. *What's she up to*, she thought. Ellen saw her looking and scowled.

Thursday, 21 September

A Day of Letters

There were two letters on the sideboard in the hall when Lorna came down for breakfast. One was local but the other was postmarked Mintlaw. A shudder of apprehension ripped through her. She took them upstairs and sat at her table overlooking the window and braced herself. The local mail was another demand from Salmond's for payment of the hire purchase on her gramophone player. She tore up the letter and threw it in the bin, then opened the second letter. It was from Reverend Duncan of Mintlaw. 'Dear Miss Carrington,' he wrote, 'I received this communication addressed to you today and, because I believe this to be your new address, I am forwarding it to you. I hope you are well.'

Anger rose within her. *How could he possibly know my address?* She recognised the handwriting on the envelope of the enclosed letter immediately and let out a low, measured sigh. She put Tommy Dorsey's *East of the Sun* on the gramophone player, filling the room with a lightness she knew she would need before opening the letter. Her mother's crabbed handwriting filled a single sheet of paper, the lines on an increasingly extravagant slant.

Dear Lorna

I thought you ought to know that your father is extremely unwell. His cancer is advancing and he is in a great deal of pain. I fear the situation may be grave.

I know you have your difficulties with Daddy, but he is your father. I would so like you to come home and see him. I know he would like that too, even if he finds it hard to say so. We all know he can be difficult, but he does love you in his way.

I hope your keeping well, my darling, and I hope to hear from (see) you soon.

With much love

Mummy

Lorna stared at the letter for some moments, letting her eyes fall out of focus until the words became a black spider-scrawl, meaningless, unimportant. 'I know you have your difficulties with Daddy.' *Really Mother? Did you know back then, too, when he. . .When he. . .When you didn't. . .You didn't. . .You never opened your mouth, Mother, neither with wisdom nor with anything else. There were no teachings of kindness on your tongue.*

The stupid bitch couldn't even spell 'you're' properly.

She screwed up the letter and threw that, too, in the bin.

*

Miss Cranston, secretary to Eddie McMurray at the Dallerie Laundry, opened the letter, admiring the florid handwriting. Good quality paper, too. She unfolded the paper and read it, then placed it on her desk and sat back, distancing herself as though it were poisonous.

'Mr McMurray,' she called through the partition into her boss's office. 'You need to see this.'

Eddie McMurray waddled from his office to Miss Cranston's desk and took the letter.

You came face-to-face with me. Rest assured, when I return to complete my mission you will not be so lucky again. Your laundry will be destroyed. I will raze it, raze it, even to the foundations.

'Do you think it's genuine?' Miss Cranston asked.

'Who knows?'

'What should we do? Call the police?'

'I suppose so. Get Danny Rudd involved. That'll make me us all feel safe. . .'

*

'And you did nothing to provoke Mr Johnstone?'

'No, your honour. . .'

'You don't need to call me your honour. I'm not a judge.'

'Sorry. He misinterpreted a comment I made and overreacted.'

'Just as Mr Denham described it?'

'Exactly.'

Justice of the Peace Kenton studied Thingwie, weighing up this latest assault. 'Last time, you tried to speak on Mr Johnstone's behalf. Is there anything you wish to say this time?'

There was indeed a matter preying on Bob's mind. Thingwie's explosive and unprovoked bursts of temper, his overreactions, were highly reminiscent of Bob's grandmother when she started succumbing to dementia. She would lash out and Bob knew it was frustration rather than any genuine anger. Thingwie was famous for being absent-minded, but that seemed to be changing. Before, it was names he couldn't remember but his forgetfulness now was of a different ilk. He was forgetting how to be human.

Bu how could Bob say that? How could he stand up in court and say that Thingwie was going daft?

'No,' he said. 'Nothing.'

'Very well,' said JP Kenton. 'Mr Johnstone, I sentence you to four weeks' imprisonment.'

*

As he exited the Masonic Hall after the hearing, Bob bumped into Sandy, on his way to John Low's with a gamebag full of rabbits.

'Been up in court?' Sandy asked.

'No me. Thingwie. Got twenty-eight days for assaultin me.'

A look of confusion overtook Sandy's face. 'He's already done time for that?'

'That was the first time.'

'He did it again?'

'Yesterday. In the Coop.'

'He ay was a persistent wee bugger.'

'Once he gets a notion.' They crossed the road at Scrimgeour's corner and walked up the High Street. 'I was meanin to ask,' Bob said, 'can you eat squirrel?'

'Aye. Tastes like a chicken that's eaten ower mony nuts. Why, you want ane?'

'I wouldnae say no. Gettin ready for rationin. We'll be eatin all sorts afore long. Have you filled oot your registration form yet?'

'No.'

'I kent you wouldnae. It has to be done by Friday, mind, or you'll end up in a cell wi Thingwie. And I wouldnae wish that on onyone.' To enforce the National Registration Act, enumerators had visited every house in town, collecting forms which listed adults' names, addresses and current and previous employment. For Sandy, this was an intrusion into his private affairs he couldn't thole and he had made sure not to answer the door.

'My business is nothin to do wi them,' he said.

'You'll no be sayin that in six months when you've nae ration card.'

Sandy raised his gamebag. 'I'll no starve, will I?'

'It's no just food. Coal's been rationed. . .'

'I've never bocht a sack of coal in my life. I live on the edge of the Laggan Wood.'

'And petrol next week.'

'Shanks's pony.'

'You ken this, you micht be the only person in the hale country that winnae be affected by this war.'

'That's the plan.'

*

Lorna intercepted Ellen before she was called into the headmaster's office. 'Think very carefully what you say, Black Alice,' she said.

'Whit does that mean?'

'What I say. Choose your answers with care. Mr MacLean may be the headmaster, but I'm your teacher. I do whatsoever I please.'

Ellen was still pondering Lorna's warning when she stood in front of the headmaster. She should have felt frightened but she wasn't. The man seated before her looked frightening enough, and there was a cane on the bookcase behind him, but she got the sense that, despite skiving the day before, she wasn't in trouble.

'Did you enjoy your afternoon off?'

'No really.'

'What did you do?'

'Went up the park and watched the traffic. Loads of army vans.'

'Yes, they're requisitioning some of the local hotels and billeting the men there. Lap of luxury, lucky chaps. What made you run off?'

This was the moment she had to decide. What would she say? 'It was arithmetic. I dinnae like sums.'

Mr MacLean's expression told Ellen he didn't believe her.

He fixed her with a penetrating stare. 'You had long hair,' he said, gesturing to her short bob.

'I cut it aff.'

'Off. Why?'

'It reminded me of hame.'

'And what does that mean?'

Ellen had no idea. The words were out of her mouth before she'd considered them. 'I want. . .' she said. 'Here. . . I want to make a fresh start. It's different here. I'm learnin stuff. . .'

'What are you learning?'

'About nature and that. Wildlife. The country.'

'You are interested in the natural world?'

'Aye, am are.'

'Yes, I am.'

'Me an aa. I'd never seen the country before. It's. . . it's so big.'

'It is, indeed. How do you get on with Miss Carrington?'

Choose your answers with care. . .I do whatsoever I pleas. . .

'Fine, sir.'

'Yesterday had nothing to do with her?'

'No, sir.'

Mr MacLean studied the child. Nothing she had said was credible, except for the interest in nature. That felt genuine. She was a child worth watching.

But what for? That was the question.

'Well, Ellen Laing, I urge you to behave yourself in future or you'll find yourself grounded and you won't be able to indulge your pleasures in the countryside.'

'Aye, sir.'

'Yes, sir.' He smiled at her.

She smiled back. 'Yes, sir.'

*

'Now then, Mr McMurray.' PC McAnuff, red-faced after a hike through town to the Dallerie Laundry, stood at the entrance to Eddie McMurray's first-floor office overlooking the main laundry operations. 'You've had a missive, I hear.'

'Aye.' He proffered the letter and when PC McAnuff saw it he recognised the handwriting immediately and let out an involuntary yelp. Watched by a confused Eddie McMurray, he took it with a trembling hand and pulled out the page and read it slowly, before carefully replacing it in the envelope.

'Doesnae read like Glesga bairns,' Eddie said. 'Nane of them can write, so I hear.'

'No,' said Willy. 'Looks like a crank,' he said. 'Playin aboot. Causin mischief.'

'You're probably right, son.'

Willy put the letter in his jacket pocket. 'Leave it wi me.'

'You'll investigate?'

'Oh aye. I will indeed.'

'You're a credit to your sergeant.'

*

'Everybody stand.' Lorna hated doing physical activity but the headmaster insisted on exercises twice per week. It was a waste of time, in her view: boys, who needed exercise, would surely provide it themselves afterwards. Any girls who wanted exercise were well able to do so in the playground with their poachie and their skipping ropes. Making everybody stand and stretch in the classroom merely took up time which could be better spent teaching them about the war and the need to defend their country.

'Should the Nazis ever invade,' she said, 'you will all have to be able to defend yourselves. This is why we do these exercises, to keep you fit and healthy, ready to fight at a moment's notice.'

And heaven help us, she reflected, looking at the dumb faces arrayed before her, if things ever reached such a pass.

The bell rang for the end of the day. 'Form up,' Lorna said. The class stood to attention and sang their prayer at the end of the day. Ellen and Marnie were supposed to be holding hands but a gulf remained between them.

'Black Alice, wait behind.'

Marnie saw the apprehension in Ellen's face and reached over and squeezed her hand. The class trooped out while Ellen waited, clutching her gas mask.

'How was the headmaster?'

'I didnae tell him anythin.'

Lorna scrutinised her expression. Beneath the anger she saw nothing to concern her. 'Good girl. We'll make something of you yet.'

'Your scratch is gettin better, miss.' Ellen pointed to her cheek. Lorna felt it.

'A reminder to take care at all times,' she said.

'Aye,' said Ellen.

*

Lorna was still considering Ellen and the headmaster as she walked along Commissioner Street at four-thirty. Today had gone too easily. It wouldn't do to underestimate DO MacLean. He was on the town council. He'd been big in the last war. He was an intelligent man, for all he was the headmaster of a small public school in the middle of nowhere. *Be sober. Be vigilant.*

'Miss Carrington.'

She expelled a sigh of irritation as she turned towards Mr Salmond, marching towards here once more with that sour expression. 'Did you get my letter?' he said.

'I did, Mr Salmond. And once more I must apologise. . .'

'I've heard that before, Miss Carrington. . .'

'And I meant it, most assuredly. It grieves me to think. . .'

'The next step will be repossession. . .'

Later, Mr Salmond would talk about this moment, 'the way her face switched from smilin to snarlin, juist like that. Like twa different people.'

Lorna rounded on him. 'Nobody will take that gramophone player from me, Mr Salmond. You have my word on that. If I can't have it, nobody will.'

She pushed past him and marched away, giving her best impersonation of someone who did not care. That was not how she felt. Her breathing was tight again. The walls were closing in. First Henderson and the witch-nurse. Now somebody had had the temerity to write to her, to forward a letter from her mother. To bring up. . .*All that*.

Remember not my sins.

She felt the strongest desire to scream. She wanted something to burn but it was too soon after the last debacle.

She needed a different release, and she knew just the thing.

Strange flesh.

*

'I do believe that was your best yet,' Lorna said an hour later as she fixed her suspenders and smoothed her frock. 'I almost felt something.'

Willy McAnuff, buttoning his trousers, said nothing. He was accustomed to Lorna's insults. Every time, he thought he should walk away, assert himself, end this nonsense, but the sight of Lorna, the sound of her voice, the touch of her hand, they held him in thrall. He came running whenever she called. Now, though, there was something else. There was the letter.

'Did you hear anythin from Dallerie Laundry?' he said.

Lorna carried on as though she hadn't heard, combing her fingers through her hair, fastening her coat.

'Aboot your letter? Maybe they've been too busy. You ken they got attacked? Set on fire?'

'I've decided,' Lorna said, 'not to bother with them. They were of interest at one time but no longer.'

Willy tried to determine what subtext, if any, there was to Lorna's words. 'Stick to Strathearn Laundry then, aye?'

'I won't be doing further business with Dallerie Laundry.

Now, go home through the bottom park. I don't want anyone seeing us together.'

'But I only live up there,' he said, gesturing towards the high road.

'And you can still get there through the bottom park. It'll just take longer.' She kissed her fingertips and pressed them to his cheek. 'Good boy.'

She turned and walked uphill without looking back. Outside Barvick Falls she looked up. Mr Henderson and his nurse were in the day room. She turned and walked out the Comrie road. She spent an hour walking the Horseshoe Drive and up through the parks and, with dusk approaching, she sat outside the small cafeteria built into the hillside three-quarters of the way up MacRosty Park. The cafeteria was closed and a group of children were playing, climbing the retaining wall that circled the rear of the building, running from one side to the other and back again. They seemed to be parentless and Lorna didn't recognise them. She closed her eyes.

The crackle. The smell. The heat. The sounds, whoosh and whump, sizzle, hiss, pop. Fire was liberation, deliverance. *Who among us shall dwell with the devouring fire? Who among us shall dwell with everlasting burnings?* Fire eased her troubles, freed her mind. Fire tempered the pain, assuaged her misery. Fire was life. Since she was six and first tormented by those night visitations, Lorna had used fire to heal the sores of daily living. All that agitation, the tumult, the disruption of the physical realm, it allowed her to purge agonies from her mind. Become unfettered. Serene. *And the God that answereth by fire, let him be God.*

She opened her eyes. Fatigue left her enervated, vulnerable. She hated this feeling. The cafeteria loomed before her, a challenge, a provocation, an opportunity. She imagined it wreathed in flames, the light of destruction surging into a black night sky. How beautiful that would be. How peaceful.

'No.' She spoke aloud and the playing children stopped

and turned towards her, recognising her as a teacher and fearing a rebuke. She ignored them and looked at the cafeteria, scene of this fantasy, and knew she had, somehow, to exercise moderation. The scratch on her cheek still throbbed. She had come close to failure twice now. Too close to exposure, capture. The police would be suspicious. They would investigate. She had left Glasgow newspapers at the scenes but even the local police were too stupid, surely, to believe Glaswegian children were capable of these crimes? No one had identified her, of that she was certain but, while she had no faith in the ability of the local constabulary, she had to exercise caution. Save the release of arson for another day. Another day when, perhaps, the vexation might be even greater than it was today. She had, after all, spent years trying to escape that vexation and still it came, insinuating, extirpating.

'No more fires,' she said. 'For now.'

She had no idea how long 'now' might last but feared it may be not be as long as it ought.

Saturday, 23 September

A Day of Detection

On their way to the Knock, Bob honoured his promise to Mrs McLaren and brought Annie and Ellen to try the dairy's new ice creams. They walked through the terraces, lapping enthusiastically, and all three ices had vanished by the time they reached the bowling club.

'Best ice cream I've ever tasted,' said Annie.

'Braw,' said Ellen, a moustache of ice cream caking her upper lip. They carried on uphill out of town and into countryside, passing dozens of people on their way to the summit of the Knock, families picking blaeberries, children shouting and running, mothers calling them to attention. The way grew steadily steeper.

'This better be worth it,' said Ellen, puffing hard.

'Juist you wait,' said Bob, puffing even harder.

Eventually, the steep slope levelled off and they emerged from trees onto the summit of the Knock, a wide expanse of heather and blaeberry bushes. In the middle, on the highest point, was an octagonal granite pillar, about four feet high, known to locals as the Indicator. Inscribed on it was the shape of the world around them, the world that is, the world that was, the world yet to be, palimpsest of eternity. Ellen detached herself from Bob and Annie and stared in silence at the mountains surrounding them, the Ochils and the Grampians, stretching from Dunsinane and Kinnoull Hill in the east to Ben More and Beinn Each in the west. She circled the Indicator three times, trying to understand the magnitude and the majesty of this towering landscape. It wasn't just the distance, or the height of the hills that was impressive. It was the depth, miles and miles of existence compressed into the frame of her vision. Like nothing she had ever seen.

She looked at Bob and Annie and made to speak but no words emerged. She turned another circle. Mountain ranges stretched in every direction. Shades of green and brown merged into one another beneath a pale blue sky, the lower reaches occupied by fields, bounded by hedges and dykes. Patchwork of activity. Horses pulling reapers, stookers following, collecting the last of the harvest. Above them, in high ground, heather and woods, rising, rising. Snow already on the upper reaches of Ben A'an. For Ellen, who had never been outside Finnieston, had never seen anything but tenements and cobbled streets, had never breathed anything but coal smoke and petrol fumes, the width and wonder of the world was glorious. As she had the other day, on Lady Mary's Walk, she felt something stir inside her, a connection with an environment which only five minutes before she had scarcely known existed.

'It's like a dream,' she said. 'It's everywhere.' She started running around the flat peak of the Knock, stopping and staring, as though paying homage to each mountain and hill in turn. Bob laid out their tartan blanket and he and Annie sat and watched her.

'I dinnae think I've ever seen onyone that excited,' Bob said, picking at a piece of heather.

'Aye,' said Annie. 'Look, is that Sandy and Mary?' She pointed down the Knock path at a man in a deerstalker and a woman from whom palpable discomfiture emanated.

'I telt him we were comin here the day,' Bob replied. 'I thocht he micht turn up.'

'How?'

'Sandy's no awfae keen on bein alane wi Mary.'

'How no?'

'He doesnae ken what to say to her.'

'Juist talk.'

'Aye, but what aboot? I was the same wi you, mind? But at least you did the talkin, kept us goin. Mary's that timid, she never opens her gab. And Sandy, if it's no aboot shootin or huntin, he hasnae a clue.' He waved and Sandy changed direction and headed towards them.

'Grand day,' he said.

'Will you jine us?' Annie asked, moving up to make room on the blanket.

'We wouldnae want to be any bother,' said Mary.

'Nae bother. Ellen, is that Marnie Bennett ower there? D'you want to go and play wi her?'

'Nut.'

Bob laughed at the abruptness of her answer. 'Has she been takin lessons in plain speakin fae you?' he asked Sandy.

'Doesnae need lessons, that ane.'

Ellen was still marvelling at the scenery. 'Do all these hills huv names?' she asked.

'Aye,' said Sandy. He took her to the Indicator and pointed out the engraved circle of polished metal on its surface. 'You see the outlines of the hills goin roond the side? Look up now, and you'll see the hills themsels in the same place in front of you. There, awa in the distance, that's Ben More. And that's Ben Chonzie. See in front of it, just aboot a mile awa fae here, that's Barvick Falls. That's a grand place for swimmin when the weather's good.' Ellen leaned against the Indicator, head close to its surface, reading the names and looking up to identify each peak in turn, seemingly trying to memorise both the names and the shapes of the land.

'Hello.'

She recognised Marnie's voice and didn't look up. 'Fuck off,' she said.

'I wanted to say sorry.'

'Whit did you do it fur?'

'It wasnae mw. . .'

'Shite. Wha else kent I've got etzemer?'

'My sister. Pattie. I telt my faimly aboot it that nicht, aathin we did oot at Monzie, what a grand time we had and how much I enjoyed it. I mentioned you had a rash. My sister heard, and she clyped aboot it at school.'

'And the curlin stanes?'

'I wasnae makin fun of you, honest.'

'The hale class was makin fun of me.'

'I ken. And I'm sorry. It's my sister. She's a brute.'

Finally, Ellen looked up at her. There were tears forming in Marnie's eyes.

'Shall I show you how to mak warpaint?' Marnie asked.

Ellen thought for a moment, deciding whether or not to continue the feud. Marnie was the only friend she'd made in Crieff, the only person to show any interest in her. Usually, when she fell out with somebody there was no prospect of reconciliation, but there was nothing to be gained from shunning Marnie. She nodded. Marnie clutched her hand and started to run downhill towards a large clump of blaeberries. Ellen bounced alongside. Marnie picked half a dozen plump berries and deposited them in the palm of her left hand. She spat on it, then squashed the berries with her index finger until they formed a purple pulp. She gathered some of the mixture on her index finger, then took hold of Ellen's jaw and drew a line across her left cheek with the mixture. In this fashion, she affixed three stripes on each cheek, then sat back on her heels and, patting her mouth with her hand, let out a series of whoops.

'Now me,' she said, and Ellen copied what Marnie had done, decorating her cheek with the purple warpaint. 'We're real injuns now,' Marnie said and she whooped again and ran off, brandishing an invisible tomahawk, her hair bouncing expansively. Ellen followed once more and caught up with her as she climbed into a sweet chestnut tree, using the banking behind to reach far enough to get her leg onto the lowest branch. She climbed again until she was nine or ten feet above the ground.

'Come on,' she said, and Ellen copied her technique to pull herself alongside. 'From here, we can see aathin,' Marnie said. 'We can see the cowboys and attack them afore they even ken we're here.' She picked at pieces of bark and waited until a group of four young laddies approached, running ahead of their families, then threw the bark at them, hitting them on the head and chest. She whooped again.

'You're deid,' she shouted. 'I shot you wi my bow and arrow.'

'No, you didnae,' said one of the lads, wearing his grey school jumper over a pair of shorts. 'You missed.'

Ellen picked another piece of bark and threw it at him, hitting his chest again. 'Aye, we did. Twice over.'

The parents of the boys reached the scene and the mother looked up at the girls with disdain. 'Bloody Glesga keelies,' she said. 'Keep awa fae them, Hamish. They'll gie you lice.' She took the hand of the youngest boy and marched past, yelling at the others to follow.

'Sorry,' said Marnie. 'That really was my fault this time.'

'No it wasnae,' said Ellen. 'It was that bitch-woman's fault. We were only playin.'

They marched downhill and found another couple of trees to climb. Ellen loved the texture of the bark on her skin, laying herself flat on the bigger branches and resting her head on the bark as though listening to the tale of the tree. After an hour, when it was starting to get dark, they sauntered back to the Indicator and Marnie made to rejoin her family.

'Best be getting hame to see if the dairy's been burned doon,' she said.

'You're no still bothered about that?'

'My faither is. Today's the first time he's been aff the farm since it happened.' She took Ellen's hand. 'Listen, I dinnae care if people see us talkin,' she said. 'Your Glesga freends. Or Crieff bairns.'

Ellen could feel her warpaint dried on her skin. It made her feel powerful, in control. 'Me neither.'

'Thocht you didnae want to play wi her?' said Bob when she settled herself on the tartan rug a few moments later.

'I can change my mind.'

'Look at the state of you,' said Annie. 'You'll need a bath when we get hame, to get that stuff aff your face.'

'It's warpaint.'

'Enough to put the fear of God into onyone,' said Bob.

'That's the point.'

Starlings were squabbling in a nearby plane tree like delinquents looking for a fight. A brace of pheasant flew by. Sandy pointed them out to Ellen, named them. She asked why their wingbeats were so loud compared to other birds.

'They do it on purpose. To mak a noise that acts like an alarm if there's ony other pheasants nearby. If you see ane fly aff, you'll probably see twa or three others nearby.'

'And why do they make such a racket the rest of the time?'

'That's the males. They mak that tuit-tuit sound aa day, but especially noo, when it's comin to dusk.' They studied the hills for some moments. 'How did your essay aboot me go?'

'It didnae. My teacher hated it.'

'How?'

'Cos she's stupit.' Ellen was still thinking about Marnie's farm, and her dad still in fear of reprisals. And she thought about Miss Carrington, and her curiously scratched face.

'Tell me aboot the hayrick fires,' she said. 'Did the person who did it really threaten to burn Marnie's faither's dairy down?'

'He did, aye.' Sandy pulled the folded letter from the inside pocket of his tweed jacket and handed it to her. She held it close and peered at it. The handwriting was elaborate, all expansive loops and whorls, probably to disguise the writer's usual style. The legs on the letters y and g were distinctive, though, oddly angular compared to the curving style elsewhere.

'It's been near three weeks noo,' Sandy said, 'so it's probably safe. But he really did burn doon Malky's hayricks, so Malky's still sure he'll go for the dairy.'

'Why wid he no huv done it already?'

'When we nearly caught him, that probably gied him a fleg. And Malky's still organisin a watch twenty-four hoors a day. Stop him afore he can strike, he says.'

'Wid it no be better to find oot who he is first?' And then stop him, instead of waitin fur him to attack? Ye cannae keep watchin twenty-four hours a day forever.'

'If we kent how to, we would.'

Ellen nodded at the letter. 'There's yer first clue.'

'Is that right?'

'He's threatenin to burn doon Fairmer Bennett's dairy, aye?'

'Aye.'

'But he put that warnin letter through *your* door?'

'Aye.'

'Why?'

'I dinnae ken.'

'Work it oot. Wan, for some reason he must think ye're the high-heid-yin on the farm. Which ye arenae. And, two, he must huv a grudge against *you*, no the fairmer.'

'Dinnae drag me into this.'

'It's no me draggin ye into anythin. It's him. So the question is, whit huv ye done to rile him?'

Sandy Disdain was not a man who went out of his way to make enemies, but nor did he make any attempt to be amenable. Folks could take him or leave him, and mostly they left him, which suited Sandy just fine. But who could he have made so angry? He tried to think of anyone he had argued with recently. And then he remembered. . .

'Ye've just thought of someone, haven't ye?' said Ellen. 'I can tell by yer face. . .'

'I was oot snaring the other Saturday. Horseshoe Drive. Someone had a richt go at me. Telt me killin animals was criminal. . .'

Ellen sat upright on the blanket. 'She said that?'

'Wha said it was a she?'

'What was she like?'

'Skinnymalink. Hacket-faced. Called me a poacher. . .' He stopped.

'And?'

'And I telt her I was the fairmer. . .'

'So now she's attackin the farm, because she thinks ye're the farmer, and ye go aboot killin innocent animals.'

'Well, that micht be. . .'

'Ye know it is. And I'll tell ye somethin else – I know *who* it is.'

It all made sense to Ellen. Miss Carrington was the anonymous arsonist. She had suspected as much the other night, when the useless policeman was talking about the Dallerie Laundry fire and mentioned the Avenger had a scratched face. The day after that fire Miss Carrington had come into class with a scratch and a nonsense story about picking fruit.

'She used the same words to me – "killin animals is criminal".' She nodded as if to give extra credence to her words, and then she told them about Miss Carrington's scratched cheek.

'Gibby Owen did say he scratched the guy,' said Bob.

'Aye, and when I asked that polisman if he was certain it was a wean, he said no.'

Bob scratched his head. This was an enormous accusation against a well-respected member of the community. 'You've nae proof. I couldnae go to the polis. . .'

'Leave it to me,' said Ellen.

'Dinnae you go gettin yoursel into trouble,' said Annie.

Ellen gave a rousing Red Indian whoop and jumped up and ran into the gloom of the Knock.

*

After tea, and after the bath Annie had insisted she have, Ellen took one of Bob's razor blades and carefully cut out the pages in her school jotter in which she'd written her latest punishment essay for Miss Carrington. She sharpened her pencil and lay on the bed and started to write a new piece, smiling all the while.

Thursday, 28 September

A Day of Progress

'Black Alice, you really should wear a hat until that ridiculous hair grows back.' Lorna stood in front of Ellen's desk and glared down at her. 'That hairstyle is not becoming on a child. Especially you, Ellen Laing. It emphasises the cunning in your nature. Sleekit, you probably call it. You're like a weed, growing where no one wants it.'

Lorna tossed Ellen's jotter onto her desk. 'I really don't think an essay about buying ice creams is in any way suitable. You veer from one extreme to another. What's more, this one is spoiled by a silly spelling mistake. I expect better of you.'

Ellen opened her jotter. One out of ten. She smiled in satisfaction.

*

'Mrs Kelty.'

Mrs McNeill hailed Annie as she emerged from Halley's Emporium on King Street. She had a small poodle on a lead.

'New dug?' Annie said.

'There has been a shocking epidemic of people in the big cities killing their pets because of the war. I took Daisy here from an old woman in Glasgow.'

Annie laughed. 'It's no just the bairns we're evacuatin, then?'

'It is the evacuees I wish to discuss with you. You'll be aware that the Perthshire Committee for the Supervision of Evacuees has set up a Conciliation Committee? The Earl of Mansfield has been asked to chair it.'

Annie snorted. 'I'm sure an Earl's the ideal person to investigate the lives of people riven wi poverty and ill-health.'

Mrs McNeill gave her a disdainful look. 'There have been so many complaints, there was no alternative but to investigate. Lord Mansfield will be looking at the unhygienic condition of the children, and their conduct both in the homes where they are staying and in the town generally. There's a feeling they're simply unmanageable. They're nearly all verminous. Ringworm, impetigo, even tubercular sores. Most of them arrived in the clothes they stood up in. As often as not those had to be burned.'

Annie knew that much of this was true of Ellen. She did have ringworm and eczema, and Bob had burned most of her clothes when they bought new in Perth. All the same, the picture being painted by Mrs McNeill was melodramatic and one-sided, deliberately partisan. It was in no way fair on the Glaswegian incomers.

'And,' Mrs McNeill continued, 'some of their behaviour has been deplorable. We've had windows smashed, chickens killed, Mr Cheney's horses were stoned in Madderty, passing vehicles have been set upon with stones and sticks. There was a pillar left on the railway line outside Comrie. Could have caused a catastrophe.'

'I'm sure there's one of two rotten eggs.'

'The appropriate metaphor would be rotten apples, Mrs Kelty. Because one rotten apple poisons them all.'

'I dinnae believe that's true.'

'Nevertheless, it *is* true. And for that reason the Conciliation Committee has been set up. The main committee will meet in Perth, of course, but I've been asked to set up a Crieff branch.'

'To do what?'

'Hear the complaints. Adjudicate.'

'And then what?'

'It's our role to alleviate friction, settle problems, offer advice. I know you have one of these Glasgow children. And you've applied to join the WVS, I understand. I wondered if you would care to join the committee. In an administrative role, naturally.'

The mention of Annie's WVS application was surely intentional. An interdependence was being established. The success of her application to join the WVS was contingent on her response regarding the committee. Annie stepped past Mrs McNeill.

'No,' she said. 'I winnae hae onythin to do wi your committee. If you ask me, the "friction" you talk aboot is as much doon to the locals as it is to the Glesga folk.'

'I don't think. . .'

'They're bairns. They're frightened. Confused. They need a bit of lookin efter. Kindness. Love.'

'Love?'

'Auld fashioned notion. Some mannie called Jesus Christ used to blether aboot it.'

*

Ellen pushed Bob's bicycle uphill to Eppie Callum's tree and turned onto the Laggan and tried to mount once more. The cycle was far too big for her and she couldn't sit on the seat and reach the pedals so she stood on the pedals the whole way, cycling for a mile until she saw, as Marnie had described, halfway up the hill, the Disdains' whitewashed cottage. Sandy was digging potatoes and he stopped as she came to a halt and crashed to the ground, the only way she knew to dismount. She propped the bicycle against his fence.

'I've somethin to show you,' she said.

'Come ben.' He showed her into a dark kitchen, the air

much colder than outside, the walls and floor bare. A pot of broth dangled over an open fire beneath a contraption Ellen had never seen before, a sort of funnel stopping halfway down the wall, through which smoke from the fire escaped. It was black with soot. Sandy lit a Capstan and they sat at the kitchen table.

'I thocht you werenae allowed oot for a fortnicht?'

'I'm at choir practice.'

'So you are. So what d'you hae to show me?'

'My hamework.'

'What would I want to see thon for?'

'Because of this.' She opened the jotter at the essay in which she described going with Bob and Annie to buy ice creams on the way to the Knock to pick blaeberries. Ice creams bought from McLaren's Dairy.

Or, as Ellen had deliberately written it, *Diary*.

And, in the margin, in red pen, was Miss Carrington's correction: "spelling – Dairy".

Sandy took the anonymous letter from his jacket pocket and compared the handwriting. In both versions of "Dairy", the legs on the letter y were sharp and angular.

And identical.

Sandy smiled. 'Well done, Miss Holmes. You're a smart wee besom.'

'Am are. And to think, that hellhag called me a weed.'

'A weed, aye? Well, let me tell you, a weed is only a plant that does what the hell it likes, whaur the hell it likes. Weeds are the strongest plants you can get. So you should tak that as a compliment.'

Ellen pondered for a moment. Weeds were strong. Not "undesirable" as that woman from the WVS had described them on the moss-collecting expedition, or "sleekit" as Miss Carrington called her. She liked that.

'So whit do we do now?' she said.

'Oh, you leave that to me.'

'Dinnae go gettin intae trouble.'

'Me? I never get intae trouble.'

'You and me baith.'

They went outside and Sandy picked up Bob's bicycle. He gripped it between his legs and rocked first the seat and then the handlebars from side to side, gradually sliding them down as far as they would go. He held it out to Ellen. 'You'll probably reach the pedals, noo,' he said.

Ellen tilted the bicycle and stepped onto it and sat on the seat. She could indeed – just –reach the pedals. 'Thanks,' she said, beaming.

'Mind, your uncle Bob'll be smashin his face wi his knees every time his pedals go roond.'

'It'll make a change from Thingwie Johnstone.'

*

Sandy accompanied Ellen back to Cloudland, jogging alongside. She sped ahead as she took the downhill past Mungall Park and the entrance to Lady Mary's Walk but by the time she reached Milnab Mill Sandy was catching up and at McLaren's Dairy he had to wait for her as she pushed her bicycle across Burrell Street.

Bob and Annie listened politely to Sandy's obvious haivers about chancing on Ellen as she came out of choir practice. 'And she showed me her hamework,' he continued quickly, moving the conversation on and gesturing to Ellen to take out her jotter. They compared the handwriting on the word "dairy" with that in the letter and both Bob and Annie were equally convinced there was a match.

'So Ellen's teacher really could be the arsonist?' Bob said.

'We had her sayin killin animals was murder, and then the scratch on her puss,' said Ellen. 'Now we've got the handwritin. It all ties up.'

'I hae to say it does,' agreed Bob. 'I'll maybe awa doon to Dallerie and hae a chat wi Eddie McMurray.'

'Aye,' said Sandy. 'Ask aboot the Glesga paper. And if she used milk bottles to start that fire an aa.'

'What milk bottles?' said Ellen.

'We found three milk bottles at the Laggan fires,' said Bob. 'She'd filled them wi paraffin, used them to start the fires. . .'

'Why did ye no tell me that before?'

'I didnae realise I hadnae.'

'Well, ye hadnae. Have ye got them?'

'Ane of them, aye, under the sink.'

'Get it.'

Sandy ran his huge hand over his face to conceal a smile at Ellen's belligerence. Annie sighed and resolved to give another telling-off later about being rude. Bob thought to say something, yet again, but her impassioned expression persuaded him otherwise. He went upstairs to the kitchen and used his handkerchief to grab the bottle by the neck and took it back downstairs.

Ellen stood up when she saw it, as though trying to make an escape. 'That's it,' she said.

'That's what?' said Bob.

Ellen stopped. This was awkward. How could she tell them the bottle was Miss Carrington's without admitting it was she who had washed her hair in paraffin? The embarrassment would be too great.

'Alison McGillivray got lice,' she said finally, 'and Miss Carrington washed her hair in paraffin. Oot of a bottle exact same as that.'

Bob studied her insouciant gaze. Another hair-washing-in-paraffin incident, after Ellen's schoolfriends did the same to her? That seemed most improbable. This wasn't the moment to broach the matter, but Bob now suspected it was more likely that Miss Carrington, and not Ellen's friends, had been responsible for her hair dousing.

'Well,' he said. 'Mair evidence. Maybe worth a wee chat wi Sergeant Rudd an aa.'

'Can I come wi you?' said Ellen.

'You're grounded, mind?'

'Maybe she could go efter her next choir practice,' said Sandy.

Bob watched the exchange of glances between Sandy and Ellen, remembered Sandy's patent nonsense about bumping into Ellen earlier, felt sure the pair were in cahoots.

*

Sergeant Rudd passed the anonymous letter and Ellen's school jotter across the interview table to Bob. He sat back on a creaking wooden chair.

'Aye, very clever. If we ever get women police officers, God help us, I'm sure the wee lassie could get hersel a job.'

'She's smart, aye.'

'But there's three problems here.' He lit a cigarette and blew smoke from his nose. 'First, it's pretty flimsy evidence, on its ain.'

'Circumstantial.'

'I forgot you'd been a bobby. Aye, circumstantial. You would need somethin mair to convince a jury. Second, and mair important, naebody's goin to believe a wee Glesga keelie ower a respected schoolteacher. Aye?'

'Aye.' Bob had already pondered Sergeant Rudd's points. 'And third?'

'Third. . .If. . .If I was to go and see this Carrington woman and ask her if she's been involved in arson, she'd want to ken the evidence that drew me to her. And I'd hae to tell her.' He gestured to Ellen's jotter. 'That would mean she would ken it was your wee lassie clyped on her. That's grand if she goes to trial and she's fund guilty. But if she isnae – and I'd reckon that's a very big "if" – what happens then? The lassie's life'll be a misery. I mind I had a teacher at the school, Mr Rawlinson, didnae like me. Made my life hell for twa year. That's naethin to what the lassie would get.'

Bob collected the letter and jotter. 'You're richt, as always, sergeant. I'm sorry I wasted your time.'

Sergeant Rudd pulled his cigarettes from his jacket pocket. 'I'm sure we'll get to the bottom of this arsonist nonsense,' he said.

'We need to,' said Bob. 'He's no stoppin. Dallerie Laundry an aa, Willy McAnuff was tellin me.'

'PC McAnuff should keep his gab shut aboot polis matters. We dinnae ken the laundry was the same man as Malky's hayricks. Nae note nor nothin.'

'But paraffin to start it, aye? Same *modus operandi*.'

'"*Modus operandi*"? Hark at him wi his fancy words.'

Friday, 29 September

A Day of Arrangements

'I wasnae sure if you'd mind me?'

'Of course I do. The Cuddies Strip. Barossa Street. I still say you're a great loss to policing. Or detecting, anyway.'

'It's funny you should mention that. . .' Bob explained the story of the hayrick arsonist to Detective Lieutenant Bertie Hammond of Glasgow City Police, a man who had helped him previously when he was a police officer with the Perth City force. 'I wondered,' he concluded, 'if I could maybe ask for your assistance?'

'It would be a pleasure.'

*

Arrangements for Sunday made, Bob explained his thinking to Annie and Ellen. 'We dinnae tell Miss Carrington what we ken yet,' he said. 'There's other stuff we need to do afore we can speak to her.'

'Like whit?' said Ellen.

'We need mair evidence. Your jotter and the letter, that's what they call circumstantial evidence. It's grand, but we'll need mair than that. Lots of different bits of circumstantial evidence, aathigither, can build a strong case, but a couple of pieces on their lane winnae. So I need to sort that. But first, I need to see Malky Bennett, ask if I can borrow his car.'

'Can I come wi ye?' said Ellen. 'See Marnie?'

'No, I'm takin my bike.'

He went to the yard and fetched his bicycle from the lean-to and rolled in onto the side entrance to James Square. Something felt odd about it and he studied it, puzzled. It seemed to have shrunk. He sat on it and his feet trailed on the ground. His right knee was against his chest. He looked up at the windows of the flat above and saw Ellen staring down at him. She looked like she was laughing.

*

'You do ken they brought in petrol rationin last week?' Malky Bennett was studying Bob's bike as he spoke, having watched Bob wobble up the Laggan road to the farm, his legs jutting out at an angle to stop his knees from hitting his face.

'Aye. I can pey you for the petrol.'

'You certainly can. But that's no what I meant. Wi the rationin, we're under instructions to use vehicles as little as possible. "Only when essential", they say.'

'This is essential. We could find oot wha your arsonist is.'

'Sunday then. But mind and mak sure you're back afore it gets dark. Bloody near impossible drivin in the blackoot. You cannae see five yards in front of your face.' He grabbed the bike and wrestled with the handlebars. 'Wha did this to your bike?'

'I dinnae ken, but I hae my suspicions.'

Malky pulled at the bars but they wouldn't budge. 'I'll need a wrench to fix this. Whaever did it must hae been a bloody gorilla.'

'That probably confirms my suspicion.'

*

The Comrie train was crossing the viaduct as Bob freewheeled his bicycle down Dallerie Brae to the laundry. There were speugs in the greenery and a gang of starlings swooped over the millowner's house and landed *en masse* in the garden. They were still squabbling as Bob passed.

He entered a first-floor office overlooking the laundry. The smell of bleach and detergent was almost overpowering, even here.

'Now then, Eddie,' he said to a chubby man seated at his desk.

'You here to sort oot Tommy Crabb?'

'No. How?'

'You're ARP are you no? Tommy Crabb, at night the mill hoose is lit up like a brothel in Soho. No that I've ever been in a brothel in Soho.'

'Is that right?'

'You boys obviously cannae be arsed comin aa the way doon here.'

'Dallerie's maybe been missed aff the rotas. I'll hae a check the morn. I was interested in your fire the other week.'

'Bloody Glesga keelies.'

'You sure it was bairns?'

He picked up a copy of the *Glasgow Evening Times* with parts of the first few pages torn out. 'What mair evidence do you need?' he said. 'And Gibby caught ane of them a scratch on the cheek. Skin soft as a bairnie's arse, he said.'

'Could it hae been a woman?'

'What would a woman set a fire for?'

'What would a bairn set a fire for?'

'Pure divilment.'

'Well, maybe it's the same for a woman.'

'Ach, awa man.'

'But could it?'

'I suppose so.'

They descended from the office and made their way round the corner to the room that had been attacked. The bottom pane was still boarded. Bob looked through the remaining panes. Damage was still visible, scorched garments piled against the wall, awaiting a visit from the insurance company.

'He went running that wey,' said Eddie. 'Into the fields. In the dark we couldnae find him.'

'Or her.'

'Or her.'

'I'm thinkin it's the same person set the Laggan dairy fires. Same approach, paraffin to start it. Glesga papers. But there's ae difference. Sandy Disdain got a letter fae the arsonist. But you didnae?'

'Aye I did. Last week. Sayin he failed this time, wouldnae fail next time.'

'You sure?'

'I'm hardly goin to mak that up, am I?'

'Sergeant Rudd said you hadnae got one.'

'Aye, and there's a man wi his finger on the pulse.'

'Fair point. Have you got the letter?'

'No. I gave it to Rudd's wee puppy.'

'PC McAnuff?'

'That's the boy. He has all the makins of a grand successor to Danny Rudd, that ane.'

'How?'

'I dinnae think he likes to exert too much energy, ken? We found a bottle lyin by the road where the fire was started. We showed him it but he wasnae interested. "It's a fire we're lookin into, no a cup of tea," he says. Damned thing reeked of paraffin.'

Bob felt he was missing something, something which could link all these events together, but he couldn't make the connection. 'You still got the bottle?' he said.

'Back in the office.'

'Can I hae it?'

'How?'

'I've a wee notion wha the arsonist is.'

'A woman, you think?'

'Aye.'

'It's a funny world, gettin.'

*

'Hoi.'

At four o'clock, Lorna Carrington was walking up Pittenzie Street from the school to the High Street when she heard the voice. Behind her was the horrible hunter-chap who worked on the Laggan farm and hunted rabbits. She turned to face him.

'Well?'

'I've been waitin for you to come oot of the school. I've a message for the arsonist.'

Lorna felt a stab of panic and struggled momentarily to remain calm. She thought what an innocent person would do in the circumstances. She affected a sort of squint, raising her left eyebrow as though in puzzlement.

'I beg your pardon?'

'I've a message for the arsonist,' Sandy repeated slowly. He was unblinking, fixing his gaze on Lorna. She found it most disconcerting. Smoke from his cigarette was trailing upwards into her face. She coughed.

'I don't know what you're talking about.'

'You dinnae ken aboot Malky Bennett's hayrick arsonist?'

'No.'

'You must be the only person in Crieff wha doesnae, then. The man's famous.'

'I've seen you before, haven't I?'

'You have.'

'You were surly then, too.'

'And you were rude. So there you are, then. We mak a grand pair.'

'I'm very busy. . .'

'I ken you're the arsonist.' He leaned towards her. 'You dinnae need to deny it or confirm it. We baith ken it's the truth.'

Lorna exhaled heavily. *Be careful. He might know, but what proof can he have? Admit nothing.* 'I'm a primary school teacher. Do you really think I would go about setting fires?'

'I ken what you did at Malky's fairm. And at Dallerie. And at Lochearnhead. It's nane of my business. And it'll stay nane of my business. . Juist as long as nae other fires start mysteriously in the toon. You ken what I'm sayin?'

He lit his Capstan and walked back the way he had come. Lorna watched him go. *Peasant. Dullard. Nothing to fear there.*

But she didn't like being told what to do. Not at all.

Sunday, 1 October

A Day of Fingerprints

'You've been in my room.'

'No, miss.'

'You've stolen one of my lipsticks.'

'I dinnae wear lipstick.'

'Looking to sell it to one of your common friends, no doubt.'

'It wasnae me, miss.' Mary felt an instant dizziness, as always when faced with confrontation. She couldn't fathom Lorna Carrington, the way she could be charming one day and make up lies like this another. She knew she hadn't stolen a lipstick and, what's more, she was fairly sure no one had. Mary had been in Lorna's room and knew there were valuable trinkets lying about. Who would bother to steal a lipstick?

'Have a lipstick on my desk by tomorrow and I'll say no more about it. A new one. I couldn't use the old one again now that you've contaminated it with your lips.'

Mary's overwhelming thought was relief that she wouldn't be reported to Mrs Mitchell and sacked. Beneath that, there was outrage. And beneath that was resignation. However unfair this was, she knew she wouldn't resist.

'Yes, miss.'

*

Bob and Ellen got lost once on the way to the Identification Bureau in Glasgow's Pitt Street, at the same spot that Bob had gone astray the last time he had visited, in 1936 as part of the investigation into the Barossa Street murder.

'Whaur do I go here?' he asked Ellen.

'How should I know?'

'You come fae Glesga.'

'I come fae Finnieston. I'd never set foot oot of the place till I came to Grief.'

'Crieff.'

'You call it what ye want.'

They were only half an hour late when Bob finally recognised the street layout and the austere outline of the police building. He pulled up Malky Bennett's Ford on the street opposite and prised his fingers from the steering wheel.

'D'ye want us to mind yer car for ye, mister?' a lad of around eight or nine asked when he stepped onto the pavement. With him were half a dozen children, practically feral, leering at him and pointing at Ellen.

'No, you're fine. It's no goin onywhere.'

'Ye need to pay,' whispered Ellen.

'How?'

'Cos if ye dinnae, it'll huv nae wheels when ye get back.'

'We're in front of a polis station. What's goin to happen?'

'Well, you can explain to Marnie's faither how his precious car got wrecked.'

Bob reflected. Malky had only had the car a matter of weeks. He pulled a shilling from his trouser pocket and handed it to the lad.

'Two bob.'

Bob extracted another coin and completed the transaction.

'Sucker,' said Ellen as they walked away. 'It was only worth sixpence.'

'Could you no hae said?'

'You're the boss.' She looked up at the police building. 'God help us.'

Detective Lieutenant Bertie Hammond was waiting for them when they finally made it inside the building, his hair Brylcreemed, his suit precisely ironed. He shook Bob's hand warmly and bent down to Ellen.

'You must be the detective Bob told me about?'

'Am are.'

Bertie shook her hand, too. 'Right, then. Let's get to work.'

Bob opened a knitted bag he'd brought with him and Ellen pulled out the McLaren's Dairy milk bottles from the hayrick fires and the Dallerie laundry, followed by Ellen's school jotter.

'These are the bottles that held the paraffin used to set the fires?' said Bertie.

'Aye.'

'And this is your school jotter?' he said to Ellen. She nodded. 'So this will certainly have your teacher's fingerprints on it, if she's been marking your homework. We'll check for that first. And then, if we can match those fingerprints with any we find on the bottles, we'll know she touched that as well.'

'I know she did,' said Ellen. Bob knew she was thinking about Lorna's use of paraffin stored in McLaren's milk bottles to wash the hair of Alison McGillivray in front of the class. Although Ellen supposed that might help their case, Bob knew it would, in fact, be a hindrance. If her fingerprints were found on the bottle and events turned sour for Lorna Carrington, in court she would argue that she used the bottles in school and somebody else must have taken them and used them to set the fires. However improbable that might be, doubts would be sown in the minds of the jurors. That was all that was required – a doubt, a chink in the case against the accused.

'I'm sure you're right,' said Bertie. 'But as detectives we have to prove things, not just believe them. Evidence, that's what this is all about. Make sure there's no way she can deny anything. Now, your fingerprints are going to be on your jotter as well, so we'll have to take those first, to eliminate them. Have the police ever taken your fingerprints before?'

'No,' Ellen giggled. 'They've taken my faither's, but.'

It was Bertie's turn to laugh. 'We'll draw a veil over that, maybe.'

'D'you need to tak mine an aa?' said Bob.

'No, we'll have yours from Barossa Street.'

'You've still got them on file?'

'Oh, yes.'

'Better no be gettin into bother, then,' said Ellen.

'Just what I was thinkin.'

Bertie took out his fingerprinting pad. 'What I'm going to do,' he explained, 'is press each of your fingers in turn against the ink pad and then press them onto this piece of paper. You can see it's already been marked out with squares for each finger. Ready?'

Ellen couldn't conceal her excitement as Bertie took her left hand and started the process of fingerprinting. When he had finished she stared at her filthy fingers and waved them at Bob, grinning. Bertie pointed to the sheet with her fingerprints neatly arrayed.

'That's you, that is. Totally unique. Nobody in the world has the same fingerprints as you.'

'No even ma mam?'

'Not even her. Now, it's time to do some dusting. Have you ever seen fingerprinting done?' Ellen shook her head. 'Well, first we identify where we think there will be a good quality fingerprint. On your jotter, probably about here, where someone would hold it when they were opening it. Yes? So I'll dust it here and – yes, look, there's a fingerprint. See it?'

Ellen was so close to the jotter her forehead was almost touching it.

'This one's yours, I think, judging by the size.' He held up her still inky finger and compared it to his own. 'Let's try again.' He affixed powder to another section and shook it and another print emerged. 'This looks more promising. Definitely too big to be your finger. Now we fix tape to it like this.' He carefully slid a piece of clear tape over the fingerprint and pressed and peeled it away. The fingerprint came with it.

'And now I'll stick this onto a piece of white paper so that it shows up more clearly and, hey presto, we have a fingerprint, ready for inspection. With any luck, one of these will be a match for one on the bottles.'

'How can you tell?' Ellen asked.

'A fingerprint shows up the ridges on your finger. The print is left by moisture and grease, and it's an exact image of what's on your hand. As I said, that's unique, so what we can do is examine the fingerprint in microscopic detail, looking at the patterns of the ridges and valleys in the print. There'll be different whorls or loops or arches. Sometimes a ridge will just end, sometimes it will bifurcate – split in two – and sometimes it will merge with another ridge. Sometimes you even get little circles, like islands. If we put it under the microscope it's easier to see. Want to see?'

Bertie took them over to a side desk on which was mounted a microscope and he placed the fingerprint from the jotter beneath it. 'This is the one we're most sure belongs to your teacher, so we'll start with this,' he said. 'What we're doing is looking for distinguishing features in the ridge details.' He bent over the microscope and studied it for some moments.

'There,' he said. 'Have a look, on the top right, can you see a very short ridge, all on its own?' Ellen peered into the microscope, adjusting her vision until the sample came into view, and she saw that there was, indeed, a very small ridge bounded on either side by longer ridges.

'That's called a ridge characteristic,' Bertie said. 'An identifying feature. And just below it, can you see where there's a ridge that splits like a letter y into two different ridges?

That's another characteristic. Now we have to study the complete fingerprint and see how many of these ridge characteristics we can find. If we find more than a dozen, say, we will have a very strong chance of identifying the individual who made it.'

He turned to Bob. 'It'll take me a bit of time to finish this fingerprint and then the ones on the bottles. It's not very exciting to watch, an old man bending over a microscope. Why don't you take Ellen into town and get some tea and cake. I'll carry on here.'

'Will there be onywhere open? It's Sunday.'

'This is Glasgow. Hansen's Tearoom on Sauchiehall Street will be open.'

'Are you sure you dinnae mind?' said Bob. 'It's your day aff...'

'It's always a pleasure to do something that might apprehend a criminal. I'll need about an hour.'

Sandbags lined the pavements on either side of Sauchiehall Street, the air filled with the smell of jute. Even on a Sunday, the street seemed full of people and Bob and Ellen dodged them as they searched for Hansen's. They found it, near the city centre end, and Bob ordered tea for himself and lemonade for Ellen and two scones.

'Bet the scones arenae as good as yours,' he said.

'Of course no.'

They finished the scones – somewhat smaller than those in Cloudland – and Bob sat back on his seat. 'I tak it back,' he said. 'They were much better than yours.'

'Yer arse in parsley. Mines are much lighter than them.'

Bob knew she was right. She was becoming a proficient baker with a delicate touch, much better than his own. He was too heavy-handed and Ellen's more patient approach did make for a lighter scone.

'Aye,' he conceded. 'Yours are the best. Apart fae Auntie Annie's, obviously.'

'Ye never say anythin bad aboot her.'
'I've never needed to. Never will.'
'Ye're a bit soppy.'
'It has been said.'
'No like Sandy.'
'You seem to be gettin on grand wi Sandy.'
'He doesnae fuss.'
'Do I fuss?'
'Aye, but no as much as Annie.'
'Sorry. Thing is, we're no used to livin wi bairns. We're probably a bit over-protective. . .'
'Yous are.'
'I'll try and bear it in mind.'

*

Lady Mary's Walk looked as though it was ablaze, the canopy of beeches and oaks an extravagant autumnal tableau of oranges and reds and browns. Earlier rain had enlivened the greenery beneath, a mixture of freshness and dust still filling the air. Sandy and Mary walked down the wide path in silence, the river Earn flowing beside them, serene in sunshine. Their absorption was interrupted briefly by the passing of the Comrie train, chugging slowly towards town to disgorge day trippers in search of normality and families intent on engagement. Silence returned.

Mary had been debating whether or not to tell Sandy about Lorna. She was sure she was being foolish, overreacting. This was probably her own fault, somehow. But there was still the question of buying a replacement lipstick: she couldn't decide whether to do so, and she sore wanted to talk it through with somebody.

The trouble was that Sandy would take matters into his own hands. He'd go to the school and confront Lorna and that would only make a terrible situation worse. All Mary wanted was for the problem to disappear. Sandy would make it bigger. She let out a yawn.

'Are you bored?' said Sandy.

'I'm just a bit tired. Bessie's an awfae snorer, I didnae get much sleep last night.'

'You should ask for a room of your ain.'

'Ach awa. I'm juist a hoosemaid.'

*

When they returned to Pitt Street, Bob could tell immediately that Bertie had found something, his beaming smile telegraphing the news.

'I have a match,' he confirmed. He pointed to a spot near the top of the bottle Bob had collected from Dallerie. 'There was nothing on this first bottle, from the dairy fire. Everything's too smudged and dirty. But this one, just here, there's a perfect match.'

Ellen clapped her hands. 'I knew it, I knew it.'

Bertie showed her the fingerprint from the jotter. 'Look at these ridges, the ones we saw first off. And look there, and there and there. I've marked off fourteen ridge characteristics that are clear and unique. Now compare with the print from the bottle.'

Ellen hunched over the microscope, focusing, bringing it into view.

'You see? The same patterns.'

'You've no doubt?' said Bob.

'None. It couldn't be clearer. The same person made both of these prints. Of course, that may not be your suspect. *Someone* touched both objects. We now know that. But we'd need to get your teacher's fingerprints next to prove they are hers.'

'And how do we do that?' said Ellen.

'Bob is going to have to take all his evidence to the local police.'

Bob saw the delight on Ellen's features and needed to temper her excitement. 'And as Mr Hammond kens only too well,' he said, 'the Perthshire Constabulary tend to work at their ain speed.'

*

Three hardy bairns were paddling in the pond in the top park as Sandy and Mary passed through on their way to Barvick Falls after their long walk round the Horseshoe Drive. Both were lost in thought and didn't spot PC McAnuff sitting in the shelter shed by the tennis court. Sandy was debating whether he'd have time to snare the top field at Callum's Hill before dark and constantly had to stop himself from speeding up. Mary was still deciding whether or not to buy the lipstick. They were both pulled from their thoughts by the sight of Lorna Carrington passing through the iron gates at the top of the park and walking towards them. The two women gave a start when they recognised one another but Lorna was first to regain her composure, smiling as she approached.

'Lovely afternoon for a walk,' she said. 'After that horrible rain this morning.'

'We need the rain,' said Sandy. 'Ground's dry as dust.'

Lorna fixed him with a stare that Sandy couldn't fathom. Hatred certainly, but surprise too, he reckoned. She had no reason to know, of course, that he and Mary were an item.

'I'm sure you're right,' she said.

'I usually am.'

'I'm just off for my afternoon constitutional,' Lorna said to Mary. 'Perhaps you'll join me for a sherry later?'

'Oh. . .well. . .I need to get back to work.'

'The offer's open.' She smiled broadly at them and walked on. 'I'll see you soon,' she called behind her. 'That matter we discussed this morning.'

When she was gone, Sandy swore. 'You need to watch that woman,' he said.

'She's a teacher at the school.'

'I ken. She's a nasty piece of work. You cannae trust her.'

'How no?'

Sandy thought it best not to mention the arson, not just yet, not until Bob had got more proof. 'There's mair to her than meets the eye.'

'What?' Mary felt a surge of alarm. Again, she thought of telling Sandy about the lipstick but that felt even more difficult now. *Mair to her than meets the eye.* Mary had always been nervous around Lorna Carrington.

Now she was positively scared.

*

Bertie made them tea before their journey back and Bob took advantage to check his map of Glasgow. He and Annie had decided, the night before, to give Ellen a surprise by taking her home before they returned to Crieff. Although she seldom talked about her family, after nearly a month away on her own they felt sure she must be missing them. Finnieston was west of Pitt Street, along the north bank of the Clyde and Bob was apprehensive about driving into residential areas. He'd heard so much – particularly in recent weeks – about the deprivation and near slum-conditions of the neighbourhoods along the river and he wondered anxiously about Malky Bennett's Ford. If it wasn't safe outside a city centre police building, what might befall it in nether-Finnieston?

'Let's get goin,' he said, and he and Ellen, clutching her string bag of evidence, said farewell to Bertie Hammond and headed for the car. It was still there, wheels intact, although the supposedly on-guard children were long gone, and Bob took that as a good omen. He set off, looking for Argyle Street. Follow that west and it leads to Finnieston, he'd read.

Ellen sat beside him, watching the streets pass by with little interest. Then she spotted a giant crane by the riverside and jolted as though being prodded by a sharp stick.

'Where are we goin?' she said.

'Just a wee detour afore we go hame.'

She continued to stare out of the window with increasing agitation. They passed a blackened tenement that ran the length of a street, the river behind it. Children were playing on the roadside.

'No all you Glesga bairns have been evacuated, then,' Bob said.

'Hauf of them have gone hame again.' This was true. Over forty per cent of the children who had arrived in Crieff had already abandoned the arrangement and returned home, victims of the culture wars between city and country. Ellen turned and did a double-take once more.

'Where are we goin?' she repeated, more loudly and more slowly.

'It's a surprise.'

'No!' she screamed. She turned to him, mouth open, a mixture of fear and anger in her expression. 'No!'

'We thought, since we're here in Glesga, we could just drap by at your folks and hae a wee visit.'

'No! No! No! Turn round. Turn round. *Turn round*!'

Bob had become accustomed to Ellen's fast-shifting mood swings but this was the most intense emotion he had ever seen from her. She was red-faced and breathing heavily, agitation seething through her. She was fisting and unclenching her hands. Her legs were shifting reflexively. Bob stopped the car.

'I. . .am. . .no. . .goin. . .back. . .hame. . .' she said. 'Get me back to Grief or I'll bloody scream until the polis come and take ye away. I mean it!'

Monday, 2 October

A Day of Policemen

Bob didn't broach the subject of Ellen's refusal to go home on the return journey to Crieff because he could tell she was still agitated, but the next morning, making scones in the Cloudland kitchen, he asked her.

'How did you no want to go and see your faimly?'

'It was Sunday.'

'Aye?'

'My faither wid huv been jakied. On the booze since Friday afternoon. Aff his heid wi the drink.'

'Every weekend?'

'Aye.'

'I'm sorry.'

Even more than normal, Ellen was avoiding making eye contact and Bob reflected that, bad as it was her father should get drunk every weekend, there was probably more to her discomfort than that. 'Does he hit your mum?'

'Mair often the other way round.'

'She hits him?'

'She has a temper.'

She was biting her lip, staring at the flour she was kneading. Her scones were too large. Bob took the dough and re-kneaded it to make smaller ones.

'Ye'll overwork that dough,' Ellen said.

'I usually do.'

'I hud it just right.'

'Aye, you did. Sorry.'

'Naebody listens to me.'

'Your mum and dad – do they hit you?'

She didn't reply. She walked out of the kitchen into the café and stared out of the window at James Square. Rain had started to fall and the dusty road surface was beginning to slick. After a couple of minutes, she returned to the kitchen.

'Better get on wi my jobs,' she said. 'Or the boss-witch'll gie me pelters.' She put the resized scones on trays and set them in the oven. 'It's just how it is,' she said over her shoulder.

*

Mary's hands shook as she knocked on Lorna's door at five o'clock. She could hear Lorna moving around inside but there was no response. She knocked again, more quietly than the first time.

'Enter.'

Lorna was seated at her desk overlooking the Comrie road. A large schooner of sherry sat before her. She was staring out of the window and made no effort to greet Mary. Mary stood with her arms behind her back, feeling like a schoolgirl. Memories of Mr Black resurfaced, the dominie at Madderty school who hated her because she was stupid. Finally, Lorna looked round.

'Well?'

Mary took her hands from behind her back and reached forward. She placed a lipstick on the table beside the sherry schooner.

'Clever girl.' Lorna studied the lipstick. '*Tangee*. A good brand. Not the cheapest.' She threw it onto her bedspread and looked out of the window again. Mary waited awkwardly, uncertain what to do.

'You do realise this is as good as a written confession?'

'What d'you mean?'

'Why would anyone buy me a lipstick if they'd done nothing wrong? You have, so it proves you stole it.'

'I didnae.'

'And yet you've spent good money to buy me that. Don't you think the authorities will find that suspicious? When I tell them?'

'Please. . .'

She turned round. 'Is there any reason why I shouldn't go to the authorities?'

'I didnae do it.'

'And what difference does that make?' Mary, unable to answer, looked at the floor. 'Very well, Mary Kemp. You're mine now. Because if you ever displease me it's off to the police I go.'

'Please. . .'

'Don't whine. It's irritating.' She sipped her sherry, then waved her hand airily towards the door. 'Out.'

*

'Does nothin normal ever happen to you?'

'I'm aboot the most normal person I ken.'

'So normal that Thingwie Johnstone, the quietest moose of a man you'll ever meet, pans your heid in every time he claps eyes on you?'

'Twice.'

'Pardon my exaggeration.' Sergeant Rudd gestured to the knitted bag containing the milk bottles, Ellen's jotter, the anonymous letter and the fingerprints. 'What you're tellin me is that a primary school teacher – weel-kent, weel-respected – is an arsonist, settin fire to Malky Bennett's hayricks because she had a to-do wi Sandy Disdain? Sandy Disdain? If aabody wha had a run-in wi Sandy Disdain started torchin things the hale of Crieff would be a smoulderin ruin. It maks nae sense.'

'But we hae evidence. The writing in the anonymous letter and the markin in Ellen's hamework.'

'Ae letter. Ae single letter.'

'And her fingerprints are on the bottle found at Dallerie laundry.'

'So *you* say. You havenae actually fingerprinted the woman, have you?'

'No.'

'So the fingerprints belong to *somebody*, but you cannae say for sure that they're *hers*.'

'The same fingerprint's on Ellen's jotter. Wha else but the teacher would be touchin her jotter?'

'You?'

'Thon's no my fingerprint. Mines are on record. They dinnae match.'

'Your missus?'

'It's no Annie's.'

'I suppose her fingerprints are golden?'

'I'll go and get her if you want, and you can fingerprint her the noo.'

'I'm aa oot of ink.'

'We hae a motive. She wanted to punish Sandy. And we hae evidence of her fingerprints on ane of the bottles used to set the fires. And we ken thae bottles were previously in Lorna Carrington's possession.'

'How?'

'Ellen saw them. At school. Fu of paraffin.'

'What would a teacher be doin wi bottles of paraffin in the school?'

Bob explained about the lice and Lorna washing Alison McGillivray's hair to kill the nits. Sergeant Rudd sat forward, a pleased expression on his face. He reached into his jacket pocket for a Lucky Strike. He offered the pack to Bob but Bob declined.

'That puts a different complexion on things,' Rudd said, blowing smoke from the side of his mouth.

'I'm glad you agree.'

'I'm glad you're glad. But I dinnae agree. This Ellen, she's ane of these Glesga bairns, is she no?'

'Aye.'

'These Glesga keelies who've been on the bloody rampage since the day they got here. I'm aboot demented wi the little bastards. Vandalism, theft, bullyin, punch-ups, you name it.'

'Ellen's no like that.'

Rudd examined the end of his cigarette. 'So. This teacher, she washes the hair of ane of your lassie's chums, in front of aabody? Bloody embarrassin, that. I bet the Glesga kids didnae like it?'

'No.'

'And how long efter this was the Dallerie fire?'

'Couple of days.'

'Couple of days. So how's this for a scenario? Wee Ellen and her chum go back intae school, pinch the bottles, torch the laundry – usin a Glesga newspaper, which isnae awfae smart – then plant the evidence at the scene – the bottle wi the teacher's fingerprints on it – and concoct a daft story about the teacher haein a fall-oot wi Sandy Disdain. Then wait for you, Sherlock McHolmes, to ride in and save the day.'

'The hayrick fires happened afore Ellen even started at the school.'

'So maybe they were done by a different person.'

'Crieff just happens to hae twa arsonists at the same time?'

'The bairn's a copy-cat. Heard aboot the fires at Malky's, used that to get her teacher into bother.'

'How would she?'

'How does she get on wi her teacher generally?'

'She doesnae like her.'

'There you go, then.'

'The circumstantial evidence – it's aa mountin up. We hae the writin in the letter and the hamework. And the fingerprints. Dinnae forget them.'

'I'm no forgettin them. I'm discountin them, because there'll be somebody else's fingerprints on thae bottles.'

'Mines?'

'Aye. And somebody else's.'

Bob faltered. 'Ellen's?'

'Exactly. Her fingerprints'll be on the bottles an aa. Noo, the teacher, we ken why her fingerprints would be there, because she used them as shampoo bottles, but what reason is there that the lassie's fingerprints would be on them?'

'When we took it to Glesga for fingerprintin. She took them oot of the bag.'

'That's awfae handy. Or maybe they were already on it. From when she torched the Dallerie laundry.'

'That's ridiculous.'

'No as ridiculous as Hoity Toity Lorna Carrington bein an arsonist.'

'The bairn's only twelve.'

'She's a keelie. They breed their criminals young in Glesga. Sleekit wee bastards, the lot of them.'

'Will you speak to Lorna Carrington?'

'I will not.'

'Surely there's enough here for at least a chat wi her?'

'The person I'm maist likely to haul in for questionin is your wee Ellen.'

'Leave her alane.'

'And since when did you tell me how to do my job?'

'When you started makin a complete arse of it.'

'I'm beginnin to see what Thingwie means.'

Bob stood up, toppling his chair in the process. He picked it up and packed his evidence back into the string bag. 'You do ken I'm goin to carry on investigatin?'

'Is that meant to bother me? Thon murder in Barossa Street you were investigatin. Never solved, was it? And the deid tinker on the Monzie estate, that you insisted was ane of thae Rover Scout laddies, murdered. How did that investigation work oot for you?' Rudd stubbed out his cigarette. 'You carry on investigatin, son. I'll sleep sound, nae worries aboot you takin my job fae me.'

*

PC McAnuff was manning the counter when Bob emerged from the interview room. He gave Bob a sympathetic smile, as though familiar with how the conversation with Sergeant Rudd would have proceeded. Bob passed through the counter opening but turned as PC McAnuff closed it behind him. He leaned forward.

'I was speakin to Eddie McMurray the other day,' he said. 'He was tellin me the arsonist sent him a letter efter he tried to burn doon the laundry, warnin him he'd be back.'

PC McAnuff faltered. He blustered. Bob watched this curious performance with some surprise. It was a straightforward question, surely? 'Is that right?' he said.

'It is, aye,' McAnuff said finally.

'Only, when I was speakin to Sergeant Rudd, he telt me there wasnae a letter. Unconnected to the hayrick fires, he reckoned, on account of that.'

'There was a letter.'

'Why did Rudd no ken aboot it?'

'I dinnae ken. I telt him, I'm sure.'

The tone of that "I'm sure" made Bob certain that PC McAnuff had done no such thing. 'Could I hae a look at it?' he said.

Another awkward silence ensued. 'I dinnae ken. It's evidence in an ongoin case. . .'

Bob was baffled by PC McAnuff's apparent unwillingness to discuss the letter. He pressed again. 'I've seen the ane he sent to Sandy Disdain, so I'll be able to verify if it's by the same person.'

PC McAnuff looked deflated. 'Aye,' he said. 'Gie me a minute.'

Once PC McAnuff started searching through the cupboards

behind the counter it was immediately obvious to Bob he wasn't genuinely looking for anything. His actions were exaggerated, designed to give the impression of someone hunting for an object.

'Nae joy?' he said.

'No yet.'

'When did you last see it?'

'Couple of days.'

'And whaur do you usually put your evidence?'

'In the evidence tray.'

'So how are you looking in thae cupboards?'

Willy's head bobbed up from the cupboard he was pretending to search. 'The sergeant sometimes shifts stuff around,' he said.

'Shifts stuff he doesnae even ken aboot?'

Willy grimaced. 'I'll keep huntin,' he said. 'It's bound to turn up.'

'Aye, anonymous letters dinnae usually up and tak their leave aa by themsels.' Bob put his bunnet on and slapped the station counter. He couldn't understand why Willy McAnuff had just put on such a dreadful pretence of looking for something he knew wasn't there.

'Willy,' he said. 'I hae to get the bus to Lochearnhead so I havenae got time for this palaver. I dinnae ken whether you've lost the letter or destroyed it, and I dinnae care. But I'm tellin you this, it's easy for a good polisman to become a bad ane. And once it happens there's nae wey back. So think very carefully aboot what you're doin.'

*

Bob descended from the bus in Lochearnhead and put on his bunnet to protect his balding head from a steady drizzle. The police station was a former domestic dwelling and only the blue light outside gave any indication of its current purpose. That was the way Sergeant Braggan liked things.

'Well, well, well.'

Sergeant Braggan, standing behind the counter, gave no indication of being pleased to see him. He had put on weight, Bob fancied, and looked older than the last time he'd seen him.

'Sergeant,' he said breezily. Sergeant Braggan had been Bob's senior officer during his unhappy employment as a police constable in Perth. Neither liked the other, nor made any pretence to the contrary. For Bob, who generally looked to find the best in everyone, this was an unaccustomed position.

'I'm sure this isn't just a social visit?' said Braggan.

'Lochearnhead Hotel fire the other week.'

'You come to confess?'

'No my style.'

'Pity. I'd enjoy locking you up.'

'You think it was Glesga laddies.'

'I do.'

'Ony proof? Or is it juist your usual blind prejudice?'

'And what would I be telling you for?'

'Because I hae some information that might be useful to your investigation.'

'You never could keep your neb out of police business.'

'Well, I see this mair as community business than polis, but no, when I see somethin wrang I'm no good at turnin a blind eye.'

'Is that a dig at me?'

'Only if you think so. Thing is, these Glesga bairns are getting the blame for aathin. A lot of it probably is them, richt enough, but no aa. And this fire, I hae reason to believe it wasnae Glesga bairns.'

'That's no what the witness said.'

'What witness?'

'Woman. Came in, told me she saw something suspicious at the back of the hotel, and a group of Glasgow kids were hanging about.'

'A woman? Young, was she? Well-spoken?'

'None of your business.'

'But she was, wasn't she? I bet she didnae hang aboot long, either. In and oot, am I richt? Probably all covered up an aa. So you wouldnae be able to identify her.'

Braggan sniffed. He had found the woman's behaviour odd that night, but he wasn't prepared to admit as much. 'That isn't the only thing,' he said. 'The fire was set using pages from a Glasgow newspaper. We found it at the scene, pages of it ripped up, and there were traces in the remains of the fire.

'You're sure it was a Glesga paper?'

Braggan bent beneath the counter and pulled out the copy of the *Glasgow Evening Times*. Strips had been torn from it to help the fire catch light. Bob inspected it. There was still a strong smell of smoke.

'What date was the fire?'

'Second of September.'

'Probably the first or second or nicht the bairns had been here.'

'Didn't take them long to start their criminal behaviour.'

'This is dated the thirtieth-first of August.'

'So?'

'If they came here first or second of September, why would they be carryin a one or twa-day-auld newspaper? To be honest, I cannae imagine bairns bein interested in ony newspaper, but certainly no one that's oot-of-date. That maks nae sense.'

'And yet, there it is.'

'Did you happen to find a McLaren's Dairy milk bottle?'

Braggan faltered and Bob knew he had. 'Why?' Braggan asked.

'Because there's been twa arson attempts in Crieff, ane at a fairm and another at the Dallerie Laundry. Baith of them were started wi paraffin poured fae McLaren's bottles. Coincidence, eh? And juist like I cannae see a bunch of bairns bringin an auld newspaper wi them, I cannae see them travellin atween Lochearnhead and Crieff to set their fires. The Dallerie Laundry – man, that's so oot of the way even the ARP wardens havenae fund their way there yet. And a bunch of bairns straight oot of Glesga did? No a chance.'

'Well, if you've evidence of wrongdoing in Crieff, I suggest you take it up with Sergeant Rudd.'

'I have. I telt him what I'm tellin you, that a woman called Lorna Carrington, a primary school teacher in Crieff – and the woman who came in here to report these bairns – is the arsonist.'

'And was Sergeant Rudd interested?'

'About as interested as you.'

'That must be right vexing.'

'It is.'

'Good.'

*

Lorna's door opened as Mary was heading downstairs to make supper and Lorna gestured to her to enter.

'I can always tell when it's you passing,' she said. 'You sound like an elephant on the rampage. I was in Scrimgeour's on Saturday. You know they've started selling gramophone records?' She gestured to her new gramophone player in the corner of the room. 'I'm trying to build up my collection but they're rather expensive. On a teacher's salary.'

'I'm sure they are, miss.'

'They've got Glenn Miller's *Little Brown Jug*. I love that tune.'

'Me too.'

'It costs 2/6.'

'My, that *is* dear.'

'It is. That's why you're going to be a sweetheart and buy it for me. I'll give you until Friday, to give you time to get the money together. Don't say I'm not fair.' She swung her door open and leaned against the frame.

'One more thing,' she said. 'Your boyfriend. . .'
'Sandy?'
'Sandy. I don't like him. He's a bad influence on you. You're not to speak to him again.'
'But. . .'
'That will be all. Close the door on the way out.'

Friday, 6 October

A Day of Punishment

When Sandy got home from snaring the Colony fields there was a postcard waiting for him. He felt a momentary stab of trepidation until he reflected that call-up papers wouldn't come in the form of a postcard. He picked it up and turned it over.

ARP WARDENS
CRIEFF REPORT CENTRE
James Square, Crieff
APPEAL FOR VOLUNTARY ASSISTANCE
Difficulty is experienced in filling the Daily Roster.
If you are willing to assist, please call at above address
and fill in Your Name, selecting a shift to suit your
convenience.

In blue pencil beneath the typed note was written: "WHAT ARE YOU DOING? WHY ARE YOU NOT FIGHTING?"

Sandy put the card in his jacket pocket and went into the kitchen, where his mother and sisters were already eating.

*

Mary waited until Friday before going to Scrimgeour's. Even the act of buying the gramophone record seemed troublesome, as though this were somehow illegal or wrong, as though the assistant would know she was acting under duress. 1939 had been a difficult year for her family, her mother's appendicitis costing them a considerable amount with Doctor McNeill, and she had only managed to save £2 so far in her Christmas tin. She was reconciling herself to the knowledge that most of that would surely now evaporate to satisfy Lorna Carrington. She couldn't understand how she had reached this position, nor could she see any way out, other than Lorna going to the police. She didn't believe there was enough evidence against her for theft – how could there be? – but even so the resultant fuss would almost certainly see her dismissed. And Crieff was a small town. News would travel. She would be unemployable. All week she had given serious thought to flitting to Perth. The idea terrified her. Perth was so big. She would be lost there. But, right now, perhaps being lost was her best option.

When she finally approached the gramophone record desk the assistant, a young woman with a perfectly tight perm and bright red lipstick, smiled at her.

'Could I have a copy of Glenn Miller's *Little Brown Jug*,' Mary said, returning the smile.

'I'm sorry. I sold the last copy this morning.'

Mary felt a stab of panic. 'Are you sure? Could you check?'

'I'm quite sure. Mr Sartorius, the schoolteacher, bought it. We'll be getting more copies in next week. And we have some others by Glenn Miller, if you'd like to look?'

Mary shook her head and turned away, feeling herself tear up. She ran onto Comrie Street and pondered what to do but her heart was racing and she couldn't concentrate. *Think, stupid girl*, she chastised herself. She would have to confess to Lorna and trust that Lorna would be willing to wait until new supplies came into stock. Even as she made her plan, Mary felt sure it was doomed to failure.

'I'm so sorry,' she said to Lorna half an hour later. 'I'll go in every day next week and check if they have new copies.'

Lorna's expression was cold. She waited for some moments

before speaking. 'Sold out today, you say?' Mary nodded. 'So if you'd gone earlier in the week, you'd have got a copy?'

'I suppose so.'

'That means this is the result of your carelessness.'

'I'm sorry.'

'Sorry isn't good enough. You will indeed go and check every day next week and get me my record as instructed. What's more, you will go back today and get me a copy of *Sunrise Serenade* instead. I don't like it as much as *Little Brown Jug* but in view of your fecklessness it will have to do. Have I made myself understood?'

'Yes, miss.'

She continued to stare at Mary, then shook her head. 'That's not enough. You need to be punished.'

'I'm sorry. . .'

She opened her satchel and pulled out her leather tawse. 'I warned you not to cross me. Hold out your hand. . .'

'No. . .'

'Hold out your hand! Every time you refuse I'll add another stroke. Do it!'

Mary looked blankly. She couldn't possibly be given the strap. She was a grown woman, not some little bairn in school. Mary had never had the strap in her life, never caused a moment's trouble throughout her school career. This was unthinkable.

'One more added.'

She started to cry as she held her arm out. Her hand shook. Lorna stepped back and raised the tawse and kept her arm aloft for a good three or four seconds before she brought it down with a resounding crack on Mary's hand. Mary screamed.

'Quiet. Do you want the whole house to know you're being punished like a naughty little girl?' She raised her arm again and once more, after a manufactured pause, brought the tawse down on Mary's hand. A red weal had already formed across the palm. 'One more,' she instructed. She strapped Mary's hand a final time, this time even harder, and Mary lowered her hand. Tears were streaming down her cheek.

'Now the other hand.'

'I thought you said one more.'

'On that hand. Raise your other hand.'

Slowly, Mary stretched out her left hand and Lorna strapped her three times. By the time she had finished, Mary's pain was excruciating, her palms hot as though they were on fire, and red, already starting to bruise. She felt she would have to steep them in a bucket of cold water. She felt like she would never be the same again.

'Now, get back to Scrimgeour's and buy me my record. Come back without it and you'll get the same thing again. Out of my sight.'

*

Early evening, a draughts game was in full swing on the giant board built into the ground at the Murray Fountain. Sunny Petrie was using a large metal hook to move one of his pieces towards those of Daft Tam. Sandy smoked his Capstan as Sunny Petrie cheated twice in succession without Daft Tam – cross-eyed and short-sighted – noticing.

'Your lassie stood you up, Sandy?' said Daft Tam.

Sandy glanced at the town hall clock. He inhaled heavily. 'Looks like it,' he said. Mary was usually first to arrive, five minutes early for everything as a matter of routine. This was the second time this week she hadn't made their usual rendezvous. He wondered when he ought to start worrying.

'Women,' said Daft Tam. 'Mair bother than they're worth.'

Sandy was certain Daft Tam had never entertained a woman in his life but he played along. 'As long as they get your tea on the table.'

'Aye, that's ae thing they're good for.'

Men were toing and froing from the ARP Wardens' office. Sandy waited five more minutes and then, marvelling at how

Sunny Petrie could cheat against Daft Tam and still lose, he waved the men goodbye and sauntered downhill.

An extra door had been fitted directly behind the front door of the ARP Wardens' offices, allowing entrants to close the front door before opening the inner door to prevent light from escaping. Fat men need not apply for ARP duty, it seemed. Sandy negotiated the tight space and entered the first office. Half a dozen men, preparing to go out on their evening rounds, were grouped around the table in the middle of the room. Among them was Bob, chatting to Ronnie Francis. Sandy recognised Gordon Eadie standing beside the large map and he pulled the postcard from his pocket.

'Did you send me this?' he said. Eadie took the postcard and studied it curiously, turning it over a couple of times before returning it to Sandy.

'That's one of our postcards, right enough,' he said. 'We have a batch of them typed up for us by Mrs Liversedge at the Public School. We send them out to people we think might volunteer. We're always short of men. But that. . .' He gestured to the handwritten text at the bottom of the card:

"WHAT ARE YOU DOING? WHY ARE YOU NOT FIGHTING?"

'We'd never write anything like that,' Eadie said. 'We're looking to encourage people, not aggravate them.'

'That's what I thocht,' said Sandy. Bob approached and Sandy showed him the card.

'That handwritin. . .' Bob said.

'Aye,' said Sandy. 'Looks suspiciously like our anonymous friend.'

'Have you been rilin her again?'

'Me?'

*

Mary sat on her bed in the narrow bedroom she shared with Bessie Molloy. She was convinced, hours later, she could still feel the pain from her strapping. Along the raised part of her left palm the skin was still reddened and tender. Mary had spent the whole evening thinking about her punishment and, in the end, she realised the humiliation of being disciplined like a child was far, far worse than the pain of the strapping itself. She felt as though what had happened to her must somehow be evident to everyone who saw her, from her expression, her posture, the way she spoke. When she had faced Miss Carrington again, to give her the gramophone record, she felt utterly mortified. There was a deviant intimacy to what happened, an exposure that left her feeling naked. She could see no end to this torment. She would have to resign from Barvick Falls, move to Perth. She stared bleakly at the floor and began to cry. What she wanted was for Sandy to hold her, tell her things would be grand, tell her to stop being daft. And now she'd lost him, too, banned from meeting him by Miss Carrington. Sobs began to rack her body and she had to fight to catch a breath.

*

Bob put aside his library book, *The Case for Federal Union*, when the BBC Light Orchestra came on the wireless and he, Sandy and Annie sat with a cup of tea listening to their performance. It was jolly stuff, but Bob sensed that Sandy was on edge, shifting in his seat as though he wanted to say something. Coyness was not something Bob usually associated with Sandy Disdain.

'What's up wi you?' he said.

Sandy blew smoke down his nose. 'I'm. . .It's Mary. I havenae seen her aa week. We've taken to meetin Mondays and Fridays when she finishes, but she hasnae shown this week. Nae message, nothin.'

'Have you gone to her hoose?'

'Her faither cannae thole me.'

'Well, you did leave him lyin in a ditch ae time.'

'He deserved it.'

'Aye, Pat the postie's no an easy man to warm to. So what do you want me to do?'

'Go and see her. Find oot what I've done wrang.'

'You think you've done somethin?'

'I usually have.'

Sandy finished his tea and Bob saw him out, clapping his shoulder and telling him things would work out. Bob returned upstairs and picked up his library book. He'd extended the loan twice and it was due back tomorrow so he wanted to finish it. The remedy for war, the book argued, was effective world government. Bob reflected on governments, their own in Britain and those abroad. Weakness all around. He picked up a pen and started to compose a letter to *The Strathearn Herald*.

*

The telegram from Reverend Duncan arrived late in the evening and Lorna knew what it was before she read it. MESSAGE RECEIVED FROM YOUR MOTHER. YOUR FATHER DIED 4 PM. FUNERAL MONDAY. MOTHER SAYS "PLEASE COME. MUM."

She held the telegram over her ashtray and flicked her lighter alight and watched the paper burn. When the words had disappeared she crushed the remains with her fingers, powdering them into ash. She closed her eyes.

'What did you say, Daddy? "And everyone who lives and believes in me shall never die. Do you believe this?"' She opened her eyes again and smiled.

'Sorry, Daddy, no I don't. You've gone. You really are dead. For ever and ever, amen. Your precious God's got something right at last.'

Monday, 9 October

A Day of Internment

Mary's hours were from six in the morning until eleven, and then from three in the afternoon until seven. Bob knew she was in the habit of returning home mid-morning for dinner with her mother.

Just after eleven, he was playing draughts on the giant board at the Murray Fountain when he saw her approaching Harley & Watts. Abandoning the game, much to the annoyance of Sunny Petrie, he crossed the High Street and intercepted her as though this were a chance encounter. Her expression was pinched and her eyes red-rimmed, and he knew immediately something was wrong.

'Mary, how are you?'

She gave a curt nod and bustled on. Bob watched for a moment, then chased after, catching her outside the Drummond Arms. He took her arm and she stopped, looking fixedly at the pavement.

'Come on,' he said, leading her to the edge of the road. 'I need a wee chat.' He took a firm grip of her elbow and led her across the High Street and down the Square to Cloudland. He closed and locked the door behind them.

'Could you gie us ten minutes?' he said to Leslie Comer. 'Go upstairs and hae a cuppie wi Annie. See if you can gie her some tips on how to manage a wild bairn.'

He poured two cups of tea and placed them on the table by the window and gestured to Mary to sit. Hesitantly, she did, smoothing her coat over her thighs.

'What ails you?' he said. He waited, watching her shifting expression, the way she opened her mouth to speak, only to close it again, the experience too difficult, too fraught to articulate. 'Sandy's worried,' he went on. 'He's aside himsel, tell the truth. You havenae seen him aa week, havenae been in touch. He doesnae ken what he's done wrang...'

'He hasnae done onythin wrang.'

'No?' There was a pause. Bob took a sip of his tea. 'What is it, then? You twa were doin grand. I was thinkin I'd need to get my good suit pressed for a weddin...'

'Oh, I dinnae think it'll come to that.'

'"Come to that"? You mak it sound like merryin Sandy would be a trial.' He reflected for a moment. 'Mind you...'

She smiled and he patted her hand.

'So, what's goin on? How can I help?'

'You cannae.'

'I probably can. Folk think I'm useless and in maist weys I am, but ae thing I can do is fix other folks' problems.'

'No this ane.'

'So there is a problem?' Again, he waited. He sensed that she wanted to open up but something – shyness, embarrassment – was preventing her. 'You havenae been in touch wi Sandy. Is that your choice?'

'No,' she said quietly.

'So what's stoppin you?'

'I just cannae...'

'You're no...pregnant?'

'Certainly no. We've never...No.'

'So what is it?' He tried to imagine what might have happened to make Mary refuse to meet Sandy when she evidently wanted to. Then a thought occurred to him. 'Or wha is it?' he said. The look of alarm in her startled eyes confirmed he was right. 'Wha?' he repeated.

'Miss Carrington.'

'Ellen's teacher?' Bob cursed himself for not working this out by himself. As soon as Mary mentioned her name it seemed obvious. Who had a spat with Sandy? Who was so angry with him she set fire to Malky's hayricks? Who sent him a letter, ostensibly from the ARP? And who lodged at Mary's workplace? Bob had assumed the problem lay with Mary but no, it was with Sandy.

And with Lorna Carrington.

'What's she said?'

Mary tried to pick up her tea but her hands were shaking and she abandoned the attempt. 'She telt me no to see him again.'

Bob screwed his eyes in confusion. Mary was a timid soul, certainly, but why would she accept something so outrageous? 'Well,' he said, 'I can see why she would say that, since she cannae stand Sandy, but I dinnae understand why you would listen to her.'

'She'll get me the sack.'

'How?'

'She just will.'

Bob knew that if Lorna was really the arsonist she would not be above issuing threats but, even so, why would Mary be so cowed she would accede? There had to be more.

'Is there somethin in particular she's threatenin to get you sacked ower?'

'Aye,' she whispered.

'What? Ye ken me, no a word of this'll pass my lips.'

'She accused me of stealin her lipstick.'

'Which you didnae?'

'No.'

'So?'

'She telt me to buy a replacement and if I did she'd say nae mair. And I thocht, if it stops aa this fuss. . .'

'So you did?'

'Aye.'

'And then she said that was as good as a confession?'

'Exactly.'

'Onythin else?'

Mary's face crumpled. 'She's made me buy her a gramophone record. And I've to get another next week when it comes into stock. *Little Brown Jug*.'

'Hell, lassie, you cannae afford to go on doin that.'

'I ken.'

'Listen, this is juist the start. She'll no stop. She's got her claws into you. You need to stand up to her. . .'

'I cannae.'

'There'll be mair and mair. . .'

'Fine.'

He could see she had closed her mind to reason, could not get beyond her immediate predicament. And, again, he felt there must be a reason for that. 'Are you scared of her?' he asked. She stared at the table. He took her hand again. 'Mary, has she hurt you?'

Her eyes started to brim. She wiped her hand across them and gave the merest nod of her head. Bob leaned forward and hugged her.

'That changes aathin.'

*

The funeral was already underway when Lorna stole in at the rear of St Andrews Free Church. An usher tried to direct her to a pew but she waved him away with irritation and stood by the doorway. As befitted a man of the cloth, the congregation for the funeral of David Porteous Carrington was large. There was no coffin, such objects raising the risk of idolatry among the mourners. Reverend Peter Rogers, from Crail, led the proceedings and Carrington himself was strangely absent from the content of a sermon which focused more on the mourners than the deceased. After a brief, almost truculent, encomium Reverend Rogers devoted the majority of his comments to an admonition of the living.

'"For man also knoweth not his time",' he preached. '"As the fishes that are taken in an evil net, and as the birds that are caught in the snare; so are the sons of men snared in an evil time, when it falleth suddenly upon them."' Reverend Rogers looked around at the bowed heads. He spotted Lorna at the back and Lorna, fearing she might be exposed, turned to leave. 'Death,' he continued, 'awaits us all. We learn from Hebrews: "And as it is appointed unto men once to die, but after this the judgment."'

Lorna retreated from the church and made her way the mile or so to the cemetery for the interment. *Judgement*. What was this judgement in her father's religion? His God, in his eternal and immutable counsel, was the one who determined who would be admitted to salvation and those whom it was his pleasure to doom to destruction. What judgement was that? Where was the human worth in that? The animals trapped in their snares were blameless, judged worthy only of death. But the humans, trapped in their existence, were judged unworthy of salvation. What difference was there? What difference?

*

'What are you doin here?' Ellen was playing poachie in the school playground after school as Bob walked towards the entrance. She kicked the lump of stone and scowled at him.

'I've come to see your teacher.'

'Whit fur?' Ellen's voice raised in volume and pitch and she hurried after Bob and tugged his sleeve.

'Nothin to do wi you, dinnae worry.'

'Good. Ye're wastin yer time anyway. She's no here. She's sick.'

'What's wrang wi her?'

'Somehin deadly, I hope. We got Mrs Paterson instead.'

'How was she?'

'Best day's school ah ever hud.'

*

Mary gave a forced smile as she approached the Murray Fountain after work and spotted Sandy lolling on the benches.

'Hello,' she said.

'You made it.'

'Aye.'

Sandy rose. 'A wee daunder?' he said.

'How no?'

He started to walk down King Street and Mary followed. Bob was standing in the doorway of a darkened Cloudland and he gave them a wave. Mary returned the wave.

'Good to hae you back,' said Sandy.

'Aye.'

'You'll maybe tell me what was wrong.'

'It was nothin to do wi you.'

He knew he should pursue the matter, talk to her, understand what had caused her so much consternation. But, in truth, he couldn't be bothered. 'Maks a change,' he said, 'me no gettin somethin wrang.'

Just carry on, Mary thought. *You're doin just grand. Carry on.*

*

Lorna watched the interment from across the road, hidden behind the low-hanging branches of a willow tree. There they all were, gathered round the graveside. The lowered heads, the wafted handkerchiefs, ramrod postures. Reverend Rogers clutching his Bible. All of them united in hypocrisy, surrounding that hole in the ground, six feet long, six feet deep, to be filled for eternity with the detritus of a life lived at once in public and in secret, in honour and in shame, in good and in malignity. She watched the ceremony to its end and she saw the mourners depart. Her mother and brother, pale-faced, stoic. Reverend Rogers, affecting to care for a man he had met no more than a handful of times. Parishioners, acquaintances, neighbours, associates. Anyone but friends. Silence settled on the cemetery. In time, gravediggers arrived and they did the world the service of removing from its view the last vestige of David Porteous Carrington. Spadeful by spadeful his presence on this earth was erased.

At half past eight on the evening of the ninth of October 1939, Lorna Carrington walked across the road and into the cemetery and stood at the graveside of her father. She recalled the words Reverend Rogers had used earlier, from *Ecclesiastes*: "For man also knoweth not his time". Lorna, practiced in family worship, morning and evening every day of her childhood and adolescence, knew the verse, and she also knew what came before it: "For the living know that they shall die: but the dead know not any thing, neither have they any more a reward; for the memory of them is forgotten."

Lorna stepped onto the recently flattened grave. She *would* forget him. Her memory of him *would* be lost. And, through this, she would gain her revenge. Throughout her life, music and dance had been forbidden, Christmas and Easter banned. All her years she had been condemned because of her sex to a second-rate existence, a drudge worthy of nothing but the honour of breeding a new generation of passionless freaks. All those beatings. All those humiliations. Disappointment. Fear.

Failure.

No.

She raised her hands in the air and in the dark chill of evening she danced, she danced, she danced on her father's grave.

Tuesday, 10 October

A Day of Accusations

Bob entered Lorna Carrington's classroom at eight-thirty, before her first class of the day were called in from the playground. Lorna was applying lipstick, peering into a small compact mirror at her desk.

'Want to be careful no to mislay that,' he said.

Lorna looked up at him and pasted on a smile. 'I didn't see you there,' she said as she slid the lipstick into her handbag. 'Can I help?'

'I'm Bob Kelty. Ellen's guardian.'

'Ah yes, I met your wife.'

'Did you?'

'Charming lady. We had a lovely chat. I'm surprised she didn't mention it.'

Not as surprised as me, thought Bob. The woman opposite him seemed – normal. He had created this image of the anonymous arsonist as a brute and a thug, and the demure, attractive woman smiling at him was decidedly not that.

And yet.

'I brocht you a present,' he said. He placed a copy of *Little Brown Jug* on her desk. Immediately, he felt foolish. *What if this was a mistake? Could a schoolteacher really be an arsonist?*

She picked up the record, her smile overtaken by a momentary frown. And then the smile returned.

'Why?' she said.

Bob felt his resolve beginning to evaporate. Could he be right? Could this elegant woman be a criminal? It seemed ridiculous. What he was about to say seemed ridiculous. A fear of humiliation began to take hold. She was watching him, smiling, but it was a smile that seemed to begin and end with the curve of her mouth, and with a flash of clarity Bob realised that it was growing less sincere with every passing moment. He heard himself speak.

'That's what you were bullyin Mary Kemp into buyin for you.'

'I beg your pardon?'

'Well, you winnae need to now, so you can leave her alane.' He gestured towards her handbag. 'And buy your ain lipstick in future.'

'I'm sure I don't understand. . .'

Bob needed to shut this down, before she managed to infest his mind with doubts. Mary had told him, explained what had happened. He trusted Mary implicitly, which meant that, whatever appearances suggested, Lorna Carrington was a bully and a scoundrel.

At the very least.

'And there's one other thing I wanted to speak to you about.'

She gave a nervous laugh and this time it was as though Bob could see the joins in her act.

'Sandy Disdain,' he went on. 'Mary's click. They mak a braw couple. I think you ken Sandy?'

'Hardly. I don't move in such circles.'

'If you dinnae ken him, how would you ken what circles he moves in?'

'Circles that maids like Mary Kemp move in.'

'The mask slips, Miss Carrington. Well, if you dinnae ken him, why did you tell Mary no to see him again?'

That laugh again, tinkling, too high pitched, strained in its attempt at effortlessness. The smile. The eyes that didn't smile. The anger beneath.

'Why would I possibly say that?'

'To mak her do your biddin.'

'Do I look the bullyin sort?'

'Maybe you dinnae. But you would, though. If you werenae gettin your own wey. Aye?'

She snatched her handbag and thrust it into her desk drawer. All pretence of bonhomie had disappeared. The intensity of her stare almost caused a physical reaction in Bob.

'People generally learn to cross me only once,' she said. She looked away, at the blackout curtains, and Bob knew immediately she regretted saying that. A momentary lapse. A loss of control.

'Sandy crossed you mair than the once, did he?'

'Do you know, you're almost as boring as little maid Mary? Her with her life of constant failure and embarrassment. The worst thing in the world is to be humiliated but Mary Kemp makes it a vocation.'

'Mary's a lovely lassie who's bein bullied because she's too nice to say no. . .'

'Nice wins nothing. . .'

'And neither does nasty, no in the long run. The thing is, whether Sandy and Mary get thegither, that's no your decision.'

'Are you leaving?'

'I've said my piece, aye.' Bob turned and walked out of the classroom, terrified and elated.

*

Ellen and Marnie exited the Market Park on the Broich Road and walked towards King Street. Opposite a row of small cottages, on a triangle of green land, sitting on a wooden bench, were the Misses Seaton, Beaton and Miller. Ellen and Marnie approached them warily.

'You lassies,' called Miss Miller, 'why are you no in school?'

'I ken you,' shouted Miss Beaton. 'You're Bampot Bennett's bairnie.'

'And you're ane of thae Glesga keelies,' said Miss Seaton, pointing an arthritic finger at Ellen. 'We'll tell Dandy MacLean on you. You should be in the school.'

Ellen and Marnie instinctively knew there was no point explaining to them that they didn't have to attend school until afternoon. They turned and fled in the direction of Braidhaugh.

'This wey,' said Marnie, turning right off King Street. They ran until they were out of sight of the three crones and stopped, resting their hands on their knees and panting. They looked at one another and laughed.

'This place is called Gallows Hill,' Marnie said. 'It's where they used to hang people.' Ellen recognised the building where she had undergone her physical examination that first day and shivered. Marnie misinterpreted her action. 'They dinnae do it now,' she said.

'Pity.'

'We cannae go back that way because of thae witches,' said Ellen. 'What's doon there?' She pointed to the path bounding the cemetery. They could hear, in the distance, the sound of the river Earn.

'Dallerie,' said Marnie.

'Where there was the fire?'

'Aye. Like faither's.'

'Come oan. I need to see.'

They walked by the edge of the cemetery. Some of the land below them was freshly ploughed as part of the war effort, but most of the expanse was flower meadow, now scruffy as winter set in and most plants started dying back. They walked on until they reached Dallerie.

'Whit's that smell?' Ellen said, screwing up her nose.

'Bleach. That's the laundry ower there.'

'Christ, I wouldnae want ma clothes smellin of that. That's mingin.'

'It washes aff.'

'Why pit it on in the first place, then?'

'Kill the germs.'

Both girls immediately thought of lice and hair washing. They fell silent as they walked round the side of the building. Ellen peered into each window in turn, but there was nothing interesting to see. One pane was boarded and inside there appeared to be fire damage.

'What would you torch a place like this for?' said Ellen.

'Hey you!' Gibby Owen yelled and limped towards them, cursing all the while. 'Little bastards! Back for mair of your mischief.'

'Run,' said Ellen and they hared away from Gibby following, although they didn't know it, the route that Lorna Carrington had taken during her escape from the same man weeks earlier. They came to the same incline and the same impediment, the lade. Unlike Lorna, they spotted it and didn't fall in. Instead, they realised they were trapped. They turned. Advancing towards them, still cursing, was Gibby Owen.

*

'Gibby, this is a piece of nonsense and you ken it.' Bob gesticulated with frustration.

'Caught them red-handed.'

'Doin what? Keekin through windaes? Since when was that a crime?'

'It juist happens to be the very windae they broke last time when they tried to set the place on fire.'

'If they were settin the place on fire they'd need somethin to do it wi. Matches. Paraffin. Look at them. They havenae a match on them. He patted their pockets to demonstrate.

'They could hae thrown them awa when they ran aff.'

'Right, let's retrace their steps. See if we can find onythin. Whaur did they go?'

Gibby gestured towards the rear and he and Bob, followed

by Ellen and Marnie. Ellen looked close to ignition point and Bob pondered what he could do to pacify her later. They made their way to the point at the lade where the girls were caught. On the way, they found nothing.

'See?'

'They were up to somethin. These Glesga bairns are nothin but trouble.'

'I'm no a Glesga bairn,' said Marnie.

'No, she's a teuchter,' said Ellen.

'Wha are you?' said Gibby, peering at her.

'She's Malky Bennett's youngest,' said Bob.

'Why did you no say? Say hello to your faither for me, hen. He hasnae been to the boolin for a few weeks.' Gibby turned and walked away. Ellen stared at Bob furiously.

'Can we go noo?' she said. 'I'll be late for school.'

'In a minute. I juist need to do somethin while I'm here.' They walked back to Dallerie and Bob stopped outside the old millowner's house. He walked round to the front door and knocked loudly. A maid arrived and he explained his business. A couple of minutes later Tommy Crabb appeared, old and grizzled, hair unkempt, cardigan full of holes, trouser hems halfway up his shins. He smelled of body odour and alcohol.

'Did the ARP no come and see you?' Bob said. 'Aboot the blackoot?'

'Aye. Pain in the arses.'

Bob gestured to the large windows facing them, none of them blacked out. 'So how come you havenae got any blackoot curtains up?'

'Have you seen how mony windaes I've got? I cannae afford it.'

'If you dinnae, the court'll mak you and you'll hae to pay a £2 fine on tap.'

'They wouldnae dare.'

'Did it to Bert Sharples yesterday.'

'£2 fine?'

'£2 fine. And that was only the ae windae.'

'Bastards.'

'I'll get Jack McOmish to come round, measure you up.'

'Ah man, I cannae cover they windaes. I'll miss aa the excitement.'

'What excitement?'

'Ootside.'

Bob looked around them. Fields and the laundry and the cemetery and the river. 'There cannae be hellish much excitement here, man.'

Tommy knew there was plenty excitement after dark. That woman the other week, for example, running away from Gibby Owen and falling in the lade and just sitting there for a full five minutes like a daft puddock. 'I could tell you a thing or two,' he said.

*

That evening, Ellen thought the best bit about going to see *The Thirty Nine Steps* at the Ritz was when Sandy was told off by an ARP Warden for smoking in the queue to get in. 'Bloody good eyesight, these German bombers,' Sandy had said, 'if they can see one wee fag underneath all that cloud.' The film itself had been boring, just old people running about and talking to each other in posh voices.

'I thocht it was braw,' said Annie later. 'Thank heavens they've allowed the picter hooses to open up again.' The government, realising an imminent threat of disorder if people were prevented from enjoying any entertainment, had greatly relaxed the initial ban on public events, and cinemas were now allowed to show films once more. Annie and Bob, Mary and Sandy and Ellen were drinking tea in the flat above Cloudland after the performance. The presence of two extra bodies seemed to make the room darker than ever, or perhaps that was Annie's perception because she wanted to be the perfect hostess.

'Certainly kept you guessin,' said Bob.

'I could hardly breathe at times,' said Mary.

'Mind you,' said Sandy, 'thae Scottish accents. . .'

'Aye, I ken,' laughed Bob. 'Eh'm from Gleeesgooow.'

'They never get Scottish accents richt in the picters.'

'Och. Hoots mon. It's a braw, brrricht moonlicht nicht the nicht.'

'And there was ae bit that was daft,' said Annie. 'When Hannay was in thon croft in the middle of naewhere, and they had that day's national newspaper. . .'

'Aye,' Bob agreed. 'Oot there, they'd probably hae to get that posted. It'd be a day auld.'

'At least a day,' said Mary. 'Miss Glass, in Barvick Falls, she has the *Glasgow Evening Times* delivered every day by post. Sometimes it taks twa days and she gets twa copies at the same time. Especially noo they've reduced the number of deliveries for the war.'

Bob placed his mug on the table with such force a wave of tea slopped out of it. He leapt up and wiped it with his handkerchief.

'*Glasgow Evening Times*?' he said. He turned to Sandy excitedly. 'The paper we fund at Malky's hayricks, have you still got it?'

'I've been using it to light the fire.'

'Aa of it?' Bob tried to keep the outrage from his voice but his words came out shrilly all the same.

'There micht be a page or twa left.'

'Man, you need to find them. Check the dates for me.'

'How?'

'Juist do it.'

Wednesday, 11 October

A Day of Interviewing

Bob stood at the counter of the police station and watched PC McAnuff searching through the disarray behind him. Bob wondered whether, as he had with the Dallerie letter, Willy would obfuscate and pretend not to be able to find what he was looking for but, with a cry of triumph, the young bobby snatched up a newspaper and took it to the counter. The *Glasgow Evening Times*.

'This is the one you fund doon at Dallerie?' Bob said.

'Aye,' confirmed Willy.

Bob checked for the date. Thursday, 14 September. 'What was the date of the Dallerie fire?' he asked.

Willy checked his notebook. 'Sunday nicht, Monday morning.'

'Sunday seventeenth, Monday eighteenth. Why no use the Friday or Saturday edition?'

'Maybe they were still readin them,' said Willy.

'Aye, I suppose they micht be slow readers, bein bairns,' said Bob. He could tell Willy didn't spot the facetiousness in his delivery. 'The fire that was started at Malky's fairm,' he said. 'It was started wi a *Glesga Evenin Times* an aa. That fire was on the fifth of September. Guess what date the paper was?'

'The fourth?'

'You'd think so wouldn't you?' Bob shook his head triumphantly. Sandy had sent word through Marnie Bennett that morning of the date on the paper. 'Saturday the second,' he said. Willy looked blank. 'An auld newspaper.'

'I suppose so.'

'Aye. Can I use your telephone?'

'I dinnae ken...'

'I'm phonin the Lochearnhead polis. It's official.'

'Okay,' said Willy reluctantly. 'But if the sergeant comes back...'

'I'll put it doon.'

Bob hated telephones, couldn't reconcile the fact he couldn't see the other person's face, judge their responses, assess their emotions. He snatched the receiver from Willy and asked to be put through to Lochearnhead Police Station.

'Police,' came a bored voice on the other end.

'Sergeant Braggan, it's Bob Kelty...'

'You must be psychic. Much against my better judgement, I was just about to call you.'

'You were?'

'This woman you say torched the hotel barn...'

'Lorna Carrington.'

'Well, I've had a sighting. Pops Barton, poacher from St Fillans way, he was chatting to me last night in the pub and told me he saw a woman the night of the fire, acting peculiar.'

'That'll be her,' Bob said. 'And did you tell me the fire had been started wi a copy of the *Glesga Evenin Times*?'

'Yes.'

'But from three days afore ony Glaswegians arrived in toon?'

'Apparently.'

'There's somebody wha stays in Barvick Falls, whaur Lorna Carrington lives, has the *Glesga Evenin Times* posted to her every day. So it's ay ane or twa days late.'

'So this Carrington woman could have picked up a copy...'

237

'Used it to try to implicate the Glesga bairns.'

'Except the dates don't work.'

'Exactly! Three days too early.' Bob felt a surge of excitement. Sergeant Braggan believed him. 'And I've juist checked. It was the same thing for Malky Bennett's hayricks and for the fire at Dallerie Laundry. Aa *Glesga Evenin Times*. Baith twa or three days oot of date. And we now ken how Lorna Carrington got hold of them.' He gave Braggan Lorna's address. 'Will you speak to her?'

'Not me. I don't have enough petrol ration to come gallivanting to Crieff. I'll get Sergeant Rudd to do it. He can ask about your Crieff fires at the same time.'

Bob wasn't sure how receptive Sergeant Rudd would be, but with Sergeant Braggan arguing his case he felt more hopeful. 'Sergeant. . .Thank you. I mean it.'

'Right.'

*

'Miss Carrington, I was sorry to hear about your father.'

Lorna was at the breakfast table spreading butter on toast when Mr Henderson arrived for his breakfast, copy of *The Courier* under his arm and his nurse trotting behind him. He smiled at Lorna, one of those simpering smiles that people used when they wanted to ingratiate themselves. Lorna recoiled from this expression of intimacy.

'I beg your pardon?' she said.

'Your father. Reverend Carrington. Miss Salter was in St Andrews on family business yesterday and she saw the announcement in the local paper. Miss Salter and I offer our sincere condolence.'

'You're mistaken.' She glowered at Miss Salter. 'My father is alive and well and living in Mintlaw.'

'But. . .'

Lorna rose, leaving her toast uneaten and tea undrunk. 'Good morning, Mr Henderson. If you'll excuse me I'm very busy.'

She went to the kitchen in search of Mary and, when she didn't find her, tried the laundry room. Mary was piling sheets into a bag for the Dallerie Laundry to collect, and she gave a start when she saw Lorna.

'You've been speaking about our arrangements,' Lorna said. 'To Mr Kelty. That's very naughty of you.'

'I was scared, miss.'

'Scared? Of what? Not me, surely?'

'I cannae afford to keep buyin you things, miss. I'm sorry.'

Lorna flashed a momentary smile. 'Of course not. I forget you're just a housemaid. That's remiss of me. I've been asking to much of you.'

'Thank you, miss, for understandin.'

'Think nothing of it. I'll wait a little while longer before asking you again. A few weeks, perhaps. How does that sound?'

Mary felt a wash of failure sweep through her. She'd hoped the situation was resolved. Now, it seemed, it was only delayed.

'Thank you, miss.'

'As for that man of yours, he's a nasty piece of work. I was simply trying to protect you. I have your interests at heart. You ought to listen to me.'

Nasty piece of work. That was exactly how Sandy had described Lorna. Mary turned away in confusion.

*

Most of the children, including Ellen and Marnie, were still milling around the playground when Sergeant Rudd marched up the path into the school. Ellen followed him and scurried to the foot of the stairs to watch his progress. He turned right and without knocking entered the Miss Carrington's classroom. Ellen ran back outside and told Marnie.

'D'ye think he's goin to arrest her?' she said.

'What for?'

On Bob's instruction, Ellen had never mentioned to Marnie their suspicions about Miss Carrington being the arsonist. At times like this, though, she had the strongest urge to reveal all. And then she remembered Marnie's sister, blabbing about her eczema.

'For bein a witch. No, worse than a witch. Witches are nice. She's a bitch. A cow and a bitch.'

'It'll be the Jardine twins he's efter. They were up the allotments the other nicht, lightin a fire on my uncle Pally's patch.'

'Ye don't know that was the Jardines.'

'Faither says it was.'

Privately, Ellen conceded it probably was, but she was irritated by the casual way Glasgow children were still being blamed for everything.

'Last one to McKenzie's buys the penny chews,' she said and sprinted along Commissioner Street.

*

Bob and Annie sat at one of the tables in an otherwise empty Cloudland. Bob turned to the inside pages of *The Strathearn Herald*. There, in "Letters to the Editor", under a pseudonym, was the letter he had submitted the week before. He read it to Annie:

Sir,
  War is the ultimate evil. We must debunk the notion that power politics of Sovereign States can lead to any permanent peace. It leads only to the peace of exhaustion between successive struggles of ever-increasingly destructive character, until at length the lights of civilisation have their "blackout".
  The only method of introducing any effective international morality into the relationships between nations is by abrogation of Sovereign Power in favour of a Federal Union of Democratic States.

My suggestion is:
1. Declare a General Armistice immediately
2. Call a World Conference of all Powers
3. Institute an International Court of Justice
4. Develop a Federal Union of Democratic States.

Pax Ad Omnes

'Will you no get the jile for writin that kind of thing?' Annie said.

'I'm only statin my opinion. Since when was that a crime?'

'Since we went to war?'

*

Sergeant Rudd was seated uncomfortably on a child's size chair, his embarrassment evident. 'Could I ask, Miss Carrington, where were you on the second of September?'

'Goodness, that's over a month ago. I'm not sure I can remember.'

'It was a Saturday. The day before war was declared.'

'That was before school started again. I would have spent the day in my room listening to my gramophone player. It's my fondest possession. . .'

'Any witnesses?'

'In my room? Certainly not.'

'What about the fifth of September? That would be a Tuesday.'

'I'd have been marking homework. School began that week.'

'I thocht it started the week efter, because of the evacuees arrivin.'

Lorna silently upbraided herself. 'You're quite right, sergeant. You'd think I'd remember that. I'm having to teach two classes at once because of all the Glasgow children.'

'They're a trial to us all.'

'They're much maligned, and often unfairly so. I'm growing very fond of not a few of them.'

Sergeant Rudd gripped his notebook. Teachers were predisposed to see the best in people, he imagined. 'And where were you on the fifth?'

'At home.'

'Witnesses?'

'No.'

'What about the seventeenth of September? Sunday into Monday.'

'Then I'd be at home, marking homework.'

'You don't seem to have a very active social life, miss.'

'I'm a schoolteacher. It's a vocation. It takes up all of my time.' Lorna smiled sweetly at him and twisted in her seat, pushing up her bosom, pulling in her stomach. She slid her fingers through her hair. 'What is all this in aid of?' she asked airily.

Sergeant Rudd pulled at his collar. He wouldn't have had anything to do with this nonsense but for that blowhard Braggan from Lochearnhead. Braggan was just the sort to complain to headquarters if he didn't get his way. But interviewing a schoolteacher – a woman at that – about arson was plain foolishness. One look at the woman – demure, elegant – told you she was not the sort to do such a thing.

'I'm investigatin a series of arson attacks,' he said.

Lorna laughed as though this were a joke and then, seeing Rudd's expression, she stopped. 'You can't imagine I'm an arsonist?' she said.

'I'm just makin enquiries.'

'How extraordinary. Quite exciting, in a way.' She gave a coquettish giggle. 'About the most daring thing I'm usually accused of is putting an extra sugar lump in my Horlicks.'

'It does sound rather far-fetched, miss.'

'What was it sent you in my direction, if I may ask?'

'I'm not at liberty to say.'

Lorna clapped her hands. 'That's what they say in the detective novels. How exciting.'

'You're a fan of detective fiction?'

'I'm rather fond of Miss Marple.'

'Not my cup of tea. They always make the police out to be idiots, these books.'

Lorna lifted an eyebrow. 'Yes, they do lack a certain realism.' She remained calm. This was that interfering Kelty's doing, she surmised. She was conscious that she felt no fear and that was invigorating. The fat policeman clearly knew nothing, had no evidence, just the word of a busybody café owner. She politely answered Rudd's questions. No, she didn't have access to milk bottles. She had only sufficient paraffin to fill her lamp at home and a small heater in the classroom. She'd never been to Lochearnhead but she supposed it was very beautiful. This was as easy as swatting flies. The biggest fly, though, her greatest irritation, was this man Kelty.

And ye shall chase your enemies, and they shall fall before you by the sword.

Monday, 16 October

A Day of Attacks

Following reconnaissance missions all morning, at two thirty-five on the afternoon of Monday the sixteenth of October, two squadrons of Heinkel HE III, Junkers Ju 88 and Dornier Do 17 bombers, around fourteen in number, flew up the Firth of Forth, their intended target probably the Rosyth naval units. Cruisers Southampton and Edinburgh, docked in the firth, and destroyer Mohawk, returning from convoy duty, instigated anti-aircraft fire, and Spitfires from 602 and 603 Squadrons of the Royal Air Force made their first engagement with the enemy at May Island. In the ensuing action, the enemy planes were beaten down from 4000 feet to virtually sea level and chased out to sea. One enemy plane fell in flames into the sea off Dalkeith and fifteen minutes later a second crashed into the sea off Crail. A third plane crashed into the Pentland Hills. Two German airmen were rescued by Royal Navy crew. One later died. A small fishing boat, the Dayspring, picked up a further three airmen. No casualties among civilians or the Royal Air Force were reported at the time, although in subsequent years a different tale would emerge. Thirty-five sailors suffered minor shrapnel injuries from the German bombing. The Southampton received minor bomb damage to the bow. No air raid warnings were sounded and civilians watching the action were reportedly unaware that this was anything more than a training exercise. Passengers on the Edinburgh to Turnhouse train, crossing the Forth Rail Bridge as the events unfolded, were treated to a grandstand view. The bridge was undamaged.

The Battle of the River Forth was the first Luftwaffe attack on the British mainland of the Second World War.

*

'Might I have a word, Miss Carrington?'

'Of course, headmaster.' Lorna followed Mr MacLean into his office, her mind whirring. Word must have reached the headmaster about the oaf Rudd and his nonsense last week. No doubt, the sneak, Mr Smith. She tried to formulate an appropriate response.

'You were off sick last week,' said Mr MacLean. He gave her a reassuring smile. 'I hope it was nothing serious.'

'Not at all, headmaster. Just. . .ladies' concerns. . .'

'I understand.' Mr MacLean appraised her, felt sure that was not an honest response but one conceived to discourage further enquiry. 'I'm not aware of you being afflicted in this way previously.'

'Until now, I've been able to grin and bear it. Last week, alas, the nausea was too great and I succumbed. I shall not do so again, I assure you.'

'If you are ill, Miss Carrington, you are ill. How are things generally? How's your family?'

Lorna faltered. This was not the conversation she had anticipated. The headmaster had never enquired into such matters before and she didn't understand why he would now. 'Quite well,' she said crisply.

'Mother?'

'Feeling some aches and pains, of course, with age, but apart from that fine.'

'Father?'

'Fine, too.' Realisation dawned. This must be that troglodyte

Henderson. He must have gone to the headmaster behind her back, concerning himself in matters which were nothing to do with him. Anger spiked inside her.

Mr MacLean, watching her intently, saw that anger manifest itself, for only the merest moment, but long enough. Although everyone in town seemed united in their admiration of the young schoolteacher, there was something about her that made him uncomfortable. He decided there was no point in continuing the conversation. Absolutely nothing Miss Carrington had told him was true.

'No matter,' he said. 'I won't detain you further, I'm sure your class are anticipating your arrival.'

*

Mid-afternoon, in a fleeting moment of fair weather, Sergeant Rudd entered Cloudland and waited while Bob finished serving Betty Copeland tea and a scone.

'Mr Kelty, have you a minute?'

'Mr Kelty is it? Sounds ominous. What have I done wrang noo?'

'A wee chat.' His expression was sombre and Bob immediately called upstairs for Annie to take over. He gestured to a table at the rear of Cloudland, some distance from the watching Betty Coleman. Outside, the Misses Seaton, Beaton and Miller were passing and they stopped when they saw Sergeant Rudd with Bob. They stared at them through the window as though studying zoo exhibits.

'That'll be the news aa ower toon,' said Sergeant Rudd.

'Aye, they'll hae me in the jail afore nightfall.' Bob rested his arms on the Formica table top. 'What can I do for you?'

'I've had an anonymous tip-off.' Rudd did not appear comfortable imparting this news and Bob waited to hear the cause of such evident unease. 'Malky Bennett's been sellin you butter on the cheap.'

'How would he do that?'

'To bypass the Food Control Committee.'

'You're no allowed to do that.'

'Hence the anonymous tip-off. He sells to you cheaper than you can buy it officially, but for mair than he gets fae the Committee. You baith win.'

'Cunning plan.'

'Agreed. So, are you?'

'No.'

'Can you prove it?'

'It's hard to prove somethin you arenae doin. But I'm registered with the Local Food Control Committee. Did it last week. And my butter supplier is McLaren's Dairy. I hae the paperwork. You can see how much I buy fae them. Ten pounds a week. I wouldnae need ony mair than that. We're just a wee café. So why would I be buyin extra fae Malky?'

'I'll need to see your paperwork.'

'Come upstairs.'

Outside, the sight of Rudd and Bob ascending to the flat sent the Misses Seaton, Beaton and Miller into a frenzy of excitement.

'I cannae wait to hear what they say you've done,' Rudd said.

'Somethin juicy, I hope. Might enhance my reputation.'

Bob gathered his documentation from the sideboard drawer and handed it to Rudd and they sat at the kitchen table while Rudd gave it a perfunctory inspection.

'I dinnae think you were much persuaded of my guilt onywey,' said Bob.

'No. Seemed a heap of shite to me. Seemed like somebody tryin to cause trouble for you. Again.'

'Again?'

'I never telt you this at the time, but you mind the Moot, the deid man in the tent and then the Rover disappearin and Norrie toppin himsel?'

'Aye.'

The Rover Scout Moot at Monzie, back in July, had been blighted by the unexplained death of a man in a tent outside the official campsite and the disappearance of an acquaintance of Bob's, a Hungarian named Zoltán Tóth. At the same time a local man, Norrie Smith, apparently committed suicide. Although Bob was convinced all three were the result of foul play, the authorities, Sergeant Rudd included, had shown no interest in investigating.

'No long efter Norrie deed, I got a queer telephone call. Some woman fae Embra. Bellamy, Bellany. . .'

'Miss Bettany?'

'That's the woman.'

'No a cheery sowel.' Miss Bettany was one of three government agents, roles unspecified, who had spent all night interrogating Bob in a musty office at Murrayfield Stadium in the aftermath of the Moot. She was not a woman he recalled fondly.

'Hard-hearted bitch,' said Rudd.

'I expect her mither loves her.'

'If you telt me she'd had her mither put in the jile I wouldnae be surprised. She started tellin me that Norrie's death was difficult. "Delicate", she said.'

'National security?'

'Aye, she mentioned that. Telt me it had aa been dealt wi. Paperwork and that. Nothin for me to get involved in.'

'Keep your neb oot?'

'Aye. And warnin me aff you an aa.'

'Me? How?'

'"Mr Kelty has a tendency to cause trouble," she said.'

'To be fair, she's no wrang.'

'No, she isnae. You can be a richt pain in the arse. But I dinnae tak kindly to bein telt what to do by some wee lassie...'

'She's quite tall, actually. . .'

'You ken what I mean.'

Bob nodded. 'There's murky stuff oot there. Stuff we ken

nothin aboot, and never will. You like to think oor government are the good guys. Overall, they probably are. But. . .'

'But indeed. So when I got this tip-off yesterday, implicatin you, well pardon my suspicious nature. . .'

'You think it was the government people, makin mischief?'

'Aye.'

Bob suspected that the identity of his anonymous informant was much closer to home, but he decided to leave Sergeant Rudd with his theory. He would deal with Lorna Carrington himself.

*

'Excellent news,' Mr Eadie said to the gathered ARP Wardens. 'After lengthy negotiation with the Town Council, they have agreed they will work the ARP water pump for us, conditional on the County Council paying the firemen's fees. I have spoken to Lord Kellett this morning and he confirms the Council have agreed to do that.'

'Splendid,' said Mr MacNaughton.

Mr Eadie picked up a clipboard and studied it. 'The blackout is being very well observed at nights,' he said. 'However, it has been brought to my attention that the early morning observation of blackout is far less comprehensive. British Summer Time will soon be ending – in November, I ask you! – and the clocks will be going back. This will make early morning a little brighter for a short period but that won't last. We shall need to introduce patrols in the hour before dawn. Dawn this week is just before seven, so I propose we patrol from half-five until seven. By the time the clocks go back, I am confident we'll have the same level of compliance in the mornings as evenings.'

'Grand,' Ronnie Francis muttered to Bob. 'Now I can get soaked to the skin afore I start work as well as efter.' Bob smiled ruefully.

'We begin tomorrow,' said Mr Eadie.

Tuesday, 17 October

A Day of Injury

Blackout darkness engulfed the bedroom and Bob had to lie still for a couple of minutes until his eyes adjusted to allow him to make his way to the chair where his clothes were spread. He dressed as quietly as possible but Annie stirred in bed.

'Sorry, I tried no to wake you.'

'I need to get up to mak the scones onywey.'

'I thocht the bairn was doin them?'

'I'm letting her lie in. She was at the homework aa nicht. Thon teacher of hers is a slave driver.'

'Aye, she's a wrang ane in every regard.'

He passed through to the kitchen and slurped a glass of water before pulling on his boots, coat and bunnet, and made his way through the gloom to the front door of Cloudland. He thought of locking it but Annie would be up and dressing the moment he closed the bedroom door and she would be downstairs in a matter of moments.

*

Mary was fixing her hair at the dressing table mirror when she heard the front door open and close. Her alarm clock registered five-thirty. She crept across the room, taking care not to wake Bessie, who would probably use an early awakening as a reason for being too ill to work. The bare floorboards around the room's edge were icy cold and she shivered as she pulled aside the blackout curtain.

Walking down the path to the Comrie road, smoking a cigarette, was Lorna Carrington.

*

Annie padded downstairs and checked Cloudland's blackout curtains were closed. It wouldn't do for ARP Warden Kelty's own premises to be found wanting. When Ronnie Francis's mother had been discovered with a light on in the upstairs rooms the week before Ronnie had been ceaselessly teased by the other wardens. The early morning air was brutally cold and Annie felt light-headed. She blinked and opened her eyes wide, trying to rouse herself. Another hour in bed would have been grand. She had been tired these past weeks, no doubt the winter darkness affecting her body clock. She switched on the lights and went into the kitchen and gathered the ingredients for the scones.

She bent over the oven and turned on the gas and struck the pilot light. There was a flash of light which seemed to emanate from inside her skull and a deafening whoosh of air. She felt herself falling and then she was on the floor, the linoleum cold against her cheek. Cold. Cold and dark.

*

It seemed to Bob that the darkness in the hour before dawn was more intense than during his evening patrols. He had seen nothing untoward and was looking forward to a cup of tea and one of Annie's fresh scones when he got home. He leaned back to slow himself on the steep descent from Craigard Road and, as he turned onto the Comrie road, he almost walked into PC McAnuff, heading out of town.

'Mornin Willy,' he said. 'You're oot early.'

Willy McAnuff looked flustered but then, Bob reflected, flustered, terrified or confused were Willy's standard expressions.

'Forgot my truncheon,' he said. 'Goin back hame for it.'

'What did you tak it hame for?'

'Oh,' he said, faltering, 'I had a nail that needed bangin in.'

'And you used your truncheon?'

'Aye.'

'Dinnae tell Sergeant Rudd. He'll hae you on a charge for that.'

'Aye. . .I'll see you later.' And Willy sped off, leaving Bob baffled. Yet again, Willy McAnuff was telling him haivers.

*

Mary sat and regarded her reflection in the mirror. Her perm was loosening. She looked tired. She pulled her mouth into a rictus smile that that would fool nobody. There was something about early morning that made her maudlin. Once she was up and about, busy with the chores of the day, she was grand, but these early minutes, alone with her thoughts, were a trial. More so these past weeks, of course, with Lorna Carrington insinuating herself into her existence. And Sandy, of course. Thoughts of Sandy. When she feared she had lost him, after Miss Carrington had forbidden her from speaking to him, she had felt a sense of loss she didn't understand. The loss of something good. Nice. Hopeful. She sighed and returned to the window and for the last few minutes before she started work she watched the day unfold, inky darkness gradually giving way to charcoal grey.

Half an hour after she had watched Lorna Carrington leave the house, she saw her return. There was a jauntiness in her step that Mary found disturbing.

Whose life had she been ruining now?

*

Bob smelled gas the second he walked into Cloudland. 'Annie?' he shouted. He had an immediate sense of dread and he flicked on the lights and ran through the café to the kitchen.

The oven door was open, gas hissing from it but not alight. Annie was lying on the floor in front of the oven, face down. He leaned over and turned off the gas and knelt down. Annie was spreadeagled, one hand above her head, the other parallel with her body. She wasn't moving.

'Love!' He grasped her shoulder and took her head in his hand. He bent over to feel if she was breathing. His own breathing had stopped in the terror of the moment. He looked for any sign of injury, any explanation for what had happened. There was blood beneath her head, pooling on the linoleum floor, dense and blackly purple. Panic rose inside him. A hideous thought overtook him. He looked back at the front door. He hadn't bother to lock it when he went out.

Had Annie been attacked?

Was this the work of Lorna Carrington?

'Love, love, love.' The room still reeked of gas and it was beginning to make Bob feel light-headed. Whatever had happened to Annie, remaining here and breathing these fumes could not help. He slipped his arms beneath her and cradled her body and staggered to his feet. He dragged her across Cloudland to the open front door. Light escaped into the darkness of James Square. Fresh air blew in.

He kicked the door open wider and lay Annie on the floor, sitting behind her and resting her motionless body against his. He stared into the darkness outside, trying to think, trying to remain calm.

'Please love, you'll be alright. Just breathe. Breathe.' He caressed the back of her head and his fingers became slick with blood. She'd been hit by something, that was for certain. But what?

Annie groaned and Bob felt a surge of relief. He hugged her, kissing the back of her head, stroking his fingers across her cheek.

'It's grand,' he said, 'it's grand.'

Annie's eyes flickered open and she stared ahead, trying

to understand why she was sitting at the front door of Cloudland.

'I'm cauld,' she said. And then, after a moment, 'What's happenin?'

'I dinnae ken. Just wheesht. Wheesht.' He rocked her gently, his arms gripping her. 'You're fine, that's aa that matters.'

But in his mind there was fury. Fury against Lorna Carrington. Fury that she could do anything to harm his precious Annie.

And, as soon as the fury arrived, it was accompanied by guilt. This was his fault. For confronting Lorna, sticking his nose into other people's business. And for leaving the door unlocked.

'Hoi,' came a voice from outside which Bob immediately recognised as belonging to Ronnie Francis. 'What are you doin wi aa these lights blarin?'

*

By the time Annie was despatched by ambulance to the Cottage Hospital on Pittenzie Street she was fully conscious, deeply embarrassed and insistent there was no need for any of this fuss.

'I only fainted when I bent to turn on the gas. Hit my heid on the side of the oven and knocked mysel oot. Could happen to onyone.'

Doctor Hodge took her temperature and checked her eyes and tongue. 'You may be right, Mrs Kelty, but we've no idea how long you were there, how much gas you ingested. My guess is that you're very, very lucky. If you're husband hadn't come back when he did. . .' He left the sentence unfinished.

'Will she be alright?' Bob asked.

'I believe so. But we'll keep her today and overnight. For observation.'

'I cannae do that,' Annie protested. 'I've that much to do.'

Doctor Hodge would brook no argument and Bob realised that, regardless of her protestations, Annie must have been at a low ebb to allow herself to be browbeaten in this manner.

He leaned across the bed and kissed her and promised to come back later.

'Bring my knittin,' she said.

*

Ellen spotted Sandy and Mary on their evening promenade and rushed across James Square to give them the news about Annie. She could barely contain her excitement – this was even more sensational than the fires, with Annie in hospital and Bob so worried he hadn't fussed all evening. Sandy and Mary crossed to Cloudland and made their way to the flat.

'I hae to go and see Annie soon,' Bob said, 'but come awa in.'

'Is she okay?' said Mary, her lively imagination concocting sundry nightmare scenarios.

'Aye, they're juist keepin her in for observation.'

'What happened?' Sandy asked.

'Annie says it was an accident.'

'But?'

Bob shook his head. 'Maybe I'm bein dramatic, but that woman, Lorna Carrington. Tryin to get me into trouble wi the authorities ower the butter. Stirring it up for you with the ARPs. And Mary. . .' He stopped himself before he revealed to Sandy any of Mary's vexations with Lorna. 'I juist wonder. . .'

'You think this could hae been her?' said Sandy, scandalised.

Mary laid her cup down on the table carefully. Even through the gloom of the blackout, Bob and Sandy saw the alarm on her face. 'What time did this happen?' she said.

'No sure. Some time efter five-thirty and afore seven. I was on my roond.'

Mary let out a gasp.

'How?' said Bob.

'I saw Miss Carrington go oot this mornin, at half-five. She came back half an hoor later.'

Sandy and Bob exchanged glances.

'We need to speak to Rudd,' said Bob.

Wednesday, 18 October

A Day of Recrimination

When Bob awoke at six o'clock, after a night of fitful and restless sleep, he was determined he would confront Lorna Carrington. Every time Annie had moved in bed, or let out a sigh or a moan, his rage against the woman was redoubled. He imagined scenarios where he would confront her, loudly denounce her, threaten her with the authorities. Face her down. Stand his ground. Every time he created this scene his anger grew until it formed a concentrated ball of animus deep inside him, spreading, infesting his nervous system, his brain, his motor facilities. He hated these thoughts. He hated himself. His right hand tensed into a fist. He would never use it.

But he could.

*

As she walked to work, Lorna spotted Sandy Disdain on his way to Low's with his latest cargo of liquidated life. Lorna felt a distaste bordering on hatred. She could have walked away but she was drawn to him, as though confrontation was inevitable. She crossed the road and fixed him with an acid stare.

'Murdered many animals today?' she said.

Sandy gestured to his gamebag. 'Only a dozen or so. Burnt ony hayricks?'

'I think it's time you were called up. Use all that energy on something more useful than butchering innocent rabbits.'

'It's what you use your energy on I'm mair interested in.'

'And what is that supposed to mean?'

'At half-five in the mornin, that kind of thing.'

Sandy tilted up his deerstalker. 'Have a grand day,' he said and walked off. Lorna watched him depart, her heart pumping.

There are some which walk among you disorderly, working not at all, but are busybodies.

What did he know? And how?

*

'Good heavens, sergeant, here again. You'll have people talking.' Lorna's delivery was light and jocular. She fixed Rudd with her most beguiling smile as she studied his own expression. She wondered why someone so evidently uncomfortable with confrontation should ever have entertained the idea of a career in policing. 'I fear I was very little help to you last week. Perhaps I can be more useful today?'

'Perhaps indeed. Yesterday. Between five-thirty and six-thirty in the mornin. Whaur were you?'

Rudd was astonished by the change that overcame Lorna's demeanour. The cheery expression disappeared and the fixed smile that replaced it was clearly forced, unnatural, uncomfortable.

'May I ask why you wish to know?'

'No, you may not.' Her response to his question, and the expression that overtook her face, were more than odd. There was something to be divulged here, of that he was certain. He cocked his head.

'I think you'd better sit down,' Lorna said.

*

Bob, Annie and Ellen were finishing dinner when Sergeant Rudd arrived, helmet under his arm. He stood stiffly in the kitchen of the flat.

'I've spoken to Miss Carrington and I'm satisfied she has no involvement in what happened to Mrs Kelty yesterday.'

'Wha said she did?' said Annie, turning to Bob in confusion.

'I just wanted to be sure,' Bob said. 'Given aa that's happened recently.'

'You didnae speak to me aboot it.'

'I didnae want to worry you.'

'It was juist an accident.'

'I needed to be sure.' He turned to Sergeant Rudd. 'What did she say?'

'That doesnae matter.'

'But she has an alibi?'

Rudd looked at Annie, then at Ellen, and finally at Bob. 'Aye,' he said.

'What is it?'

'I'm no at liberty to say.'

'I dinnae understand.'

'I'll see mysel oot.'

He clambered downstairs as quickly as he could and Bob followed. Rudd stopped at the door and glanced upstairs at the flat. He gestured to Bob to come outside.

'She definitely was oot at that time,' he said. 'She admitted as much.'

'And?'

'She telt me whaur she was. And what she was doin. And I've had that verified by a third party.'

Bob threw up his hands. 'What?'

'She was wi PC McAnuff.'

'Willy?'

'An assignation in the shelter shed by the tennis courts in the tap park.'

'Lorna Carrington? And Willy McAnuff?'

'I went and asked Willy. He admitted it to me. I've never seen onyone mair embarrassed in my hale life. They go to the park because Lorna Carrington insists on doin it ootside, apparently. Even in this bloody weather.'

'But I mean, Lorna Carrington and Willy McAnuff?'

'I ken. Thing is, there's nae harm, as such. They're neither of them merried.'

'But Willy? That woman'll eat him alive.'

'Aye, it's the strangest match-up I've seen since Mae West and Cary Grant in *I'm No Angel*.'

'I was thinkin mair Lady Macbeth.' Bob thought for a moment. 'I saw him, richt enough. He must have been on his wey there. Puir laddie.'

Sergeant Rudd raised his hand in agreement. 'He's a nice sowel, Willy. But he joined the polis far ower young. Scared of his ain shadow. You need some wool on your back in this job. Well, I dinnae need to tell you that.'

Bob thought back to his nocturnal imaginings, his confrontations with Lorna Carrington, his besting of her, and he felt shame that he had allowed his emotions to run wild. Whatever she was, she had nothing to do with Annie's accident. He looked at his open hand as though it were a traitor.

*

Mr MacLean was waiting at the station when Sergeant Rudd returned from Cloudland. Rudd greeted him cheerily and invited him to the interview room.

'I understand,' said Mr MacLean, 'that you had cause to question Miss Carrington earlier today.'

Rudd faltered. 'That is so,' he said.

'Are you at liberty to divulge the reason for this enquiry?'

Had Miss Carrington been responsible for an attack on Mrs Kelty, or had they more substantial proof of her identity as the arsonist, Sergeant Rudd would have felt able to discuss these matters with Mr MacLean, who was, after all, Miss

Carrington's employer. But the conversation with Miss Carrington had taken an unexpected turn and, while he deplored her behaviour with PC McAnuff, if the police were to arrest every courting couple taking advantage of outdoor cover they would have to ship all the other offenders out of the prisons to make way for them.

'There was a particular line of enquiry I wished to discuss with Miss Carrington,' he said, 'and she managed to allay any fears I may have had. There was nothing untoward and we ended the discussion there and then.'

'No thought of malpractice?'

'None.'

'I do have some concerns about this individual, you see, for various reasons, and if the police were maintaining an interest. . .'

'No interest, Mr MacLean. None at all.

'Thank you sergeant. I am greatly relieved.'

*

Miss Salter laid a porcelain cup of tea in front of Mr Henderson.

'Sit with me, my dear,' Henderson said. He patted the cushion of the chair next to his, overlooking the garden of Barvick Falls. 'I wish to discuss something.'

Miss Salter, not accustomed to sitting with her employer in the afternoon, nonetheless did so without demur. She smoothed the skirt of her uniform.

'Miss Carrington,' Henderson said. 'I cannot shake off my concerns about her.'

'Indeed,' replied Miss Salter.

'This story about coming from Mintlaw, her father being alive and well – you're quite sure she is from St Andrews?'

'Quite sure.'

'And the late Reverend Carrington was her father?'

'He was.'

Henderson frowned and reached for his tea. He sat it on

his lap without attempting to drink from it. 'Reverend Duncan from Mintlaw was very discreet but I am convinced there is a story there. Something happened.'

'Perhaps we should go to Mintlaw. Check the local newspapers, ask around.'

'I was thinking the same thing. Next week. Can you make arrangements?'

'Of course.'

'In the meantime, I'm minded to speak to the headmaster of the Public School. See if he's aware of anything odd in her background. What do you think?'

'Perhaps wait until we've been to Mintlaw. See if there's anything relevant.'

'Quite right, Miss Salter. It's a boon having someone so clear-headed to talk things through with. Make sure we make the correct decisions.' He sipped his tea and gazed out of the window.

*

Downstairs, Bessie and Mary were lying on their beds listening to the wireless and resting their aching feet during the brief lull between dinner and supper preparations.

'I fancy goin to the picters,' said Bessie.

'Well, dinnae go to *The Thirty Nine Steps*. It's ower creepy.'

Their door swung open and Lorna stood in the doorway. She smiled broadly at Bessie. 'Mrs Mitchell has asked if you could go downstairs for a moment,' she said. 'Sorry to drag you away from your rest period.'

'Thank you, ma'am,' said Bessie. She jumped to her feet and ran downstairs without stopping to put on her shoes. Lorna advanced to Mary's bed, her smile replaced by an eerie froideur. Mary sat up in alarm and Lorna gripped her hand around Mary's throat.

'I had the buffoon police sergeant come to see me today. Again.' Mary cringed and tried to escape Lorna's grip. Lorna squeezed more tightly. 'I ended up having to tell him something intensely private to prove I'd done nothing wrong.'

'I'm sorry.'

'It was humiliating. Demeaning. All because some little snitch reported I'd left the house early yesterday. Now, who could that be?' She slapped Mary across the face.

'I dinnae ken, miss.'

She slapped her again. 'Maybe somebody whose repulsive boyfriend seemed to know about it as well.'

'I dinnae ken, miss.'

'Was it you?'

Mary continued to struggle but couldn't break Lorna's grip. Tears were forming in her eyes. 'Aye,' she said, sobbing.

Lorna slapped her again and released her grip on her throat. She stared into her eyes. Nothing but weakness and fear.

'I've just been playing with you up to now,' she said. She slapped Mary a final time, the hardest of all. The sound reverberated around the small attic room.

'But now I'm serious.'

She turned and walked out of the room. Mary listened to the sound of Lorna's door opening and slamming shut and she threw herself back on the bed, pulling the pillow over her head to shut out the world.

Thursday, 19 September

A Day of Bullying

Fresh rain and humid air raised the earthy smell of jute from sandbags deposited outside the North of Scotland Bank. James Square was quiet. Thingwie Johnstone walked down the middle of King Street, causing Roy's the butcher's van to swerve past. Sunny Petrie was losing at draughts to Habbie Gaudie. Bob tapped PC McAnuff on the shoulder as he passed Harley & Watts.

'Willy,' he said, not sure how to broach the conversation he needed to have. Willy McAnuff's expression suggested this was not a discussion in which he was keen to engage, either. 'Lorna Carrington. . .' Bob continued.

'That's nane of your business.'

'Indeed it isnae. And you can rest assured you'll hear nae mair aboot it. . .Except ae thing.'

'What?'

'The letter, to the Dallerie Laundry, have you fund it yet?'

'How?'

'I'm sure Sergeant Rudd telt you my theory that Lorna Carrington is the arsonist?'

'Aye.'

'You see, that puts you in a difficult position. Chances are you ken what her handwritin's like. And now this important piece of evidence, which could implicate your girlfriend. . .'

'She's no my girlfriend. . .'

'However you want to describe her, that evidence has disappeared on your watch.'

'Are you sayin I had somethin to do wi it?'

'No. But plenty folk might. I'm tellin you, whatever your feelins for Lorna Carrrington, dinnae let your career get ruined acos of this.'

'I dinnae ken what you're talkin aboot.'

'You ken fine what I'm talkin aboot. I've said my piece. But I mean it – it'll be best all roond if that letter miraculously reappears.'

*

Mary took a deep breath as she emerged from her bedroom and joined her parents and brother Dick in the smoky living room of their Millar Street home. After the incident with Lorna she had been too frightened to remain at Barvick Falls. Her first thought had been to resign but she had only been there a matter of weeks and prospective employers would view such a short engagement with suspicion. Besides, she couldn't afford to be unemployed while she looked for another placement. The only option, then, was to keep working at Barvick Falls but return to live at home. Mrs Mitchell had been unwilling at first, and warned Mary that if she was late for work, even once, she would be dismissed. Mary accepted the condition. Now, she had to face her father.

'Bloody ridiculous,' Pat Kemp said the moment she entered the room. 'Perfectly good lodgins and you're back here stayin wi us.'

'I'm sorry, Dad.'

'You'll pey board. I cannae go on lookin efter a grown woman.'

'Aye, that's fine.'

'I tak it you negotiated a rise in your wages?'

'No. How?'

He gestured to Mrs Kemp in exasperation as though this was the response he had anticipated. 'Because, you silly lassie, you were getting that wage wi board and lodgins thrown in. So your pey was lower. Now you're no boardin it needs to go up.'

'I dinnae think I can do that.'

'You need to speak to Mrs Mitchell. She's takin a len of you.'

'She'll sack me.'

'Tell her you'll get the polis on her.'

'What for?'

Pat rubbed his temple. 'You ay were a useless bairn. Nae gumption. What the hell are you leavin your digs for onywey? Just acos a schoolteacher was nasty to you? Belt her across the lug and hae done wi it.'

'I couldnae hit anyone.'

'You'll get walked ower aa your life, lassie. What's that feckless boyfriend of yours doin aboot it? Should he no be stickin up for you?'

'I havenae telt him. He'd go and do something stupit and get me sacked.'

'I'll tell him mysel.'

'No dad, please. Let me do this my wey.'

'Your wey? Cowerin in a corner till the nasty world goes awa? What wey is that?' He picked up *The Strathearn Herald*. 'Awa to the pantry and get me a bottle of beer.'

*

Bob was attracted by the headline "War and Civilisation" in the *Herald*. This had been the headline for his letter the previous week and he studied the response, from someone styling themselves *Macedon*: 'There's another letter here,' he said to Annie, 'haein a go at mine.'

As an excuse for doing nothing in the way of National Service, *Pax Ad Omnes* declares a belief that war is the ultimate evil and suggests an alternative – a Federal Union of Democratic States – that is utterly facile and completely impossible to implement.

Germany – and Russia – have not progressed far along the road from primitive savagery. That being the case, the only arbiter can be force. These people have no honour. Their word cannot be trusted. The League of Nations proved impotent in the face of such barbarity and the notion of a Federal Union is pie in the sky. If we cannot make the League of Nations work as an effective bulwark, how can we possibly aim to implement a system that is more ambitious (and naïve) yet?

War wins nothing, we are told. Cassandras such as *Pax Ad Omnes* would do well to reflect on history. Greek civilisation was saved by it from devastation by the multitudinous armies of Asia. War enabled Rome to build a great empire and spread her beneficent influence over the greater part of the known world. The destruction of the Spanish Armada saved European freedom. Marlborough "settled" Louis XIV; Wellington "settled" Napoleon. The last war is often cited as an example of war's futility, yet it "settled" German attempts at world domination for thirty years and would have done so for far longer had it not been for post-war diplomacy and peace-making, the abysmal Treaty of Versailles which created the political and economic climate in Germany that Hitler harnessed to his advantage. Peace then, not war, is what brought us to the pass we face today.

And war, only war, will relieve us.

Macedon

'That's a bit strong,' said Annie.

'Tempers are gettin frayed. Folk are gettin mair extreme in their views and in the wey they express them. And mair extreme in what they do. This is what comes of war.'

'It's getting far ower close to hame.'

'I ken.'

For two days, there had been Luftwaffe raids on the north

of Scotland. One ship had been damaged. Scapa Flow, a symbolic site for the German Navy, had been attacked and HMS Royal Oak sunk while at anchor. Bob threw down the *Herald* and shifted on the settee. He picked up his pipe but laid it down again and sighed. 'You've got Stalin threatenin Finland. China and Japan fechtin each other. Merchant ships bein sunk. I tell you, the hale world's goin mad.'

'We juist keep oor heids doon,' said Annie.

'I'm no sure we can for much longer.'

*

'Children, there are craven shirkers among us. In our country's time of need, when our men are required to fight, there are people clinging to false notions of pacifism in order to disguise their cowardice.'

Lorna strode up and down the classroom's central aisle waving the last two editions of *The Strathearn Herald*. She could see some heads nodding in agreement but most remained motionless. She checked for expressions which betrayed disagreement. Black Alice, she thought. Black Alice always adopted contrary views.

'In the local paper last week,' she continued, brandishing the *Herald*, 'a pathetic coward dared to talk of war as "the ultimate evil". No, children, pusillanimity is the greatest evil. Allowing oneself to be pushed around, turning the other cheek, choosing self-interest over national duty – that is evil. This person – this poltroon, this dolt – wants an armistice. Does he truly believe a man like Herr Hitler would observe such a thing? He wants a "Conference of World Powers". We have one of those: it's called the League of Nations and it sat on its hands while Germany led the world into conflict. He wants a "Federal Union". What sort of madness is this?'

She paused, challenging the class to respond to her rhetorical question. No one did.

'Fortunately,' she went on, 'in this week's paper there is a redoutable rejoinder to this craven cowardice. An excellent piece of reasoning. I urge you to read it, and get your parents to read it.'

She walked across the classroom. 'Black Alice, what do you say? Do you think the man you are staying with – a young man, fit, in his mid-twenties – do you think he should be cowering in a café in Crieff or fighting for his country?'

'I don't think he'd be very good at fightin.'

'Then he would die. Somebody has to. That is the nature of warfare. But, even in death, a soldier advances his country's cause. Is that not noble?'

'Not for him. He's deid.'

Instinctively, Lorna slapped Ellen across the face. The class gasped. Ellen stared at Lorna in horror. Lorna knew she had gone too far but there was no possibility of backing down now. On the contrary, having provoked an attack she had to redouble her response. She slapped her again.

'Get out of my classroom. Stand in the corridor, facing the wall. When you wish to rejoin the class you may enter and apologise.'

*

Ellen didn't much mind being sent out of the classroom because running the length of the corridor was a wooden-framed glass cabinet containing as many as fifty stuffed birds posed on a tangle of tree branches. She wasn't keen on their eyes, which looked evil, but she was fascinated by their bodies. In the wild you couldn't get close and they didn't stop in one place long enough for her to study them in detail. The red breast of the robin. The intricate patterning of the starling. The elegance of the sparrowhawk. She was deep in thought when she heard footsteps approach.

'Now then, missie, have you been in trouble?'

Mr Smith smiled down at her. The peak of his hat gleamed.

He wore round-rimmed spectacles. He smelled of tobacco. His expression was kind.

Ellen gestured with her head towards the classroom door. 'Miss Carrington.'

'Enough said. What did you do to get sent oot here?'

'Nothin. I disagreed wi her.'

'Aye, I'm coming to see she's no a woman to be argued wi.' Mr Smith bent and inspected her still reddened cheek. 'She didnae hit you, did she?'

Ellen thought of telling him what had happened but reasoned annoying Miss Carrington even further would only ever have one outcome. Before she could answer, the classroom door swung open and Lorna strode into the corridor.

'What's the meaning of this?' she said.

Mr Smith looked her up and down, making no attempt to hide his disdain. 'I was askin the lassie what she's oot here for.'

'Because she's a disruptive wretch.'

'Bairns, eh? They will insist on actin like bairns.'

'I'm sure you have duties to attend to, Mr Smith.'

'Aye. We've mice in the oothooses. I'm juist aff to kill them.' He walked away without waiting for a reply. He knew her sentimental attachment to animals of all description and was satisfied that any plan to kill mice would greatly anger her.

'If only she loved her bairns the way she loves the beasts.'

*

After school, Lorna put a note through Willy McAnuff's door, instructing him to be in the shelter shed at six in the morning. She needed to know what he had said to Sergeant Rudd about their liaison and, in any case, she suspected she would need to provide his backbone with requisite support. Rain was falling heavily and she pulled her coat collar around her neck. She didn't notice Pat Kemp following her until he was upon her. He gripped his arm around her neck and forced her to her knees on the pitted and sodden path.

'You're the schoolteacher, Carrington?' Unable to speak, Lorna nodded her head. 'Well, I've a message for you, stuck-up bitch. Go onywhere near my lassie again and I'll tie you in a sack and drop you in the Earn. Understand?'

Lorna couldn't breath and she feared he might break her neck. She was growing nauseous and was on the verge of passing out but she managed to nod her head once more and Pat Kemp pushed her away, sending her sprawling over the doorstep of the little cottage in the middle of the lane.

Pat strode back the way he had come, satisfied with his efforts. Lorna watched him go, her eyes watering, her breathing laboured. Anger seethed inside her.

'Who the hell was that?' she said.

Friday, 20 October

A Day of Association

Lorna's cheek was grazed for the third time in a matter of weeks, this time a large patch near her left ear where she had hit the ground during the attack. She still had no idea who her attacker was, or what his motives were. "You're the schoolteacher", he'd said. That suggested a parent, but which parent she couldn't determine. Although most of her ire was directed at the Glasgow urchins she discounted any of them because she couldn't imagine any of their parental proxies being annoyed enough about the children's treatment to respond in such a fashion. That meant a local child, but Lorna couldn't identify anyone to whom she had meted out harsh treatment in the current term. Edward Soutar, perhaps? She dabbed the graze with surgical spirit from a piece of cotton wool and winced. Provocation therapy her father would have called that: any injury or ailment only has so much pain inside it, so provoke it and get it out more quickly.

'Get out of my fucking head, father. Moulder in your grave.'

She put on her swagger coat and slipped outside Barvick Falls. She lit a cigarette and waited on the path for some moments, looking up at the first floor to see whether anyone was watching, but she knew that the simple maid had moved back home and she wasn't surprised when nothing stirred.

She made her way to the shelter shed, anticipating the assignation. If only the sap wouldn't treat her like a fragile doll, he would do so much better.

He was waiting for her, the usual gormless expression on his face. She kissed her fingers and planted them on his cheek, then reached for the buttons of his crotch. He stepped away.

'I'm too busy the day,' he said. 'I havenae time.'

'No time for me? I don't think so, darling.'

'How did you get on with Dallerie Laundry?'

'What?'

'You wrote to them. About their prices. For the school.'

Lorna studied him curiously, his innocent face, frightened features, nervous of life itself. 'I told you. It didn't work out,' she said. She dropped her cigarette end and ground it into the gravel with her stiletto. 'We might go to the cemetery next time. Wouldn't it be fun to have sex on a grave?'

'No.'

'No? Do you say "no" to me, lover boy?'

'You're using me.'

'I beg your pardon?'

'You don't love me.'

'Of course I don't love you. Who said anything about love?'

'I want love.'

'Well, you won't get it here, silly boy.'

'No, I won't.' Willy turned on his heel and walked away, hoping fervently that she wouldn't call him back because, if she did, he knew he would obey.

She didn't.

She watched him walk away, her chest constricted with tension. Matters were coming to a head. She would need a release.

'No fires. No fires.'

But their lure was growing ever harder to resist.

*

Sandy tapped his Capstan against the round ashtray in Cloudland and blew smoke down his nose. Mary, just started her midday break, sat beside him cradling a cup of tea.

'Whaur's the feisty wee madam this mornin?' Sandy said to Bob.

'In Annie's bad books again. Confined to her room.'

'How?'

'The Misses Seaton, Beaton and Miller were in yesterday dennertime. "We just thocht you ought to ken. . ."'

'Oh aye. What's she been up to?'

'Her and Marnie on their bikes, burlin doon Lodge Street and ower Burrell Street wi-oot stoppin to see what traffic's comin.'

'Ah.'

Bob narrowed his eyes and took his pipe from his mouth. 'What d'you mean "ah"?'

'Oh, juist that I can see why Annie would be bothered by that.'

'Aye, so can I. But that's no what you meant when you said "ah". I ken you. The wey you said it. . .'

'It's juist that, when I was a laddie, we used to run oor carties doon Lodge Street exactly the same.'

Bob relit his pipe. 'Now, is that no a coincidence? A bairn newly arrived fae Glesga comes up wi the exact same game you played as a laddie twenty year ago?'

'I micht hae mentioned it to her in passin.' Bob rolled his eyes. 'Well, I didnae ken she'd go aff and do it hersel.'

'What, the feisty wee madam?' He shook his head. 'Juist watch what you say to her. And dinnae let Annie ken it was you put her up to it or she'll send you to your room an aa.'

*

During her lunch interval, Lorna walked uphill into town, wandering aimlessly. She entered Muir's the Ironmongers and pretended to look at kitchenware while she inhaled the shop's unmistakeable aroma. That sweet smell of dust and oil always calmed her. As she left, she saw the sap Mary and her brute of a boyfriend leaving Cloudland. The maid was looking up at him, doe-eyed, while he walked on regardless. They were an odd couple, to be sure. What on earth did he see in her? Lorna couldn't stand the man, hated everything he stood for, but there was something about him. That long gait. Permanent frown. He was a man who lived life by his own measure.

She didn't have the patience to talk to her afternoon class so she set them an hour's silent reading. She studied each child in turn, trying to recall if there was anything she had done to warrant a parent's anger. No likely candidate emerged. Not even Edward Soutar. She hadn't strapped him in weeks. She seethed. The trouble with people was that they had no perspective. Wouldn't live in the here and now. Why couldn't they understand? "Man that is born of a woman is of few days, and full of trouble." This, she believed, was the most misunderstood statement in history. For two millennia, sheep-for-men had read those lines and wept for their own mortality. "So man lieth down, and riseth not: till the heavens be no more, they shall not awake, nor be roused out of their sleep." That was the truth of it. Yet what did they do, these mortal men of women born? They waited. They waited for the end, the endless sleep, a resurrection that would never come. They traded the glory of the present for the folly of the future. Why? Why forswear the moment, the experience, life itself? Foolish little McAnuff, more child than man, wanting love, bleating regret, whimpering from the stage like a lovelorn cuckold. Lorna didn't want a future, she wanted the present, and she wanted it to be astonishing.

She studied her face in her compact mirror. The compressed light in the classroom caused by the blackout curtains was unforgiving. She knew she was pretty but at this moment she didn't look it and didn't feel it. She was thirty-two years old. She didn't want to become an old maid, turning into a harridan like the Misses Seaton, Beaton and Miller, but the idea of marriage was equally horrifying. Giving up her career. Bearing children. Becoming a domestic drudge. This town was insufferable, these little people, sappy Willy, gormless Kelty, his shrew wife, moronic Mary. Sandy Disdain. Unthinkingly, she stood and began to walk around the room, almost in a dance, a listless waltz. The children watched her nervously. The smallness of her world was encapsulated by those steps, a procession of little movements and little moments, a dry cavalcade, a life demarcated by circumstance and happenstance. If she hadn't been born a woman. If her father hadn't been a Wee Free minister. If she hadn't been the cleverest child in her class. If she could have been happy, even once. If the simpleton boy hadn't panicked and instead got out safely. If she'd never set foot in Mintlaw. If she could be rid of her past. If she could fall in love. If she could unravel what happiness was. How to attain it. Keep it. If she could only settle. Settle – stay. Settle – enough. She made a resolution there, then, stepping through the classroom, solitary and lonely, that she would never chase the dream of love. Love was not for the likes of Lorna Carrington. She didn't care enough about anything – most of all herself – to allow such intimacy to take hold.

But relationships could be forged from more than love. It was commonly said that the opposite of love was hate. Lorna knew that wasn't true. The opposite of love was indifference. No relationship can thrive on indifference. But love and hate were bedfellows, emotions that bring people together. She would never form a loving relationship, that much she knew.

But she could form a hating relationship.

Oh yes, she could.

Saturday, 21 October

A Day of Invitations

Lorna had come to realise the gamekeeper was a creature of habit and she waited at Scrimgeour's Corner in the minutes before William Low's opened. She spotted him sauntering along Comrie Street, hand in his pocket, bulging gamebag over his shoulder. She waited until he was almost upon her before stepping onto the pavement.

'I wanted to speak with you,' she said. She smiled at the surprise that registered on his face. He was handsome, in a rustic sort of way. Those deep-set eyes had an intensity that Lorna found intriguing. They were challenging. Forceful.

'Well?'

'Not here. Meet me in the shelter shed in the top park at seven tonight.'

'How?'

'I'll see you then.' She smiled and walked up the High Street, swaying her hips, not waiting to see his reaction.

*

Annie, her hair covered by a knotted scarf and with a pinnie tied around her waist, stood on one of the kitchen chairs and reached with a duster to clean the top shelf of the cabinet. About eight feet high, the shelf was no use for everyday items and had become a dumping ground for a jar containing buttons and ribbons, two vases left to her by her grandmother and sundry utensils too good to throw away but never used. She was fretting about Cloudland, how they would manage to keep operating when food became scarce. She would need to find work, she thought, and resolved to ask Mary Kemp if there were any vacancies at Barvick Falls. She felt a sudden wave of dizziness, a hot flush sweeping across her brow, and she became instantly disorientated, as though the room had started whirling around her. She looked upwards and nausea overtook her and she slipped, falling from the chair and landing heavily on her back on the kitchen linoleum. Winded, she lay there, uncomprehending and unable to move. As quickly as it had come, the dizziness disappeared and she felt pain from the fall but she was otherwise fine, and she was left wondering what on earth had happened.

'Annie!'

Leslie Comer dashed into the kitchen and knelt beside her and took her hand, staring into Annie's confused eyes. 'I heard the clatter fae doonstairs. What happened?'

Annie closed her eyes and opened them. 'I juist lost my balance,' she said. 'Must have stretched ower far.'

Leslie helped her to her feet and pushed the chair back to the kitchen table and sat Annie on it. 'I'll mak you some tea,' she said. 'You gave me an awfae fleg.'

'Ach, I'm grand.' Annie gripped the kitchen table. Her back and shoulder were sore where she'd fallen but her head was fine. No dizziness. No nausea. Just like the last time. 'Dinnae go sayin onythin to Bob,' she said. 'You ken how he fashes.'

*

Marnie and Ellen watched the dairy cattle process stolidly up the Laggan road to the farm for afternoon milking.

'How do they know where to go?' Ellen asked.

'They do it twice a day. They juist mind the wey.'

'And how do they know it's milkin time?'

'When their udders are fu. Look.' She pointed to the cows' heavy udders, swaying from side to side as they walked. 'If you had aa that sloshin aboot underneath you, you'd mind it was milkin time an aa.'

'Can I watch?'

'There's nothin to see.'

They entered the whitewashed dairy and Ellen studied the dairy hands as each cow in turn was fastened to a mechanical milker which droned away like a car engine, while behind them three girls bottled the milk and loaded it into crates.

'Is that what we drink at school?'

'And in your tea, aye.'

'It comes oot of a coo?'

'Whaur did you think it came fae?'

'I've never thought aboot it.'

'Dinnae tell me, you're never goin to drink milk again?'

Ellen watched the dairy hands, their deft touch, listened to the sloosh of the milk entering the pails. 'Why wouldn't I?'

Farmer Bennett pointed to the waiting cows. 'D'you want a go?' he said.

'Can I?' said Ellen, grinning.

*

Lorna was already waiting in the shelter shed when Sandy approached from the direction of the bottom park a couple of minutes before seven. She eyed him sardonically.

'Glad to see you made the effort to get dressed up.'

Sandy looked at his jacket and trousers. 'I own what I have on and my funeral suit,' he said.

'You must go to more weddings than funerals at your age, surely?'

'My friends are too sensible to get merried.'

'And you?'

'Me an aa.'

'Surely you want a good woman to look after you?'

'No.'

'Not even little Mary?'

'Mary's a fine lass.'

'A "fine lass". Sounds like you're describing a dog.'

'She's a fine lass.'

Lorna patted the bench. 'Have a seat.' She was wearing lipstick. Beneath her swagger coat, Sandy thought she was wearing a blue frock. She seemed to have different clothing every time he saw her. Must be a good-paying job, the teaching. He sat down, his breath swirling like fog in the chill of the evening.

'I imagine you're in a reserved occupation?'

'Twice ower. Farmhand. Gamekeeper.'

'Lucky you. While all the lads your age are off fighting, you'll have the pick of the girls. Little Mary had better watch out – you'll be in demand.'

'Me in demand? That'd be a first.'

She turned and studied him. 'I wouldn't say that.' She stroked his thigh. 'You're quite a handsome chap.' Feeling no resistance, she rested her hand on his thigh and squeezed. Still, Sandy didn't respond. She slid her hand upwards to his groin and leaned across to kiss him. Sandy swayed away and shifted on the bench.

'Don't you want me?' she said.

'No.'

'What do you mean "no"? Don't you find me attractive?'

Sandy stood up. 'You're a bonny lassie, richt enough. But I wouldnae gie you the time of day, hen. You've an ugly soul.'

He walked away into the darkness, reaching for his cigarettes.

Sunday, 22 October

A Day of Accusations

Lorna Carrington held herself erect as she waited at the counter of Crieff Police Station. 'I wish to make a complaint,' she said.

Sergeant Rudd picked up his notebook. 'Go ahead,' he said.

'I was physically assaulted. Violated.'

Rudd put down his notebook and opened the counter flap. 'Come through,' he said, and he escorted her to the interview room and, once she was seated at the table, he sat opposite.

'Tell me,' he said.

'I was sexually assaulted last night in the shelter shed at the top park. I was passing on my evening walk about seven o'clock and I was dragged into the shed and attacked.'

'Was it a full sexual assault?'

'No, I managed to escape.'

'And do you know who the attacker was?'

'I do. His name is Sandy Disdain. From the Laggan farm.'

*

Sandy watched Sergeant Rudd's bicycle wobble up the path to the Disdains' cottage on the Laggan Hill. He rested his arm on the handle of his graip as Rudd came to a halt and staggered from the bike.

'Dinnae see you oot here very often,' he said.

'I'd like a wee chat.'

Sandy gestured to the back door. 'I'll put the kettle on.'

'I've had a complaint,' Rudd said once they were seated at the kitchen table, pot of tea infusing beside them.

'Wha's land have I been poachin on, noo?'

'A complaint from the primary school teacher, Miss Carrington.'

'That was ages ago.'

'What was?'

'She had a go at me aboot shootin rabbits. That's what started aa this arson nonsense at Malky's. I had it oot wi her.'

'This is mair serious. Says you assaulted her. Sexually assaulted.'

'You ken fine I didnae.'

'I'd be gey surprised, I'll say that.'

'When was this supposed to hae happened?'

'Last night.'

'In the shelter shed in the tap park?'

Rudd closed his eyes. 'That hasnae helped you, son. It was in the shelter shed, aye. Care to guess what time?'

'Seven?'

'How d'you ken that?'

'She invited me there yestreen. And she made a pass at me. Pit her haund on my thigh, sweet talkin. . .'

'Lorna Carrington? You?'

'Dinnae ask me. I cannae fathom the woman. She's been makin Mary's life a misery for weeks, noo. Mary's even gone back to live at hame wi Pat the postie.'

'Man, that is desperate.'

'I've nae idea what game she was playin last nicht, but it was nothin to do wi romance. And I never laid a finger on her.'

Rudd scratched his scalp as Sandy poured their tea. 'I dinnae believe for a second you touched the lassie, but I hae to ask mysel how she would lee aboot it.'

'Because she's a heidcase.'

'Thing is, you've nae alibi. Worse than that, you actually admit you were there.'

'And maybe that's what this is aa aboot. She made a pass, kennin I'd say no, so she could make accusations against me.'

'How?'

'She hates me. The arson thing. I warned her aff.'

Rudd closed his eyes 'What do you mean you "warned her aff"?'

'Telt her I kent it was her. Telt her no to start ony mair fires.'

'Or what?'

'Or I'd come and see you.'

'Did you threaten her?'

'No exactly.'

'Bloody hell, Sandy. I'll hae to investigate that an aa, noo. I'll hae to ask her aboot it. If she says you did threaten her – and I've nae doot she will – I may need to charge you.'

'What wi?'

'Threatenin behaviour.'

'She needed tellin.'

'Will you wheesht. You're no helpin yoursel.'

Rudd drank his tea noisily. Sandy sat back on his chair. 'So what do we do?' he said.

'I'll hae to do some investigatin.'

'Sorry to put you to ony effort.'

'I ken you aa think I'm a lazy gype. But this time it's you I'm thinkin aboot, no me.'

'I ken, Danny. I appreciate it.'

*

Bob and Sandy sat downstairs in Cloudland during a mid-afternoon lull. Bob poured them each a tot of whisky.

'They'll hae to do a physical examination of her,' Bob said, 'if they havenae already. Look for signs of violence.'

'She says it wasnae rape.'

'Well. . .' Bob sipped his whisky, trying not to wince. It was a taste to which he'd never become accustomed, but a tot felt the right thing right now. 'That was smart of her, unfortunately. But it doesnae really help her. There's nae wey of provin onythin, so unless she could conjure up a witness. . .'

'Which she couldnae, because it didnae happen.'

'Aye. Although there could be a witness says you were there.'

'I say I was there. I'm no denyin it.'

'Good. So in the end it comes doon to her word or yours.'

'They'll side wi her. She's a teacher. I'm a poacher.'

'No necessarily. If she cannae provide a shred of evidence what is there to prosecute?'

'And that's your considered judgement, as an ex-police officer?'

'Aye.'

'Given your record, I'm mair worried than ever.'

Bob laughed, pleased that Sandy could still find humour in his situation. He knew he was right, though, the lack of evidence made it most unlikely charges would ever be brought. That wasn't the problem. The problem was that mud stuck. When news of the allegation escaped into town – and it would – the likes of the Misses Seaton, Beaton and Miller would scatter it far and wide. And a lack of evidence was no impediment to gossip. Not where there was ripe speculation to take its place. Bob studied his friend's glowering face and worried for him.

*

Mary lay on her candlewick bedspread listening to her father downstairs. He had returned from the Pretoria ten minutes after it closed for the afternoon and had been banging drawers in the kitchen ever since. He would be looking for bottles of beer and Mary hoped fervently he would find one. Those hopes vanished when she heard his tread on the stairs. Her door flew open.

'You little bitch, you've hidden my beer.'

'I havenae touched your beer. You've drank it all. There's four empties in the pantry waitin to go back.'

'There you are, then,' he said rounding the bed and thrusting his face towards her, 'I bocht six bottles fae Lipton's on Friday. Whaur's the other twa?'

'I dinnae ken, faither. How would I touch your beer?'

He grabbed her hair. 'Whaur are they?' he shouted. Spittle landed on her cheek.

'Faither.' Mrs Kemp stood in the doorway, peenie tied round her waist. 'There's twa bottles in the breid bin. You pit them there when you got hame last nicht. Lord knows how.'

Pat grunted and let go of Mary's hair. He pushed past his wife and lumbered downstairs, muttering.

'I'm sorry,' Mrs Kemp said.

'I'm goin back to Barvick Falls,' Mary said. 'Even Lorna Carrington's better than this.'

'Get yoursel merried, hen.'

Mary lay on her back and stared at the ceiling. Her mother was right. Sandy Disdain was a good man. He wasn't a drinker. He was steady. Good prospects. He would look after her. She allowed herself, for a brief moment, a fantasy future life, Sandy and Mary Disdain, bairns, a wee place of their ain.

'Please, Sandy.'

*

When he left Cloudland, Sandy cycled to the foot of Turleum, where he left his bike and climbed four hundred metres to the summit. He stretched on the damp heather and studied the Strathearn valley. North-east was Crieff, the only town he'd ever known. His family had moved from Panbride in Angus when he was a bairn, too young to remember, and they'd flitted from farm to farm, house to house, maybe fifteen or sixteen times in his twenty-six years, but always around Strathearn, always with Crieff the nearest town. He used to think it some kind of metropolis – all those churches and pubs – but the lustre had dimmed over time. The fuss with Lorna Carrington would subside, he knew. There was nothing to concern him there. But Mary. . .Mary. . .He was increasingly certain that he and Mary would marry. She wouldn't have the gumption to look elsewhere and he didn't have the patience. A marriage made in. . .passivity. They would marry, make a home, have children, grow old. Die. He lit a cigarette.

From here, the whole of Crieff was visible and it wasn't so big at all.

*

Sergeant Rudd placed a cup of tea on the table in front of PC McAnuff. Willy eyed it warily. The sergeant had never made him tea before.

'Your fancy woman. . .' the sergeant said.

'It's ower.'

'Dumped you, aye?'

'I dumped her.'

'Is that why you've been a miserable bastart the past twa days?'

'I said I dumped her. I didnae say I was happy aboot it.'

'Richt enough. It's a bugger when you get the tap turned aff.'

'It wasnae like that.'

'No? What was it like, then?'

Willy pondered the question. He didn't have enough experience to answer. He knew he was being used by Lorna, knew their relationship was out of the ordinary. Basically, he provided sex when she demanded. Nothing else. No intimacy, not even conversation. Just sex, mechanical, perfunctory, followed by some insults and tidy up your clothes and be off.

Reflecting like that, he couldn't understand the attraction, yet he knew if she called him now he would come running.

'It's ower,' he repeated

Rudd lit a cigarette and stretched back on his chair, arm around the back. 'Good,' he said. He offered Willy a cigarette and Willy took one, lighting up nervously. He'd never smoked in front of anyone before.

'She came to see me the day,' Rudd continued. 'Made a complaint.'

'Aboot me?'

'Sandy Disdain. Says he sexually assaulted her.'

'Sandy Disdain? Sandy's only interested in onythin he can shoot.'

'Exactly. It's aa lees, I'm sure of it. That woman bothers me. There's somethin no richt aboot her. She's cauld. Thin. I dinnae ken if she's the arsonist and a few weeks ago I would never hae believed it. Noo? I wouldnae like to say. I'm thinkin onyone wha could make an accusation like thon against Sandy is capable of onythin.' He tapped his cigarette against the ashtray.

'So, I'm asking you, son, is there onythin you can tell me aboot that woman? Onythin I need to ken?'

Willy was feeling dizzy from the cigarette and his brow was flushed and clammy. He knew he should tell the sergeant about the letter to Dallerie Laundry. But that opened the door to too many questions. He shook his head.

'No sergeant. Nothin.'

He would deal with this in his own way.

Monday, 23 October

A Day of Decisions

'I knew you'd come crawling back.'

Lorna exited the playground and began walking along Commissioner Street, not waiting for PC McAnuff.

'I havenae.'

She turned and regarded him coldly. 'No? You will.'

Willy was carrying a thin, square parcel wrapped in brown paper and he anchored it with his elbow while he felt in his uniform pocket. He pulled out the letter to Dallerie Laundry. 'You recognise this?' he said.

She looked at the letter and then at Willy. 'Never seen it before in my life.'

'You gave it to me to post for you. What were you thinkin? Did you imagine the laundry wouldnae report it to the polis? That I wouldnae get to see it? And recognise it?'

'No to all of those. Particularly the last one.'

'D'you realise what a position you've put me in?'

'Poor baby.'

'Poor me. But also poor you. There's already proof you're the arsonist. Maybe no enough to stand up in court.' He brandished the letter. 'But this could mak it stand up.'

"There's already proof". *What did they have? Keep calm, keep calm.* 'What is this?' she said. 'Are you threatening to do your job properly?'

'If I did my job you'd be up in the court.'

She leaned forward and caressed his cheek with the palm of her hand, then scratched it lightly with her fingernails, raising the faintest of marks. 'Which is why you won't. Will you, lover boy?'

Willy wiped his cheek. 'I couldnae care less aboot the arson,' he said. 'But I winnae stand by and watch you tell lees aboot Sandy Disdain. That's goin too far. Go to Sergeant Rudd, tell him you're withdrawin your complaint aboot Sandy, and this letter disappears.' He put it back in his pocket. 'If you dinnae, I go to the sergeant mysel, and hae a wee discussion. If that gets me into trouble, it's nothin compared to the trouble you'll be gettin.'

Willy saw the anger in her eyes and wondered how he could ever have become involved with this woman. He handed her the parcel.

'What's this?' Lorna said.

'A leavin present.' Willy tipped his helmet in salute and walked back towards the school, leaving Lorna to stand and stare.

*

Lorna placed the gramophone record PC McAnuff had given her on the player and eased the needle on to it, Guy Lombardo and His Royal Canadians, playing *Little Coquette*. She lit a cigarette and lay on the bed, eyes closed, mind at bay, as Guy Lombardo began to sing.

> Tell me, why you keep foolin, you little coquette,
> Makin fun of the ones who love you.
> Breaking hearts you are ruling, little coquette,
> True hearts tenderly dreaming of you.

Poor McAnuff, she thought, too young, too innocent, too nice. Life requires collateral damage. People like McAnuff didn't understand that, didn't realise that was their predestination.

> Someday, you'll fall in love, as I fell in love with you.
> Maybe, someone you love will just be foolin you, too.
> And when you're all alone with only regrets,
> You'll know, little coquette, I love you.

She opened the palm she had kept fisted while the record played. In it was a small piece of now crumpled paper. She smoothed it out and read, in Willy McAnuff's handwriting:

"You'll know, little coquette, I loved you."

Lorna screwed her eyes shut. Be strong. *She would not tear herself in mourning, neither would she drink from the cup of consolation.*

*

Sergeant Rudd sat forward in his chair, hands clasped tightly in front of him. 'I will ask you to consider, miss, before goin on wi this. You made a serious accusation and if you're going to withdraw it I want to mak sure you're doin so for the right reasons. Has anybody tried to force you?'

Lorna stared him down. 'I have reflected, sergeant, and I have concluded that what happened was not serious enough to be considered sexual assault. The man is a lout, but I'll go no further than that. I wish to withdraw the accusation.'

Rudd was half inclined to charge her with wasting police time but there was something about her behaviour he couldn't decipher. The cold self-assurance didn't ring true. The way, even when she was presenting herself as an upstanding member of the community, she somehow managed to insinuate she was apart from and even above the hoi polloi, was baleful in its detachment. This was how she exercised power over people. Rudd had seen toffs behave this way all his life, been on the receiving end more often than he cared to remember, but Lorna Carrington was not a toff. Hers was an act, but what was she concealing, or compensating for? She was clearly odd, but he had to decide whether she was dangerous. And that was difficult because her hauteur was like a carapace.

'Very well,' he said. 'But if onythin like this happens again, I want you to come to me immediately. Me personally.'

'You are such a solace, sergeant.'

'I dinnae ken what that means, so I'll hope it's good.'

*

'I want to speak to the bairn,' said Sandy.

'Dinnae go giein her ony mair daft notions.' He called for Ellen and she emerged from her room, copy of *Culpepper's Herbal* in her hand.

'I'm readin aboot sweet cicely,' she said.

'Licorice,' said Sandy.

'Aye.'

'Saturday mornin, early, I need you to come up the Knock wi me.'

'Whit fur?'

'You'll see when you get there.'

Bob marvelled at the way Ellen accepted Sandy's air of mystery. If Bob had tried something like that, she would have flounced off in a huff.

'You've a way wi her,' he said when Ellen had retreated back to her studies.

'I juist speak to her. I've news: Lorna Carrington's withdrawn all charges.'

'How?'

'Nae idea. But at least I'm oot of trouble.'

Bob twisted his tea cup on its saucer. Everything he knew about Lorna Carrington suggested she must have some ulterior motive: she did not seem a woman inclined to unilaterally change tactics, or to make life easy for others. He was happy that Sandy's immediate problem had been resolved, but he was far from reassured that this would be the end of the matter.

'Keep awa fae her,' he said.

*

Mr Henderson and Miss Salter waited on the pavement outside Mintlaw Public Library for the doors to open at two o'clock. Once inside, they enquired after local newspapers and were directed to the *Buchan Observer*.

'We're interested,' said Mr Henderson, 'in a fire, about two years ago. Would you recollect such an event?'

The library assistant looked momentarily startled. 'Station Road,' she said. 'Late thirty-seven. Terrible thing.'

'What happened?'

'Puir wee Celia. Celia Young, eighteen year auld and, oh, a bonny quine. Killed in a fire at her ludgins. She'd only started workin there a few weeks afore.'

'Were there any suspicious circumstances?' asked Miss Salter.

The library assistant turned to her. 'Faa are you?'

'We're just interested in what happened,' said Mr Henderson.

The library assistant clammed up, clearly uncomfortable with the conversation. 'Ye can read aa aboot it in the paper.' She pulled a large, bound volume of the *Buchan Observer* from the shelf and laid it on a table and flipped through to October 1937. The headline read: "Tragic incident at boarding house". Mr Henderson and Miss Salter bent over the paper and read about a raging fire in which Celia Young, a maid, was trapped in an upstairs room and succumbed to smoke inhalation before a group of men from the nearby public house could attempt a rescue. She was already dead when they reached her. There was no mention of Lorna Carrington, or of suspicious circumstances. Mr Henderson rifled through the next few weeks of the newspaper but the incident was never referred to again.

'Well,' he said to Miss Salter. 'I'm not sure we're any the wiser.' He closed the volume with a thud and they stood and prepared to leave. The library assistant approached and addressed them quietly.

'You micht speak tull Maisie Campbell. In the grocer's doon the wey.'

'Does she know anything about the fire?'

'She was there.'

They thanked her and went onto the street and headed towards the centre of town. On the right was Robbie's Grocery and they entered and waited until the young woman behind the counter had finished serving an old lady in a grey headscarf.

'Are you Miss Campbell?' Mr Henderson asked.

'Aye,' the woman said suspiciously. 'Fit can I dee for you?'

'I understand you were in the boarding house on Station Road when the fire happened in 1937?'

Maisie Campbell did not appear eager to reminded of the event. She flushed and shook her head.

'I'm sorry,' said Mr Henderson. 'I don't want to rake over what must be painful memories, but I'm most concerned about what happened in that fire.'

'Fit do ye mean?'

'I've heard rumours that it wasn't entirely accidental.'

Miss Campbell looked as though she might tear up. Miss Salter reached out and stroked her arm.

'Does the name Lorna Carrington mean anything?' said Mr Henderson. The effect was instantaneous, a look of horror overtaking Miss Campbell's face and an involuntary cry rising from her throat.

'Did she have something to do with the fire?' Mr Henderson continued.

'There was nivver ony proof.'

'But you believe so?'

She stared into Mr Henderson's eyes as though trying to

read his thoughts. 'There's the deil in thon wumman. I never want ti hear her name again.'

'Could. . .'

'Please, gang awa!' Miss Campbell turned and rushed into the back room of the grocer's. Mr Henderson and Miss Salter looked at one another, perplexed.

*

They debated what do next on a tense journey back to Crieff. 'That poor girl,' Miss Salter said. 'She was so upset. Something terrible must have happened.'

Mr Henderson sighed. 'Something terrible certainly did happen. A house fire is a disaster, and any loss of life must be insufferable for those who remain.'

'Should we do something? Speak to Miss Carrington's employer? The police?'

'And say what? You saw the newspaper. There was no suggestion of foul play, not officially. . .'

'But Miss Campbell. . .'

'Is broken by grief and perhaps seeing things that aren't there. Lashing out in anger and pain. We have no evidence for what she says.'

'But St Andrews. . .the same thing. . .'

'And we don't know the precise facts about St Andrews either. . .'

'Somebody died.'

'Coincidences are a part of human life. I've seen it often enough, men accused of vile things on the battlefield, all for the sake of the coincidence of being in the wrong place at the wrong time. . .'

'But. . .'

'You can't rely on coincidence, Miss Salter. It's the cruellest thing. People are predisposed to see patterns. But two does not make a pattern. Sometimes it's sheer bad luck.'

Jane Salter knew plenty about bad luck. Her fiancé, Thomas

Booker, had experienced bad luck in the last war, at Mons, shrapnel-shaped bad luck that ripped him in two. The official telegram didn't say as much but his RSM, over tea and crumpets in Bearsden one afternoon at war's end, explained the final moments of her love's existence. Jane Salter never recovered, never married, never laughed again.

Bad luck, Thomas Booker. Thirty-four of his comrades, pals all from Hamilton and Motherwell, knew the same bad luck that day. Privates and corporals, every single one. Working lads. Numbers on a roll. Jane Salter was approaching fifty, her heart set on retiring at sixty. She already had a tidy amount set by and another ten years' scrimping would see her comfortably through old age. She hoped Mr Henderson would live long enough for her to not need to seek another employer in that time. She was comfortable with him, now, and that was as much as she could ever have expected. The failure she had felt all her life had been neutralised by the grind of daily existence and now she was waiting, waiting for different days, a better ending, quiet contemplation, afternoons in tea shops and evenings with sherry and a book. Good luck. Hosanna.

'So we don't say anything?' she said.

'I don't see that we can. Do you?'

Miss Salter looked at the Aberdeenshire countryside slipping past. She most certainly did. She saw scruple. 'I suppose not,' she said.

Saturday, 28 October

A Day of Eclipses

At six in the morning, Sandy and Ellen stood on the summit of the Knock Hill. The moon was full and the sky was cloudless. Lambent light fell on the Strathearn valley, as though the world was returning to consciousness.

'Watch,' said Sandy. 'Tap left of the moon.'

A minute elapsed and a crescent-shaped sliver of the moon seemed to disappear. More minutes passed – three, five, ten, twenty – and as the moon drifted westwards with each passing moment the gap grew larger.

'It's like someone's takin bites oot of it,' said Ellen. The bite grew until almost all of the moon had disappeared, only a small crescent remaining, diametrically opposite where the first bite had been taken.

'Now watch.'

Just as the moon was about to disappear from view, it re-emerged in full, red and ethereal, while the last visible crescent shone brightly. The ghost of the moon floated through the morning sky for quarter of an hour until it gradually began to fade into nothingness once more and the brightness of the bottom crescent dimmed and the process began to reverse itself. Slowly, bite by bite, the moon returned to its full form.

'Eclipse of the moon,' Sandy explained.

'What happened?'

'The moon went behind the shadow of the earth. It was still there, but we couldnae see it because we got in oor ain wey.'

'Story of ma life.'

'You and me baith, hen.'

Ellen viewed the hills and mountains surrounding her, the Strathearn valley below. It was all so massive, so perfect, and she was merely a speck within it. Within it, but part of it. She had had no idea such beauty existed, but now she did, and she was inside it, and it was inside her, and she knew, then, that she never wanted to leave.

Sandy lit a Capstan and studied the same view. He had pondered all week, what was right, what was best. Lorna Carrington's retraction had freed his way and last night, sleepless and agitated, he made his decision. It was probably the wrong decision, certainly the perilous one.

But Sandy Disdain never took the obvious course.

*

Bob sat at the window table of Cloudland with a cup of tea and *The Strathearn Herald*. He had ten minutes before opening time, enough for a read of the paper. Two British ships, *Sea Venture* and *White Mantle* had been sunk. German aircraft were sighted over the south of Scotland. The Soviet Union and Finland were no closer to agreement and war seemed inevitable. On page two there was a new letter in the "War and Civilisation" correspondence, from Mr Henderson of Barvick Falls, in response to *Macedon*'s letter the previous week.

Sir,

As a society, we ignore the implications of the Sermon on the Mount. The war spirit enfranchises all sorts of evil. I was in the last war and I hate everything that militarism stands for. Apart from the pointless waste of life, wealth and human energy, it gives power to the greedy and base, sustains a cult of blind obedience in a crowd of mischievous blockheads such as *Macedon* and puts our lives at the mercy of trained bullies. The ruling class has drifted and floundered, taking us into this mess, and behold the spectacle of world Statesmen screaming to the young to get them out of it. Always the old, silly, childish cry – "On to Victory" which they know perfectly well is impossible. Last time it took four years with the entire world on our side to subdue Germany. How is it to be done now with only France in support? Even if we were to force a victory, it would be quite pointless unless we knew the cause and cure of what has produced Hitlerism. Otherwise, another Hitler will arise and the butchery will have to be gone over again. *Macedon*, the gomeral who recommends the study of history as a means of understanding the present, might wish to consider that point. Augustus Caesar's *Pax Romana* brought peace to the world. Such a statesman would never have presided over the folly of the Treaty of Versailles.

'I'd like to see Macedon's face when he reads that,' Bob said to Annie. 'A "blockhead" and a "gomeral".'

'Seems quite accurate to me,' Annie replied.

*

Lorna turned to the letters page of *The Strathearn Herald* to see whether her *Macedon* letter the previous week had provoked any response. Indeed there was, and she read the letter with rapidly growing anger which exploded into full-blown fury when she saw the identity of the author, none other than the old buffoon upstairs, Henderson. She glared at the ceiling, as though trying to see through it and find the man himself.

'"Blockhead"? "Gomeral"? We'll see who's the gomeral.'

*

Early afternoon, after crossing Perth's South Inch and making his way the length of Shore Road, canvas bag over his shoulder, Sandy arrived at the Lower Harbour. The place appeared deserted, metal gates held shut by a giant padlock on a rusting chain. He rattled the gate. It would not open. Disappointed, he lit a Capstan and pondered his next move. A short man in an oversized bunnet was walking towards him with the most bandy-legged gait Sandy had ever seen.

'Hello,' he said to the man. 'Is the harbour open?'

'No,' said the man, his voice high and reedy. 'Shut doon twa month syne, when the war started. The Upper Harbour's still open, for sand and gravel, but aa the fancy trade goes to Dundee noo.'

'Is there a Merchant Navy office still here?'

'It's in Dundee an aa.'

Sandy checked the position of the sun. Still early afternoon. If he was quick he could get a train to Dundee before evening. He said goodbye to the man and turned and retraced his steps back to the General Station.

*

Willy McAnuff saluted the Misses Seaton, Beaton and Miller as he walked along Comrie Street towards the terraces. This wasn't on his path, but who was going to check if a policeman did more than his regulation beat? Why, since it was he who had ended things with Lorna Carrington, did he feel so bad? Why did he miss a woman who cared nothing for him? Why would he crawl over drawing pins to be by her side? He reached Barvick Falls and looked up at the house, proud on the hill. Lorna's room was on the first floor, above the portico.

And there she was, looking out. Willy felt instantly sick, a flush rising up his face. He tried to walk normally but his legs had turned to jelly. She gave no indication of having seen him and he turned and walked back the way he had come. She shouldn't see him like this, like a lovelorn puppy staring up at his mistress. He passed the Misses Seaton, Beaton and Miller again.

'You can do better than her, son,' said Miss Beaton.

'You can, aye,' said Misses Seaton and Miller.

*

Mary sat in the Kelty's' living room, cradling a cup of tea. She could scarcely think straight, wasn't even certain how she had ended up here. The news about Sandy had left her dumbfounded and she struggled to control her emotions. It wasn't as though she loved him but the thought he was gone was too massive to comprehend. Her future. Her dreams. Where was she going to find another laddie? Her? Mousy Mary? With the laddies all off to fight, anyway. Women like the Misses Seaton, Beaton and Miller had been left over at the end of the last war, not good enough for the laddies who returned from the fighting. Surplus. That would be Mary Kemp.

Surplus.

'What d'you mean he's gone?' Bob took Mary's hand. She had been crying and her eyes were still red.

'Jined the Merchant Navy. Audrey came roond and telt me. Left a note for his mither and went aff to Perth to sign up.'

'He's done whit?' Ellen jumped up from her chair and advanced towards Mary, who shrank back in alarm. 'How could he? Who's gonnae teach me about nature and stuff now?'

'That's maybe no the number one concern juist noo, Ellen,' said Bob.

'Aye it bloody is. He's no business doin that.' She turned and stormed out of Cloudland, slamming the door behind her. Through the window, Mary and Bob watched her stride uphill to the fountain.

'I'm awfae sorry, Mary,' Bob said.

He knew this was bad news, on every level. Already, only a couple of months into the war, it was obvious that merchant shipping was coming under constant barrage, Germany intent on starving Britain into submission. Sandy could scarcely have chosen a more dangerous occupation. It was typical of him, Bob thought. Sandy was a man who found his own way in life and bridled whenever anyone tried to tell him what to do. He had chosen not to wait for a call-up he had no control over, and instead decided his own future, even when that meant forgoing the reserved status he could easily have claimed. In his head, Sandy had won. He had got one over on authority.

At what cost, Sandy?

Monday, 30 October

A Day of Revenge

'Black Alice, turn round.'

Without thinking, Ellen stood and turned three-hundred-and-sixty-degrees while the class watched, horrified. Everyone turned to Lorna. Lorna dropped her bag on her desk and pulled from it her tawse.

'Come here!' she said, her voice crisp and cold. Ellen stepped towards her desk, her ears ringing with fear. 'Hands out!' Ellen stretched out her hands, one on top of the other. She stared at Lorna and refused to break eye contact even as the tawse was brought down three times on her palm.

'Now the other hand.'

Ellen took her punishment without a word and sat with her hands palms-upward on the desk for the rest of the lesson, staring at the map of the world on the wall and planning her next move.

*

Playtime, and Commissioner Street was alive with the sound of girls' voices, shouting and laughing as they played skipping games and poachie. Marnie was bouncing a ball in time to the rhyme she was chanting:

One, two, three-aleerie,
I spy Mrs Peerie
Sittin on her bumbaleerie
Eating chocolate babies.

Ellen watched morosely from the low wall dividing the girls' and boys' playgrounds. She slipped away and sneaked unnoticed into the school. This was forbidden during breaks and she crept upstairs, all the while looking out for any passing teachers. In the open expanse of the wide stairway she would have nowhere to hide if anyone arrived but she made it to the top unseen and tiptoed to her classroom and listened at the door. Hearing nothing, she opened the door and leaned in.

Empty.

She took the metal waste bin from beneath Miss Carrington's desk and checked the cupboard where the paraffin had been stored. There was a single milk bottle filled with paraffin for the classroom heater and she took it out and poured half into the bucket. She snatched Miss Carrington's tawse and dropped it into the bucket, ensuring it was completely dowsed in the paraffin. She lit a match from a box of *Scottish Bluebell* she'd found in Mr Smith's hut and dropped it. The paraffin exploded and a whoosh of flame leaped two feet into the air before hissing and subsiding. Ellen watched with satisfaction as the tawse was engulfed by flames. It smelled vaguely of burning animal flesh. She wanted to wait and watch its complete incineration but she knew she had to make her escape. She checked the stairs for activity and, seeing nobody, raced back to the front door and the playground and re-took her seat on the wall beside Marnie.

She didn't spot Mr Smith watching her from the cloakrooms.

*

The classroom reeked of burning when the children returned after playtime. They took turns examining the charred remains of the tawse in the bucket, each speculating on who could have done this. Marnie stared at Ellen but Ellen's face remained blank.

'What on earth?' Lorna dashed into the room, looking for the source of the smell and saw the bucket on the floor. 'Sit down, all of you,' she shouted as she bent over the bucket and pulled out the remains of her tawse. Her face clouded with fury.

'Who. . .did. . .this?' She stood at the front of the class and repeated the question. No one spoke. She turned to Ellen. 'Black Alice. Are you responsible for this?'

'No, miss.'

'I strapped you earlier and now the tawse has been ruined. What a coincidence. Admit it, child, this was your doing!'

'No, miss.'

Lorna grabbed her hair and lifted her to her feet. 'Headmaster's office, now. You'll be expelled for this. Class, write one hundred lines: "I shall not have an heart that deviseth wicked imaginations." She gripped Ellen's shoulder. 'You, come with me.'

Mr MacLean, irritated to have his afternoon interrupted by an over-excited Miss Carrington, listened to her explanation and studied the tawse. 'A disgraceful thing to happen,' he said. 'And you think it was this child?'

'She's a constant source of trouble, headmaster. An absolute ruffian.'

'I was given to understand she's clever.'

'She is, but she's difficult.'

Mr MacLean adjusted his spectacles. 'What do you have to say, child?'

'It was nothin to do wi me.'

'I know it was her,' said Lorna. 'Guilt written all over her face.'

'Excuse me, headmaster.' Mr Smith stood outside the open door of the headmaster's office, hands in his overall pockets.

'I couldn't help overhearing the conversation. I can vouch for the lassie. She was wi me all through playtime. She's an interest in horticulture. She was helpin me plant some cabbage and cauliflower seeds. I grow them in the boiler room, where it's warm.'

Mr MacLean clasped his hands and rested them on his desk. 'Is that correct?' he said to Ellen.

Ellen didn't understand what was happening but she wasn't about to pass up an alibi. 'Aye,' she said.

'Poppycock,' said Lorna.

Mr Smith flashed her a hostile look. 'Are you calling me a liar, Miss Carrington?'

'Enough,' said Mr MacLean. He handed the ruined tawse back to Lorna. 'This was a vile act indeed. Perhaps you should reflect on what would drive anyone to do such a thing.'

'I hardly think. . .'

'We have a duty of care to our children. If we are driving them to such extreme acts then we ought to wonder why.'

'But. . .'

'That will be all. We shall put this unfortunate event behind us.' He smiled at Ellen. 'Keep developing those green fingers. We shall have need of them, with this war.'

*

For the third time that afternoon Mary picked up the letter addressed to Lorna Carrington, as though checking whether it had somehow changed. "REPOSSESSION NOTICE: SALMOND'S EMPORIUM" was stamped across it in red ink. Mary put the letter back on the sideboard by the inner door and returned to her duties. She had a feeling this would cause ructions. Lorna hadn't made any monetary demands on her since the gramophone record but that would surely change.

*

'Lassie.'

Mr Smith was holding a broom at the door of his hut as Ellen and Marnie left school for the afternoon. Ellen told Marnie to walk on and she'd catch her up, then sidled up to the janitor's hut.

'Thank you,' she said.

'Next time you pull a stunt like thon, do it ootside. You could've burned the school doon.'

'Why did ye help me?'

'Because thon woman's no fit to be a teacher. She'll come to a bad end, but I wouldnae want to see you get hurt alang the wey. Juist keep awa fae her.'

'Oh, dinnae worry,' said Ellen. 'I've plenty on her. I could ruin her if I needed to.'

'Is that richt?' Mr Smith sensed an opportunity to do something about this vexatious woman. 'And what do you hae on her, exactly?'

'Nah. I was telt no to say anythin. I'll just hing on to it in case I need it.' She skipped away in search of Marnie and Mr Smith watched her go, full of foreboding.

*

'You wanted to see me, headmaster.' Lorna stood before Mr MacLean's desk, still struggling to control her anger over Mr Smith's obvious lie and the way the headmaster had sided with him, brushing off the destruction of Lorna's personal property with a warning as to her own conduct and not a word of censure to Black Alice. She stared at the headmaster balefully.

Mr MacLean looked up. 'You've been with us since January last year, Miss Carrington?'

'Yes, headmaster.'

'And how have you found it?'

'Very edifying, headmaster. I have such lovely children to work with.'

'How have you settled in in Crieff? You're not from here?'

'No, from Mintlaw, Aberdeenshire. I find Crieff a charming town. Very friendly.'

'So you have friends?'

'I have acquaintances, yes.'

'Close girl friends?'

'Not close, no.'

'Boyfriends?'

'No, headmaster.'

Lorna looked around the headmaster's office as though in search of something to calm her. There were books on mountaineering, on lifeboats, biology and botany, on history, literature. The headmaster was a man of eclectic tastes. Lorna tried to focus but she did not feel in control of the conversation and not being in control was her greatest fear.

Mr MacLean adjusted his glasses. He stared directly at her. 'I'll get to the point, Miss Carrington. I have observed your manner this term, your demeanour with our children, your lack of communication with your peers. I don't believe you have integrated in the way I would have wished, either in the school or the wider community. Today's incident with the tawse was a portent. Never in my career have I seen a child do such a thing and it is impossible to avoid the conclusion that this was a calculated act, and your tawse was deliberately targeted. Why would that be?'

'I think, headmaster. . .'

'That was a rhetorical question, Miss Carrington. Why would that be? The tawse is a symbol of your power. Someone felt the need to curb your power. That suggests to me a poisonous atmosphere in your classroom.'

'I take great pride. . .'

'I have spent the past hour telephoning some of the parents of the children in your class. What I heard was most alarming. . .'

'I should have. . .'

'I have made my decision. You are not the calibre of teacher we require in Crieff Public School. You will leave at the end of term.'

*

The walk from school to Barvick Falls did nothing to calm Lorna. All these little people getting in her way, blocking the pavements as they indulged in their inane chatter, gormless schoolchildren running amok, vacant mothers pushing prams, old men long devoid of any useful function, soldiers strutting about in oversize boots and ugly uniforms. She was glad to reach the sanctuary of Barvick Falls but, on entering, she spotted the letter.

Repossession? Never!

She scrunched it in her hand and headed for the stairs. No more bad news today. She flung open the inner door and entered the hallway. Heading upstairs from the living room, humming tunelessly, was Mr Henderson, trailed by Miss Salter. Lorna tried to overtake them without speaking.

'Did you see my letter in *The Herald*?' Mr Henderson said.
'No.'

He gave her one of those looks that old men of his generation always gave, sincere and solicitous and, as always, it made Lorna want to punch him.

'Let me fetch it for you,' he said. 'I'm sure you'll be interested. It touches on a conversation we had with those soldiers. . .'

'Thank you, but no.' She continued to the first floor landing and looked back. 'Actually, I did read your letter. Full of pacifist nonsense.'

'I beg your. . .'

The rage that was inside Lorna spilled out. 'There are enough cowards in this country already, without doddering old buffoons encouraging craven defeatism. War is the only way to counter tyranny. *Pax Romana* my foot. It shouldn't be lawful to write such nonsense. All you Cassandras and your conscientious objector friends, you're the gomerals. You should all be shot.'

Mr Henderson reached out his arm and pointed to her. 'You,' he said, 'you're *Macedon*.'

'And you are a fool.'

'Rather a fool than a warmonger.'

'Go to hell.' She grabbed at the handle to her bedroom door and threw it open. Mr Henderson called out to her.

'Celia Young.'

Fear surged through Lorna's body. *What could the cretin know of Celia Young?* She composed herself and turned back to him. 'Who?' she said.

'Eighteen-years-old. Killed in a fire in Mintlaw two years ago. Terrible tragedy.' He climbed the stairs and crossed the landing and stood next to her. He spoke quietly. 'So they say. Not everyone, though. Some say it was no accident.'

'What are you talking about? Are you senile?'

'Very much *compos mentis*. *Compos mentis* enough to make some enquiries about you, your activities since you left St Andrews. Suddenly. A child dead. Went to Mintlaw. Left suddenly again. A young woman dead. There's a cloud hanging over you, Miss Carrington. All your life. You left St Andrews to escape it. Left Mintlaw to escape. Still it hangs over you. The cloud of justice, decency. It's going to jettison its load on you one of these days.'

'Was that a threat?'

'No. A meteorological observation. Or an ethical one. You decide.' He fixed her in his gaze before turning away and he and Miss Salter climbed the second flight of stairs to his rooms.

Lorna watched, enmity seething inside her, until they were out of sight and she sought sanctuary in her room, slamming the door behind her.

Mary Kemp, having observed the whole scene from the

living room, closed the door and made herself busy to calm her nerves.

In her room, Lorna snatched her letter opener from her desk and opened the crumpled letter in her hand.

"Repossession of the gramophone player tomorrow morning at eleven o'clock."

Lorna looked up at Mr Henderson's room above her, and then at the gramophone player. Dismissed from her employment. Her property repossessed. Now, her history scrutinised. Trespassed against. A violation. Intrusion. Memories of her father resurfaced, the brute, hating through love, love, an abstraction, a parody of human sensibility. She sought to escape him but where could she run, when his seed was inside her? The Sermon on the Mount, the fool Henderson wanted to recall. Very well. *Every good tree bringeth forth good fruit; but a corrupt tree bringeth forth evil fruit.* Lorna stared at her reflection in the dressing table mirror. I am my father's child. Any guilt is not mine, it is his. I was forced into this. *A good tree cannot bring forth evil fruit, neither can a corrupt tree bring forth good fruit.* She threw herself onto her bed and pulled the pillow over her head and shut her eyes tightly. Temptation was insinuating itself into her mind. Oh, oh, dread temptation.

Behold, how great a matter a little fire kindleth! A fire, just a little fire, providing great release, the sanctity of the flames.

For these be the days of vengeance. Sandy Disdain, common little man, had refused her. *An ugly soul.* Willy McAnuff, hapless fool, had spurned her. *A coquette.* A stranger had assaulted her. *Stuck-up bitch.* The headmaster had dismissed her. *Not the calibre.* She had no friends. No comfort. She would not cry. Self-pity was no pity. *I will not speak in the bitterness of my soul.* She had no family. Her father was rotting in the dirt. Every unkindness he had ever inflicted on his daughter she remembered now and would avenge. The living trump the dead. The dead are of no consequence. *They sleep in death. What do you think, Daddy?* She squeezed her eyes more tightly shut. She would not let him in. She would not let him in.

You're too little to be proud. You're a worm in search of love. You need to turn that regard for yourself towards God, wretched child. You'll go to hell. There is no repentance. God knows all.

Her skin itched as though it were going to crack open. A succession of little explosions was turning her brain to pulp. *He healeth the broken in heart and bindeth up their wounds.*

'Who will bind my wounds?' she shouted. Flames abounded, flames in her heart, flames in her head, flames in her memory.

Flames in her future.

When thou walkest through the fire, thou shalt not be burned; neither shall the flame kindle upon thee.

Lorna felt a sudden clear-headedness such that she had never previously known. Everything made sense. Her father, the false prophet. And now the new ravening wolf upstairs. Finally, the answer was obvious.

And thrilling.

Monday, 30 October, 10 pm

A Night of Catastrophe

Lorna had never felt more alive. Never more frightened. Never more happy. The top floor of Barvick Falls was in darkness. The blackout curtain taped over the large skylight in the roof billowed loosely. She thought of her father, and this time his presence was not unwelcome. *Watch, father, watch what you've made your daughter do. What you've turned her into.* She pulled a rag stopper from a milk bottle and poured turpentine onto the curtains drawn across the east-facing window. She opened another bottle and threw the turpentine against the blackout curtain on the skylight. Most of it fell onto the stairway curling beneath. She breathed heavily, three times, four, five, staring at the closed door to Mr Henderson's room. Her hands shook as she struck a match and watched a flame dance from the sulphide. She dropped it against the base of the curtain.

Watched.
Smiled.
Walked downstairs.
A flame of fire.

*

In light snow, Bob passed the site of the new air raid shelter and the halted works on the Abbots Buildings housing scheme.

His inspection of the frontages of Milnab Street found nothing amiss and at the bottom of the street he took the rough path behind the terrace to check the backs of the houses. There was a light showing in the skylight window of number twenty-seven and he rapped on the back window and waited. The window opened and the silhouette of a woman appeared in the darkness.

'Mrs Duguid?'

'Who is it?'

'ARP Warden, ma'am. Juist advisin you there's a light showin in your upstairs. If you could shut it aff, please.'

'I'm sorry, son.'

Bob heard a quaver in her voice and realised she was crying. 'Are you alright?'

'Aye. Heard the day my laddie, Jack, he's been sent oot to France wi the Black Watch. Twenty-year-auld. A bairn.'

'I'm sorry. It's a hellish thing, this war.'

'You no been called up yet?'

'Winnae be lang.'

'What's that?' Mrs Duguid pointed behind him at an orange glow in the distance, behind the trees at the end of the Duguid's garden.

'Fire,' he said. 'That's the Comrie road is it no?'

'Aye.'

'Can I get there fae here?'

'Tap of the gairden, there's a fence atween us and Barnkittock. Then you're on the Comrie road.'

'Fix your light,' Bob said as he ran into the darkness. He became entangled in the Duguids' washing line and extricated himself and lumbered upwards, his hands outstretched in search of obstacles. The garden was steeply raked and the top half was given over to vegetables, with a path running around the edge. He could see fire glowing through the heavy line of trees marking the border between the Duguids' and Barnkittock, and he located the fence and pulled himself over it. He ran up the curved slope to the Comrie road. Flames were visible now, round the corner, and he ran towards them. A house towered over the road and flames were leaping twenty feet in the air from first and second storey windows.

The house next door was in darkness and he dashed up the snow-covered driveway and banged heavily on the front door. After a good minute, a disgruntled man appeared at the door, poker in hand.

'Call the fire brigade,' Bob shouted. 'Next door's on fire.'

'Barvick Falls?' The man ran barefoot onto the snow and peered round the corner of his house. 'Dear God.' Bob left him to telephone for help and made his way next door. There was a stentorian roar of combustion and crackling of timber and paint and varnish. Flames were funnelling in heavy waves out of the windows into the black night sky. The heat was profound in comparison to the coldness at ground level from frost and light snow. Through the noise of the flames a scream rose and Bob looked up. Above the portico was a balcony, twelve feet or so in length, and behind that an open window. The room beyond was ablaze and a woman was clambering out of the window. She staggered onto the balcony and took three or four heaving breaths of fresh air.

'Here,' Bob shouted up at her and waved his arms. 'Climb over and let yoursel doon. I'll catch you.'

'I can't. It's too high.'

'Try. Climb over. Grip the railin. Let yoursel drop. I'll be there.'

A sharp concatenation sounded inside the room as something collapsed, and the woman screamed again. She climbed the balustrade and crouched over it. Fear overtook her and she stayed like that, unable to move.

'Grab the railin at the bottom. Slide your hand doon. Noo, let your foot go.'

Slowly, the woman did as Bob instructed and she tumbled from the balustrade. At the last moment she gripped it and was left hanging in mid-air. Bob positioned himself five feet below her and prepared himself to catch.

'Let go,' he shouted. 'I'm here.'

After fifteen or twenty seconds, unable to keep her grip any longer, the woman fell and Bob braced himself. She landed on his chest and he gripped his arms around her and they both fell to the ground, Bob taking the weight of her fall. They rested motionless for a moment before the woman rolled away and got to her hands and knees and pulled herself upright. Bob groaned and winced as pain lanced his shoulder, and then he, too, pulled himself to his feet.

'My hero,' the woman said and it was only when she spoke Bob realised she was Lorna Carrington.

'Is there anyone else in the hoose?'

'I have no idea.'

The neighbour loomed out of the gloom carrying a twenty-foot ladder. 'Fire brigade's comin,' he said. He held out his hand. 'Geordie Lauchlan. Plumber. Is aabody oot?'

'We dinnae ken.'

A peal of breaking glass and loud screams pierced the darkness, coming from the rear of the house. Bob and Geordie ran towards it. The west gable had fewer windows and initially the fire didn't seem as fierce but as soon as they turned onto the rear elevation they saw the flames were now out of control, far worse even than when Bob had arrived only a few minutes earlier. The entire roof was ablaze and in danger of collapse. Another scream rang out and Bob saw a shape at a first storey window, waving frantically.

'We cannae wait for the fire brigade,' Bob said. 'Will your ladder reach?'

'Just aboot.' Geordie set the ladder against the wall next to the burning window. Beneath it, the ground floor window was broken and flames were licking around the frame. 'I'll haud it,' he said.

Bob looked at the ladder and at the window, twenty feet

above them. He blew out his cheeks and stepped onto the ladder and started to climb, fear creating an excess of lactic acid which was causing his calves to seize up. He felt more tired than he had ever known. There was a blast of heat as he passed the first floor window and the blaze was so intense the stonework was hot. Each step took him closer to the epicentre of the fire. Trying not to think about how far he had climbed, he reached the first storey window. Inside, Mary Kemp and Bessie were holding each other for comfort. Flames were leaping from the beds behind them and licking around the base of the wardrobe. The bedroom door was open and beyond that was a seething mass of flame. The window was their only exit.

'Can you climb doon?' he shouted.

'I'm too scared,' Mary replied. 'I'll fall.'

'I'll haud on to you.'

'I cannae.'

Bob looked around helplessly. Everything beyond the house was in complete darkness, while the house itself was haloed by the orange glow of a fire that was devouring it.

'Climb oot,' he shouted. 'Hang on to me. Ower my shoulder.'

'I'm scared.'

'Me an aa. Juist do it.'

Bessie started to push Mary forward as the flames drew closer to them and Mary clambered onto the window ledge, whinnying in terror. She pulled herself over Bob's shoulder and gripped the back of his jacket.

'Ready?' he shouted.

'No.'

His foot groped in the air in search of the next rung on the ladder and he lowered himself until he found it. Mary's entire weight was now rested on his shoulders. They already ached. His foot searched for the next rung and he began his descent. He tried to think of nothing except the next step, aware that if he thought too much about their predicament he would panic. He had no idea where he was on the ladder, how far he had descended, how far he had still to go. He drove on, step by step, shoulders throbbing with fatigue. Below him, flames from the first floor had settled on the ladder and it was beginning to burn. Geordie Lauchlan shouted up to warn him but he didn't hear. He carried on until his foot reached the point of the flames and he looked through his legs, horrified at the sight of the burning ladder. He kicked at the flames as though trying to push them off. There was no alternative but to climb through. Flames licked at his trousers and he felt them hot against his skin. He climbed down until his hands needed to grip the burning rungs. Three of the rungs were aflame and he tried to pull his jacket sleeves over his hands and took a breath before descending once more, resting his hands on the burning rung. Pain shot through him and he groped with his foot for the next rung to pass through as quickly as he could. He missed it and his foot swung helplessly in the air. Mary, sensing the jolt, screamed and Bob steadied himself as he searched for the rung again. He lowered himself once more, this time forced to grip the rung that was completely ablaze. He screamed and pushed himself down again, searching in the darkness for the next rung, and then he was clear of the burning section of the ladder. It was beginning to creak and he feared it might break apart soon.

'Five more steps,' Geordie shouted up at him and he forced himself down, each step an agony of burning and fatigue, until he reached the ground. He felt Geordie's hands on him pulling Mary from his back and settling her on the ground.

Bob bent over and pushed his hands into the light snow. He took a deep breath and looked up at the window, knowing there was no way he could get back up there to rescue Bessie.

'There's another ane up there,' he said to Geordie.

'The fire brigade's just arrived. I'll get them.'

Bob collapsed to the ground and sat spreadeagled on the

snow-covered drive. Mary sat beside him, dazed. Behind him, a fireman toppled Geordie's ruined ladder and replaced it with one of their own.

Suddenly, Mary looked up as though woken from a stupor. 'Mr Henderson,' she cried. 'Miss Salter.'

Bob couldn't take any more consternation. His head felt heavy and he wanted only to sleep. He pushed his hands into the snow once more and looked up. Lorna Carrington was standing over him.

She was laughing.

*

Bob awoke in the Cottage Hospital in Pittenzie Street with his hands bandaged and gauze over his cheek. Annie was seated beside him and Sergeant Rudd was standing at the foot of the bed, cap under his arm.

'The hero awakes,' Rudd said. Annie reached forward and stroked Bob's forearm.

'Did Bessie get oot?' Bob asked.

'Aye, she's fine.'

'I'm sorry I couldnae get her.'

'The Fire Brigade did. You did fine, son. You saved a lassie's life.' He paused, as though weighing whether or not to continue. ' Pity the others werenae so lucky,' he said finally.

Bob felt a jolt of fear run through his body. He tensed as pain flared up in his shoulders and hands.

'Others?'

Rudd bowed his head. 'Hellish thing. They must have been trapped on the tap floor.'

'Wha?'

'Mr Henderson and his nurse.'

Tuesday, 31 October

A Day of Investigation

The instant Bob woke up from a confused and muddy dreamscape his mind was overwhelmed by a surge of thoughts and emotions. He had hoped, with his rescue of Mary, that last night would be remembered as a terrible event with a happy ending, but now it had become a tragedy. Never to be forgotten. Mr Henderson, with his letter of hope for humanity in the face of war, now lost. Miss Salter dying alongside her employer, The country was at war but, it seemed, the true dangers were closer to home.

'You alright?'

Sergeant Rudd was seated by the bed. His bulk overspilled the narrow wooden frame of the chair.

'You been here aa night?'

'Dinnae flatter yersel. Juist arrived to see how you were doin. See if you mind onythin. . .'

Rudd was stony-faced. Bob identified a resolution in his expression he hadn't seen before. 'You're thinkin this wasnae an accident?' he said.

'Aye. The Fire Brigade are still there, dampin doon. But it looks suspicious, Eddie Weston telt me earlier. To go up that quick somethin must hae started it. Probably on the tap flair.'

'How do they ken that?'

'The way the tap flair burned and fell through to the first

flair, and then the first flair fell to the ground flair. In that order. They found Mr Henderson's body on what was left of the first flair, the nurse's on the groond flair.'

Bob closed his eyes. In his imagination, he had turned the horror into something almost passive, Mr Henderson and Miss Salter succumbing to smoke and falling where they stood, the flames claiming them only as an afterthought. That was the sanitised version, restricted, suppressed, designed to make the truth easier for him to digest. Now, the violence of their demise was clear. He started to cry for people he had never met, for their lost hopes, for their tribulations and woe.

'Sergeant. . .' He hesitated, the thought that was forming in his mind too horrible to contemplate. 'Lorna Carrington was there last night. I rescued her. . .'

'I ken.'

'And you ken she's an arsonist. . .'

'I dinnae ken that.'

'She's started three fires we ken of. And now the hoose she bides in is burnt doon.'

'That might be suspicious, aye, except for the fact she was caught in the fire an aa. If you were goin to burn doon a place, you'd mak damned sure you got oot. Stands to reason.'

'Maybe the speed of it surprised her.'

'And maybe she was just an unfortunate victim.'

'A fortunate ane. Mr Henderson and Miss Salter are the unfortunate anes.' Pain from his burned hands was making him light-headed but he persevered with the ugly thoughts in his head. 'When I saved Mary and we were lyin on the grund, Lorna Carrington was there.'

He grimaced.

'She was laughin.'

*

Sergeant Rudd was still cursing himself for stopping to see Bob as he made the short walk down King Street later from the station to Salmond's Emporium. Because of the fire, he was having to field agitated calls from the Procurator Fiscal and the Chief Constable, and now he had Kelty's weird notions to consider. He didn't have time on top of all that for fools' errands but Mr Salmond had insisted he had something important to relay and needed to speak to Rudd personally. Mr Salmond was repairing a clock at his wooden counter when Rudd entered the shop.

'Sergeant,' he said, looking up. 'How's your new wireless doing?'

'Just grand. Reception's clear as a bell.'

'You made a good choice. *GEC* are fine machines.'

'You've somethin you want to tell me?'

'Lorna Carrington.'

Rudd rolled his eyes. 'Please dinnae try to tell me she was responsible for the Barvick Falls fire.'

'That's just it. I think she might be.'

Rudd pulled out his notebook. Where Bob Kelty was known for his active imagination Mr Salmond was not a man given to flights of fancy. 'You'd better tell me,' he said.

'Yesterday mornin, I sent her a letter advising her I was repossessin her gramophone player. She hasnae made any HP payments for near three month. I warned her numerous times. The repossession letter was the last resort. But then, last nicht, the fire...'

'You cannae think she'd burn the hoose doon just because her gramophone player was bein repossessed?'

'It sounds ridiculous, I ken. But she's an unco woman. Comes across all prim and proper but there's a side to her. I saw it for mysel, otherwise I wouldnae hae believed it. I went to the school to see her, afore we sent the repossession letter. I wanted to tell her to her face, like. "You'll never get it back," she says to me. "If I can't have it, no one will."'

'She said that?'

'She did.'

'"If I can't have it, no one will"? Those precise words?'

'Those precise words.'

*

'That backs up what I said.' Bob studied his bandaged hands and then looked up at Sergeant Rudd. 'Lorna Carrington had a motive for burnin doon Barvick Falls.'

'No much.'

'No for a normal person. But Lorna Carrington's a pyromaniac. Burnin things doon is what she does.'

'Twa people deed.'

'She didnae mean that. Probably didnae mean for the hale hoose to burn doon.'

'Just the gramophone player?'

'"If I can't have it, no one will." That's what she said.'

Rudd reflected for a moment. 'But,' he said triumphantly. 'Eddie Weston says the fire started on the second floor. How would she start it up there, if it was her gramophone player she wanted to destroy?'

Bob had already considered this and didn't have a plausible answer. 'To deflect attention?' he said. 'Avoid suspicion?'

'But the fire could hae been put oot afore there was ony damage to her room. The gramophone player could hae been left untouched. Why risk that?'

Bob acknowledged the point. If Lorna had set the fire on the second floor she must have had a reason. But he had no notion what that reason might be.

'And. . .' Rudd stood up as though to emphasise his point. 'As I said last nicht, the woman was caught up in the fire hersel. You had to rescue her. What kind of arsonist would get trapped in their ain fire?'

'A useless ane?'

'Whatever you think of Lorna Carrington, I dinnae think useless is a word you'd ever use to describe her.'

*

Lorna sat in temporary lodgings in Burrell Street. In her wardrobe were clothes that had been donated by the WVS, hideous things, presumably unsold leftovers from some jumble sale. There was a single mirror by the rear wall and nothing else. No pictures, no ornaments, like a prison cell. She studied her hand to see if it was shaking. The faintest tremor. She didn't know how to process these feelings, this disorientation, disconnection from reality. Her entire life had been punctuated by crises, some created by her father, others by herself, but through them all she had retained her equanimity. *For God hath not given us the spirit of fear; but of power, and of love, and of a sound mind.*

Today was different.

After a peremptory knock at her door and, before permission to enter had been granted, her landlady, Mrs McInnes, peered in. Her simpering smile caused Lorna to recoil. 'Miss Carrington,' she said, 'the polis are here to see you.'

Sergeant Rudd strode into the room. He removed his helmet and waited while Mrs McInnes reluctantly closed the door and retreated downstairs.

'I hope you're settlin in,' he said, 'after the shock of the fire.'

'This isn't permanent.'

'May I ask, miss, were you defaultin on your hire purchase with Salmond's for a gramophone player?'

Lorna looked at him with distaste. 'I've lost everything in the world. Surely Salmond's aren't still hounding me for that blasted gramophone player?'

'If they are, that's nane of my business. But he's a good man, Eric Salmond, I doubt he'll cause you much bother on that score.'

'Then why the question?'

'We've discussed afore, aboot whether you might be the arsonist. . .'

'And you imagine, because I was about to have my gramophone player repossessed, I'd burn down the whole house and kill two innocent people?'

'It sounds far-fetched.'

'It sounds insane.'

'I hae to investigate. . .'

'Then investigate away, sergeant. Prove what you will. But don't expect any help from me. Good evening.' Lorna picked up her cigarettes and, turning her back on Rudd, lit one. She exhaled and stared out of the window onto Burrell Street while she listened to Rudd opening and then closing the door. She turned back to an empty room and smiled. If their only line of enquiry was a repossessed gramophone player, she had nothing to fear. These yokels were even more stupid than the police in Mintlaw.

And what a dance she led them.

*

The door of Cloudland opened and DO MacLean entered, smiling firmly. 'Mr Kelty,' he said, 'I'm glad to see you're on the mend. You were quite the hero, by all accounts.'

'Onyone would hae done the same.'

'Perhaps, but you're the one who did. Actions speak louder than words. May we talk?' Leslie Comer poured two teas as Mr MacLean and Bob took a seat by the window. Mr MacLean laid his trilby on the table and adjusted his bow tie. 'I've spent the morning debating whether to speak with you. I'm troubled, and I would benefit from some advice.'

'Advice? From me?'

'Don't sound so surprised.' The headmaster's smile was encouraging. 'I believe Ellen Laing is staying with you?'

'Smashin lassie.'

'Somewhat feisty.'

'She knows her mind.'

'How does she get on with Miss Carrington?'

The question took Bob by surprise. He deliberated how to respond.

'I'm seeking honesty, Mr Kelty, not diplomacy.'

'Miss Carrington doesn't strike me as a very good teacher. She uses fear. And she seems to have it in for Ellen, We don't know why.'

'Can you give me any examples?'

'She washed a bairn's hair in paraffin in front of the hale class. . .'

'She did what?' Mr MacLean's voice rose and Leslie Comer, behind the counter of Cloudland, turned in surprise. 'Why?'

'She had lice, apparently.'

'Was this Ellen?'

Bob shrugged. 'Ellen said it was another lassie, but I have my doubts. She came home one night, upset, hair reekin of paraffin, and said it was some Glesga bairns did it. Then, later, she told us Miss Carrington did the same thing to another lassie. Doesn't seem likely there would be two separate occasions a bairn got her head washed in paraffin so I'm thinkin it only happened the once and it was Miss Carrington did it to Ellen.'

Mr MacLean turned his teacup on its saucer. 'I wish you had come to me about this at the time. I'd have put a stop to it. Did you know Ellen burned Miss Carrington's tawse on Monday?'

Bob stifled a laugh. 'No, she didn't mention that.'

'I would like to know what provoked such an act.'

'I can ask her.'

'Explain she's in no trouble.'

'I will. If I may ask, why are you interested in Miss Carrington?'

'I'm troubled by the fire at Barvick Falls last night. I have spoken with the Fire Brigade and they suggest there was foul play.'

Bob studied the concern etched on the face of the headmaster, the grimace of a smile, the tired eyes. This was a man wrestling with his conscience. 'And you think,' he said slowly, 'that Miss Carrington may have something to do with it?'

'It's a notion too horrible to contemplate, but that is precisely what I am thinking.'

Bob took a breath, then outlined his theory about Lorna being the arsonist. He explained the evidence, and described Lorna's subsequent behaviour, targeting both Bob and Sandy.

'And now a fire at her lodgings,' he concluded. 'It's too much of a coincidence, surely?'

'It raises suspicions, certainly.'

'I said as much to Sergeant Rudd, but he's convinced she had no part in it because she was trapped in the fire herself and had to be rescued.'

'I understand his logic.'

'And what's more, he says the motive doesn't hold water.'

'What motive is that?'

'Miss Carrington was goin to have her gramophone record repossessed today. And she told Mr Salmond that if she couldn't have it, nobody would.'

'Sergeant Rudd suspects that burning down the house is not a proportionate response?'

'Correct.'

Mr MacLean slid his spectacles up his nose. 'Again, I see his logic. However, this is the precise point that is exercising me. Yesteday afternoon, I spoke to Miss Carrington and informed her that I was terminating her contract at the end of the school year.' The two men stared at one another. 'Might Sergeant Rudd consider dismissal a sufficient motive?'

Bob ran his bandaged hand over his thinning hair. 'I think you need to ask him,' he said.

*

'I should like to speak with the headmaster.' Lorna addressed Mrs Liversedge firmly, knowing the secretary's tendency to rebuff requests to see Mr MacLean.

Mrs Liversedge didn't deign to look up from her correspondence. 'The headmaster has gone out on urgent business,' she said. She paused. 'To the police station.'

'The police station? What business has he at the police station?'

'I wouldn't know.' She spoke slowly and deliberately, making it evident to Lorna that she did, indeed, know. The only inference Lorna could draw was that the reason had something to do with her. She felt a burst of trepidation. Her disposition was veering between confident indifference and a near certainty that she would be uncovered. Even after the initial flush of triumph following her conversation with Sergeant Rudd, she had sunk once more into despondency. This was something she had never experienced, a fatalism that was enervating and debilitating. Her headache was oppressive, shutting down rational thought, making sleep the only agreeable option. She turned on her heels and exited the secretary's office.

*

'You have no alternative, sergeant.' DO MacLean was a man used to being in positions of authority and he had no time for small talk. 'The evidence against Miss Carrington is slight, I accept, but given the seriousness of this incident it is surely sufficient for further investigation. I am sure the Procurator Fiscal would expect to be appraised of this turn of events. I recommend he is, very quickly.'

Sergeant Rudd felt himself being backed into a corner. He had to concede Lorna's dismissal was a more convincing motive than repossession of a gramophone player. Moreover, the Fire Brigade had officially confirmed the fire was arson. Eddie Weston was certain it was started with turpentine and, while the anonymous arsonist's accelerant of choice had been paraffin, Kelty's previous evidence and the word of DO MacLean meant he had no alternative but to question Lorna Carrington again.

'I'll telephone the Procurator Fiscal.'

*

Lorna experienced a crisis that evening, alone in her room, listening to a convoy of army lorries heading for Glasgow. She began to tremble uncontrollably and felt more cold than she had ever known, despite wearing four layers of clothing and having a shawl wrapped around her. DO MacLean's voice was ringing in her head, denouncing her to Sergeant Rudd, calmly listing the evidence against her compiled by the fool Kelty and his wastrel friend. Her secret was known, her lust for flames. Now the fire at Barvick Falls. They would trace her back to Mintlaw. To St Andrews. Investigate again. Jeopardy. Exposure. A daft child dead in St Andrews. A foolish maid in Mintlaw. Now, the coward Henderson and his nurse dead in Crieff and Lorna could be accused. She could be tried. She could be. . .

'No, no, no, no.'

She pulled the shawl more tightly round her shoulders and began to rock backwards and forwards, thinking furiously.

A plan was forming. She didn't like it, not one bit.

But there was no alternative.

Wednesday, 1 November

A Day of Revelations

Sergeant Rudd had figured it would be best to send PC McAnuff to bring Lorna Carrington in for questioning, reasoning his familiar face would offer reassurance. Their demeanours as she followed him into the station told him his plan had been misguided.

'The Parkies have been complainin aboot vandalism in MacRosty Park,' he said to a sullen McAnuff. 'It'll be thae Glesga bairns. Awa up and speak to the heid Parkie, then round up the little bastards.' He smiled at Lorna. She didn't smile back and he gestured towards the interview room in the rear.

'We're tryin to understand the cause of the fire,' Rudd said when they were seated. 'The Fire Brigade have some suspicions. I'm sorry to mak you go over aa this again, miss, but ony information you hae would be very helpful.'

He watched in astonishment as Lorna's face crumpled, her mouth quivering and her eyes brimming. She buried her face in her hands and started to cry, huge, sobbing wails bursting from her chest and tears sliding down her cheek.

'It's all my fault,' she said finally.

'What is?'

'The fire. It was a terrible accident.' She stared at her lap, her hands fisted against her green pinafore, a picture of misery.

The assured – even cocky – woman to whom he had become accustomed was so transformed it was like confronting a different person. She looked like a child. Sergeant Rudd sat back on his chair for a moment and gave her time to compose herself. She continued to stare sightlessly in front of her for some time before finally looking up at him.

'Tell me what happened,' he said.

'I was making floor polish.'

'Floor polish?'

'For my classroom. The floor gets into such a state with the children's feet, especially in winter. I had some beeswax and turpentine and I was heating it together. . .'

'Where?'

'On the top floor of Barvick Falls.'

'How?'

'There's no carpet up there. I thought it would be the safest place, if anything happened.' She paused and sniffed and passed a handkerchief over her nose. 'Which, of course, it did. . .'

'Go on.'

'I was heating it on the little camping stove from the kitchen. . .'

'How did you no do it in the kitchen?'

'Cook doesn't like anyone in there.'

'Go on.'

'I lost control. I've never made it before, only read the instructions. Everything seemed to be going absolutely fine, but suddenly it boiled over and jumped out of the pan and landed on the flame underneath. There was an explosion and the whole thing went up. Flames shot along the floor and onto the curtains and they went up just like that. . .'

'What did you do?'

'I tried to put it out. Pulled the curtains down and tried to stamp on them. I think that might have made it worse. All that dust. . .'

'Did you call for help?'

'I didn't think there was anyone around. I thought Mr Henderson was out – I saw him going out earlier with Mrs Salter and I didn't know they'd returned. If only. . .' She stopped and stared down once more. She took a deep breath. 'I looked around and the whole of the top floor was ablaze. It's so dry and dusty up there, the flames just got out of control. So I ran downstairs to my room to put on my shoes and go for help. By the time I got them on, when I opened my door there were flames everywhere on the landing. I couldn't even see the stairs.'

'And how long did all this take?'

'Two minutes. If that.'

Rudd reflected. Eddie Weston confirmed the fire must have taken hold with uncanny speed. Her story at least confirmed that.

'And in my panic I didn't shut the door behind me. I was still thinking what to do. But then the fire got into my room. Across the carpet. Onto the bed. I had to climb out of the window onto the balcony. . .'

'And Bob Kelty helped you doon?'

'Yes, he saved my life.'

'He probably did, aye.'

Lorna looked round the room as though only suddenly aware of where she was. She looked at Rudd and Rudd saw a different woman from the one he'd come to know, tremulous, vulnerable.

'You didnae mention this yesterday,' he said.

'I was frightened. You were asking questions about this blasted arsonist. I thought people would jump to conclusions. Think it was me. Think I could. . .'

'So why tell me noo?'

She fixed him with a stare. 'Guilt. I can't live with it. Knowing what I did. . .'

'You're no just tryin to talk yoursel oot of trouble?'

'It seems to me I'm doing the very opposite.'

Rudd sat back and lit a cigarette, watching her all the while. There was something intensely dislikeable about the woman but that didn't make her a murderer.

'I'll never get over this,' she said.

'I dinnae suppose you will, lass.'

'What will happen?'

'I'm glad to say that's no my decision. I'll hae to speak to the Procurator Fiscal.'

'Could he charge me?'

'He could hae you charged, aye.'

'Oh my God.'

*

At eleven o'clock, Sergeant Rudd sat down in the interview room once more. Opposite him were Bob and DO MacLean.

'I interviewed Lorna Carrington this morning,' he said. 'And she explained to me how the fire started.'

Bob looked at him in amazement. 'She confessed?'

'No. She explained how the fire started.'

'How?'

'An accident. She was makin floor polish.'

'Floor polish?' said Mr MacLean.

'For her classroom.'

'Nonsense. Mr Smith has a plentiful supply of floor polish. His brother keeps bees. We have to give jars away every year in the Christmas raffle.'

'The mixture boiled over, set fire to the stove, the fire spread to the curtains and overran the hoose.'

'And whaur did this happen?' said Bob.

'On the second floor.'

'How would she do it there?'

'She thought it would be safer, on account of there bein nae carpet.'

'And you believe that?'

'Of course I dinnae believe it. I've never heard such blethers in aa my life. Thon hoose was destroyed in less than half an hoor. It would hae taken a sicht mair than a wee pot of turpentine to do that.'

'So you think she did it deliberately?'

'She's admitted responsibility. Presumably thought we'd work it oot, so came up with this haivers for an alibi.'

'What happens next?'

'The Procurator Fiscal's made it clear. He wants answers. He wants arrests. He wants charges.'

'You'd better get on wi it, then.'

'That's why you're here. Thon milk bottles you hae, and the fingerprints from your man in Glesga. You'll need to bring them in. I need to get them checked. Headmaster, I need a statement.'

Bob and DO MacLean exchanged glances. Things were coming to a head.

*

In mid-afternoon, Mary Kemp sat beside Annie on the settee in the flat above Cloudland, smiling unconvincingly. Bob sat in the armchair. This was the first time Bob and Mary had been together since the fire and initially both were inexplicably shy, as though their shared experience had assumed some form of intimacy. At first, their conversation avoided mention of the fire, instead covering platitudes of Crieff living, weather, war, blackouts. Rumours of rationing were a source of vexation all round. 'Have they seen how much my faither eats?' Mary complained. Finally, Bob broached the subject of the fire and relayed to Mary what had happened in the past two days.

'I had to go to the polis earlier and hand in the milk bottles and fingerprints. Sergeant Rudd's fingerprintin Lorna Carrington. Gettin it checked by the Glesga polis.'

'You cannae really think Miss Carrington set fire to Barvick Falls?' Mary said.

'The Fire Brigade say there was turpentine poured ower the tap floor. Much mair than you'd need for makin a pot of floor polish. So she's the main suspect. The only suspect.'

'But how?'

'Sergeant Rudd thinks it's because on the same day she heard her gramophone record was bein repossessed and she was sacked fae the school. Combination of events tipped her ower the edge.'

'And you believe that?'

'No. I believe she did it. But that's no the reason. Or no all the reason, onywey.'

'How no?'

'If it was, why would she start the fire upstairs? Why no in her ain room? Next to the gramophone player? If that's what she wanted to destroy, that's where she'd start the fire. There has to be a reason for startin it on the second floor.'

'Mr Henderson?'

'What would he hae to do wi it?'

'I dinnae ken. They had an argument that day, though.'

'Lorna Carrington and Mr Henderson?'

'Well. . .' Mary flushed, seeing Bob's reaction and worrying she was making too much of it.

'Did you tell Sergeant Rudd?'

'He never asked me. . .It didnae seem important. It wasnae an argument as such, juist a disagreement, on the stairs. . .'

'What aboot?'

'She was callin him for aathin. Aboot the war. Bein a coward. Somethin aboot a letter.'

'What letter?'

'I dinnae ken.'

'And then what happened?'

'Miss Carrington went up to her room. Mr Henderson said somethin, somebody's name. Then he followed her to the landing and carried on speaking but I couldnae hear what he said. Him and Miss Salter went to their rooms. Miss Carrington watched them go and then went into her room and slammed the door.'

'Mr Henderson said a name? Wha's?

'I cannae mind. I didnae ken it.'

'Man or woman?'

'Woman.'

'And she watched him goin upstairs?'

'Aye.'

'Was Miss Salter there?'

'Aye.' Mary frowned at Bob. 'It was nothin, really.'

'No,' said Bob. 'That was definitely somethin. But what?'

Thursday, 2 November

A Day of Predestination

Under instruction from Ellen, Bob went to the children's section of the Taylor Trust Library in search of new nature books and pulled out *Curiosities of Natural History*. A coloured picture of a lion next to the title page suggested this would be ideal and he took it to the counter, pulling one of Ellen's library tickets from his wallet. As Eliza Burrell stamped the due date on the date label he requested copies of the last three weeks' *Strathearn Herald*. He still had the edition his letter was published in but the others had been used to light the living room fire. Eliza pointed to a shelf in the reference section and Bob gathered the papers and set them on a table by the window. He read again the letter from Mr Henderson. "Mischievous blockheads such as *Macedon*". "*Macedon*, the gomeral". Whoever *Macedon* was would have felt mightily aggrieved. Bob checked the previous edition for the letter by *Macedon* which had so rankled Mr Ferguson and realised it was the letter published in response to his own, calling him a Cassandra. "And war, only war, will relieve us."

Bob felt a heaviness in his heart. Things were beginning to fall into place. A truth was emerging. He knew how this would end.

And he knew he had to prevent that.

*

Bob poured two teas and ushered Willy McAnuff to a seat at the rear of Cloudland. Willy looked terrible, drawn and haggard as though he hadn't slept in days, much older than his twenty-two years.

'You think she did it?' he asked.

'Aye. Sorry.'

'So do I. She's. . .she's no richt in the heid.'

'I'm comin to see that.'

'D'you think she'll get convicted?'

Bob sipped his tea. 'There's no much evidence. Her defence'll pull the prosecution case to pieces. I've seen it happen. They'll say why would she start the fire awa fae the very thing that allegedly brocht her to commit the crime, the gramophone player? They'll convince the jury it's a load of haivers.'

'There's the arson stuff and aa. Malky's, Dallerie, Lochearnheed.'

'Aye. That could prove she's a pyromaniac. But we're no plush wi evidence there, either. Fingerprints on the bottle, that's aboot it. Again, the defence'll pull that to pieces.'

McAnuff sniffed. 'There's the letters,' he said.

'Letter,' corrected Bob. 'We've got ae letter, sent to Sandy Disdain.'

'And the Dallerie letter.'

'Which has never seen the light of day.'

'She gied me it to post for her.'

Bob looked at him in disbelief. 'So you kent aa along it was her? How would she do that?'

'I dinnae understand it. She must hae realised I'd end up seein it. Recognise it.'

Bob took his pipe from his jacket pocket. 'D'you think she was tryin to get caught? Cry for help?'

'That's what I'm thinkin. And. . .And I hid it, thinkin I was helpin her. And noo. . .'

'Nane of this is your fault, Willy. Dinnae start takin on someone else's guilt.'

'Twa folk are deed.'

'And it wasnae you lit the fire.'

'What do I do?'

'D'you still hae the letter?'

'Aye.'

'I think it would be best if it reappeared. Got sent aff wi aa the other evidence.'

'Won't that look suspicious?'

'I've a feelin your sergeant winnae ask ower mony questions.'

Willy sat back, relief evident in his expression. Bob smiled encouragingly.

'As it happens,' he said, 'I was hopin to run into you the day.'

'How?'

'I've a wee job I want you to do for me.'

*

Reverend Duncan threw the *Press and Journal* onto the circular living room table, greatly vexed by what he had just read, a filler paragraph in the middle pages referring to a tragic fire in Barvick Falls, Crieff, Perthshire. Colonel Henderson and his nurse perished. No suspicious circumstances.

No suspicious circumstances. So why was Reverend Duncan suspicious? Mr Henderson had been the gentleman who enquired about Lorna Carrington. Well spoken, almost certainly ex-military. And he'd said he shared lodgings with Lorna Carrington.

In Barvick Falls.

Could the fire be suspicious? Even as he posed the question he knew the answer. He knew Lorna Carrington's history. Fire and Lorna Carrington were unhealthy confederates. He went into the hallway and picked up the telephone. The operator asked him which number he required. 'Which number, caller? Sir?'

Reverend Duncan replaced the receiver in its cradle and buried his head in his hands.

'He that is without sin among you, let him first cast a stone at her.'

*

The Strathearn Herald office appeared small and insignificant from the front but extended into a sprawling machine-room at the rear, into which, in 1907, had been built the *Cossar* newspaper printing press on which the *Herald* was produced. PC McAnuff was escorted through the machine-room to a glass-fronted office at the rear in which David Phillips, the editor, was working behind an ink-stained wooden desk.

'I'm enquiring,' McAnuff said, 'about the identity of one of the "War and Civilisation" letters you published a few weeks back.'

'Is this part of a criminal investigation?' said Mr Phillips.

'It is.'

'Whose identity do you wish to know?'

'Went under the name of *Macedon*.'

'I don't need to check the records for that. I remember well, it was Miss Carrington, the schoolteacher.'

'You're sure?'

'A most charming young lady. But very single-minded. I shouldn't like to get on the wrong side of her.'

'No. You wouldnae.'

*

Willy sat in Bob's living room that evening, nursing a bottle of Younger's Pale Ale. The news had just concluded, reporting heavy German artillery bombardment of the French lines. Now, the newly-formed BBC Scottish Variety Orchestra was playing a selection of dance tunes. Willy relayed his findings from the *Herald* office.

'That's that, then,' said Bob. 'He called her a blockhead

and a gomeral in the local paper. They had a stand up row aboot it on the stairs and hoors later she sets fire to the landing richt outside his room.'

'You think that's enough motive?'

'No, I dinnae. Mr Salmond thocht the repossession of his gramophone player was sufficient motive. It wasnae. Mr MacLean thocht him sackin Miss Carrington was sufficient motive. It wasnae, either. Mr Henderson callin her a gomeral, that would annoy her richt enough, but no enough to kill him and his nurse. But aa three thegither? One efter the other? Is that enough?'

'It is,' said Annie, gripping her sherry glass. She usually only drank sherry on Sundays but tonight felt different. Important. Bob was looking unhappy, she noticed, withdrawn.

Willy refilled his glass and sipped some beer. 'As long as they get her, doesnae really matter what the motive was,' he said.

'I suppose no,' said Bob. To Annie's ear, long trained to the intricacies of Bob's thought patterns, his agreement sounded unconvincing. She raised an eyebrow to attract his attention but he paid no heed.

'I'll tell the sergeant aboot the *Herald* letters the morn, said Willy. 'See if it gets me back in his good books.'

'I'd hing on,' Bob replied. 'It's no exactly proof positive. Pretty circumstancial.'

Annie knew Bob well enough to know he was using the word circumstancial in an oddly pejorative sense. He understood the meaning of the word perfectly, and that wasn't what he had just conveyed.

'Onywey,' he continued, 'the sergeant's got enough on his plate wi aa my evidence. We wouldnae want the man owerworked. That never turns oot well.'

'Good point,' said Willy.

*

Annie rounded on Bob as soon as Willy departed. 'What was aa that in aid of?' she said.

Bob's brow furrowed as he finally allowed worry to show on his features. 'When Willy said it doesnae matter the motive, as long as they get her. . .'

'Aye?'

'It really, really does matter.'

'How?'

Bob felt sick in the pit of his stomach. He could foresee a catastrophe – another one – approaching.

'If the motive was juist the gramophone bein repossessed or Lorna bein sacked, that would be ae thing. She'd be charged wi culpable homicide. She didnae mean to target Mr Henderson, didnae mean for him and Miss Salter to dee. A terrible accident. She'd get five year, maybe.'

'Aye?' said Annie.

Bob sighed heavily. 'But if the motive was revenge because of thon letter. . .'

'Then it was a deliberate attack. . .'

'And therefore it would be murder.'

Bob switched off the wireless and they sat in silence. The fire was dying in the grate, a chill descending on the room.

'And if it was murder,' Bob said finally, 'then she'll hang.'

Saturday, 6 November

A Day of Finality

Bob blew out his cheeks as he knocked on the door of DO MacLean's house on Carrington Terrace. Mr MacLean himself opened the door, sporting a tweed suit and a bright red bow tie.

'Miss Carrington,' Bob said when they were settled in Mr MacLean's living room with a pot of tea.

'I have been sorely vexed about that young woman these past days, I can tell you,' Mr MacLean replied. 'You know her background? Her father was a minister, Free Church.'

'The Wee Frees?'

'Yes. Very strict. Have you heard of the Dornoch case?'

'No.'

'Two or three years ago. The Provost of Dornoch, he was thrown out of the church because he allowed his daughters to sing and dance on Christmas Eve.'

'Seems severe.'

'Doesn't it? You wonder what it does to the minds of young people. That kind of upbringing. How do you differentiate between right and wrong, if everything's wrong?'

'Aye. That's a Scottish thing, to be sure.'

'And I can't help thinking that, had I not terminated her contract so abruptly, this disaster might not have happened.'

'PC McAnuff is torturing himself with the same thoughts.

Something he could have done but didn't. But would it have made a difference? How can you say it was you sacking her that tipped her over the edge? Maybe it was the gramophone player?'

'That seems a less serious matter. . .'

'To you maybe. Me as well. But we're not obsessed like Lorna Carrington. Maybe she'd already decided that's what she was going to do, even before you sacked her. Maybe she was going to do it anyway.'

'We'll never know.'

'Exactly. So stop torturing yourself.'

Mr MacLean smiled. 'Wise words, Mr Kelty. Do you propose to heed them yourself?'

'Eh?'

'I've spent a lifetime studying the faces of people who're trying to conceal something from me, or tell me something surreptitiously, or even just understand something themselves. People who only want to talk to me to work out what they think.'

Bob smiled back. 'You're a clever man, heidie.' He smoothed the arm of his jacket. 'This is a difficult time for me. The war and all that. Thing is, I think I'm a pacifist. I can't be doin with killin. And that includes the state. . .'

'The death penalty?'

'Aye.'

'I would have thought it highly unlikely a death sentence will obtain in this case. Pure and simple manslaughter, surely? She never intended to kill anyone.' DO MacLean waited but Bob didn't reply. 'She didn't, did she?'

Bob thought about Leslie Comer, to whom he gave a second chance three years before when she, too, could have faced a capital charge. Nowadays, he trusted Leslie to manage Cloudland without a moment's hesitation. He happily left Ellen in her charge. But Lorna Carrington was different, surely? Leslie Comer found herself an innocent victim of another man's rage. It was possible, though, that the deaths of Mr Henderson and Miss Salter were premeditated. Was that not evil? Did evil not need to be destroyed? Wasn't that what this wretched war was all about, removing an evil from Europe and the world?

'I don't think the fire had anythin to do with the gramophone player or you dismissin her,' he said.

'Are you trying to suggest that Mr Henderson was the intended target?'

'Possibly.'

'Therefore, are you suggesting that this was cold-blooded murder? Capital murder?'

'I don't know.' Bob wanted to explain to the headmaster about the letters to *The Strathearn Herald*, seek his advice, reach a conclusion, but he knew if he did Mr MacLean would be drawn into the same dilemma he was now facing. And it was evident the headmaster felt enough guilt already without Bob piling on more. 'I do have reason to believe,' he said, 'that Miss Carrington targeted Mr Henderson.'

'And did she intend to kill him?'

Bob bit his lip. 'No.'

'Is that your belief or your wish?'

'I'm not sure.'

'You must be sure, Mr Kelty. Principles are fine things. But they must never be used to obscure the truth. The truth is the truth, whatever that may be.'

'I know. I've been wrestlin with that for the past two months.'

'The war?'

'The war.'

'You can't twist the truth so that it fits more easily your point of view. Can pacifism ever hope to defeat an evil like Herr Hitler? Can you be sure that Miss Carrington meant no ill to Mr Henderson and his nurse?'

'It's Miss Salter that makes me think she didn't. Lorna

Carrington harboured a grudge against Mr Henderson, aye. But that wouldn't extend to the nurse. And she knew they were both at home because Mary Kemp saw her watching them going upstairs to their rooms. I just don't believe Miss Carrington would deliberately kill her for no reason.'

'Don't believe or don't want to believe?'

'I genuinely don't believe.'

DO MacLean rose to his feet and examined the bookcase behind him, pulling a small paperback from the middle shelf. He handed it to Bob. 'On the matter of the war, this may help you make up your mind.' Bob took the book, *An Encyclopaedia of Pacifism* by Aldous Huxley. 'I think most of it's bunkum,' Mr MacLean said, 'but it's well-argued bunkum.'

'Thank you.'

'As to the other question, I think you already know what you're going to do. What I ask is that you do it for the right reason.'

'I will.'

*

Bob felt sick as he followed Mrs McInnes up the stairs to Lorna's room. Mrs McInnes had been reluctant to permit him entry, but Bob found the name DO MacLean had powerful properties. Mrs McInnes knocked on Lorna's door and introduced Bob and closed the door behind her.

Lorna was seated at her desk, staring across the room. For the first time, he discerned no arrogance in her posture. She looked frightened. Distressed. She groaned when she saw Bob enter.

'Who said you could come here?'

'I dinnae need permission.'

'Do you enjoy making life difficult for me?'

'No. But I'm about to mak it even mair difficult.'

'You're quite the investigator, aren't you? Such a clever little man.'

'I get the impression you don't like men very much.'

'How remarkably observant of you.'

'And I dinnae think you like authority that much, either.'

'Are you trying to paint me as some modern-day Suffragette, railing against a male-dominated world?'

'No. My thinkin's probably no sae far fae yours on that matter.'

'Oh, you share our pain, do you? Understand what it is to be a woman?'

'I'll never understand women, I'll tell you that for nothin.'

Lorna laughed, and it was perhaps the first genuine sound Bob had ever heard come from her mouth.

'Your faither was a minister?' he said.

'Yes.'

'Wee Free Church?'

'Yes.'

'Hard, that.' Lorna didn't reply. 'No much fun. No much love.'

'There was plenty of love. Don't presume to know the lives of others.'

'What I mind fae my ain childhood is that there's a difference atween love and *showin* love.' He watched her, her small movements, internalised. 'And you need baith.'

Lorna snatched for her cigarettes and lit one. Her hands were shaking. 'Are you trying to redeem me? Say I'm not so bad after all, it was just my upbringing?'

Bob pushed the ashtray towads her. 'No. I think there's evil inside you, richt enough. Juist, I couldnae presume to say what put it there.'

Do it for the right reason. Until now, Bob had been uncertain whether he truly was acting for the right reason. Now he was sure. While others, assuredly, would disagree, he was convinced. Murder was murder, however it was procured.

'But somethin put it there,' he said, 'and you cannae tak aa the blame for that.'

'My,' she said, clapping her hands theatrically. You really

are a knight in shining armour. Maybe I should have tried to seduce you.'

'Instead of Sandy Disdain?'

'Yes.'

'Trying to seduce Sandy was plain daft.'

'It worked. I got rid of him.'

'He would hae been plannin on jinin the Merchant Navy, onywey. You juist speeded it up.'

'They say life expectancy in the Merchant Navy is lower than the Royal Navy.'

'You're wishin him deid?'

'I'm sure his family would be devastated.'

'And me. And plenty others. He's a good man. That's why naebody believed your story. That's why he'll ay be welcome here. Unlike you.'

'Don't worry. The headmaster has dispensed with my services at the end of term.'

'You'll be gone long afore then.'

She was maintaining her flinty demeanour but Bob could see moments of doubt in her expression. She wants to know what I know, he thought. She wants to know how much trouble she's in.

'And why does the great investigator believe that?'

'You're goin to be arrested and convicted for the Barvick Falls fire.'

'You're sure of that?'

'I *am* sure of that.'

'Because of the HP repossession? Or because I was sacked? That's nonsense and you know it. No one's going to believe I'd burn down a house out of spite because of those things. If this goes to court – and it won't – they'll never be able to prove the fire was anything but an accident.' She looked away and then back at Bob. 'Because it was.'

'You're going to admit that you set the fire because of the repossession.'

She laughed harshly. 'The repossession? That's trivial. Even the sacking would be a more credible motive than that. Are you insane?'

'I think you might be, but I'm not, no.'

'Why would I admit to something that isn't true?'

'Because it's better than the truth.'

That stopped her cold. She clenched her jaw. A pulse throbbed in her neck. Her voice was quieter, weaker. 'What do you mean?'

'You're goin to plead guilty to culpable homicide by setting a fire to spite Salmond's and make sure they couldnae repossess your gramophone player. If you dinnae, I'll see to it you're charged wi the murder of Mr Henderson and Miss Salter.'

'Murder?'

'You didnae set the fire because of the gramophone player. Or for bein sacked. You set it because of Mr Henderson. He wrote a letter in the *Herald* ridiculin you and callin you a blockhead and a gomeral. You telt me aince, the ae thing you cannae stand is being humiliated. You regretted sayin that the moment it came oot your gab, I could tell. Noo I see why. Because it's true and because you cannae control your anger. You lost your temper and poured turpentine ower the second floor landing. Second floor, whaur only Mr Henderson and Miss Salter lived. The fire brigade are certain there was mair turpentine used than you'd hae needed for a single pan of floor polish. You meant that fire, and you meant to kill Mr Henderson in it.'

'I didn't even know he was in.'

'You did. You'd no long had an argument wi him. And you watched him and Miss Salter goin back up to their rooms.'

'And how do you propose to prove this?'

'You were seen. On the stairs.'

'By whom?'

'Doesnae matter.'

'The wretched maid, Mary, no doubt.'

'And I hae evidence that you are *Macedon*. *The Strathearn Herald* office confirm it.'

'They wouldn't tell you that.'

'No, they didnae. They told PC McAnuff.'

'He wouldn't do that to me.'

'He would. He's growin into the job, that lad. He's got the measure of you. Here's the thing, Miss Carrington. If you admit to culpable homicide you'll probably get five year in the jail.' He stepped forwards and leaned over her.

'If you get convicted of murder, you'll hang.'

He pulled himself upright again. This was the right thing. He knew it was. He knew.

'So the best thing you can do is go to the polis and mak a confession to Sergeant Rudd. Cry a bit. Look remorseful. I'm sure you can do that. Then let the law run its course.'

'And if I don't?'

'I reveal the truth.'

'Your "truth" doesn't amount to very much does it? I killed him because he called me a blockhead? That's stupid.'

'But you are a blockhead.' He saw a blaze of anger in her eyes and laughed. 'See? Mind you said to me ae time: "People generally learn to cross me only the once". I can see why. Do you really think they wouldnae try to rile you in court, mak you lose your temper? Believe me, I've seen them do it, thae prosecution lawyers, and they're a damned sight smarter than you, you daft gomeral.'

'Sticks and stones. . .'

'The other thing thae prosecution lawyers do, they go into every single detail of your life. Drag it aa oot in court. Mak it sound really, really bad. So think aboot this: is there onythin else you've done in your life, somethin similar maybe, onybody who really did cross you, that thae lawyers could use in court against you?'

'I've lived a blameless life.'

'A woman, maybe. The woman whose name Mr Henderson shouted at you on the stairs of Barvick Falls the night of the fire.'

Lorna was breathing heavily, her face and neck flushed. 'You're fishing. You don't know anything.'

'No, I dinnae. I dinnae need to. Because believe me, *they* will. If there's onythin, they'll find it. And they'll crucify you wi it in court.'

Lorna turned and stared out at Burrell Street, quiet in a mid-morning lull. 'Why do you want me to confess to the gramophone repossession? Why not the sacking? Wouldn't that be more realistic?'

'Your headmaster doesnae deserve that. The guilt it would leave in him.'

'What about Mr Salmond's guilt?'

'There is no guilt. He could never have guessed how you would react ower somethin so trivial. You said as much yoursel.'

'But as a motive it would stand up in court better, wouldn't it? The sacking?'

'It winnae go to trial. You're goin to confess. Nothin for a jury to debate.'

Lorna closed her eyes. 'If I confess, you'll keep *Macedon* quiet? The .. any. . .names?'

'You hae my word. Which is worth an awful lot mair than yours.'

'And why would you do this?'

'I dinnae want to see you hang.'

'Just moulder in prison?'

'It's better than the alternative.' Bob put his bunnet on his head. 'I'll gie you till the morn. If you havenae been to the polis, I'll go mysel. Good day, Miss Carrington.'

*

Lorna sat in darkness staring out of the window at Burrell Street rising towards the Comrie Road. Main road south and west. Escape route. She felt an impotent rage. There was no escape. She would have to confess to some ridiculous – humiliating – crime in order to. . .In order to. . .

In order to conceal the other crimes.

A child badly maimed in St Andrews, died. A maid locked in her room in Mintlaw, dead. And now these two, the coward and his simpering nurse. Lorna could justify each of them. Henderson and his nurse deserved to die. So did the Young girl in Mintlaw, who couldn't obey orders. The child in St Andrews was a simpleton, expendable. People like that, little people, herd people, they didn't deserve the consideration you would give to a real human being. Setting the fire at Barvick Falls had been the triumph of Lorna Carrington's life. It was a blow for freedom. For humanity. For right.

I will send a fire on the wall of Tyrus, which shall devour the palaces thereof.

They were the sinners, the ones who needed punishment. Lorna Carrington was without sin. She was sinned against. Her father, her church, her sex, the smallness of the world around her, conspired to make her what she was – a fighter for justice, a conscientious slayer of wrongs and wrongdoers. Her father was responsible for this. Her father, with his beatings and lectures and punishments and his hate dressed as love. Her father and his religion, a religion of predestination in a world of the moment.

And her mother, for her neglect. For taking his side. For not loving her.

Lorna Carrington was innocent. Her crimes were not her crimes.

And, tomorrow, she would confess just as the little investigator said she would. Five years in jail. And then?

And then. Then, the world.

Suppose ye that I am come to give peace on earth? I tell you, Nay; but rather division.

*

Bob and Annie sat on the settee in the blackout gloom of their living room. Ellen was reading cross-legged by the fire.

'You think she'll do it?' Annie asked.

'Aye.'

'Are we doin the richt thing?'

'This story is already terrible. We can at least stop it gettin mair terrible. Another needless death.'

'Will she go to jail?' Ellen asked.

'Aye.'

'Good. She does things oot of pure nastiness.'

Bob squeezed Annie's hand. Pure nastiness. Was he strong enough to cope with pure nastiness? The coming months would let him know.

Wednesday, 6 March 1940

A Day of Change

News of the arrest of Lorna Carrington for arson and manslaughter exploded through Crieff. The Misses Seaton, Beaton and Miller had never known anything so exciting. The children in Lorna's class were unteachable for a full week. Ellen couldn't hide her satisfaction. Malky Bennett instructed Mickel's Solicitors to sue Lorna for damages over the loss of the hayricks. Weeks passed. Thingwie Johnstone was arrested and sent to jail for a month for assaulting Sunny Petrie, a lifetime's unblemished record tarnished for the third time in a year. Justice of the Peace Kenton expressed concern about his mental facility. Mrs Drysdale was killed by a runaway horse on Commissioner Street and her grandson thrown from his pram. The news turned. Life moved on. January of 1940 saw the longest, coldest spell of weather in living memory. Because of the war, this went unrecorded.

On the sixth of February the government launched an advertising campaign. "Careless Talk Costs Lives". Bob received a poster and stuck it on the wall of Cloudland. A month passed.

The steak and kidney pie Bob was making contained considerably more kidney than steak, rationing already making an impact. He looked up as Annie emerged from upstairs, carrying that day's *Courier*. He could tell immediately something was wrong. She handed him the paper. At the bottom of the page was a notice:

NATIONAL SERVICE (ARMED FORCES) ACT 1939
NOTICE TO MEN BORN BETWEEN
2nd OCTOBER 1914 AND 2nd OCTOBER 1915
Requirement to Register at Local Offices of the Ministry of Labour and National Service on 23rd March 1940

'You've been called up,' Annie said.
'Aye.'
'What now?'
'I dinnae ken.'
'Will you go?'
'I dinnae ken.' Bob looked out of the window at the tranquility of James Square in the early morning. A thunderous commotion behind him heralded the arrival of Ellen, barrelling down the stairs from the flat. Her face wore its usual, furious expression but she smiled when she saw Bob watching her.

'I'm awa to Marnie's,' she said. 'There's baby lambs.' And she ran out of the door.

Bob watched her sprint up James Square to the fountain. He embraced Annie.

'Life goes on,' he said. 'It ay does.'

. . .

TIPPERMUIR BOOKS

Tippermuir Books Ltd is an independent publishing company based in Perth, Scotland.

PUBLISHING HISTORY

Spanish Thermopylae (2009)
Battleground Perthshire (2009)
Perth: Street by Street (2012)
Born in Perthshire (2012)
In Spain with Orwell (2013)
Trust (2014)
Perth: As Others Saw Us (2014)
Love All (2015)
A Chocolate Soldier (2016)
The Early Photographers of Perthshire (2016)
Taking Detective Novels Seriously: The Collected Crime Reviews of Dorothy L Sayers (2017)
Walking with Ghosts (2017)
No Fair City: Dark Tales from Perth's Past (2017)
The Tale o the Wee Mowdie that wantit tae ken wha keeched on his heid (2017)
Hunters: Wee Stories from the Crescent: A Reminiscence of Perth's Hunter Crescent (2017)
A Little Book of Carol's (2018)
Flipstones (2018)
Perth: Scott's Fair City: The Fair Maid of Perth & Sir Walter Scott – A Celebration & Guided Tour (2018)
God, Hitler, and Lord Peter Wimsey: Selected Essays, Speeches and Articles by Dorothy L Sayers (2019)
Perth & Kinross: A Pocket Miscellany: A Companion for Visitors and Residents (2019)

The Piper of Tobruk: Pipe Major Robert Roy, MBE, DCM (2019)

The 'Gig Docter o Athole': Dr William Irvine & The Irvine Memorial Hospital (2019)

Afore the Highlands: The Jacobites in Perth, 1715–16 (2019)

'Where Sky and Summit Meet': Flight Over Perthshire – A History: Tales of Pilots, Airfields, Aeronautical Feats, & War (2019)

Diverted Traffic (2020)

Authentic Democracy: An Ethical Justification of Anarchism (2020)

'If Rivers Could Sing': A Scottish River Wildlife Journey. A Year in the Life of the River Devon as it flows through the Counties of Perthshire, Kinross-shire & Clackmannanshire (2020)

A Squatter o Bairnrhymes (2020)

In a Sma Room Songbook: From the Poems by William Soutar (2020)

The Nicht Afore Christmas: the much-loved yuletide tale in Scots (2020)

Ice Cold Blood (2021)

The Perth Riverside Nursery & Beyond: A Spirit of Enterprise and Improvement (2021)

Fatal Duty: Police Killers and Killer Cops: the Scottish Police Force 1812–1952 (2021)

The Shanter Legacy: The Search for the Grey Mare's Tail (2021)

'Dying to Live': The Story of Grant McIntyre, Covid's Sickest Patient (2021)

The Black Watch and the Great War (2021)

Beyond the Swelkie: A Collection of Poems & Writings to Mark the Centenary of George Mackay Brown (2021)

Sweet F.A. (2022)

A War of Two Halves (2022)

A Scottish Wildlife Odyssey (2022)
In the Shadow of Piper Alpha (2022)
Mind the Links: Golf Memories (2022)
Perthshire 101: A Poetic Gazetteer of the Big County (2022)
The Banes o the Turas: An Owersettin in Scots o the Poems bi Pino Mereu scrievit in Tribute tae Hamish Henderson (2022)
Walking the Antonine Wall: A Journey from East to West Scotland (2022)
The Japan Lights: On the Trail of the Scot Who Lit Up Japan's Coast (2022)
Fat Girl Best Friend: 'Claiming Our Space' – Plus Size Women in Film & Television (2023)
Wild Quest Britain: A Nature Journey of Discovery through England, Scotland & Wales – from Lizard Point to Dunnet Head (2023)
Guid Mornin! Guid Nicht! (2023)
Madainn Mhath! Oidhche Mhath! (2023)
Who's Aldo? (2023)
A History of Irish Republicanism in Dundee (c1840 to 1985) (2024)
The Stone of Destiny & The Scots (2024)
The Mysterious Case of the Stone of Destiny: A Scottish Historical Detective Whodunnit! (2024)
Salvage (2024)
A Most Unsuitable Game: Celebrating Scottish Women's Football Fifty Years After the Ban (2024)
The Scottish Murder Book: Sensational Scottish Murder Trials. Book 1: Perth, Angus and Fife (2024)
William Soutar: Collected Works, Volume 1 Published Poetry (1923–1946) (2024)
William Soutar: Collected Works, Volume 2 Published Poetry (1948–2000) (2024)
The Road to Mons Graupius (2025)

'The Wheesht' The Best o Scots Hoose Yaldi (2025)

'The Perth Steamies': the Story of the Fair City's Public Washhouses, 1846–1976 (2025)

The Lass and The Quine (2025)

Balkan Rhapsody (2025)

The Royal Edinburgh Military Tattoo: 'The Show Must Go On' – Travels of the Tattoo Producer (2025)

A Wildlife Guide to Edinburgh (2025)

'The Old Divide': A History of Sectarianism in Scotland (2025)

Perth Academy: A History (2025)

William Sandeman (1722–1790): Perthshire Entrepreneur and Cotton Pioneer (2025)

FORTHCOMING

An Odious Campaign: The Ross and Cromarty By-Election of 1936 (Rob McInroy, 2025)

Disasters, Accidents & Enquirers in Scotland (Gillian Mawdsley, 2026)

City Lives! A Dundee GP's Memoir of the NHS at its Height (John Hulbert, 2026)

The Black Watch From the Crimean War to Coomasie and Beyond (Derek Patrick and Fraser Brown (eds), 2026)

William Soutar: Collected Works, Volume 3 (Miscellaneous & Unpublished Poetry) (Paul S Philippou (Editor-in-Chief) & Kirsteen McCue and Philippa Osmond-Williams (eds), 2027+)

William Soutar: Collected Works, Volumes 4–6 (Prose Selections) (Paul S Philippou (Editor-in-Chief) & Kirsteen McCue and Philippa Osmond (eds), 2028+)

Roger Crofts, Scotland's Natural Heritage: An Insider's View (2026)

All Tippermuir Books titles are available
from bookshops and online booksellers.

They can also be purchased directly
(with free postage & packing (UK only)
– minimum charges for overseas delivery)
from **tippermuirbooks.co.uk**

Tippermuir Books can be contacted at
mail@tippermuirbooks.co.uk